For everyone

PROPHECY WITH THE MOONS

NEVAEH BRAGG

PROPHECY WITH THE MOONS

Prologue

The all silver car hadn't been bothered to be parked in the lot beside all the other hundreds of vehicles. The moonlight was making them shine with an exquisite sparkle, giving them depth besides a plain monochromatic black. It was halted in the front, drove recklessly, and hit the curb. The couple sitting within it became startled. It added to the already steady increase of anxiety that was shooting from the very tips of their toes, to their racing heart. But once knowing that their vehicle wasn't going to tip over (because of a minor piece of concrete only a foot off the ground), immediately pushing the driver-side door open was a man.

He was tall. A height that towered over people, giving them terror, and forcing most to look up in order to meet his dark umber eyes. He was bulky, with muscles that didn't like the restraint of clothes, yet was kept within them with a tight squeeze. His huge form matched well with his dark skin, smooth always managing to catch the moonlight just like the cars. His expression was firm, hasty and scared as he rushed to the other side of the car—meeting with a beautiful woman on the other side. She was shorter than the man, head coming to reach just below his pecs. She was never underestimated, her feisty and independent nature pushing her confidence. She looked like a goddess, one descending from the clouds and making her mark the minute she let her foot touch the grass. With hair a brown that resembles dark chocolate and skin that might as well be the embodiment of caramel, she could also resemble one of candy. Luckily the man who opened her door, holding a hand out as she struggled to leave her seat, had a sweet tooth.

"Let me help you, my love." The woman wobbled as she made it onto the sidewalk. Her face twisted into one of pain, hazel eyes squeezing shut as she cried out. One hand went to her stomach, clutching the round shape for support, while the other held on tight to her lover's forearm. Her nails dug into his skin with strength that left crescent marks. Any tighter and they would have possibly drawn blood. She shook her head to his words, waiting for any more waves of agony before returning to her normal posture. With sweat dripping down her temple and lungs gasping for air, she encouraged the man to just start following her into a hospital.

The building was ginormous. The windows that took up the majority of the brick walls were painted white. Seen through them could be people of all kinds, being rushed to and fro for medical issues that only they could explain.

With swollen feet and a back that has been sore for every day since she was willing to carry a child, the woman tracked her way to the hospital doors. They were glass as well, metal frames that were connected to a bunch of wires therefore they could be moved on their own. Immediately once the couple was close enough, with a faint whoosh and a blast of the air conditioning, the two were being greeted by ringing landlines, crying children, nurses bustling, and the overwhelming scent of antiseptic.

The woman felt a kick to her stomach then. She doubled over at the jab, once again using her husband as a means of support as she groaned. The couple didn't even have time to call out for help, because almost immediately showing up to their side was a nurse. She held a clipboard close to her chest, a look of worry creasing her forehead even when her onyx black hair is pulled back tightly into a bun.

"You bare a child!"

The pregnant woman cried out once more, her legs almost buckling. It had the nurse momentarily surprised by her outburst.

"And you're about to give birth to said child. I must hurry. Let me get a wheelchair" She rushed to the left of the entrance, clipboard shoved under her armpit as she briefly struggled to open one of the many folded wheelchairs. Once her nimble fingers had managed to pry it open, she quickly brought it over, urging the lady to take a seat within it.

It only made the feeling worse. The pressure she was putting on was making the birth progress faster. She grabs onto her stomach and almost glares at it. While she knew that she would love her child the minute they came out of her, as of right now, while she struggled to keep her composure (because it felt as though she was being teared open), the awful thoughts she kept thinking was enough to put a sailor's mouth to shame.

The nurse guided her to a secluded room, capturing the attention of many other employees and patients along the way. Another nurse began walking alongside them, questioning what exactly they're dealing with when it comes to the pregnancy. Not many answers were being given as of course the nurse pushing the wheelchair had just met this couple; the pregnant woman was more of a mumbling mess; and the husband was clueless. He's been to all of the doctor visits with his wife, but none of what has been said about their child pertains to what is being asked of them. Or at least he doesn't think so. Medical terminology sounds like a foreign language.

"And are there any health risks, scares, or certain procedures that we have to take in order to successfully deliver your baby?" Nurse two was a lot less warm than nurse one. Her black ponytail was tighter, and her aura was stricter. The husband racked his brain. Never were the couple introduced to any potential health problems during their monthly check-ups. His wife was as healthy as could be. She ate all the right things (with the occasional cheat), and made sure she had a pregnancy safe work-out routine. If anything, the husband is the one they should fear. Fear and nervousness just might lead him to have a heart attack.

"Not that I know of, no."

"Well then, we shall proceed like normal. I will get the doctor in right away" Nurse two nods. She moved stiffly, professionally. "In the meantime Amora," Attention was directed to nurse one. Momentarily she stopped rushing to look at her colleague; but remembering the circumstances, she pushed forward, entering an empty room seconds later. "Check the mother's and child's vitals, get her hooked up to an IV drip. And keep us updated with any potential abnormal pain or complications. I will try and get the doctor in as fast as possible. Understand?"

Amora nodded, her determination giving one of a soldier to

their captain. Once nurse two left, Amora was in the clear to proceed with her orders. First step: getting the crying pregnant lady into the uncomfortable hospital bed. Thankfully with the help of her husband (almost) being as large as a bodybuilder, lifting her, and then gently settling her on top of the cotton fabric sheets was a lot faster and easier. The nurse rushed to a cabinet, pulling a few items that resemble the ugly blue hospital gowns from within.

"Before I start checking your chart, and guaranteeing this a smooth birth, I need you to change into this" She held out the gown. The husband took it. "I know you just laid down, but you can either get up and put it on, or your husband can help you while you lay. It's your preference. I will give you guys your privacy while also fetching a few required items. Okay?" *Yeah, Amora was a lot warmer than nurse two.* A sympathetic grin stretched to her face, only walking out of the room with light steps when she got confirmation from the couple.

"Here, let me help you," The husband whispers. He approaches his wife's side, smoothing back strands of her hair that begin to stick to her forehead. She melts into the touch, heart yearning for more of the comfort that her lover was already providing so much of. She wishes that she could be more for him. Also give him the solace that he might need in a time like this— but she's helpless. She can't do much other than groan because of what she's experiencing. But she tries anyway. She makes it less difficult by moving in every way that her husband wishes for her to, just so that stripping and then putting the gown on will be trouble-free. And when they're done she looks at him. Watches as he neatly folds her previous shirt and sweatpants before placing them on a nearby table. Then he takes a seat in an empty chair.

It's quiet then. She doesn't feel the harshness that is her child trying to escape. Doesn't have the perturbation that is this entire experience becoming a nightmare. It's just her and her husband. They lock gazes, smiling, before she's reaching out with a weak hand. He does the favor of holding it, running his thumb over her knuckles to help soothe any last remaining pain. And she loves him for it—loves him all the more for it.

"Did you want to help because you wanted to see me naked?" Her typical confident and lively laughter was left to nothing but a breathless chuckle. He's never seen his wife so drained before. It was concerning yet endearing. While he hopes that she recovers fully after birth (returning to her former dignified self), it's nice to see her have to rely on someone else for a change. She can take this moment to be vulnerable.

Her husband chuckles.

"We have the rest of our lives for me to see your gorgeous body. I don't think I need to use this as an opportunity."

He's still scared. Fear could be seen in his eyes. Worry that something will go wrong, and not only will he lose his wife, but a child that they've tried so hard to create. That's why she squeezed his hand. Tugged it closer to her face, leaving a peck to his knuckles before holding it close to her chest. He looked at her with admiration and wonder, leaning in closer before falling to his knees so they were eye level and in each other's space.

"You're going to be a great father. Don't stress too much, my love" With her other hand, she brought her palm to his face, caressing his cheek with shaking yet light fingers. Before he was able to respond, thank her for the sweet words of encouragement to their future, she was throwing herself back against the bed. Tears left their eyelash barrier, carelessly falling down her cheeks as she moaned and groaned. Her grip on her husband grew stronger. Her knuckles were white, crushing his limb until black and blue bruises began to appear where her fingertips touched. "Ah, the baby's coming! They're coming right now and—AH!"

She tried to grab onto the bedpost. Use it as some sort of stability and stop the awful ache. But the metal was only falling victim to her strength; with the trick of the eye, looking as though she was bending such a sturdy material.

"Get the doctor!"

"Just one more push Mrs. Whitmore!" The delivery doctor shouted over the pregnant lady's screams. The demand was gentle though. Motivation for her to continue with the intense suffering just a little while longer.

Then his hands held the squirming child in just the same way that he talked to the mother. He made sure that his grip was firm enough to pull the newborn out, but also soft enough to cause them no physical harm.

"One more big one and-" He was abruptly cut short when almost with a pop, a bloody child now laid in his arms, staining more than the latex gloves he wore. The baby squirmed and cried hard with their lungs. They were completely unfamiliar with the bright and cold world that they had just been brought into. One of the nurses, the nice one: Amora, made her way over to the doctor and handed him a blue blanket. "It's a boy. Congratulations."

He was ready to hand the child off to the parents. Allow the newborn to be greeted by smiles that couldn't be happier. Only, just as the doctor was leaning down to be the one to connect a mother and its child, said mother was yet again screaming out in pain. Amora immediately ran over, taking the child from out of the doctor's hold, giving him the opportunity to figure out the problem. The husband clung to her side more than ever, desperately asking for what could be making her react this way. Clutching her stomach, eyes screwed shut and ripping shouts pouring from out of her mouth, luckily an answer was given when the doctor gasped at the discovery that was another bloody head peeking through.

"Twins!" The couple looked at him as though he had gone insane. Especially Mrs. Whitmore. Not once during any of her pregnancy check-ups, was she given the news that she could be carrying a second child. Neither has she felt it. And *she knows* she would have felt it. It's always been one—the gender kept hidden as a surprise, but all other medical results meant to be said immediately. So even with dimming brown irises, she narrows them in on the man who just helped her deliver her son. She grows angry. Frustrated. Sweaty and undeniably in discomfort. "Were you not aware?"

"We would have told you if we di—aagh!" She twists to her side, face pressing into the pillow. A vein was popping out of her forehead, cheeks painting red as she swears she's never had to experience this amount of pain in her life. And no amount of strength she grips the metal bars with, or how many times her husband promises that it'll get better with a caress of her head, Mrs. Whitmore feels as though she is being ripped apart.

"Well this baby is coming. And they're coming fast."

Everyone returned to their stations. Amora swapped places with the previous much colder nurse. With the first born still in her grasp, he was growing quite agitated by all of the loud sounds and it was beginning to intermingle with high tensions that were already spreading about the room. That's why she decided to take him to the neonatal intensive care unit—the N.I.C.U—where she will calm him before continuing on with her duties. Bathing and making sure he gets the extensive care that is needed for records. So now nurse two: Emry Young, stood beside the doctor, taking orders.

Unlike the boy, this child didn't take long. There weren't long hours of preparing, or a few more of getting the baby out. This one practically slipped into his arms, with wails just like their brother, and arms flailing because they too couldn't comprehend the world. Emry dashed up to the doctor with a white blanket, covering the second born from the dropping temperatures in the room. Mr. Whitmore brushed his wife's sticky hair out of her face before placing a delicate kiss to her forehead.

"You did amazing," It was whispered as he watched her slow her breathing from the heavy and hasty intakes from before. Her eyes gently fluttered closed and her muscles relaxed. The doctor handed the child to the father.

"It's a girl" Mr. Whitmore looked amusing holding such a small and fragile child in his large arms. "From what I gathered, you had no idea you were going to be able to hold two children...Hopefully though," The doctor and father looked at one another with happy, satisfied grins. "You will care for both of them equally. Realize that this may be a surprise now, but in the future know that she is nothing but a gift."

"Thank you. I guarantee that my wife and I-" When Mr. Whitmore stole a glance at his lover, he grew concerned. Her skin wasn't glowing like usual, and her chest wasn't moving. She looked ghostly, and was as still as a mannequin. "Miriam? Miriam?" He was told to step back, give the doctor enough space to check her pulse. His eyes grew wide as he felt her heart beat grow faint.

"Doctor! I'm afraid there's severe bleeding. Surgery needs to be induced now!"

Crimson stained the bed sheets for every second the three of them scurried about trying to save Miriam Whitmore's life. Or at least the doctor and Emry did. The husband stayed glued to his wife's side, tears pricking his eyes as he stared down at her lifeless body. It hasn't been announced yet, but he can already hear the news—see the future. He had lost the one person he had come to love with his entire being. The contradiction being that he gained two new ones. To which one still lays in his arms currently; little thing having finally calmed and now sleeping peacefully.

Was it cruel to say that he blames her? The little bundle of innocence. She was the cause. The *unexpected* cause of his lover's passing. Was it cruel to say that he would trade her for his wife?

He feels sorry.

He shoves the newborn into Emry's hands, taking her off guard. Not only by the abrupt action, but how heartless his eyes appeared to shine.

"I-I-I-" His jaw clenched and an internal battle was being fought. "I'm sorry. I need to go. I need-"

"Mr. Whitmore" Emry grabbed his shoulder, stopping him

from exiting the room. Her expression was softer. Suddenly not as inhuman as before. "Your children are going to need you more than ever now. Please don't forget that."

It took an hour. Sixty minutes. Three-thousand and six hundred seconds passed before Mr. Whitmore, the husband, a man whose first name is Harrison decided to return. He'd left the hospital completely. At first it was just the room, leaving behind the body of his wife who he knows he won't be able to hold again. He took a lap around the ground floor, passing patients—passing families who will be able to go home after their care. It was too hurtful. It pulled on Harrison's heart strings until he was feeling tears start to prick at his eyes, daring to break past their barrier and just fall down his cheekbones. So he took his spiraling emotions outside. First thing he noticed was that his car had been parked next to hundreds of other ones. That should have been obvious enough, when he sometime before gave another one of the nurses his keys and sheepishly explained that he parked unprofessionally.

Harrison couldn't leave though. He was grounded, being pulled back and kept at the hospital knowing that no matter what, those kids are all his responsibility now. They were still a part of his wife. Even his unexpected daughter. That's why after inhaling fresh air, going up and down the concrete, head bustling with decisions about what path he genuinely wants to go down, he found his way back through those sliding glass doors. The heels of his sneakers padded against the clean white tile floors, making their way to the same room that his beautiful wife laid in. Only before he was able to walk in, he was being tapped on the shoulder.

"Mr. Whitmore," He turned to see Emry. She didn't have to say anything for him to know the unfortunate news. She was empathetic, blue eyes staring straight into his brown ones, pink lips pulled into a line on the brink of becoming a frown if she didn't have to be the strong one in this situation. "I'm sorry...but your wife didn't make it" She took a breath for him. Had shown some sort of emotion for him, because like expected, he was as stoic as a rock. Nothing was said or done on his part, and it was honestly a little scary. "I know this is a difficult time, but we have to inform you that we are preparing your wife for transportation to the morgue. We cannot allow you in her room at this moment, so if you'd like to see your children for the time being, I will escort you back when you are able to give your last goodbyes."

It took a minute. Took Harrison a minute to debate whether he should fight and demand that he see his dead wife, or continue being tranquil and just take this moment to relish in the fact that he has two innocent newborns awaiting to meet him properly for the first time. Eventually he nodded.

"Yeah, I understand. I would love to see my children."

Emry mocked his head nod before guiding him to the N.I.C.U. He was allowed in his own secluded room where two incubators were placed in the middle; two bundles of joy laying within them as Amora affectionately stared down at them. Gurgling noises were heard, some shuffling and then Amora was seen leaning forward slightly to console the boy. Emry knocking on the door is what gathered her attention, immediately turning around with this expression that didn't know whether it wanted to be happy that Harrison came back or worried because something was on her mind and she just had to say it. She decided on being glad that the father of the twins came back, and ushered that he come join her. Emry left the two be, commenting that she needed to help finish with Miriam Whitmore's release.

The room fell quiet then. Harrison stared down at the twins who lay about in their incubators, holding back the waves of depression that were waiting to burst out of him. He doesn't think he can continue to look at them knowing that it'll just be a trio from here on out. The woman that was supposed to be their mother is no more, and they'll never be able to meet her. They'll never have that relationship with her and feel that love she was always willing to give. His feet were ready to step back and take another hour break. This hurt more than anything or anyone he has ever faced. But then Amora was keeping him there by lifting the first born, his son, and handing him over. Harrison went stiff. While he was open to holding his child, he couldn't help but feel his heart squeeze. And those grueling tears finally began to fall when said baby opened his round eyes and stared up at the big man he was now and forever supposed to look to for safety and support.

"I'm so sorry," Harrison said. It came out choked. "I'm sorry that you'll never be able to meet your mother. I promise you would have loved her."

He sniffled, using his giant hand to smooth back dark brown hair that is already so full on a newborn's head. The baby cooed at the affection, squirming happily in his hold.

"Beautiful, aren't they?"

Harrison nodded. Diverting his attention from his son, he looked at the nurse before looking down at his sleeping daughter.

He felt regret then. Never should he have blamed his child for the passing of his wife. Nothing she had done purposely killed the woman. And now he will spend the rest of his life making it up to her.

"She looks just like her."

"I'm so sorry for your loss. Genuinely. But I believe your wife is now looking down on all of you and using her own method of protecting" Amora sucked in a breath and tightened her smile. "Especially now that you'll be needing as much as you can get."

Mr. Whitmore stopped watching his children fondly to look at Amora with confusion and slight alarm.

"Excuse me?"

"Your daughter," Amora sighed and Harrison placed his son back down in his incubator. The child briefly whined at the loss of his father's warm arms, but fell silent when a green pacifier was placed in his mouth. Immediately all attention was back on the nurse then, eyes needing an explanation for the worry Amora released. "When casting my gift, your daughter...I could feel her power. It's different from your son's."

"Isn't that a good thing? It means she'll grow to be an alpha. And we all know that's quite rare for women."

"No Mr. Whitmore, I'm afraid—has your wife ever claimed to be anything other than part wolf?"

"My wife isn't a wolf at all."

"That'll explain the power difference! Your daughter's energy, while I do experience that werewolf gene, I can also sense something magical."

"My wife is fully human."

"I'm sorry?"

Amora was baffled. Taken completely aback, her eyebrows furrowed as she looked down at the baby girl. Fear might have taken her expression. Harrison on the other hand raked a hand over his buzzed hair. He never expected that he would be telling his love story to a nurse after getting the frazzled news that his family might be in danger.

"I met Miriam in the human world. My job gave me the opportunity to travel there about seven years ago. I was supposed to be doing some of the first research on life over there—to see if our kind would ever be able to merge with theirs."

"You work for the Raba?" Amora couldn't contain her gasp. The Raba are their kings. There are three of them. Fakhar, Qayid, and Qua. They have all of the discussions and make all of the decisions for the people in Kariq Leada. They're rarely ever seen though, only making appearances when it comes to extreme problems or threats that will be needing power that stems stronger than their underlings the Junud.

The Junud are who the people see on a day to day basis. They're the ones who spread the word about what the Raba plans to move forward with. And years ago, it was announced that research about other realms will be conducted. Said it was to help with expanding their realm. Prove to other worlds that they are the most powerful. It wasn't a plan that was taken lightly by the citizens—most if not all afraid that wars would be caused if all of Kariq Leada decided to start rampaging against the innocent. Especially when everyone is already satisfied with where they live now. No move has been made, but research hasn't been stopped either.

"*Worked.* I do construction now" Harrison shook his head,

wringing his calloused hands, reminding himself that he couldn't go on a rant about his transfer of employment and what he liked and disliked about it. "But basically as I was fulfilling my task, I happened to meet Miriam. I told myself that I shouldn't, it'll never work out and if anyone finds out, she's doomed. But I just couldn't stay away. There was this pull to her, I couldn't resist" If there wasn't an uneasiness still lingering, Amora would have cooed at how lovestruck Harrison is. "We fell in love and eventually I revealed who I was. I said I didn't live in the human world. I said I would have to eventually go back home. It was surprisingly easy, but she agreed to come with. All we had to do was lie and say that she was also a werewolf."

"But that doesn't make any sense," Amora speaks. "Your daughter. She holds the same power as one of a prodigy witch."

"You must be reading her energy wrong. There's no way-"

"Take it from someone who is also a witch my dear. Your daughter is far more powerful than one can imagine. Makes me believe that your wife might have lied to you. Are you sure she's only human? Has she ever done anything that might have reminded you of one?"

Harrison wracked his brain. He looked distressed at what was being told to him. His wife? His Miriam? A liar? She would never hold something so important from him. There was no reason to.

"No. I mean she drank a lot of tea. Meditated. And unless you witches are religious when it comes to yoga, I believe my wife was nothing but human."

"Mr. Whitmore, look I know this may be conflicting, un-believable if one will, but you have to at least try to understand what I'm saying" Her hand went to his shoulder for brief comfort before she was stepping back to slide up beside the baby girl's incubator. "If your daughter possesses as much power as I'm-" Amora reached down to lift the child into her arms. Just as her hands touched the newborn's body, her head was being thrown back, eyes rolling into the back of her head. Harrison became frightened by the sight, calling out her name multiple times. No response was given, instead just low mumbles that he couldn't quite make out. So with rather slow thinking, he decided to just pull Amora away from his daughter. He tugged her back a little too hard, his strength knocking her to the ground where her head ended up colliding with the hard floors; and ultimately forcing her unconscious.

Harrison rushed to her aid, shaking her shoulders and yet again calling out her name in hopes of waking her. Not only did he wish for her to be okay, but he needs to know what happened only seconds ago. Was she witnessing a vision? Does she know the danger?

"Nurse Amora! Wake up! What did you see?"

"Us perhaps?" With a smug look, there stood beside his children were the Raba.

Chapter One

TWENTY ONE YEARS LATER...

"...happy birthday *dear Maeve!* Happy birthday to you!" There was immediate clapping, some cheers, and the enthusiastic exclamation of making a wish before blowing out the yellow-orange flames that danced from the wic of the wax candles. They were shaped into the age that Maeve turned.

The number candles sat upon a supposedly round cake—one tier, and sloppily decorated in blush pink frosting. Then in front of the candles is what's supposed to be the cursive writing of the generic celebrational phrase in black edible gel. It's questionable whether or not it actually said anything, the words having been written in a rush, leaving some of the letters mushed together or unreadable. There was minimal arguing that happened in the kitchen about who had the steadiest hands and deserved to write it; and then how the writing looked terrible and should be wiped before starting over. That led to whether or not scraping the already scribbled phrase would ruin the home-baked cake.

How extremely sentimental of all them to do this for her.

Maeve couldn't have been any happier to witness her family greet her with their own creation of a baked treat. Gentle smiles stretched at her parents' elder faces, and eager grins plastered on her younger siblings'. But that probably had to do with the fact that they weren't allowed a slice until they watched her blow the flames into smoke.

She smiled back. With plump lips that she glossed over with makeup, she let her teeth show as she genuinely thanked her unofficial-official family with tight hugs and unwanted kisses to the cheeks (that most definitely left a mark in her wake). Her adoptive mother, Athena Ross, who held the cake in her pale wrinkly hands carefully slipped it onto the wooden dining room table. Immediately her husband, James Ross, guided three young children towards the same table, joyfully slicing them all equal triangular pieces with the occasional licking of his thumb whenever some of the frosting touched. And while they were preoccupied with eating the delicious dessert (more than happy that they get to endorse in sugar before heading off to bed, where they'll do anything but sleep), Athena approached the eldest. She's cared for Maeve ever since she randomly appeared on her doorstep all those years ago—swaddled in a white blanket, body squirming about in a box that might have been stolen from the curb for trash day. She cried terribly, lungs about ready to combust from the pressure that she was putting them through that night. And if it weren't for her waking to the sound of her doorbell going off repeatedly, the poor child wouldn't have been found until the morning.

"*James. James. Wake up. I think someone is outside*" Athena said it groggily. With eyes barely open, she leant over to switch on her bedside lamp. The orange hue that came from the bulb had her squinting, ready to turn away and look at her still asleep husband. Or that was until he had gotten fed up with all of her whisper shouting, all of the shoving she had done to his bicep, impatient to know whether or not she was hearing things or if the doorbell was being constantly pushed. She might have even heard someone knock on their door, the rapping of knuckles being so aggressive that it might as well be the police demanding for an investigation. *"James you lazy-ass! Get up and see who's at the door!"*

"It's probably just those church kids trying to sell to us again" Maybe that's what he said. He was speaking in mumbles, body turned on his side, away from his nagging wife and the lamp that's been left on. *"Just go back to bed."*

He didn't waste another second when it came to falling back into a slumber, his congestion catching up to him, so now loud snores left his mouth as he exhaled. Athena stared at him with disgust, eyes rolling right after before she's sighing deeply. Then throwing the blanket from her body, she's throwing her feet around where the temperature change sent chills up her legs and temporarily gave her goosebumps. She slipped her feet into the fluffy cotton slippers gifted to her years ago on her anniversary. They were worn from the everyday use of them, but that just made them all the more comfortable. And with one last look at her lazy husband, she scoffed before shuffling her way out of the bedroom.

She temporarily stopped to put on her matching robe, hands tying the fabric belt in a secure knot by the time she reached the front door. One more loud knock to the fiberglass had her startled, yet extremely curious. She doesn't believe it to be a robber or a murderer, because cruel people like that don't typically carry out their mischievous plans by knocking first. So with an interest in the person or thing on the other side, she unlocked and twisted the knob before swinging the front door open. She was met with nothing but the warm night air. She momentarily heard feet padding against the ground, bushes being shook, but then the street went quiet. No one stood on her porch, on her front yard, or even in the streets. Like expected, everyone was tucked in their bed, safely in the comfort of their homes as they awaited the sun to rise once again.

It must have been a prank. She would have to scold those pesky neighborhood teenagers that liked to cause chaos everywhere they went. It was probably them wanting to create another stupid joke and then run away as they laughed about it.

But as Athena shook her head, ready to turn around and go back to bed, crying was heard. It was faint at first, just loud enough for someone nearby to hear. Looking around in absolute confusion and slight worry for somebody who might be hurt, Athena stepped further out of her house. That's when her foot accidentally hit something. Gaze falling to her wooden porch, she was met with a box. It was ripped, torn to create a large enough hole. And placed inside of it was a big bundle of some white cloth. Or that was until the cloth started to move and Athena was fast to realize what was presented before her. Bending down to move the cloth from what she assumes to be the top, she was met with the insane sight of a sobbing baby. She looked around, desperate to find the person who left a child on her doorstep. But again, the street was bare. Not a person in sight.

She'd be a horrible person to leave a helpless baby all alone.

So with a good heart, Athena pulled the crying child from the box, carefully coddling them in her arms.

"Oh don't cry" She pushed the blanket further down the baby's face, getting the adorable view of screwed shut eyes leaking tears and chubby cheeks fainting red. She couldn't help but caress the child's cheek, comforting coos given in order to calm the upset baby. *"You have nothing to worry about. I'm sure I can take care of you while your parents are away."*

The child slowly let their sobs de-escalate into whines, before settling into light breathing. They had fallen asleep in a stranger's warm arms. Arms that carried them back into an even warmer home.

Letting her much older hands rest on Maeve's shoulders, the two women stared at one another.

"Mother, what's that look for? I've already told you over a hundred times that I'm not staying home tonight. Elise and I already made plans" It was said with a chuckle. With much younger hands reaching for the same ones that have held her for roughly twenty-one years, Maeve detached them from each other, laying pecks to Athena's knuckles. Thin pink lips became tight against the elder lady's face, expression becoming less celebratory and more sullen. "No need to worry about me. I've already promised to be back before the sun comes up."

"I still think that's an unreasonable time to be returning" James butts in. His left cheek was stuffed with cake, and it looked as though he was ready to shove another fork full into his right one. Maeve giggled in response before walking her way over in black stilettos, laying a kiss to his temple. She stuck her finger in her cake then, frosting coating the tip of her perfectly manicured index finger, and licked it off with a pop of her lips.

"Will Reggie be there?" Her youngest sibling Jax smiled wickedly, mouth contorting into one of a kissy face. "Maybe finally you'll tell him you're madly in love with him" Then there went the noises. Faux smooching sounds vibrated throughout the room, until shouts of help were replacing them. Maeve didn't take kindly to the teasing and was quick to chase after a pubescent boy that liked to shoot virtual zombies in his free time.

"Jax, please leave your sister alone" James said as they rounded back to the dining room and stared at one another from opposite ends of the table. "Whether or not she confesses to her three-year-old crush on Reggie from across the street is entirely up to her" He shoved another bite of cake into his mouth. Maeve looked at her adoptive father in disbelief.

"Dad!"

He shrugged in return.

"Darling," Athena came up from behind her daughter, a hand gently placed to her lower back. Her skin came in contact with a sparkly blue dress, one that stopped only inches above the knees and had thick straps that were brought down for a more elegant approach. The smokey-eye makeup look she added to her brown irises only made her appear more stunning—proof that she was ready to step out into the night and celebrate turning the legal age to drink alcohol. "I'm not worried about you going out. Well maybe that as well, because you just don't know what kind of people are out there until something bad happens..." She heaved a deep breath. "This is more of me saying, don't you think it's time that you go out into the world...on your own?"

"You're kicking me out?" Maeve raised an eyebrow that she used a pencil and concealer to make look perfect. "Well that's fun news to hear on my birthday."

"No, we're not kicking you out-"

"Yes we are" Youngest brother Aziel blurts with a wave of his fork. "Ah, does that mean I get your room?"

"No, I'm getting it" Sister Bailey replies.

"But you already have your own room!"

"Yeah, you don't know what it's like to share with someone!" Jax intervenes.

The three children's squabbling would have turned from something verbal to physical if it weren't for Athena catching their attention with a stern look and shouting for them to quit it. The trio didn't hesitate to return to their seats with zipped lips and attention diverted away from one another. Or at least that's what's seen above the table. Secretly they were kicking each other.

"Listen Maeve, we're not kicking you out. It's just you're twenty-one now. Don't you want to live on your own? Find someone? Start your own family?" Her hands went to her daughter's shoulders again. A squeeze was given and as they connected stares, only good intention was obvious from this conversation. Even if mentally Maeve kept repeating that she was still too young to settle down. "I just don't want you to stay cooped up in this shabby house forever, when you know you have so much potential. Go out and live your life! Didn't you want to be an astronomer? What happened to that?"

"Well yeah, but-"

"Then make your next step, college. Get your degree and study the one thing I've always known you to be so passionate about."

If only it were that easy.

"But mom, you know we don't have the money for that. And what happens if I don't find a proper career to pay back all those college debts? I'll still be stuck where I am."

"That should be a risk you're willing to take," Athena whispered. Then she stepped back to claim another empty chair, stealing an unused fork and began to take her own bite of cake. "Besides, who says we don't have the money? You might be a reckless spender, but I for one have always believed in trust funds" Slipping the cake into her mouth, the familiar sound of the doorbell had gone off. Maeve removed her amazed stare from her adoptive mother, to look in the general direction of the front door. That must be Elise. "Go, this can be a discussion for another time. Have fun."

Maeve nodded with a twitch of her lips.

She'd shifted her body weight from one foot to another for what seemed like the twentieth time; the heels she's wearing are beginning to create sores on the bottom of her feet, and squeeze at her toes until the littlest one couldn't even be felt anymore. She curses herself mentally for thinking that tonight would be the best time to break in a new pair of shoes.

Tonight wasn't necessarily going great so far, having to stand outside a club within a line that doesn't look as though it's moving. It's been an hour since they've parked Elise's car on the side of the road, then made their way in line in between a very touchy couple and four men who just might have come from a frat house. Maeve was about ready to throw in the towel. She was ready to complain and then suggest that they could go do something far different, yet more fun than standing about a slow moving line into a club (that'll evidently be packed with drunktards that don't know how to keep their hands to themselves as she danced). But just as she was contorting her face into something of a whine, she was feeling her ass being grabbed. Startled by the movement, she almost tripped and accidentally bumped into Elise who was busy staring at her phone. She had a scowl on her face, one that looked as though she was reading something—*read something* that had made her visibly upset. But then again, she seemed to always look like that. There were rare moments where she displayed something far softer.

"Hey!" Maeve shouts. With the accidental bump and her obviously offended tone, Elise diverted her attention from her cell phone and onto her friend. Maeve was being harassed by the frat guys. Or at least the guys, who looked as though they should be a part of one; with their shirts that are a little too tight and too odd of a color, and jeans that couldn't be any more blue than they already are. They had evil smirks on their faces, teasing mocks coming out of their mouths, and motioning to more sexual grabbing if Maeve allowed. They were laughing at how angry she was getting. Taking her protests and letting them go right over their heads. "Keep your hands to yourself, you dick!"

"Ah, but we just wanted to see if it felt as good as it looked. How about one more grab? Maybe on those nice boobs of yours as well?" The one in front, who did all of the talking, attempted to reach out, yet was stopped by a firm grip to his wrist. Sight fell on Elise. She looked dangerous; the hold she had on the stranger was at a bruising strength, with her nails rightfully digging into the man's skin and forcing him to wince in pain. They held eye contact, her blue ones burning so hot into his brown ones that she could have easily created a hole in his head.

"Don't you dare touch her" Elise pulled the man closer so they were almost nose to nose. "...ever again" She waited for the stranger to nod his head, a whimper leaving his lips before she released him. He stumbled back into his friends, creating a distance as they stared at Elise with pure terror. Then what seemed to be mumbled words, the group of men thought it was best to just leave the line completely. They pushed past other people, eager to leave behind the two women that made them look like little boys. And Elise watched them go; waited until they turned the corner before refocusing her attention onto Maeve. "Did they hurt you? Touch you anywhere else?" This was one of those moments where Elise became a lot softer than expected. She looked genuinely worried as she tried to look over every inch of her friend, looking for any marks; giving her a reason to follow those men and begin to shred them piece by piece. Maeve was thankful to have someone like her. Someone outside of the family to make her feel so loved.

"El, I'm fine. You stopped them before it got out of hand" She held the other's forearms, smiling. "Thank you."

The line started moving then. People filled the club to its maximum capacity, and Maeve and Elise were two of those people. They granted the bouncer permission to see their IDs, which granted them permission to enter, and before either of the two knew it, they were standing at the bar counter receiving drinks. It being Maeve's first time to be able to order something involving liquor she didn't know what to ask for, so she let the bartender surprise her. Elise on the other hand decided it would be best if she stayed sober throughout the night and asked for a soda. One of them had to be the designated driver. And judging by the fact that it's her car, and that she wanted Maeve to celebrate her birthday in all of the fun ways she could, Elise doesn't mind having to babysit.

Even if she knew that Maeve was already going to be a handful.

Taking a sip from her mystery drink, the birthday girl beams at the taste. It was sweet, fruity, and definitely burned going down. But she liked it nonetheless and was already ordering another one when the glass she held was still full. Or until it wasn't and she was chugging the beverage as though it was water. Made Elise wonder if this was actually the brunette's first time drinking alcohol. She never verbally questioned it; just asked that Maeve slow down or else the liquor will hit a lot faster than she expects. Then they took their energy to the dance floor. It was glowing underneath their feet, flashing all colors of the rainbow, and matching the strobe lights that would blind someone if shined directly in the eye. It was the only source of light the club had. It was dark and hot. But that probably had to do with all of the bodies that bounced about. The dancing was just another form of dry-humping, women and men coming together to hopefully leave this place with a partner to have sex with. If Maeve wasn't already having so much fun trying to get Elise to perform the sexy dance moves she does whenever they go out, she probably would have also partook in the grinding that strangers tend to do whenever sexually driven.

"I have to use the bathroom. Be right back."

Maeve wasn't listening. She was too far gone into the music, the alcohol of the two fruity drinks and a few shots she stole off a waiter's tray was building and evidently making all of her senses blurry to the environment she was in. She nodded anyway. She let Elise go, pushing past sweaty bodies until she disappeared into the sea of people. Then Maeve felt hands snake around her waist and heat blow across her earlobe. She would have told the stranger off (give the new person the same piece of mind that she gave to those supposed frat boys), but she was under the influence. She was melting under the delicate touch the stranger was giving her, loving the caress that was being done to her sides as they swayed to the fast tempo song.

"Happy birthday Mae" It was whispered, the warmth of the person's breath sending tingles down her spine. But she knew that voice. The deepness of it, the smoothness of it. It always made her smile, causing an eruption of butterflies to flutter not only through her stomach but throughout the entirety of her body. Typically she would shy away, grow nervous and not know how to properly seduce someone that she's obviously had a crush on for years. But tonight she had liquid courage. So turning around to face who she's guessing is Reggie—the cute boy who lives across the street—she smirks up at him while throwing her arms around his neck. "Sorry I couldn't make it earlier. Got caught up with something."

"Well you're here now. How about we dance? Or better yet, go somewhere private?" *Yeah, she's definitely had a lot to drink.* Even Reggie, who wasn't used to seeing her be so bold was taken aback by her words. But he finds her hot, and he's a guy, therefore he wasn't going to surpass the opportunity to make out with her. So grinning, he nodded before allowing Maeve to drag him somewhere else in the club. Only every place that they've tried to escape to already had so many other couples sucking faces or attempting to have public sex. It's frustrating and killing her buzz. If she was being honest, she really wanted to at least kiss the man before all of the liquor drains out of her; or else she fears she'll never get the chance again.

That's why she opted for outside.

Forgetting all about Elise, she pulled at Reggie's wrist until they were pushing through an emergency exit. It led to an alleyway; with a giant dumpster overflowing with trash pushed to the side of the building, and their only source of light being the streetlights that were flowing in from the far side of the alley. When knowing that they were alone, Maeve didn't waste any time. She pulled Reggie close by the collar of his shirt, colliding their lips in a kiss that was anything from sweet and gentle. The two were explicit with their actions, ready to devour one another. He moved them, motioned that they needed stability in order to keep going, so he backed her against the cold concrete club wall—the rough texture scratching her and mixing the pain with pleasure that had her moaning into all of the fast touching. Eventually they detached from the mouth and Reggie started to kiss, lick, suck all over the caramel skin that covered her neck and collarbones. She threw her head back at the sensation, eyes closing shut as she reveled in what she only dreamed about. And because drops of alcohol still coursed her, the feeling was ten times better than what was to be expected.

She became so invested in everything that was Reggie that she didn't realize just how vicious he was until she felt a nip to her neck. She groaned more than sighing out of pleasure. She pushed him back, a dopey grin on her face as she tried to read the sadistic gleam that now laced his eyes as he stared at her.

"Ow, be easy."

She brought a hand to her neck, rubbing at the skin that burned. A chuckle was heard rumbling deep from within Reggie's chest, striking her own with uneasiness. And before she could read any further into the fear that was slowly creeping from the pit of her stomach, Reggie was grabbing for her wrist, pulling it from her neck and trying to dive in for another taste. But by now, Maeve had begun to sober up. She was far more aware of her surroundings; and from what she was gathering, none of what she was experiencing was worth that euphoria. She felt sticky and grimey, her back hurt from the jagged wall, the spot where Reggie ultimately bit her was inflamed, and the headache aimed at her temples was not something she wanted to be enduring for any longer.

For the second time she was shoving Reggie off of her.

"Hey, uh, why don't we do this another time? I really need to get back to Elise."

Right there. Right then. Right now. That wasn't Reggie. The sweet guy that managed to win her over just by smiling with glimmering teeth, a wave and a greeting being shouted from their respected porches. He was someone else, *something* else. His posture became straight, chest puffing and muscles clenching. His lips pulled into a devilish smirk where his white teeth brightened under the street lights. Maeve doesn't know if it was the liquor messing with her, but she swears she saw his canines become longer. Become sharper. And his eyes. They shifted from their natural brown, to a maroon, before glowing a bright red. Then with a motion that she couldn't have even detected was coming, she was once again pressed against the wall of the club, hissing as a particular piece stabbed her in the back. Reggie had a hand wrapped around her neck, squeezing. And while she couldn't see it, she could definitely feel his nails digging into her skin, elongating into claws and itching to draw blood. Tears pricked her eyes and her lungs gasped for air.

"Oh I'm sorry *Mae*, but unfortunately you'll be coming with me" After all these years, never has he said her name so evilly. Made her hate it. Her name. If she changed it, the itch that pricked at every inch of her skin would disappear.

Then she saw them. With the sound of feet padding against the ground, and the limited movement she had with her eyes, she was able to catch glimpses of four men approaching from behind Reggie. They were the frat guys. With faces that matched the one of the guy she could probably say she's in love with, Maeve believed there was no way that she was getting out of this alive. She was trapped, and there was no way that anyone from inside the club was going to hear her scream. If she was even able to. With how tight Reggie had his grip on her neck, she wouldn't be surprised if he snapped it.

"W-What are you...d-doing?" She was desperate for some oxygen. With her own hands, she scratched and clawed at Reggie's hold. To no avail, his grip only tightened the more she squirmed.

"I don't think you know this-" He let a cackle escape, head thrown back as his laughter rang throughout the alley. "What am I saying? Of course you don't know" He looks back at the other men, seeking their agreement. "Of course she doesn't know.

Because if she did, she wouldn't have fallen so effortlessly for me" Looking back at her, he'd only gotten scarier. "I'm assuming you would have known that this attraction you have for me is all a trick. I kind of needed your trust...your love. Made it easy for me to get intel...to get you right here."

Maeve shivered out of fright. From how close he was getting again, and how she no longer has any strength to free herself.

"E-l-lise."

"Elise. Right, that stupid *witch*" Reggie laughed again. "Get it, because she's an actual witch? And it's a play off the word bitch?" He waved it off with an eye roll as Maeve was growing far more terrified and confused than ever before. What was this man on about? Who is he? What is he? "You'll understand eventually. It's okay, you can laugh later. But there's no point calling out for her. She's a terrible protector by the way. Leaving you all alone," Reggie pressed his body against Maeve's, lips brushing against her ear. This time she wasn't enjoying the shiver that runs down her spine. She whimpers, wishing that this is all some weird nightmare. "All alone where anyone can take advantage of you. What a shame."

No. Maeve refuses to go out like this. A tragedy to die on the day of your birth. She has to at least try to save herself. So with some momentum, she used her foot to press herself from off the wall, giving enough pressure to take Reggie by surprise and release her. First order of business: inhale as much air as possible. Second order of business: run away.

She didn't get very far. Reggie was almost immediately behind her, hand going to her thick dark hair and grabbing a clump of it into a fist. Maeve almost buckled at the insane pain she felt from the tugging.

"And where do you think you're going?" He began to drag Maeve down the alleyway. "When I was told that I'd get paid great money for this job, I didn't know that I'd have to deal with someone like you. Annoying and far too guarded. Made it difficult. But finally..." He pulled her head back, her wincing. "I'll be getting my money, and ridding myself of you."

That hurt. Maeve thought they genuinely had a connection. And if not on a romantic level, then at least on a friend one. There had been countless times where they had gotten together for something as small as quick chats on one of their lawns; catching each other up on what had been going on in their lives that week. They had a bond. Something that made her realize that she liked this guy for more than his pretty face and sculpted body. She wanted him for how caring and understanding he was. He made her feel less like an outsider. And that was a topic that she never took lightly when growing up in an adoptive home. It's hard growing up and seeing children with their biological parents, their blood siblings. And while Maeve had grown to love her blended family, there probably always will be a hole in her heart; yearning to know who her real mother and father is, if she's an only child. Why was she given up? For a minute Reggie was one of the few people who silenced all of those thoughts.

But none of their shared communication was real.

Who he was, wasn't real.

She could feel her heart shatter.

Reggie reached into his pocket to only a second later pull out a sphere. It was glowing yellow, blue, purple hues. It reminded

Maeve of a smaller version of a fortune teller's crystal ball. She had no idea what Reggie was going to do with it, but she tried to move as far as she could away from it. He held it within his claw for nails, beaming at the sight of it before throwing it onto the cold ground. Immediately it burst open, and then shining bright and tall was a circle. The shocking part was that on the other side was the world. A much sunnier, happier part of the world. There was this giant grass field, the faint sounds of birds chirping as the blue sky greeted the dancing sunflowers planted. The real eye-catcher though was the huge granite castle structure that dominated the piece of land it was built upon. Again, Maeve has no idea about what the circle thing is, or what it's doing, but she refuses to go anywhere near it.

"I hope you don't get realm-hopping sick?"

Realm hopping!?

"I'm not going anywhere with you! Let me go!" She tried to get his hand to release her hair, but opted to just jab an elbow into his stomach. Reggie hunched over at the attack, giving her the opportunity to twist his hand out of her hair, then quickly using her own leg to swipe his feet from under him. He goes tumbling to the ground with a moan. "Thank goodness Elise made me take those self-defense classes."

Then while at least Reggie was stunned, Maeve was going to make a run for it. Only just temporarily she had forgotten that he brought back up. She came to a halt when those same horribly dressed men were creeping up around her with wicked smiles. It's just as one of them managed to grab her wrist, it was being chopped off and the hand that once tightly held onto her turned into gray dust before sprinkling onto the ground.

"I told you not to touch her."

Looking beside her, Maeve was relieved to see Elise. Within her hand was a silver blade, shining even with the minimal lighting. The blade was sleek, sharp to the touch, and had an engraved brown handle. It read something but she couldn't get a good look. Maeve didn't know what to be more surprised by; the fact that she was being attacked by some form of creature, was about to be kidnapped and transported to a new realm, or that her friend was fighting these four men like an amazon warrior. She single-handedly took all of them on. The man who already lost one hand went to strike with his opposing, nails that could have been knives ready to claw at her pale skin. But as he got close enough she ducked down and sliced at his torso. Then she used his hunched figure as leverage to jump insanely high and stab another one of the men in the chest, digging her blade in deep before twisting it. The man cried out before turning into more of that dust. Elise went to the next guy and missed his punch by maneuvering under his arm. Then she used his same outstretched arm to throw him onto his back, where she was able to step onto his stomach. She leaned down to stab him in the chest. He fizzles away too. The final man she leaps onto, she grabs ahold of his head while he desperately scratches at her side to rid her. But Elise effortlessly twists his neck, the sound of his bones snapping being a cringe to the ears. She flips off of his body and that's when his corpse turns to dust as well.

Elise looked at her dead opponents and took a minute to recapture her breath.

"You okay?"

How was Maeve supposed to answer that? She was absolutely

terrified about what she just went through, and if what Reggie is saying is true, then her one true friend—her best friend is some kind of witch. She too can't be trusted. She's lied about who she is. But then again, it's not like Maeve would have believed her. She would have probably called her crazy before mistaking her for some really good magician. Elise did save her life just now though. So hesitantly nodding her head, the two were getting ready to meet each other halfway, maybe embrace one another. Of course there had to be one more complication though. With speed that Maeve has only seen in the movies, mastermind Reggie was holding her tight by the waist.

"Your precious guardian may have saved you from those low ranks, but I promise she's not saving you from me. See ya' later" And then with a wink to Elise, Reggie was pulling Maeve through the gleaming circle.

Chapter Two

Elise ran, the hand that was holding the sharp blade being raised and ready to throw. With Reggie and Maeve still stepping through the portal, she could have hit Reggie—stab him in the back before he managed to jump through the portal just as it was closing. But she was just a little too slow. Right as she threw the knife, the giant circle had whooshed closed and she missed entirely. The blade flew through a moment's worth of purple smoke before striking that stupid metal trash can. Animosity began to flow through her body, through her veins; and with a shout that came straight from the core of her stomach, she stomped her heeled boot down on the ground.

To a stranger passing by she would have looked like she was throwing a tantrum; and if she was being honest, she deserved to do so. Twenty-one years of being Maeve Ross' guardian; protecting her from all danger (whether that be from tripping over her own shoelace, or stopping a bunch of men from groping her in a club line), and she failed. She doesn't know whether she's irritated because of how long she was succeeding in her vow, and then some man (that she should have seen right through) took

Maeve away from her. Or if she's agitated that she didn't try her hardest in making sure Maeve was completely safe.

Now she's entered a new realm by the enemy and it could only be guessed where she was taken.

Her eyebrows creased inward and her lips that were painted over red with lipstick dropped into a scowl. Whipping around to face the one man that was still conscious and *alive*, she narrowed her blue eyes on him. *Might as well get some answers.* So stalking her way over to the man that struggled to get himself off the dirty concrete, Elise snagged him by the collar of his shirt (ever so easily lifting him inches from where he was already crouched). They stared one another in the eye, blue clashing with red and causing a storm to brew between the two. The intensity came mostly from her side though, the anger she felt being enough to make the other submit with physical cringe and hope that she wouldn't land the final strike.

"Where did that bastard take her?" Nothing was said. He just stared at her with lips sealed shut and a trembling figure. He was only making it worse for himself. And it became more apparent when with a quick flick of her wrist, suddenly her trusty knife was no longer wedged in the side of the trash can. She held it once again, fingers curling around the handle as she held it up against his neck. He tried to crane his head away from the cold metal, but could only go so far when she had a stable hold on him. He kept looking between her and the blade. He appeared loyal enough to die for Reggie, not uttering a word of his plans. But the hesitancy was also clear as sweat began to dribble down his temple as his adams apple bobbed. "I asked you a question!"

Her shout and the blade starting to cut through his skin was enough.

"Alright! Alright!" She reeled back just a little, but didn't change her strict demeanor. The man gulped. "Reggie, he's trading her. Money for the girl. She's got a huge bounty over her head. Men from all over are searching for her. Have been for a while now-" She pressed the knife tight to his throat again. Fear trembled down his back and any longer with this minor integration he would probably pass out; or worse, shit on himself. Whether or not some random low-class vampire soiled his underwear was the least of her problems though. Dread was beginning to sink so deep within her gut because the people she was supposed to be protecting Maeve from finally found her. No, they did that years ago. Reggie was merely a spy, a professional one hired because the locals weren't succeeding fast enough. Then it was a waiting game. Figure out all of the details, gather a team, and then catch her when the time is right.

She needed confirmation.

"Who did he take her to? Who promised him riches!?" Her teeth were clenched. Any tighter and her molars would turn to dust.

"The Raba."

"God fucking dammit!" She sliced the man's throat, leaving him to bleed out all over her hands, her clothes. "I had one fucking job! One job!" Her blade then began to puncture his stomach. "Shit, shit, shit" Repeatedly the man was being stabbed, blood as red as a fresh apple was covering everything. It splattered on her face, the ground. But then she left the knife in his unmoving chest, twisting with a flick of her wrist. Seconds later he was nothing but a pile of gray dust.

She stood tall then, staring down at the grueling sight that were lifeless bodies and the disgusting remains of who they used to be. As she was wiping her crimson hands on her ripped jeans, she grimaced. Not only was she now filthy from sweat, blood, and the gray particles of one's body, but she was kept transformed into the figure that was fit for the human world. It wasn't entirely too different from her natural form, but the slight changes that had to be made occasionally became uncomfortable if covered in it for too long. So dipping her head slightly, she let her hands track through her hair as she threw her head back. A grin graced her features as the feeling of any bits of magic left her rotund figure. Blue eyes that were once temporarily closed, opened and glanced over herself. Intricate marks that would be considered tattoos to any human swirled from the tip of her neck, not stopping until they were on top of her feet. Her onyx black hair magically tied itself into the tightest ponytail, giving everyone the sight of the long silver earrings that dangled from her earlobes. And prominent wrinkles etched themselves on her once perfect pale skin, her true age finally showing. The handle of the knife glowed yellow at her transformation before changing itself. It went from this majestic blade to a shiny pretty bracelet that wrapped around her wrist. It had her name etched on it, the engraving still holding some of that glow.

Emry.

"Ah, I guess it's finally time for a family reunion."

Maeve's eyes were closed the entire time. She was afraid this was all some crazy trap, and when she enters the other side of the portal, she'll be vaporized to death. Her breath was held, thinking that it'll brace her for the impact that might be lightning striking her and turning her into a roasted pile of what she used to be. Probably end up like those frat guys who fizzled into dust. Which is blowing her mind, because never in her entire life has she seen something as insane as a person turning into sand particles. But then again, she didn't expect to see her long-time crush turn out to be some monster. Kind of reminded her of a vampire. A sexy one, just like Edward Cullen—only so much scarier with cherry red eyes that could see right through her, and fangs and claws that could easily rip her throat open if wanted.

Maeve was pushed to the ground when she and Reggie emerged from the other side of the portal. She waited a second or two, still far too scared to open her eyes. But eventually when she wasn't being burnt to a crisp, entire body still completely intact, she peaked her brown irises open. It was one at first, met with that same fresh green grass as before. So from shock she was opening the other, a gasp vibrating from within her throat as she couldn't believe that she was actually in a different place. What did Reggie call it before? A different realm? Utterly baffled on how she managed to become stuck in a high field, she immediately stood to her feet, arms going around herself for some sort of protection. The place was exactly like what she saw through the circle. Blue skies, and a giant castle that dominated the grounds.

"If you're done freaking out, I'd really like to trade you for my cash prize now."

Maeve whipped around, taking in Reggie who was far too nonchalant for someone who just kidnapped another person before throwing them both into a whole new world. He stood casually, expression smug as he stopped picking at his nails to stick them within his pant pockets. He wasn't the least bit worried that Maeve would take off running. And he had no reason to be, because she wasn't about to. She has no idea where she is; there is no sign for guidance, and who knows what other creatures she might encounter. If there are ones like Reggie already in the human world, who knows what she might find in what she could only assume is their mother land.

"I'm not going anywhere with you."

She meant to sound confident. The spit she conjured to spray on his face had gotten stuck in her cheeks, swallowed right after just like her pride. She was terrified and confused, and the only face that she's familiar with is the only one in sight. He betrayed her. Maeve would rather falsely portray her courage than let Reggie take her anywhere else.

"You don't really have a choice. You either come with me, or get eaten by one of the dragons that live here."
"There's dragons!?"

She dropped her arms, face becoming one of pure shock as she stared at the other. She doesn't know whether she's scared even more now, or if she's amazed. Both seem reasonable in her opinion. Maybe she'll be able to see one before she's traded in (or whatever Reggie keeps mumbling about). The same Reggie who almost cracked a grin at her astonishment. But he kept his poise, rolling his eyes instead. He kept on track with his mission, grabbing her arm and beginning to drag her in the direction of the castle. It looked a great distance away, but that's probably just because of how massive it was. Built to almost reach the clouds and stretching long enough that it would take hours before you'd be able to see the side. Maeve didn't appreciate the hold Reggie had on her though, squirming until she was able to get him to release.

"Let me go! I already said that I wasn't going anywhere with you!"

With freedom, she made a run for it. Even though her heels dug into the dirt, getting her stuck every now and again, she never gave up when it came to getting away. When she momentarily looked back to see if Reggie was following after her, she was baffled when he was nowhere in sight. Just the distance that she managed to sprint. Or that was until she felt as though she wasn't walking on anything anymore and the sensation of falling shocked her nerves. She closed her eyes again, believing that instead of being vaporized that she'd just fall to her death.

Only she didn't.

Arms that she was quite familiar with caught her by the torso. She didn't move. She was stuck in the slanted position, dark hair hovering in front of her face, gravity ready to pull her down no matter how. Then yet again, she was peeking her eyes open, a yell leaving her mouth when she saw that there was nothing underneath the land she was standing on. It was almost like a floating platform, and a piece of her wanted to look under and see if they really were just somewhere in the sky. No wonder the castle was ready to touch the clouds. They were basically there. So far up that one slip and there is no way that you'd survive.

"I sort of need you alive for this. So please, no more running off." It was Reggie. Of course it was. No dragon was around to save her from facing her doom.

He was completely indifferent to the fact that he was standing on the edge—one push and he would be the one crashing onto whatever land that was closest—red eyes shining as he stared down at her. Once upon a time she would have swooned if he stared at her with such arrogance. It was quite a sexy look on all of his handsome Korean, slightly tan muscly body, and perfectly sculpted features. Even the way the slight breeze blew through his wavy dark hair was making his evil entity so much hotter than expected. But that's just the part of Maeve who is still deeply in love with him talking. The hatred part of her thinks he's letting this kidnapping go straight to his astonishingly large ego. That was another surprise that she doesn't think she'll ever get used to. Reggie Marks: the cute guy across the street who was the epitome of the person you would want to spend the rest of your life with. Now he was just some huge jerk.

"Only because you asked so nicely" She says sarcastically.

Reggie helps her find her balance on the ground, eyeing her as she straightens out the short dress she still wore. She wasn't as glamorous as she was when she first left her house; but even in such a wrecked state, she still held a beauty to her. Makeup slightly smudged and hair sticking out with a frizzy undertone, she still held her grace. She took off her shoes, holding them in one hand by the thin heel before taking a glance at Reggie who waited patiently. She looked around awkwardly, then taking the man off guard, she threw her shoes at him and then took off running again. He shakes his head at her, the frustration with her attempts to escape growing more and more with each second.

He caught up to her in no time. And instead of dragging her like before, he lifts her and then tosses her over his shoulder. Of course she starts to squirm in his hold, screaming that she be let go. He didn't listen and just tightened his grip on her thighs. Anymore movement and she would have slipped onto her head.

"This is kidnapping!"

"That's the point Mae."

"I could have you arrested."

"By who, the dragons?"

Maeve huffs out, body going limp in his arms...arm. She props her head up by using her hand and his back. She made sure to dig her elbow as deep as she could into his spine; chuckling when a brief hiss got swept up in the wind.

"You're lucky I have no idea where I am" If her almost falling off a floating platform hadn't made her aware that she wasn't genuinely still on Earth, then the words spoken from her lips was her wake up call. Her eyes widened and she tried to look at anything and everything she could. Kind of difficult when you're stuck in a position where the main sight is a man's ass and the grassy field that he continues to walk on. "I have no idea where I am. Oh my god, I have no idea where I am! Where are we!? Take me back home right now! My family is probably worried sick!"

That would defeat the whole purpose of kidnapping her to begin with, so he rolled his eyes again. After all these years of pretending to be her friend, a potential lover, he really does find her quite annoying. Her personality was far too hyperactive for his own. She liked to talk and be on the move—when he prefers to sit back and observe...quietly. They're opposites. He can't wait to get rid of her. Three years is far too long to be stuck on a mission. Even if deep down, in the farthest part of his body there is that tiniest bit of emotion saying that he'll miss her.

"Kariq Leada. You're in...Kariq Leada. A place where you humans would typically call monsters or weird creatures, live. It's my home. And from what I've been hearing...it's also yours."

Maeve has so many questions. But no correct way of asking them all.

"No. You're lying. I was born on Earth, Henderson Nevada, left on the porch of an adoptive home, because *parents of the year* didn't want me."

Reggie finally put her down. It wasn't grass that she felt on her feet, but stone. Looking down, gray cement was only the beginning of the mere astonishment she felt as she turned around to now stare wide-eyed at the ginormous castle. If it was physically possible, her jaw would have unhinged and fell to the floor. The architecture was beautiful from what she could see. Detailing was etched deep into the stone and gave her the itch to trace her finger across every swirl and jagged edge. But she kept her hands to her sides, actually gluing them there as fear began to strike her chest and her gut was bubbling with negativity. Everything about the building she was in front of had an evil aura, rupturing the beauty that once came with it. If she was supposed to enter that, she would have to be forced. And from the looks of Reggie's blank stare, arms crossed over his chest, he'll be the one to do it. Probably grab her by her hair again and block out the way she screamed and kicked.

"Look, I've spent years of my life dedicated to bringing you back. And for all three of those years, I've had to hear you rant on and on about how you genuinely believe that your parents are assholes and didn't want you. Well guess what? I don't care. I never did."

Why did that feel like a lie? Because it has to be one. *Right?* Reggie always listened to her problems with care. Intimacy. There was never a moment where he proved to be uncomfortable about her spilling every single worry and insecure thought that comes with abandoning parents. Maeve uses all of her willpower to hold back the way her eyes gloss over and begin to sting with tears. She doesn't know if it's from heartbreak or anger. He dedicated his life? Well, so did she.

"So *please*, save me the sob story and just enter the fucking castle already. Because if I were lying about any of this," He stepped closer and lowered his voice. Maeve didn't like it. She didn't miss the way he got close, when it gave her goosebumps and had her breath catching. "I wouldn't have chosen you."

Her chest tightened and saliva from unspoken curses built up in her mouth, it all being swallowed down until getting stuck in her throat. She couldn't swallow all of those thoughts and feelings no matter how hard she tried. It's either she says it, or lets it resonate with her a little bit longer. Her knees felt weak. Any second she will collapse. Who knows what after that. Maybe sob until her tears are no more? Just stare blankly at the stone? Lay all of her anger out through punches to Reggie's chest? Because how dare he? He comes into her life with a pretty white smile and a charming hello, just to rip that fantasy life away from her—stating so casually, so condescendingly that everything that she's ever known is a complete lie; and that right now she has to face the truth whether she likes it or not. And all because of what? Some money? She stared into his red eyes. They used to be such a pretty brown color. Right then she became absolutely defeated.

"Why not just kill me?" Her voice was low, almost unrecognizable.

"Because the people paying me need you alive."

His bland response was enough. She nodded, then slowly turned on her feet. The cold cement felt kind of nice against her burning skin. It eased some of the fiery animosity that kept building in the pit of her stomach. Now she was facing the ginormous door. It'd take at least thirty of her, stacked on top of each other in order to finally touch the top. Maeve inhaled sharply before pushing forward, ready to meet her doom. The doors opened loudly; with a squeak that was the wood scraping against the floor. Made a great way to announce that there were visitors; two who made their way in without any permission or previous notifying.

The castle was gorgeous. Something straight out of a fairytale. The ceilings were as high as could be, housing crystal chandeliers and articulate paintings that appeared to be hand-drawn from the immaculate detailing put into it all. More of the intricate design from the outside was carved also on the inside. It was like a trail, the swirls and curves eventually leading one's eye to the center where a grand staircase was built. Red carpet covered the beautiful marble, splitting onto more separate, more shorter stairwells which lead to the left and right hallways. But in the middle of it all was an arched window. A colorful one at that; the entire rainbow and specific cut pieces of glass creating a picture that was ultimately telling a story. Maeve was completely enraptured by the art. She was greedy when it came to wanting to touch it. Her fingers twitched and her feet almost lifted to get closer. The window looked to be presenting some form of worshiping. A man, maybe a king, was crowning a woman on her knees. But the crown wasn't the stereotypical shiny golden trinket everyone has seen, instead what might have been a halo. It was purple, shining the brightest out of the colors. But the woman didn't have any wings. If she was an angel, wouldn't she have wings?

The need to touch the window was interrupted by the sudden and extremely quiet presence of three people dressed in purple robes. They matched the same color as the woman's halo. The strangers were all men, walking from some place behind the stairs. That negative eerie feeling Maeve had gotten before was back and stronger than ever. She almost wanted to hide away, maybe take sanction behind Reggie and hope to all higher beings that these aren't the people she was being traded to. They could just possibly be butlers for someone else—that woman in the window. When staring at the piece of art, nothing bad seemed to resonate with it. It was pure.

Fearing behind Reggie was worse than a cowardly move. And the last thing Maeve wants to do is spend her last days, hours (whatever), hiding behind someone she thought she could love.

The three men stood beside one another in a line, in the middle of the room. Or that was until the one in the middle took a step forward.

"Ah, Maeve Whitmore. What it is to finally meet you."

Maeve thought he would sound more menacing. More evil, with a voice that booms, shaking the room and putting fear in any person or thing it was addressing. It was anticlimactic to hear him sound like a middle-aged man who was learning to quit smoking. And if she was stuck on such an underwhelming voice for a little bit longer than she would have missed out on what he had just called her. Animatedly she shakes her head, pushing strands of dark hair behind her left ear that has been pierced multiple times, silver earrings going all the way up her cartilage.

"Excuse me?" Maeve took a step closer even though she was reluctant. "Uh, you might have the wrong person...my last name isn't Whitmore, it's Ross..."

The man in the front's lips twitched. Almost as if he wanted to smirk and yet failed at doing so because he had to keep his serious evil henchman persona. He nodded instead, wrinkly hands poking through the long sleeves of the robe and clasping together in front of him.

"You underestimate me. But I can assure you," He sucked in a sharp breath, head craning both left and right, motioning to his companions who also made their presence known by stepping into the light. Just as fast as they had shown their face, they were magically gone. Maeve could have imagined the poof sound; it would have fit perfectly with how following the bodies of the men, there was a cloud of purple smoke. "You are the one that we are looking for" The other men right then appeared behind her.

Their sudden appearance had Reggie momentarily taken aback, leading him to take two steps towards the front door. And now there is space placed between him and his abductee. He lost sight of Maeve because unfortunately the three men could be mistaken for the giant species with how they tower over her with a height of nine feet. "Maeve Whitmore is your name. Born yet not raised here in Kariq Leada. And a second born to two of our own."

Maybe she should have questioned how he knows her, what

he plans to do with her. Even ask where he got the information to find out that she lived in Henderson Nevada? Instead she was rather hyper focused on the brief comment about her family. The family she was born into, and not the one that had been created for her.

"You know my family!?" Her eyes sparkled and a rush of excitement surged through her. Maybe now she could finally meet them. Ask them all of the questions that she's spent years pondering about. She could also soak in what they look like, who they are. She'd be able to finally laugh alongside them, creating jokes about which parent she looks like more. And if hearing news about her parents was enough, her ears rang from the joy that was comprehending that she had a sibling—and an older one at that. She couldn't wait to see whether they were a girl (who she could gossip with while doing each other's nails) or a boy (who she could still gossip with, but now while also seeing who was the best at playing video games...that is unless he wants his nails painted). The possibilities of hanging out with them are endless.

"*Knew*" The middle man watched her face deflate. "I'm afraid to relay the unfortunate news that is their deaths. You are the only one who survived."

Maeve did more than frown then. Her brown eyes searched the elder's, and observed his body posture. She needed to find something, anything, to prove that he was lying. So she stared. Her gaze intensified, shoulders rolling back as she looked at any movement to show that he was fibbing. And for a second her eyebrows raised when his expression drooped into a split second of vulnerability.

He was keeping something from her.

He had to be.

That is if he was telling the truth about any of this. What if he doesn't even know her parents? After all, everything that she's witnessed so far can be something straight out of a nightmare. So she laughs. Maeve breaks out into a huge grin, chest heaving up and down as giggles trapped behind her pink lips are refused to be let go as of now. It's guaranteed that she looks crazy with how she then starts to spit, not being able to hold back her laughter any longer. The man in a robe in front of her raises an eyebrow at her cackling figure—watching as she clutches her stomach, doubling over as the fit couldn't be stopped. Tears even began to brim her eyes, daring to spill the longer she laughed. The nameless man then looked at his companions silently asking for an explanation for her abnormal behavior. They could do nothing but stare as well, almost unprofessionally lifting their shoulders to silently reply that they have no idea why she so shamelessly laughed in their faces.

Reggie, also wanting to know what could be so funny, sneaks around the two men blocking him to eye over the eccentric Maeve Ross—Whitmore. He watches as she covers her mouth in an attempt to stop her fit, but it only resulted in more tears to fall. He watched those tears, saw how they fell out of eyes that held an emotion far from amusement. She wasn't laughing because she was entertained. Reggie turns his head from the sight. With the space where his heart is supposed to be, his chest clenches just like his jaw.

"I'm sorry!" Maeve manages out through more giggles. "I'm so sorry for-" She chuckles, hands now leaving her aching sides to wipe at her face that was evidently stained with salty droplets. "I'm so sorry for laughing. It's just this whole thing—this entire place, it's nothing but a dream. I'm dreaming right now and I'll wake up any second" She goes up to the man in front of her and weakly punches him in the chest. A puff of breath is released before he's regathering himself and immediately looking not only offended but angry. She's the first in so many years to be informal to someone of his power. "You all aren't real" She spins around to look at the other two men, also playing with them by messing with their robes and poking one of them on their long pointy nose. "My parents being from a different realm isn't real. And *you*," She puts her attention on Reggie. Momentarily he looks terrified of the hungry stare she's giving him, seriously becoming scared when she starts stalking her way over with hands clawing out like one would do when roleplaying some sort of cat. *Did she just growl at him?* "You aren't some evil-demon-vampire-thing that kidnapped me for some stupid money. You're an amazing guy who I can't deny being in love with anymore and will take this opportunity to be confident and just-" When close enough she grabs him by the collar for the second time that night (? Was it even night anymore? Should she be saying that day?) and slotted her lips with his. And for a moment it was believable; that this really was just some weird birthday dream that she'll wake up to and be so excited to tell her family about. But then one of the elderly men were clearing their throat, breaking Reggie from whatever trance that was Maeve Ross. He pushed her off, Maeve stumbling back as she wiped at her lips with a crooked grin.

"Maeve Whitmore," The front man goes stoic as he fixes his posture. "This isn't a dream" With a flick of his wrist, immediately being chained together were Maeve's wrist. What looked like flickering lightning, purple energy kept her hands tight in front of her, unable to break apart no matter how hard she tried. And when beginning to comprehend that the restraints only got tighter as she struggled, reality was also hitting. She looked at the men and back at Reggie who removed himself from the circle, scratching at his neck awkwardly. The apples of his cheeks were tainted red and yet that's not what worried Maeve so much. Whipping her head back around to the front man she again tried to remove herself from the magical handcuffs, nervous chuckles leaving her mouth now.

"What-?"

"Everything that's happened to you is real."

"No! That can't be!" She was shocked by the restraints then and it awfully felt real. Her eyes shook as her mind desperately tried to wrap around everything. Not only was that panic rising in her all over again, but embarrassment. There was no way that she just confessed her love for some man who was ready to kill her outside of a club.

"I've been seeking you out for quite some time, Maeve. You don't know how much power you actually possess. It's impressive really. And exactly what we need in order to fulfill the prophecy."

"Excuse me!?"

Maybe if she repeatedly blinks up at the man then a clear explanation would be said.

"You can thank Reginald Marks for that. Speaking of which," Outstretching his palm, seconds later a brown pouch appeared. Then without warning tossed it in the direction of the unexpecting man. He caught it with his chest, a bit confused by what was handed to him. Opening it, right then he had almost forgotten that he was getting paid for this. He dumped the few golden coins into his hands, eyebrows moving inward, agitation showing on his expression as he looked at the front man.

"What is this? We had a deal on fifty! This isn't even half of that!"

The nameless man rolled his shoulders back, hard stare being thrown down on the person who dared speak so carelessly.

"And you'll get what you were promised once the prophecy has been fulfilled. This is merely a portion for a job well done."

"What about the other thing we discussed!? I was promised it back!"

The man turned his back to Reggie.

"You may leave now. We must prepare for what is to come" Then yet again with a flick of his wrist, being pushed back by a force, Reggie was then taken out of the castle with the front doors slamming close in his face. The last that was heard of him was screams of protest.

Elise—*Emry* knocked on the door. It was loud, it was aggressive. It was enough force to get the homeowners to walk down their stairs so late within the night and open their door to what the possible danger is. Athena opened the door while her husband held a bat ready to swing behind her. Luckily he didn't just start waving it about, or else he would have struck Emry right in the temple.

"Elise? What happened? Where's Maeve?" The couple looked over her appearance, baffled by the change. And while there were questions that definitely needed to be asked, neither one said them aloud. Instead they waited for answers on their missing daughter. And Emry was ready to give them the explanation that they most definitely needed. But just as she was opening her mouth, interrupting her was the squeaky voice of a ten-year-old.

"Ew, why do you look so old?"

"Jax!"

Chapter Three

"We must prepare for your destiny. For now, you'll stay here."

Maeve was pushed into a cellar, a dungeon with metal bars and dirt floors where a dead rat may have taken sanction in the corner because it couldn't find a way out. Everything was rusted and disgusting, dim and extremely creepy when the only sound occupying the underground cell was the flickering of a flame from a giant torch that hung on a nearby wall, and the faint dripping sound that might be coming from an old sewer pipe. Maeve crashed to the floor with a grunt, her knees scraping against the hard ground and making her feel more gross than she already did. And she couldn't catch herself until it was too late; the front man who kept her in the magical cuffs refused to release her until she was secure within the prison. The purple handcuffs fizzled away once the screeching sound of a key twisting within a metal lock was heard. It was also a noise that made Maeve's heart pound aggressively against her chest and make her body tremble. It was when she knew that she wasn't being restrained anymore that she stumbled to her feet before dashing her way up to the bars and gripping onto them tightly. She stared at the three evil men with doe-eyes, a clear gloss coating them while her lips twitched as she stuttered out every concern she had.

"Wait! Wait! You can't keep me here!" She tried to pull at the bars, the rust coming off on her already muddy hands. They weren't moving. While the cell looked as though it needed many repairs, it kept sturdy. Maeve was officially a prisoner. "Aren't I the key to something big? You can't keep me in here knowing that something might go wrong. Why not put me in a nice bedroom? I bet you must have one to spare out of this huge castle."

The three men stared at her uninterested.

"This place might have originally been built to house the family of royalty, but not anymore. Us, the Raba will use this place to reconstruct and take back what should have been ours from the very beginning" They turned their back on her. "So no, you will not be *put* in a nice bedroom."

Then without another word they disappeared from the underground prison, closing the heavy metal door in their wake— startling Maeve as it slammed shut with an echo that might have made her go deaf in one ear. That's when she slumped. She huffed out a breath, pout taking over her features as she let all of her limbs go weak. And then she fell to the ground completely. Disregarding the fact that she still wore her sparkly blue dress (more so, she stopped caring that she wore her sparkly blue dress), she sat with her legs crossed, the thin fabric moving up her thighs and giving anyone the perfect view that was black laced panties. Or not, considering it was extremely dark and a pervert would have to actively seek for a peak at her underwear. And from what she's gathered, she's the only one even down wherever she is.

Or so she thought.

Maeve squeals from fright when a deep voice comes from across from her.

"He's quite uptight, isn't he?"

"What—Who are you!?" Maeve scrambled towards the bars of her cell once more, trying to get a better look at whoever was speaking. It only resulted in her accidentally banging her forehead against the metal, momentarily forgetting that they were the main thing that was blocking her view. She rubbed at the sore spot, feeling embarrassed when the other person, a *man, was* heard chuckling at her. Thankfully she didn't have to try too hard when it came to getting a good look at him. The flame from the torch gave his features an orange hue. His dark skin danced with the fire, creating a glow that even Maeve doesn't think a supermodel was capable of doing. He didn't have a shirt on strangely enough, so she could see the outline of abs that were on display, alongside a shaved chest that she will admit would be a fantasy to rub oil all over just to see his pecs glisten.

Tearing her eyes away from his body, she finally saw his face and almost found herself entranced by who he was. He was handsome. *Are all monsters sexy?* He had a sharp jawline that was covered in grown-out facial hair. He must have been in here for some time now. But it all trailed perfectly to his plump pink lips that were being stretched into a cheeky smile where his white teeth were shown. His nose was like a stretching effect where it starts off slim yet widens in the best way when reaching his nostrils; and it was also easy to guide anyone to the set of eyes that this man has. They were the stereotypical brown. Dark and obviously mysterious because she has no idea whether this man has been locked up for dangerous reasons or not. (Even if she highly doubts it.) His eyelashes were long, batting gracefully whenever he blinked. She has to pay for eyelashes like his. And when he stopped trailing his gaze all over her body, locking his sight on hers, she almost felt as though the wind had been knocked out of her.

She felt like her chest was compressing—her lungs being squeezed from all of the oxygen, her heart thumping, the tightening of every organ, bone and vein within her. She clutched at her chest, thinking that if she clawed hard enough then she'd be free from whatever horrible feeling she was experiencing. Maeve inhaled, exhaled, panted, and then mumbled out that she couldn't breathe. The man on the other side gave no response. Instead he was the same way...a bit more feral though. What once was brown irises shifted into a bright yellow, shining brighter than the fire ever could. They were locked in on Maeve too. If she wasn't already scared that she was going to die from everything else that was happening to her, she would have been mortified that she was about to be attacked. By what, is the question? The man fell to the ground, hands digging into the dirt as he fidgeted, grumbling incoherent phrases to himself. Then there was low growling—something akin to an angry dog. Was he some kind of wolf-man-thing? Maeve stepped away from the bars. With her back against the stone wall, she watched him eventually stand to his feet once more. He looked at her, watched her; not only could he see her fear, but could feel it too. And upon recognizing who she was, he didn't need her to be afraid of him. He never wants her to be afraid of him. The thought in itself is heart clenching and soul crushing.

"You don't need to be scared of me. I will never hurt you."

Maeve looks at him as if he were crazy. What part of this whole thing would make her believe him? He's a man who's behaving like he took one too many drugs, has yellow eyes, and suddenly has a voice that is ten octaves lower than what it originally was. She'd be a fool to smile in his face and automatically agree. Even if a part of her was claiming that she was a fool. Her emotions were in a frenzy. There was fear, sadness, joy, but poking and prodding at all of that was the faint feeling of adoration. Would she call it that? It's what she felt whenever around her family, around Elise. She was eerily calm, and for a moment thinking that those golden irises had casted a spell upon her so she would stop having what she assumes is a panic attack. So with hesitancy she crawled her way a little closer, brown eyes never breaking sight from the way his body moved, eyes darted, fingers twitched. Something about this man was pulling her in; and while she wasn't about to give up her trust so easily, she could also spare her fellow prison mate an ear.

"Am I just supposed to take your word for it?"

The stranger sucked in a breath then. He gripped the metal bars and dropped his head between his shoulders. He shut his eyes only for a second or two before he was lifting his head back up and now those yellow eyes of his had returned to their typical brown. His grip loosened and he returned to his standing height. He stopped staring at her with a crane of his neck, lips pulling into a grin as he let out a breathy chuckle.

"Judging by the fact that you aren't gasping for air like a dead fish anymore, yeah I think you should."

Was this him trying to be nice? Why use a dead fish for a comparison?

"Says the man that was quite literally on the ground ready to dig a hole" He didn't take kindly to her rebuttal and was quick to whip his head around and narrow his eyes at her. *Ooou, even his menacing stare was quite hot.* He scoffed as he crossed his arms over his chest. "What kind of monster are you anyway? I hear this place is full of kinds."

"You're not from here?"

"The human world as you people like to call it."

"Well *human*, using monster is a derogatory term in this realm."

Maeve let her eyes widen comically. How many times has she thought about these people like this and unintentionally hurt them?

"Really? I am so sorry! I didn't mean to-"

The stranger snickered then, laughter breaking through as her apology became a ramble. That's when Maeve stopped and huffed out in offense.

"I'm just pulling your hind leg, blue dress" While it was obvious that his remarks were getting under her skin just a little, she will admit that his line delivery is charming. Even when he smiles she can't help but slightly swoon from how pretty he appears. "We actually take pride in such terms around here. So call us what you want. Kariq Leada citizens will just brush it off as some weird compliment."

Well that's relieving to hear.

Brushing stray strands of her curly hair from her face, Maeve shifts the topic.

"So what kind of monster-creature thing are you?"

The man approached the bars yet again, leaning against them

as he used the biggest gap he could to look her up and down from head to toe.

"The same thing that you are, of course."

His smile was mischievous enough for her to think that he was bluffing. How would he be able to know that she was supernatural just by being able to look at her? Since she's been brought here, she's been fed nothing but the same story that she is one of them. But if that were true, wouldn't she have unlocked whatever crazy power a creature in a mystical realm should have? She's twenty-one now, if she had even a speck of something magical within her, she's pretty sure that she would have figured it out.

"And what's that? A giant dog?"

"Are you going to be upset that it's not something cooler?"

Maeve quirked an eyebrow.

"So that's it? You're a giant dog?" Now it was her turn to look him up and down, from head to toe. "Yeah, that's kind of disappointing."

"Don't worry your dirty little head, blue dress...we don't catch fleas if that's what you're concerned about" Maeve sub-consciously reached a hand to her hair where she didn't have to touch much in order to believe that she looked like a wreck. What once was a perfectly curled style for a night out, was now just a frizzy and greasy mess. "I'm a werewolf if you want the logical term for it. And *you* are also one. Ya' kind of reek of one actually, now that you look like you haven't showered in days" He made the dramatic movement that was raising a hand to wave it in front of his nose, face scrunching up as if what he was smelling was extremely distasteful. Which if she was him, she would know that was a complete lie. She actually smelled of the heavenly scent that was the combination of mandarin oranges, jasmine, peach and sandalwood. Maeve outstretched her arm, pointing an accusing finger at him while yet again she was twisting her face in offense.

"Hey! I showered this morning! I smell fantastic!"

She was taking the whole groundbreaking news of her being a werewolf kind of lightly. But then again, she's also kind of impressed that she didn't check into a mental ward yet for actually considering that this place is real. The stranger put his arms up, taking a step back to prove he meant no harm out of the comment. Gave her enough confidence to smile and quit pointing so angrily.

"I smell otherwise" It was coughed out, very quickly covered up by another topic change when she was heard shouting with a palm banging at the bars. He snickered at her frazzled state. "So how did someone like you get stuck in the dungeon of the all powerful Raba anyway?"

Someone like you? What's that supposed to mean?
"Apparently I'm some sort of chosen one" Maeve wiggled her fingers for dramatic effect. "My power can help them do what they've always wanted—I don't know. One minute I was enjoying my birthday, and then the next I was brought here through some portal...which by the way, super scary to travel through."

"It's your birthday? Funny, it's also my best friend's birthday. Just turned twenty-one."

"No way! I also just turned twenty-one. When I was born is honestly the only thing my adoptive parents said they could find in all records of me." *Adopted?* That's an insane coincidence when it comes to his best friend. The stranger really looked at her then. Looked at all of her beautiful features with an intensity that almost had her flinching. "Why are you staring at me like that?"

He was getting ready to answer when the metal door to the cellar had screeched open. Immediately both of them whipped their heads, stretching their necks and eyes in order to see who just walked in. Maeve was praying that it wasn't those Raba dudes again. Who knows what this prophecy actually was, and what they were preparing for. She was hoping for enough time to try and find a way out, really only stuck with talking to someone who she doesn't know whether she likes or dislikes. There was the sound of feet padding against the stone walkway, the steady heels being interrupted with a voice.

"Amir, we've come to save you!"

"Shut up, you moron!"

There was the sound of a hit, an exclaimed ow, and then the same feet getting closer. Before Maeve knew it, there were three men in her line of sight. She couldn't exactly see what they looked like, because they had their very large backs to her. All attention was on their friend and the guy that she learned was named Amir. And without much talking, the trio actively messed with the metal lock before swinging the caged door open. At the freedom, one of the newcomers launched himself at Amir and brought him into one of the tightest hugs. It looked extremely awkward and uncomfortable judging by the fact that it is an adult man clinging onto the body of another adult man; who had no idea that he was about to be greeted with such a warm reunion.

"We missed you so much!"

"Speak for yourself" It was said with a scoff by one of the other guys, huge arms crossing over his even bigger chest. He must be the dark hair, dark eyes, emotionally unavailable one. A contrast to the bubbly blonde with striking green eyes that doesn't know the definition of personal space. While the last guy was off to the side just glad to see that his friend, family, whatever they are to each other, was perfectly fine. Maeve stared at him the most. He was tall, six-foot at least; he had brown skin just like hers; with the body of a man who didn't skip a day at the gym. *Doesn't seem like any of these men do.* His facial features were soft though, not a piece of facial hair anywhere, while his lips were the perfect shade of pink. And his eyes were the same color brown as hers, showing that sparkle that Athena always claimed that she had whenever she talked about something she was so passionate about. Everything about the man seemed oddly familiar, and right now she wishes that she could just go up and touch his face until she is able to figure out why.

"Took you guys long enough. I could have found my own way out by now" Amir smiled after he managed to get the blonde off of him. Then he gave the other two a brotherly handshake.

"Sorry, we would have been here sooner but you know how the Junud have been recently. They won't let us out of their sight. That's why it's only us three" The final guy (that Maeve wishes would just say why she feels as though she knows him) spoke. "But we're here and we only have a short period before the Raba realizes we broke in, so we need to leave now."

The three men were about to make their leave when Maeve interjects. Rightfully so if she may add.

"Hi," The blonde one let out a shriek. Everyone faced her,

curious. Or at least everyone but Amir who couldn't keep a grin from his face. "I don't mean to interrupt your little reunion, but I'd be super grateful if you let me out of this cell as well. Kind of been kidnapped, and have no idea what they plan to do with me."

The scary man stepped forward. He looked huge—like a tower. His perfectly proportioned face never deterred from the firm eyes and chapped lips that were in a line. Maeve probably would have cowarded back from his presence alone if she wasn't already terrified of everything else. If anything, he was probably the tamest thing she's experienced all day.

"We don't even know who you are. How can we trust that you're not some ploy-" He stopped when Amir walked up to his side and leant closer to his ear. Something was whispered with a pat to his shoulder and those eyes that shifted yellow again. What must have been said was world changing, because the tough man turned to look at him with complete bafflement. With eyes that grew as wide as saucers and a mouth that wouldn't clamp shut, it was comical. His once cold exterior dropped and his true personality began to show. The cold-guy act was nothing but that; and he's just someone that needs a bit more time in order to let loose. "Micah, give me the keys."

Micah, the one who Maeve still can't wrap her head around furrowed his eyebrows. They looked at one another. His brown irises connected with hers. He looked ready to protest, wondering why someone with so much masculinity was ready to drop that just because of something said. But then he felt it. There was a pull when it came to Maeve. His heart was swelling with this newfound admiration, brain whirling with this need to keep her safe because it was his duty. He too had this strange feeling of familiarity yet can't quite figure it out. Being the leader of the group though, whether he has a strong passion for someone or not, he's still obligated to take caution. His instincts are never wrong, and he doesn't plan to ruin that now.

"But we don't know if she's a danger or not. We can't release a prisoner belonging to the Raba. They're already so intrusive of our-"

"From what Amir just told me, I think it's best that we save her. Give me the keys."

"Guys, I think the Raba have caught wind of our presence" Blondie says as he sniffs the air.

"No, I cannot release someone that we know nothing about. Now let's go. Whatever happens to her, has no concern for us" Micah replies with an assertiveness that even Maeve is struck by. Whether or not it was a positive strike, was something she would need a minute to decide. A part of her felt kind of rejected by the man.

"I promise I'm no harm. I'm not even from here. I'm human!" She gripped the bars. Micah looked at her again, a stormy debate brewing within his head.

"We really need to go now if we don't want to get caught" The blonde presses.

"She's not human, she's one of us" Amir joins in. He looked just as determined. "I'll explain when we get out of here. But she's coming with us."

"Oh, you were being serious about that" Maeve says head now whipping to look at Amir. The hurt that she once felt from Micah was being pushed to the side a little, her now being overcome by levity. Why are her emotions haywire? It's as if she had another person telling her that she needed to be feeling these things. It's a complete contrast to how she truly feels, and it's going to give her a headache.

"Of course I was serious about that. Why would I just randomly say you're a werewolf?"

"I don't know, maybe you wanted to prank me,"

"Prank you?"

"Or make me think this place is real,"

"She doesn't even believe in us!?" Micah shouts.

"Kind of a deal breaker" Mean man mumbles.

"I hate to break it to you blue dress, but this place is one hundred percent real" He looked at Micah. "And if she doesn't want to die-"

"Die!?" Maeve yells. While it was definitely a thought that crossed her mind because of all of this, the terror that it might actually happen never truly processed.

"—or whatever they plan to do with her, she's coming with us. She has to!"

"We seriously need to go. Now!" Blondie is growing a bit frustrated that no one is listening to him. So he decides to just push his fellow friends towards the door. Amir growled when he was touched. His eyes flashed that yellow that Maeve was beginning to believe looked extremely pretty, alongside his buff body going rigid. It wasn't until hands were raised in the air, surrender being given did he calm down...just a little though. Amir himself was agitated that only dark and mysterious guy was on his side. But then again, he also only told dark and mysterious guy who Maeve is. And he doesn't have time to just blurt it out. Because not only will his two friends have to process the information, but it's promised that Maeve will have a million questions before she does too.

Micah sits with his friend's intensity. He looks between the door and Maeve numerous times. His eyebrows were furrowing and he rubbed at his buzzed hair in frustration. His decision is life changing.

Having to explain to her parents, to her adoptive parents who for all of this time believed that they were gifted the miracle of precious little baby Maeve, that it was all planned for her safety was a lot more difficult than Emry expected. She's had to repeat the same thing over three times now just for the sake of James (who still was a little confused by it all). The tea that Athena made them sat on the rectangular wooden coffee table. Hers and Emry's went stale, cold from being left there at the beginning of the conversation; only being sipped on maybe once or twice before the beverage was long forgotten. James on the other hand couldn't stop drinking his, thankful that the tea was something he could use as an outlet not to freak out. Kept his hands from shaking, his mouth from urging that he be taken to look for her immediately, and his mind from bustling with worry. Even though no matter how much tea he forces down his throat, he will always be scared of the fact that his daughter was taken by some evil men and is about to be used for something.

"I hate to tell you about this now, but it's my job to protect her. The less people who knew about her true identity the better" Emry shifts her stare to the TV mantle. It was aligned with many family photos. Each child got their own picture as well, one being taken from some special moment; printed from their recent school year; or something that they took themselves: 'a selfie'. Her attention was captured by one of Maeve. It was a recent picture, nothing too special about it, just her smiling brightly. Her dark hair was pulled up into some messy version of a bun, strands loose, yet with most of it out of her face everyone was able to see the way her eyes formed into crescents from how hard her lips were pulled up. Pure joy was evident. A complete contradiction to the last time they saw each other. Her smile was nowhere to be seen—just a wobbly bottom lip that didn't know whether it wanted to be from fear or puzzlement. Maybe even betrayal. "I was doing so well. Twenty-one years…"

The sun was shining, beaming if one will, forcing its heat on anyone who dared walk outside instead of spending their day on the couch in front of a tv. The Ross couple were one of those people; taking the time where they both had a break from work and wanted to spend some time together. And they wanted to spend it with their recently adopted daughter. Having spent six years waiting for Maeve's parents to come back and claim that they just needed time before they could happily take care of their child, eventually they gave up and understood that no one was coming. Besides, by now they had grown attached to the little bundle of joy and couldn't give her up even if they wanted to. Her laughter was theirs, and her tears were theirs. So wanting another loving family moment for the books, the trio headed for the city park. A generic picnic was packed in a white and red cooler where James forgot the important part that made a cooler a cooler, and that was the ice. Athena nagged his ear off then, pushing him back in the direction of their car where he must go to the store right now and buy some. That left one less person to keep an eye on their belongings.

"Momma, I wanna go on the slide" With tiny fingers, six-year-old Maeve Ross pointed in the direction of the giant playground where many other children of all ages ran about with giggles. And with tiny feet she bounced on the tips of her toes, ones covered in flower decorated sneakers, an eagerness in the way she also let her doe-eyes widen at the admiration for the huge green twisty slide.

"Sorry hun, but you have to wait until Dad gets back" The disappointment Maeve displayed was adorable yet still heartwrenching. Athena searched an extra bag she brought that was sitting limply on the picnic table they stood in front of. Eventually she pulled out a plastic shovel and pale, alongside the few dolls that were allowed to be brought. She leant down to give them to the sulky little girl. *"Here, why don't you go play in the sandbox for now? I'll be able to see you while keeping watch of our stuff. Then when Dad gets back, I'll take you to the slide. Okay?"*

It was contemplated by Maeve for a moment. She really wanted to go to the playground. It's all she's been raving about since her parents said that they were taking a trip to the park. Sadness filled her as she watched a little boy come from out the end of the twisty one. Yet even at a young age she understood her mother's words and took what was given to her. She glumly walked over to the sandbox, plopping down on the part that seemed the most leveled. There was only one other kid there with her, but he was picking his nose and then smearing it on his shirt, so there was no way that she was about to approach him and ask to play. Maeve sat where she was, shoulders slumped and frown almost permanently on her round pink lips. Leisurely she stuck her dolls in the sand while she tried to build them a house. The sun shined directly down on her as she tried to play all alone, until it didn't. A shadow casted over her, and she was quick to look up as to why. She was met with a little girl, she looked around her age. Pale was her skin tone and it was great that she took the damage that was a tan away from Maeve's already dark skin. Her black hair was pulled back tight into a ponytail, leaving none of her facial features to the imagination. With sparkling blue eyes and the attempt at a smile, the stranger stuck her hand out.

"Hi, my name is Elise! Can I play with you?"

Maeve was hesitant at first. But that was only because she thought she would be able to pout in peace. It wasn't until Elise took the spot beside Maeve anyway that her frown began to pick up.

"Do you play with dollies?"

"Do you play with unicorns?"

Pulling out a small plastic unicorn from the pocket of her light blue overalls, Elise knew that she had the other right in the palm of her hand.

"And then they took her. They took her the one time that I let my guard down" An anger started to bubble within Emry as she kept her attention on the photograph. Not only at everyone who's involved for her capture, but herself. How dare she, for even a moment, believe that their lives weren't in danger? How could she for a moment enjoy the human world and let go of that tough persona she's built even before Maeve was born? It was her one job to protect the girl, avenge the man who didn't get to see any of her firsts. She's an absolute idiot.

A hand was felt to Emry's. That's when she turned to see Athena staring warmly at her. Her smile was gentle. Forgiving.

"Don't be so hard on yourself dear. I think you did a splendid job. You were the one person that Maeve trusted with her life. If you ask me, twenty-one years is a long time to dedicate to someone" The mood was slightly lifted when snickers were given on both ends. "And I can already tell that you would have gone for all of eternity making sure that my daughter didn't go through any harm. So thank you" Then without warning, Athena was pulling Emry in for a hug. It was oddly nice. Or well it's not odd. Emry has grown up with this family; had been treated like a daughter as well; was given the opportunity to experience what love and care actually not only looks but feels like. She never had that with anyone—as for witches, it's in their culture to only populate for the sake of keeping their species alive.

Daughters and sons are born, and then once their seventh birthdays have passed they are sent to a prestigious boarding school purposely built in order to train those same daughters and sons how to control the magic they possess. It was after the Witch Massacre in 1982 that witches deemed it necessary to only use magic for dire situations; it being the only way that they were allowed back into society. The negative of it all, children are taken from their parents and basically forced to forget about them, because they were never going back. All focus had to be on yourself, there was no time to talk with mom and dad, grow an emotional connection with them and then allow them to help guide you through life. You would be lucky to even

have remembrance of who they were before you were taken—
you would be lucky to even have parents that were actually in
love and not two people who were given a few hundred rons
after gifting a newborn to the boarding school. Because they also
did that. Took in infants to become soldiers, to use their magic
offensively just in case Kariq Leada ever wanted a rebuttal war.

Or if Kariq Leada continued to be blind to the disappearing
witch issue that was established almost twenty-seven years ago,
and they had to make sure they were fighting off anyone who
may be a suspect to why their people would be walking the
streets and then they're not. It was said that Ma'am Letita, the
representative for the witches within the council would speak
with everyone and demand that all other representatives get
their species to help find the mastermind behind the declining
of them. And yet no one has offered to help. It's almost as if
they're turning their cheeks to the issue and letting their down-
fall become the new normal.

"So tell me," Athena speaks as she releases Emry. "How old are
you really? It's interesting to see that you've been altering your
appearance this entire time" James tapped her on the shoulder.

"Honey, let's keep this on Maeve for now."

"Right. How can we save Maeve? What I'm gathering is
that she's somewhere in your realm, held hostage by your kings,
and all because they believe that she's the one to give them
something"

Emry nodded.

"And it's not we, it's me. I cannot bring you with me because Kariq Leada isn't the best place for humans" She gently
grabbed hold of Athena's hands. They were similar as she looked

at them. Wrinkly and faded of their youth. It was tugging at her heartstrings to replay all of the wonderful moments that they've shared with each other. Athena didn't see that she may have been a little girl from a different family, didn't once think that she needed to be treated differently because she wasn't her child—or even after her and James adopted three more. She was still Elise White; a name she randomly thought of when looking at a perfume billboard upon the first entry of the human world. "I just wanted to tell you the truth. You deserve to know. You've raised her like she's your own, and the guilt I'm going to feel if I'm returning with devastating news..."

"Don't say that!" Athena yanks back her hands. "Don't you dare say that!"

"But Mrs. Ross, there's no guarantee that I will be able to save Maeve. You have to understand that the Raba are people that even someone like I cannot slay."

"I don't care! You're going back there and you're going to save my daughter! You're going to save her and then the both of you will come back so I can hug you forever" She was standing on her feet now, tears brimming her eyes. James immediately went to her side, bringing her in for a hug.

"I'm sorry Mrs. Ross."

"I don't want to hear another apology from you."

"Casualties are predictable I'm afraid" Emry stood to her feet, voice leveled and voided of emotion. She tried her hardest to remain impassive, afraid that one waver and she'll be crumbling. Weeping for failing her guardian duties. For failing people that she's grown to care for, and that she hopes cares for her too. "All

I can promise you now is that when it comes down to it, I will sacrifice my life for hers."

She walks out of their home then, head straight and refuses to look back even though she could hear Athena protesting. If she blocks out the woman's voice, it won't be as painful.

Pushing the door open, in walked the Raba. It wasn't apparent but they were thrilled that they had the final thing in order to reach the amount of power needed. They practically glided across the walkway, chins high and confidence even higher. Their hands had been clasped behind their backs, chests puffed and ready to bring Maeve upstairs and sacrifice what is attached to the incredible abilities she doesn't even know she carries. They stopped in front of her cell. Irises that resemble charcoal had shown nothing when the flames of the burning torch danced close to their face. And yet they could see their future when they find themselves staring down at the woman. Laid out on the floor, she must have fallen unconscious from the exhaustion that was entering a new world and being told all of the most bizarre things.

"It was said that she and the dog had managed to escape. Only she is right where we left her" The three men turned to see the opposing cell. It was hard to tell, but there definitely was a lump of a body sitting in the corner. "And so is he. We must question the Junud who gave inaccurate information."

The front man, Qayid snapped his fingers and the cell door had swung open, an ear wrenching squeak following the move. Then with his palm facing up, a purple hue surrounded the limp form that is Maeve. She was floating not too soon after, where gravity pulled at her hair, head, clothes, arms and legs.

"Our ritual may commence."

Chapter Four

The sun was finally peaking over the horizon as a new day has finally come. The breeze was light, cooling the remains of last night's heat, yet making the horrible events so much more apparent. It was damaging to Emry's heart. She sat on a park bench, eyes glued to the way the sky was a beautiful yellow and orange; something that will eventually change into a beautiful blue, and no one but her and the Ross family will know what happened. To the rest of the world, they were living their lives— some probably recovering from a drunken hangover because they were at the same club, some waking from a peaceful slumber because they had to work. She thought about Athena as she sat, fingers tapping at her knee. She was still wearing her previous clothes. And if anyone were to go by, jog past for their morning exercise, then they would probably take a minute to question her appearance. Mentally they would ask why she looked like a wreck.They would ask why such an older lady decided to wear clothes that definitely didn't fit her age range. But it's not like Emry would care. If anything she would just continue to stare out into the distance, trying her hardest not to cry because she disappointed the few people that she never thought she would grow so attached to.

Her cell phone rang. No, it vibrated. She remembers turning it off because she wanted to be alone. No sound. Reluctantly she pulled it from her jacket pocket, eyes still on the rising sun than the glowing screen. It didn't matter who called anyway. This was something that she needed to fix on her own, and with no emotional pep-talk about how she's a lot stronger now than she ever was before. The phone vibrated in her hand once more before her thumb was swiping at the screen and it stopped. Slowly she brought it to her ear, the earrings she wore swaying at the motion.

"Emry, ah thank goodness you finally answered" Right, because this wasn't the first time that she decided to just ignore the calls she was receiving. At first it was because Athena tried contacting her. Call after call, after call, a few messages that were accompanied by capital letters, long paragraphs and exclamation marks, until she gave up. Emry didn't bother checking her phone anymore after that—no matter who was the one that was ringing. But even through the despair that filled her veins and numbed her brain, the minimal shock she felt when she was hearing a voice that didn't belong to Athena.

"Amora!?" Emry straightened her back, eyebrows creasing and grip on that stupid bedazzled case that Maeve made her buy because: *"It would just make you feel pretty!"*

"Yeah, I've called at least three times! Why haven't you picked up your phone!?" A heavy sigh was given while Emry tried to give an answer but was nothing but a rambling mess. What could she say anyway? Anything and everything that's happened so far is only terrible news. Maybe now is the right time to tell her.

"They've found Maeve...and they took her" Her tone was neutral. Spoken and just as hard to say for the second time. Made her feel weak and useless. Her eyes dropped to the ground then, ears awaiting the surprised shout that is Amora scolding her (even though it's typically the other way around). Emry watched as a wilting daisy got caught up in the wind. She raised a hand, finger swirling in a circle as she thought about bringing the flower back to its natural beauty. Only nothing happened. If anything, the daisy looked to have gotten worse—it caused anxiety to tingle those same fingers that were supposed to sprout magic. "Fuck, and I'm too overwhelmed that my magic is dwindling."

Amora giggled. That wasn't the response Emry was expecting. It kind of made her frustrated. This obviously wasn't a giggling matter.

"Why are you laughing?"

"Because for once it's not me" Amora let the laughter out loud now. It was loud enough that the other cringed at the sound, momentarily removing the phone from her ear. "Oh my— even when we were nurses all those years ago, it was always you cleaning up my mess. But now I have to clean up yours!"

Thankfully Amora was in a completely different realm right now, their only communication being cell phones that they've casted spells on in order to be able to reach each other. If she was beside Emry, the woman probably would have turned her into the hyena that she was laughing like.

"I think it's best that we finally introduce the first born into this. He could help."

"Well won't you like to hear the great news!" Amora chirped.

"What are you talking about? What did you do?"

"Ah, no need to cry about losing the one person you were supposed to protect,"

"Get to the point."

"She fell ever so gracefully in my lap" You could hear the way she smiled smugly. But pushing the way she bragged to the side, Emry stood from the bench in a haste, astonishment and bafflement making her pace back and forth.

"What!? How!?" Her shout startled a few birds, them flying away.

"Oh you won't believe it! Her brother found her."

The four strangers, the four men that were originally only there for each other, said that she had to run as fast as she could. She was supposed to follow them, to never look back and keep her mouth shut from any unnecessary sounds; all unless she wanted to end up right back in the dungeon that she was successfully saved from. So she listened, emotions heightened by the adrenaline that rushed through her veins, fueling the way that her lungs burned and legs already ached. She was never the athletic type, only spending a year of her high school career in cheerleading before realizing that it just wasn't for her. Elise was there when she tried out for the squad, not only being her emotional support but agreeing to try out if it would help ease her nerves. While Maeve barely passed auditions, Elise was spectacular. She handled the flips and cartwheels with ease; also having the strength to lift other students when newbies were asked to do a practiced routine. After witnessing Elise slice and dice those frat guys outside the club, doing the same tricks that she did years ago made sense now. She's been hiding who she really was, and with that hidden identity came with skills that no normal human could possess. Judging by the new intel Reggie ever so quickly threw upon her about her best friend actually being her guardian from a different realm, no wonder she so easily could bend backwards or flip into a split. Maeve wonders how she's doing. If she's going out of her way to look for her? If she decided to tell her parents? If once they were reunited that all of the lies from the years they've spent together would be given an explanation? She thinks she really needs one.

It'd obviously take time, but Maeve knows she'll eventually understand. She has to. Elise was her best friend. Someone she would trade her life for if it came down to it. And she probably would be able to explain Reggie. Tell her why the man she's grown this massive crush on, would turn out to be a douchebag with really sharp teeth. Or maybe she wouldn't? Only Reggie would be able to do that. Then maybe she'd be able to explain why these three old men are desperate to capture her, and use her for some prophecy. She'd be able to explain why she was following behind four other men, all of them huffing and puffing as they maneuver their way out the giant castle. Micah led them all—the five of them in a line as they rushed their way through dark tunnels that were extremely hard to see through. Maeve almost tripped a few times. Barefoot with no remembrance of where her heels have gone, she's stepped on one too many sharp things that had her squeaking out in pain. It was when Amir realized that she was falling behind from the lack of sight did he stop to grab for her hand.

The refreshing feeling she felt then. She felt anew. But it

didn't stop the way she let out a gasp, eyes moving down to the way Amir's much larger hand held onto hers. He was warm despite being locked up in that cold cell for who knows how long. And he held on tight, his fingers gently pressing into the back of her hand. There wasn't the slightest hint that he would be letting go. Or at least not until they have finally made it to safety. She moved her sight from their hands then, craning her neck so she was able to stare at the back of his head. She didn't know this man at all. Couldn't even tell you what his last name was. And yet here she was, keeping in line with his steps, matching his movements perfectly as if she was able to predict exactly what he would do next.

"The exit is up ahead!" Micah shouts. *So much for being quiet. Why was he allowed to yell but not her?* Probably had to do with the fact that he still didn't trust her—he didn't know her. Rejection was felt again, detering the way she kept up with Amir. So Amir glanced back, yellow eyes finding hers.

"You're tired."

"No, no. I'm fine. It's just been a while since I had to run away from creepy men in creepy robes" She jokes. They move around a giant rock that must have fallen from the wall of the tunnels. She stumbles but is back up once a tug at her and Amir's hands are threatened to break apart. He smirks at her attempt to hide her true exhaustion. That doesn't stop him from halting them from moving any further, to then squat down in front of her with his hands reaching behind him.

"Come on. Jump on. I'll carry you the rest of the way."

"No, I said I'm fine. I can keep going" She doesn't know whether she's rattled because a really attractive guy is asking her to get on his really attractive back, or if she's still too stunned by what is happening that she just wants to persevere on her own. Who knows if this guy and his buddies are even the good guys. They could be luring her to her death right now. But if that were true then she wouldn't already be so sure that whatever Amir says is the truth.

"It wasn't really a request, blue dress."

He nods for her to get on once more. He's grinning as he does so. He wiggles his fingers, the action giving some sort of clarification that he'll catch her. She looks at the others already nearing the end, then she looks from where they came from. If she tries hard enough, really straining her ears, then she's able to hear that someone or something is definitely following. So with a nod of her own, she gets closer and then jumps onto Amir's broad back without a warning. He pretends to groan, face scrunching which leads her to show concern.

"I'm too heavy. You're tired as well. You were locked up longer than I was" She was ready to slide down, return to her feet. Only before she could, he was already gripping the underneath of her thighs. Her breath hitches at the touch. It was just as assertive as when he held her hand. So firm yet so soft. And then he was also chuckling, body straightening as well as it could with a grown woman attached to his back.

"Pulling your hind leg again" He looked back at her as well as he could. "You really need to lighten up...try a salad."

She scoffed, arm lifting ready to hit him for such an offensive comment. Maybe even for the terrible joke when they're in a serious situation. Only before she could land it, he's continuing on with his run down the tunnel. He was far too fast for her to hold his shoulders loosely, therefore leading Maeve to wrap her arms around his neck and press herself as close to him as she could.

I'm going to fall. I'm going to fall. I'm going to fall.

She squeezed her eyes shut, only reopening them when the brightness of the outside greets them. She blinks once, then twice. She had to readjust, head lifting in order to look at her surroundings. She's back on the grassy field. The sun was beginning to go down, it was touching the horizon so the once beautiful blue sky was now turning a yellow and orange hue. Maeve then looked back at the castle they just left from. Instead of seeing the front doors, she was met with a giant stone wall. The tunnel had led to a side entrance/exit.

"Let's go! It won't be long before they catch up!" Micah shouts before he's holding up a sphere. Maeve remembers that thing. It was the same ball Reggie used in order to get her here. It was another portal, one that opened as soon as it touched the ground. She couldn't see much of where she would be going this time—just somewhere far more busy. She could hear hundreds of bustling voices, honking cars. *They had modern technology in this place?* She was expecting something more medieval...that is judging by the fact that she literally just escaped a castle that looked to have been built centuries ago.

"Last one back to the house is an ogre's ear!" Blondie smiles wide before pushing past Micah and skipping through the portal. Maeve watched him enter with wide eyes. Did he have no fear about where he would end up? If he would be vaporized?

"He could have said anything," Mysterious man says with a roll of his eyes before following after the other.

Micah stepped through after he looked back at the duo. His expression was blank.

"Ready?" Amir asks Maeve once they're in front of the portal. She could see the otherside a lot better now. There was a city on the other side. There were skyscrapers and corner stores. There were roads and traffic from the many cars that were on it. People of all kinds walked the sidewalks, and conversations about different topics were held. While it gave her a bit of comfort that she will finally be back in a scenery that she is used to, it still isn't her home and that fear still resonated with her. The people that she sees walking and talking are all kinds of creatures—ones that might be ready to gobble her up if they find out she's a human. *Part human.* Amir is still adamant that she's also a werewolf.

"Am I allowed to be honest?"

"With me?" He tapped at the back of her thigh with his fingers. "I think it's only fair that you are. I did convince my pack leader that you were worthy enough to be freed."

She couldn't hold back a snicker.

"Well in that case, no...I'm not."

"Hold on tight then. It'll help" It was the last thing either one of them could say before Amir took the ignitive to step through the portal. And Maeve took his advice once she saw him take the step. The hold she had around his neck had gotten tighter, to the point that she was afraid she might have begun to choke him. Thankfully the trip through this portal was just as fast as the first one she went though. In a blink of an eye she was once in the grassy field, and the next she was standing in the middle of a dark alleyway. It was just her and Amir though; the three others must have continued their adventure home, genuinely not taking a break until they were entering the safety of the house blondie was talking about. She glanced back at the portal, watching as it closed. But before it disappeared she was able to see a woman. She was leaving the tunnel exit as well, catching her eye and then frowning deeply.

Maeve returned her focus to Amir. He was halted in place, grip loosening as he stared off onto the busy street. She took it as a sign that he wanted her off, that she was finally getting too heavy and he needed a break. They weren't in mortal danger anymore so all of their tense muscles and heightened senses could relax as well. But as she was letting her weight go back to her feet, body shifting awkwardly so she was able to easily slide off, he kept her in place. His palms grabbed at the flesh of her thighs, fingerprints pressing even deeper. She won't admit to the flare of heat that suddenly shot through her entire lower-half. That's a little embarrassing. Instead she'll try to get down once more, this time making it known that she is fully capable of walking from here on out. He didn't stop her, gently placing her back on her feet.

"What are you doing? You're still barefoot."

He is correct. She looked down at her toes that wiggled against the cold and wet concrete. Maeve is praying that it's wet because it has rained recently...not because there is an unknown substance that may have come from anything else. She pushed hair out of her face, smoothing down her short dress. If accidentally hiked up any further, her panties would be on display, and if someone just so happened to walk by and see the two of them then there would be questionable glances. Maybe even assumptions made.

"And you're exhausted," She reached out to touch his arm. He flexed under the touch, to only go lax as she gently massaged the meat there. Thankfully she didn't give into the random impulsive desire that was to let her hand roam. To bring both hands to his still extremely visible torso and just rub at his smooth skin. Maeve removed her hand, clasping it with her other in hopes of ridding the feeling of Amir off of her—the urge to just grope him in public, because not only is that objectification of someone that she just met (and he most definitely will be calling her a creep before leaving her stranded), but this need she has doesn't feel real. The unexplainable attraction she has for this man is so intense and so sudden she doesn't understand how that could be. She's spent three years of her life pining after someone that is a complete liar, and now she's just over it because she looked a werewolf in the eye? Maeve hasn't loved many people in her life, hasn't indulged in too many romantic relationships, but she's positive that getting over someone doesn't happen so fast; so easily. "I don't mind stepping on a few rocks here and there. I can walk."

"I'm fine. I can carry you the rest of the way. No need to hurt yourself. The house is not too far from here."

He seemed just as adamant of helping her, that she is of helping him.

"Yeah, until you drop me because your arms lose all feeling. You're tired. I know you are" The look each other in the eye. It was as if electricity was her new blood and it was sparking tremendously now that she's so close to Amir. "I can practically feel it."

Unspoken words. Just an impressed and cheerful expression

taking place on his face. What's that supposed to mean? A smile took over his perfect lips and his brown eyes shifted to their pretty yellow briefly before turning back. If he had a tail, it probably would be wagging.

"I'll admit, I am a little...but only a little!" Amir chuckled when watching Maeve grin in triumph. "I guess being locked up for about a week does take a number on you."
"A week!?"

"Yeah, I was caught when trying to steal something. But that can be a story for another time. For now, let's head to my home so you can freshen up. I think either Thais or Zenaida should have some clothes you can borrow" He didn't mean to give her a once over that made her feel exposed. He just wanted to imply that she might want to get out of the clothes she was wearing now, take a shower; before nearby animals begin to think she's a dead body that they could scavenge for food later. But it appears that his stare was just a bit too intense that Maeve wrapped her arms around herself in hopes of shielding how gross she looked. It would take more than a bad hair day and a ruined sparkly dress in order for Amir to be repulsed by her. "So come on," He bent down again, arms yet again sticking out behind him.

"I already told you-"

"And I already told you that I'm fine. So hop on. If I didn't lose all sense of time, today should be Friday, and on Fridays, Ms. Loom makes her infamous chicken parmesan. And I don't know about you, but I'm starving" The goofy smile he wore was contagious. His energy was contagious. But also her stomach began to grumble at the mere thought of food—and she realizes that she hasn't ate since lunch of yesterday, being too excited to go out for her birthday so she skipped dinner to get ready—so she doesn't deny Amir any longer and happily gets back on his naked back where she places her hands on his shoulders and wraps her legs around his waist. They way they mold together so easily makes her warm.

Qyaid has Maeve's body strapped to a metal table, leather cuffs keeping her arms and legs down (just in case she finally decides to wake up and go berserk at the thought of being restrained again). And then in her left arm there was a needle pricking her skin, the needle connected to a tube, and the tube being connected to a beaker that will eventually collect all (if even any) of the magic that resides within her and then drip from it's spout into a cup that Qyaid, Fakhar, and Qua will drink from. Just as Qyaid was making sure that the preparations have all been complete, there will be no mishaps, and that their future is unstoppable, Qua had opened his mouth in order to spew some concerns.

"Brother," He stepped away from Maeve's unconscious body. He stuck his hands behind his back as he approached the eldest with a creased forehead and uncertain eyes. "Don't you feel as though we should wait until the red moon before we do this? Our chances for success are higher."

"We don't need the red moon in order to take her power," Qyaid responds.

"But we aren't positive that her magical abilities will be strong enough by the time that night approaches. We still have seven days, brother, why not try a different method in the meantime?" Fakhar steps in. He had no shown no hesitation in his words when speaking so bluntly. Unlike the youngest triplet

Qua, Fakhar has no fear when it comes to Qyaid. "It's possible that we don't even have to drain the girl. We can get her to see our side."

"Are you an imbecile!? The chosen one is destined to change the world for the better, not abuse the power given to them. There is no chance she'll agree to our greedy desires!" Qyaid looks between his brothers, realization dawning upon him. "Do not tell me you are doubting our ability? I promise this will work," He stands before them with a smile that calms only a bit of their nerves. "Once I drain her power and we drink it, no one will be able to stop us. And then when the red moon comes, we'll finally get what we've always wanted. So no need to worry, our time has officially come."

Reluctancy was still hidden within the other mens' eyes; but with silent head nods, Qyaid grinned before returning back to the machine, It whirled loudly as he turned it on—the clanking of metal hitting against each other and steam needing to be released. It's best that their castle was so high in the sky. The outrageous noises that came from the room would have had anyone eager to get a peak of what it was. And then like a mad scientist would, Qyaid cackled mischievously at the sight of Maeve's glowing purple power being removed from her form.

"It's happening! It's finally happening!"

It wasn't long before the machine turned off on its own. The room went silent then, the only sound being the faint drip of her magic landing in the cup, and the heavy breathing of the three men. But then Fahkar was grabbing the cup, holding it up like it was a prized possession. And for a minute he scolded himself for believing that even for a second that they would have failed. But here they are. They formed a circle, staring down at the magic liquid that will evidently decide what happens to their world.

"Youngest takes the first sip."

Qua was handed the cup. There was a second given before he was lifting the glass to his lips and ingesting the purple magic. It didn't taste like anything—the feeling being something akin to swallowing air. So there was no real way to tell if he was drinking too much or not. Qyaid pulling his hand back was his signal to stop. Fahkar was next. He admired the vibrant color in the cup before he was drinking his gulp. He doesn't feel any different; maybe a little tingle in his fingertips, but nothing to show that he was one of the most powerful beings in the universe. The last bit was passed to Qyaid. He looked at his brothers once more, an evil smirk taking over his face.

"This is it. Soon everyone will be bowing at our feet" And with that he was tipping his head back so he was able to down the last gulp without as much as a breath. And once all gone he was tossing the glass across the room, relishing in the way the sound of porcelain shattered against the stone wall. "And now we just kill the girl."

"Your majesties!" In rushed a woman. She stood tall and serious as she entered without a warning. She didn't bother with pushing the stray strands of ginger hair out of her face, too busy maintaining her professional image that is general of the Junud.

"You are not to barge into any room so casually!" Fakhar roars.

"I apologize, your majesty" She bowed. For a moment her face resembled one of shame. She already knew that rule. It was one of the many that is drilled into a Junud's head when given their job. And yet here she is breaking it anyway. She'll definitely have to punish herself later. Probably go do her work-out routine until she passes out. "I'm afraid your captures have escaped. I've caught sight of them leaving through the east tunnel exit."

"General Harris, I'm afraid you must be mistaken. Our capture is right here-" The three brothers turned to be met with an empty metal table. The leather straps were still locked in place, therefore there was no sign of removal, therefore there was no one to have left. "An illusion spell. She tricked us!"

"So what did we just drink?" Qua asks.

"Nothing," Fahkar growls.

"Find her" Qyaid starts low. "Find her right now and bring her to me!" He then finishes with a shout so loud that it might have shook the ground.

Chapter Five

"Here we are!"

Maeve slid off Amir's back for the second time. He helped her get her footing by lowering himself by the knees, his hands refusing to let go until he knew that she was stable enough on her own. His fingertips were loose on her smooth thighs, inch by inch leaving the molded place that they once sat, only truly missing the fleshy feeling when her bare feet had landed onto the cool pavement of the sidewalk. She pulled her blue sparkly dress down, covering what might have been the indent crescent marks from Amir's fingernails. Maeve kept behind him, palms, fingers, just barely touching the man's naked back, while her brown irises began to observe the house she was brought to. She didn't know what to expect when it was mentioned; when she had the entire trip over to think about its appearance. Maybe she imagined it to be bigger? After all, from what she guesses four grown men are living there—they're going to be needing enough space to fit all of them, each of them hopefully getting their own bedroom and probably two full bathrooms so they don't have to fight over who gets their time on the toilet first. But it was an average home. It had a nice front yard, a few sunflowers growing from the fresh green grass. There was a porch, wooden and painted gray for the sake of a nice look. There was a mat in front of the white front door, the casual *Welcome* printed on the rough brown texture. It must have been there for a few years, the black letters having faded. Then to the left was a swing. It could probably hold two adults before there would be no room left and the metal bars would start squeaking. From what she could see, there had to be at least two floors—the upstairs containing all of the bedrooms, whereas everything else was stationed downstairs. And it was all painted this pale yellow. Like the mat it must have worn from time, once being a vibrant color that could have given Amir's werewolf eyes a run for its money.

"Are you ready to go in?" He must have seen her worry. But what did she have to be so scared about? This place looked like a dollhouse. *That's how they get you. Lure you in with its cuteness and then suddenly your neck is sliced open.* "I promise nothing or nobody can get you here."

Maeve looked behind her. It was an open street, one aligned with many more houses that could have replicated the one she stood in front of if they just changed the paint color. There were a few cars on the road, passing by with or without curious looks to who she was. There was even an elderly couple in their front yard, helping each other plant tulips, while not even two houses over a few kids ran around playing with a red rubber ball. Absolutely nothing about the place was dangerous. It didn't give her the same negative feeling that she got from the castle. She almost felt safe. Which is why she turned back towards Amir with a grin and head nod. Honestly accepting the offer that was entering his home was her only option anyway. She had nowhere else to go when it came to this realm; no money to pay for that expensive looking hotel they passed on the way here; or anyone to talk to about how to make her way back to the human world. Who knows if anything bad will happen once she admits to another set of strangers that she doesn't believe she's like them? Luckily the people she has met have been extremely considerate and didn't just leave her with the Raba—three older men who screamed evil and obviously planned to use her for their grand scheme that ultimately might result in her death.

Amir didn't make her go first, didn't make her uncomfortable by grabbing her hand and dragging her up the stairs to the porch, practically forcing her into his home. He let her continue to choose if she wanted to enter, the hesitation in her movements insanely obvious to him. He did open the door though, and left it open for her slow steps. However he made it known that he's finally arrived back home by throwing his arms wide open and puffing his chest.

"I'm home!"

Maeve practically jumped from how loud he was. She could see that he had a giant smile on his face. Amir's canines began to show and she was amazed by how sharp they were. They were nothing compared to Reggie's, growing longer and pointier. They definitely weren't something she was used to seeing from people's smiles back home though. It's probably why she kept alert as she crept closer inside the house. Amir could easily grab her, pull her in and then rip her to shreds with his teeth alone. And no one would notice because he would have closed the door, muffling the sounds of her screams. The imagery had her halting her steps, only keeping in the doorway while watching the other enter further. Feet could be heard padding from all over. Marching sounded from the living room built to her right. And it was heard from the left where the dining room was, where a kitchen was connected to it, with only an archway separating the two. Noise could even be heard descending from the wooden stairs that were given the beautiful design of being in the middle, pressed up against a wall and leading up to a second floor. The first person to greet Amir was blondie. Even though he's just seen the both of them not even fifteen minutes ago, he still couldn't keep a pretty smile from spreading across his handsome face.

No seriously, is every mythical creature here super attractive?

Blondie could be a model if he wanted; with glimmering green eyes and a slanted nose bridge. His shaggy dirty-blonde hair cascaded in waves that framed his face perfectly, and his build was tall and muscular. He could throw a deer over his shoulder and Maeve wouldn't question if it was heavy or not. It's a bit surprising to see that he had a few tattoos littering his arms—symbolism of a star overlapping a crescent moon inking his left forearm is what intrigued her the most though, seeing as he wasn't the only one who had it. Amir has it as well...and mean mysterious guy (who approached in nothing but a towel, onyx hair still sopping wet and causing droplets to fall down his body; which Maeve may add is like staring at a Greek God), and Micah (who stared for a second too long at the other's glistening body, before turning away awkwardly).

"Alright, you guys just saw him. Save my brother for the rest of us, yeah?" The surprising sound that was a female voice vibrated throughout the space.

Maeve craned her neck in order to see the girl, not at all surprised to see that she resembled someone on a runway. But it is amazing to see that she almost looked identical to Amir, there being no chance that you could mistake them for siblings. The only difference had to be that she appeared younger. Her pearly whites shined bright as she greeted her brother with open arms, mushy comments about missing him was said as they embraced. Then she saw Maeve behind him.

"And who do we have here!?" Her excitement was startling. Maeve's tactic was to go undetected until she knew for sure that the people she surrounded herself with were one hundred percent good. So far there hasn't been any tips in the scale. Obviously her plan hadn't gone accordingly when she actually stood not too far in the background, sticking out like a sore thumb in her party dress and messy state. "Ah, come in! Don't just stand there! We don't bite...or at least I don't. I'm not so sure about Foster though" She said it all while guiding Maeve further into the house, forcing her to get over any fear that was being mauled by werewolves. Luckily enough the house feels cozy.

"Hey!"

Ah, so now she knows dark and mysterious guy's name. All that's left is blondie, the sister...and the two other men and women that approached. Maeve feels as though she's being overstimulated. Everything she's seen, heard, felt so far is far too much for her to handle. A migraine was beginning to form near her temple, an eagerness to sit down and drink a glass of water becoming a new focus for her. And it doesn't help that there was suddenly a loud crash sounding against the hardwood floors. All small talk that was bouncing off every wall came to a halt at the shatter, and eyes traced back to one of the women standing in the back. She was more on the elderly side, years of her life written all over her face. Maeve's stomach drops. The elderly lady is staring directly at her, a look of horror. Shock. Everyone looked between the two with confusion.

"Ms. Loom, are you okay?" Micah wonders as he rushes to her aid. Blondie bends down to begin picking up what she dropped. It appeared to be a platter, made of white porcelain. There were freshly baked cookies on it, peanut butter, made in order to greet Amir back home from being trapped in a dungeon for so long. They were now nothing but a crumbled mess, resting in front of feet encased in pink slippers. Didn't stop blondie from shoving a few undamaged pieces in his cheeks, chewing slowly.

"Yeah, yeah" Ms. Loom smiles, finally breaking her stare from Maeve and letting it settle on the concerned man. "Just surprised to see that we have such a beautiful guest."

"I think she's a bit young for you" One of the newcomers chuckles. Ms. Loom was quick to throw a glare his way, stepping out of the gentle hold Micah had on her shaking hands, to make her way closer to Maeve. What might have felt like guilt before shifted into something more bashful. All of the attention was on her, if it wasn't before, and Maeve wanted to do nothing but curl up and hide away. This is awkward.

"Ah hun, I'm sorry for that introduction. Rowan, stop eating off the ground!" She didn't bother to look back. Too busy with admiring the sight that was a grown Maeve Whitmore in the flesh. Blondie though finally did stop picking at the broken cookie chunks, returning to his feet after hurriedly gathering what was left and heading out of the room. Probably to throw it away. "I'm Ms. Loom. But you can just call me Amora" Maeve tilted her head just slightly at the woman. There was something about her. She kind of reminds her of Elise, just less frowns and scowls and more smiles and sparkling eyes.

"Maeve. Maeve Ross" Or is it Whitmore now? She'd have to figure that out later. For now she must continue to find a way home. And with finally meeting someone older who might have more knowledge of the land, she could know a way out of here. Maybe she has another one of those portal things? "I don't really know how to say this either, but I really need to get home. Like the human world home. I'm not-"

The two tried to dismiss the whispers that came from her confession. As if the majority of them didn't already know.

"Hey, it's okay. How about we get you cleaned up first? Make sure you've eaten. And I'm sure in the meantime we can figure out a way. Thais, Zenaida, please help Maeve to the bathroom. Find her some clothes to wear. I still have dinner to make."

"Oh no, it's really okay. The sooner I get home, the sooner I will be out of your hair" Maeve tries to speak. She was almost immediately shut down when the two girls grabbed hold of her arms and began to drag her near the stairs. All of the rest watched her go, indifferent to her pleas of none of the hospitality being necessary. Even Amir. He looked smug as he watched his sister gush about what clothes she could wear. *Traitor.*

"Everyone get out of my entryway now!" Ms. Loom shouts. "Foster clothes on, Amir shower and shave that unruly beard, everyone else either make yourself busy or you're cleaning dishes with Lucas!"

"But Ms. Loom!" The Lucas fellow whines as he follows the elderly woman into the kitchen.

She didn't mean for it to happen. One minute she was listening to Thais ramble happily about what clothes she believes that could fit her, and then the next she was waking up from a bed that was far more comfortable than her own. Maeve rubs at her eyes, easing away the drowsiness that came from an extremely exhausting day.

For a minute she believed it all to be a dream. From the moment she was kidnapped by Reggie, to being forced into a warm shower, none of it felt real. She remembers the soothing shower fairly well. How the bathroom was clean and yet obviously fairly used by the many people who lived in the house. Beauty products were mixed with the razors and colognes; colorful towels hung on the back of the door, drying from previous use. Foster must have taken one to wrap around his waist before descending the stairs. Zenaida had given her a spare toothbrush shoved in the back of one of the sink drawers, and then given the warning that she must engrain what it looks like in her head if she wants no mistakes in the future. Thais left her borrowed clothes on the lid of the toilet as she babbled about going to throw her dress in the wash. Then she was left alone with directions about how to work the pretty basic shower, where the spare towels were, what body wash she was allowed to use, and if she needed anything else than just to shout and someone would eventually come running to her aid. It took her a moment to figure out what she could use to scrub her body with, deciding on a loofa that looked to be brand new from how the tag still lingered.

Maeve also remembers how she made it into the bed as well.

She crept back into the room that she believed to be one shared between the two girls, bare feet padding against the hardwood and leaving wet foot prints for a path. She was in search of a pair of socks. Stupid, she knows, but after having lost her heels long ago, her feet began to ache from enduring everything from dirt to stone. She thought it be nice to warm them up with a pair of fuzzy socks that she saw peaking through a top dresser drawer when Thais was in search of spare underwear. Mission was successful when she sat down on said bed. It moved under her weight, her body bouncing just slightly as she slipped her feet into the socks. But it wasn't until she spotted a spare hair-tie on the dresser that she truly began to get comfortable. She snatched the item, hoping neither of the girls would get angry that she nabbed it. Maeve had half a mind as she tossed her hair up into a wet mess, just glad that it was out of her face and off her neck. She closed her eyes then, hand going to her nape and massaged a particular crook out. She relaxed in her spot. She felt the softness of the blanket, too pressing at the mattress and how her hand melted into it. She wondered what it would feel like for her whole body. And that's the curiosity that sealed it for her. One glance at the fluffy white pillow and she was laying down. At first she just slipped her feet under the blanket—she didn't want to intrude in a space that was never hers, nor did she get permission to use. But then she could feel the heat that she craved once she first put that dress on. Then before she knew it she was covering her entire body with the promise that she'll take a short nap.

Leads her to now. Waking because she swears she hears birds chirping outside the window. Weird, she's used to waking to the sound of cars honking because even though it's early morning, people can't keep their anger down and just have to beep. This was a different alarm, a refreshing one. Maeve was throwing the blanket off of her, ready to rush downstairs and explain to her parents how crazy her dream was—how realistic it was. But as she was lazily walking out of a bedroom that she is barely registering, she's squealing because she's tripping. It's face first into the floor, luckily a rug breaking her fall. Maeve was ready to scold Aziel. He must have left one of his toy guns on her floor again. But then she was hearing a groan. A murmur about how it is fairly too early for them to be awake and that all noise needs to be kept down. Right then Maeve's eyes shoot open and she's looking behind her. It wasn't a toy gun that she tripped over, but a person. Thais to be exact.

And oh goodness, none of it was a dream.

Thais lay on the floor, cuddled with a pillow while a throw blanket covered her. And then across the room was Zenaida, snoring in her own bed. Maeve doesn't know whether she should be guilty for taking the girl's bed away from her, or scared because she genuinely is trapped in a different realm.

Scurrying back to her feet, Maeve then makes her way out of the room and down the stairs. It was when she was reaching the ground floor that she could hear people speaking. Two women. One was Amora, the other *Elise*? That can't be. Elise was still in the human world, left there after fending off all of those evil frat guys. Maeve inched closer. Their voices were coming from the dining room. She made sure her feet were light against the floorboards, cringing when creaks were made. Eventually she successfully hid behind a wall, ears peeled for whatever the conversation was about. She peaked around the corner to see who was talking. *Yup, there was Amora. And in front of her was Elise!* She looked way older. This was not the same person she grew up with. Makes her question who she really is.

"We need to tell them, Amora. For every day that goes by from here on out, they could be in danger. Who knows if the Raba has already caught wind that she's missing? It won't be long before the Junud are banging on your door, asking to search the place" Elise says with a sigh.

"I know that! It's just you never know how they'll react. It's been twenty-one years, Emry-" *Emry? She even has a different name!?* "They'll probably be angry at us for keeping them apart for that long" *Amora knew who she was all along? Why act sweet and clueless? Or well, that explains her reaction when they first saw each other.*

"It was for their own safety. I'm sure they'll understand."

"I highly doubt Maeve will. That poor girl has been lied to her entire life. And then wait until she hears about Amir..."

"What about him?"

Yeah, what about him? Maeve inched closer trying to hear better. Only just as she was getting ready to hear an answer, a new, more masculine voice was whispering in her ear.

"Who are we spying on?" She would have jumped with a scream if she wasn't supposed to be stealthy right now. Looking back, she was met with not just one person, but two. It was blondie—Rowan, and one of the other boys that she wasn't able to meet just yet. They both smiled down at her, genuine curiosity covering their eyes as they tried to look around the corner. Of course she stopped them, pulling them back before their cover was blown.

"Ms. Loom and a friend of mine. They're talking about me. So if you could..." Maeve whispered back before putting a finger to her lips. Then she's back to focusing on the two women talking. Rowan and the other guy leant in too, playing into the stealth mission.

"Taking her back to the human world is dangerous. She'd be up for grabs then. She's already been found, by some guy who I should have known was with the Raba. It's best to keep her here, she's hidden if people already think that she fled" Emry says. It sounds like she's getting up from her spot at the table, chair rubbing against the ground. With the fear of getting caught, Maeve rushes that the two men fall back and quietly move further away just in case. The trio look at one another, their hushed bickering about how Maeve didn't have to push and shove goes silent when hearing Amora get up as well, following Emry to the kitchen. It's when the women's voices have become distant that they release breaths they didn't even know they were holding. Only just as they believed that they were safe from getting caught, rounding the corner were the same people they were just spying on.

"I knew I heard someone. Comes to find out it's just you three rascals" Amora chuckles as she places her hands on her hips. The two men returned her smile with sheepish grins and faint greetings for the morning. Unlike Maeve who was stuck staring at who she believed to be her best friend. Elise White. No, her name is Emry. Seeing her up close, the wrinkles of old age were a lot clearer now. She wasn't youthful anymore. Gray hairs lined her once striking black hair, her ocean blue eyes became dull, and tattoos could be seen sprouting from out of her clothes. Those weren't there before. "Help me with breakfast, you two" Amora must have sensed that Maeve and Emry needed a minute to talk. Or well, more than a minute if everything needs to be said. So she guided the two other spies away from the friends. And as her back was to them, some of the same markings were seen peering out of Amora's clothes as well.

"It's been a while" Emry stretches a tight smile. "I'm glad you're safe."

"It's been what? A day at most" Maeve must have sounded bitter because Emry's grin fell into her signature frown. The elder understands though. So much has happened and now all of it needs to be explained.

"I'm afraid you're wrong. I haven't seen you in three days. It's Monday."

"Three days!?" Her shout was loud enough to shake the house; birds heard flapping in distress away from the powerlines that they once sat upon peacefully. Amora, Rowan and no name guy came running back, different kitchen utensils in their grasp. They had no reason to be alarmed, ready to attack whatever may be the cause of her scream. Unless they plan to throw a spatula at Emry, then they can lower the pan, spatula, and cutting board.

"Holy—you can't just do that!" Rowan huffs. "We thought you guys were getting mauled by a goblin. Gabe, you can put the cutting board down now."

Another name down.

"Why didn't you guys wake me up!? I've been asleep for three days!"

"Because you looked so cute and peaceful" Amora coos. "Plus, we kind of thought you were dead when we slapped you twice and you didn't even flinch. Glad you're alive! Which do you prefer, waffles or pancakes?"

"Pan-"

"Privacy" Emry interrupts bluntly. "We prefer privacy. So could you give us a moment?"

She didn't bother waiting for a response, already turning her back to the three and heading towards the living room. Maeve followed close behind, catching sight of a sleeping Foster sprawled out on a couch that had the ugliest floral pattern anyone could ever create. It looked as though it belonged in an antique shop, a purchase only made by old ladies with a fashion stuck at a time they were originally born. Assuming that this is Amora's home and that she appears to be up there in age, it all aligns. Everything in the house was one for an elderly actually—the few contrasts to modern day being the gaming council connected to the giant flat screen television mounted to the white wall, and the connected cable and wifi package. It's interesting to see that even monsters enjoyed online activities. Do they ever come across things on the internet that involve their kind, or do they react to humans?

Emry seated herself on the opposing sofa to the one Foster lay upon; limbs on the brink of falling off and head stuck in the crack. Why didn't he just go to his bed? Maeve decided to keep his attention on her main (and should be only) issue, which is finding out answers involving what her life actually is and how she should return to the fake one created for her. Which is why Maeve sat down as well, keeping her distance just in case this goes south and suddenly she's having her neck slit open like those frat guys.

"I want to know the truth...all of it," Maeve said. It came out shaky, breathy when she intended for it to be stern and demanding. This wasn't the same person she grew up with, so why must she treat her like such?

"And I understand that, but this goes far deeper than you think. Even I only know so much" Emry sighs back. She tried to reach out—hopefully touch the one person that she not only had taken away from her original parents, but her adoptive ones as well. She wanted to make sure that the Maeve Whitmore that she sees in front of her isn't some figment of her imagination, fabricated because peak devastation finally hit. But Maeve moved back, pulled her hands close to her chest before staring at Emry with a sight that was foreign between the duo. Uncertainty.

"Well then start with what you *do* know."

"I knew your parents. Your mom...Miriam Whitmore, she died after giving birth to you. And your father, Harrison, is the one who tasked Amora and I to be you and your brother's guardian after the attack of the Raba not too long after you two were born" Emry didn't know where to start. From the part where Maeve is in grave danger with some of the most powerful people in Kariq Leada; or that she had to separate Maeve from her only family in order for their safety; or that her entire identity is a lie and she's actually a witch who specialized in medicine after graduating from Alsahar Boarding School.

"I thought my brother died as well? Or that's what this *Raba* told me before Amir and his friends helped me escape" This information wasn't already sitting well. Maeve had scooched to the edge of the couch, legs itching to stand back up and pace a bit.

"No, your twin brother was saved before the Raba managed to give him the same fate as your parents. Amora and I were on the run for a while before we thought it was best just to separate the two of you. So I brought you to the human realm, a place where no one would even think to look for you...or so I thought."

She tried to inch closer. Just one touch. One embrace. She needed something to show that she wasn't crazy. That this wasn't a dream and she could in the future relay the news to the Ross' that their daughter hadn't passed. But Maeve kept her distance. Her brown irises glimmered with disorientation, chapped lips pressed in a line. She wanted to keep her sight on Emry but it was getting far too difficult. She had already begun to come to terms (not that she had much choice, or a true connection with her original family to begin with, so there wasn't much she had to be upset about) with the idea that she would never be able to meet the people she was supposed to love with her entire being. But now she's hearing that one piece of her is still out there, grown just like her and probably with no clue as to who she is. Do they know about her? Or did they keep that part of his life a secret to him as well?

"So where is he?"

"Amora kept him here. Gave him a new life as well."

"So, where...is...he?"

Right then, clomping down the stairs with heavy feet and a groan was her answer. A person who helped save her life, who was hesitant and made her feel un-welcomed from the very beginning. He wasn't at his full height, having just awoken and still

a bit drained from the previous day so he slouched. He wasn't
wearing a shirt, yet occupied pajama pants that were a bright
baby blue and were decorated with cartoon cats. He raised a
hand to his puffy eyes wiping away what may have been sleep,
while a loud yawn rose from the depths of his chest, jaw basically becoming unhinged from how wide his mouth opened. He
stopped at the bottom of the stairs, turning his head to look in
the direction of the living room. He looked at Foster first, body
stiffening while dismay suddenly laced his morning glow. Upon
noticing other people in the room though he quickly changed it
into something less disapproving. Emry looked from him to her.
Maeve looked from him to her. And then she caught the hint.

"You're kidding me?" She was calm at first, a painful chuckle
vibrating out of her throat. Emry looked down at her hands in
culpability. Micah was the one. Micah was her brother. But he
didn't understand Maeve's sudden hostility and looked at the
conversating duo perplexed. "You're kidding me!?" Maeve stood
to her feet, voice reaching that starling octave again. Emry
couldn't look up, scared of what the other's reaction was. It's not
hard to tell though, judging by the anger in her voice. Micah
though was a bit cautious. He's seen Emry a few times before,
and has talked to her briefly whenever Amora was. She seems
like a decent person—very heavy on the stone-cold personality
though. So to see a stranger (Maeve) becoming provoked, he
took interest.

"Woah, what's going on here?" He slowly made his way in,
eyes darting back and forth between the two. Neither women
paid him any attention though. Short glances and then they
were back on each other.

"Twenty-one years!" No need to rub it in. Emry already knows the long term damage that's been done. Of course she planned out the possible future conversation; she was always one step ahead, ready for the consequences of her secrets. But maybe she wasn't? She wasn't prepared for the revelation talk to go like this. None of what's happened was supposed to go like this. "Twenty-one years of my life I believed that I was abandoned because *you* chose to let me think that! And then comes to find out it was all a lie! I have a fucking brother!" Tears welled up in Maeve's eyes. Her hands shook. It's surprising that this is what it took for Foster to finally stir awake. "You knew how much finding out anything about my family meant to me! And this whole fucking time, you let me sit there and believe that they gave me up because they didn't want me! How dare you!?"

"What's going on?" Foster groggily asks. He sits up from his lying position, squinting as the sunlight from a nearby window strikes him in the eye. "Isn't it a bit early to be yelling?"

"Maeve, you have to understand that I did this for your sake. I never would have intentionally tried to hurt you" Emry stood as well. Again she reached to touch the other. Maeve made it very adamant that she doesn't want to be anywhere near her.

"And you could have done that by telling me the truth! Does he even know? Does anyone know!?"

Emry shook her head. Maeve threw her hands in the air, letting them fall back down to her sides as she mumbles something under her breath. Amora, Rowan and Gabe walked in the room. Their steps were light as they didn't want their presence to cause another uproar.

"Your identities are completely confidential. No one was

supposed to know who you guys were. Not even each other" *So much for not causing an uproar.* Amora had been the one to chime in, heads turning to look at her. Typically the spotlight causes people to be nervous, but the gentle smile she let on wasn't wavering a bit. She was okay with receiving the backlash of her and Emry's actions. A lot more than Emry was taking it at least. "I know this is a lot to take in right now, but I promise this was for the best. If not, you probably would have been killed a long time ago."

"Ms. Loom, what is going on?" Micah asks.

"Yeah, what *is* going on?" Maeve spits. She was still very hyped from her vexed adrenaline and now everything for the next few minutes will either come out sarcastic or just down-right mean.

"Watch your tone" Micah snarls at her.

"No, it's fine. It's expected. And I won't expect anything but the same reaction from you once you hear what needs to be said" Amora speaks as she places a hand to his shoulder. Micah can't help but look down at her with a creased forehead and bafflement. Amora inhales sharply, taking the okay from Emry who nodded solemnly. Then she looks between the newly defined siblings. "You Micah, are the first born to Miriam and Harrison Whitmore. You are also a few minutes older than your twin sister Maeve Whitmore. You two had no acknowledgement of each other until now."

The sister and brother took the confirmation and stared at one another. No wonder they had a freakish familiarity with each other upon first meeting. The room was silent until Rowan had to let out his shocked verbal reaction.

"Well that's a twist I didn't see coming."

Chapter Six

Emry and Amora got to sit the twins down after that. They kicked everyone else out, explaining that if the rest of the pack are to finally join the fiasco, they are to go anywhere else but the living room. A job Gabe didn't take lightly because the minute Amir was about to head over and ask what not only has his best friend so upset, but Maeve as well, Gabe was yanking him by his pajama shirt collar. The big man almost went stumbling to the floor if he didn't catch himself in time. He threw the other his nastiest glare, hands ready to go around his neck for retaliation. Gabe ran off screaming as Amir trailed behind with the promise of getting even. Lucas opened the front door (coming back from his morning jog), to only have Gabe wizz by him and almost fall down the porch stairs with a scream that sounded as though he was about to be murdered. Lucas wanted to ask what had him in a state of panic, to only have Amir rushing right after him with this glimmer of maliciousness that couldn't be erased from his eyes until he had captured his prey. It didn't take long. Gabe made the mistake to try and steer left of an almost grab, but looking down he realized he was about to step all over Amora's freshly planted flowers—therefore he had to stumble his way around them, tripping over a nearby stone and going face first into the front lawn. It took roughly two seconds for Amir to then tackle him and begin to wrestle the whimpering other right there. They must have looked like fools. No one stopped them though. If anything, Lucas closed the door again and began to whistle about the match, nararating what was happening in his rich accent that sounded a lot like British.

"Look, I know this may be a lot to process, but we promise that what we're saying is all the truth. We did this out of your safety and the promise of your father that we will do every-thing we can to protect you from the Raba" Amora breathes. She wasn't like Emry, trying to reach out and touch Micah from across the coffee table where he and his suddenly brand new sister sat on the opposing sofa. Instead she let the one person she's raised for twenty-one years curl in on himself; hands clasped tightly in his lap as he did that scratching thing with his hands he's developed at a young age whenever he was nervous or uneasy about anything.

He'd ruin the skin between his thumb and index, occasionally scratching and picking at it so hard that he bled. He had his legs pressed together as well, heels bouncing against the hardwood floors at a pace he didn't know whether he wanted to be fast or slow. He was already so overwhelmed, trying to pry him out of that state with comfort he probably doesn't even want isn't going to help that. So all she can really do is remind him that he needs to stop scratching or else he'll hurt himself again.

"You have to trust us. Especially now more than ever. If the Raba finds out that not only you are here," She points at a spaced out Maeve. She was staring at an oblivious Micah, eyes keen on remembering every single detail there is about her brother's face and body. Like how he has the faintest of moles on his upper lip, and piercings that went up the ear she could see (his left), how his skin was just a shade darker than hers, especially on his arms because of a possible tan, and that on his right hamstring there was a tattoo that she couldn't see completely but looked something similar to a flower sprouting—and could even be the start of something bigger if he decides to go back for more. That is if he doesn't already have more under the t-shirt and basketball shorts he changed into. But that trance was broken when Amora motioned in her direction, so she was quick to look back at the two women. Her cheeks tinted the faintest bit of pink, a bit embarrassed that she just got caught eyeing a stranger turned family. "But that Micah is alive, it's guaranteed that you both will end up in their clutches...or worse, dead. So take this as a warning."

A pause filtered the air, it being interrupted by three rowdy men barging in through the door in lighter spirits than when they left. Everyone looked at one another awkwardly, the stare off ending once Thais and Zenaida stalked down the stairs, gossiping about something. From what was heard before they also halted in their steps, Thais was crushing on some girl who was in her high school algebra class. Rowan popped his head in explaining that he finally finished making breakfast for everyone, expression of a proud smile contorting into wide eyes and teeth clamped shut into a silent "yikes."

"I don't need to know what's going on here" Thais waved a hand around in a circle. And then she was entering the dining room with all intentions to eat the pile of pancakes that was placed in the center of the large rectangular table. The smell of fluffy buttery and chocolatey goodness wafted throughout the room. If Maeve wasn't in distress about her life flipping on its head and being threatened to be killed, she would have followed the others and indulged in a pancake or two, along with the nicely sliced fruit and the three different types of juice that was placed next to the other option that was milk and cereal.

"Can you tell me—" Micah cleared his throat, surprising Amora and Emry with speaking since this entire conversation began. "I mean, tell us about our parents?" He also finally looked at Maeve as he said it, taking this as his turn to look at his sister. Genuinely looked at her. Saw that without makeup, her right eyebrow had a small scar, almost as if when she was younger she accidentally hurt herself; and that she had a hoop in her right nostril; and that she was staring back at him with the same anguish. It was like staring at himself...and *oh my, he was about to leave her in the hands of the Raba who could have killed her right there if Amir didn't convince him.* Regret fills him, his heart tightening, his mind bustling with mere images of what Maeve would look lifeless; body completely bloody; soul gone from her eyes. But then he's sucking in a breath, turning his attention back to Amora and Emry. "You knew them enough to protect us? What were they like?"

Emry sighed.

"Unfortunately that's where our information stops. We can tell you about your separation, but we cannot tell you about who they were as people. Unfortunately we met them the day that their sacrifices have been made. We're sorry."

"But if we had to say, they were lovely people. Your mom

was in pain the whole time, but I could tell that they loved each other. Especially since your father was nothing but caring to her cries of how she did this to him" Amora chuckles. "We were their nurses. We knew you from the moment you were born. One of the first ones to hold you actually. I sadly can't say the same about Miriam."

"Our mother..."

"She wanted to. But she was gone before she could even lay a finger on either of you. It was only your father that was able to hold you" Amora sat up further on the couch, eyes finding Maeve's. She was oddly quiet. The screaming she had done before was nothing but thoughts that ran rampant in her mind, because not for a second can she seriously believe that all of this is happening to her right now. "And then I touched you...Maeve" Brown locked with blue then. There was interest yet insecurity, as if a part of Maeve knew that what was about to be said wasn't going to be good news. Amora brought her bottom lip between her teeth before letting it go, eyes closing briefly until they were fluttering open with sympathy. "I believe I know why the Raba wants you."

Maeve sat on the back patio. It's been about an hour. She said that she was going out for some fresh air. To really think everything over. She wasn't staring at anything in particular— once caught up in the way that the beautiful backyard swayed with the light breeze, how the trees and the cut grass danced as the sunlight hit it with the best golden glow she had ever seen. But now she was just staring. Zoned out, stuck in the thought about just wishing that she was back in a time where her life was normal. Her normal. Where she knew nothing about the supernatural being real, she still believed that she had no family left, and her best friend wasn't her secret guardian. This was all too much for her to handle and for a minute she was ready to cry. But she blunk those tears back, thinking that it wasn't the best time. She was surrounded by a bunch of people she doesn't know...who don't know her. Besides Elise. *Emry*.

She doesn't know her either actually. Doesn't know the real her anyway, just the one that's been curated. So all she can really do is just sit there, maybe wish that the ground will swallow her whole and finally take her from this place. It would definitely save from the possible doom that is being kidnapped for the second time, stop her from fulfilling this dumb prophecy she keeps hearing about. Why must she be the special one? Why can't it be her brother? Literally anyone else? It's when she blows out a raspberry, one hand leaving the encasing of her legs that she brought to her chest to run down her face in exhaustion that she's finally greeted with someone.

"I was told to come fetch you...get you to possibly eat something before everyone else scarfs down the leftovers" Maeve only turns her head to look at who was talking to her. Right after, she's back to facing forward, this time watching a bee land on a flower.

"What is that, some kind of dog pun?"

She chuckles but there wasn't any humor.

"Nah, Gabe wearing a collar is" Micah nudges her with his shoulder. "Look, I know I haven't been the most friendly–"

"If it wasn't for Amir, I'm pretty sure I would have been sacrificed by the Raba by now. You could use a bit of help when it comes to meeting new people. Try smiling more" She bumps his shoulder back, but at least he managed to get a grin out of her. From what he's noticed, she hasn't shown a speck of happiness since he's met her. But he understands, he too isn't the most joyful person right now. Especially not with Amora who he counted as a replacement mother.

"Yeah, yeah. If I apologize now, we can just call it our first sibling fight."

They fall into a silence then. Micah almost completely forgets what he was going to say; or well he forgets how he was going to say it without sounding like a moron. So he keeps quiet, relishing in the unexpected peace that comes with sitting with what's left of his family.

"It's weird right?"

"What is?"

"Us. Us being brother and sister. Finally meeting after all this time" Maeve diverts her sight from that bee who was now flying away. She looks at the man beside her, head cocking to the side just a bit and suddenly Micah is the one who wants to make a dog pun. She looks like a curious one with her head tilted and eyes wide, so many unanswered questions and uncertainty swarming in the pools of brown. He's positive he looks the same way. This is something new for the both of them. While they grew up with so many other people, having created their family out of others, they have each other now. The same flesh and blood, the same dead parents.

"I would have assumed you would have said being the chosen one for a prophecy, where now that you're on the run puts a bounty over our heads. But yeah, I guess that is a bit of a shocker too" He likes seeing her smile. It warms him. Gives him this serenity about the world, his future, that everything is going to be okay. Because his sister is happy and that's all he wants for her. A crazy jump from almost having her killed, but he knows it'll grow on him.

"I'm being serious" Her giggling and yet again pushing him with her shoulder lightens the mood. "We've basically spent our entire lives believing that our parents weren't coming back for us. And now we know they aren't–"

"Because they're dead."

"Don't say it like that!"

"It's the truth!" Micah raises his shoulders, hands going out in front of him in exasperation. His eyebrows even go up when his voice reaches a pitch that couldn't be considered manly. "Our parents are never going to meet us, and we'll never meet them. It's just us now. And while I do think our so-called *protectors* could have done things a bit differently, I feel like our parents would be proud of where we ended up. Because in the end, it led us to each other."

"Oh how wise" Maeve rolled her eyes with a snicker and Micah grew defensive. "But it's just—I don't know—like I said...weird. In a way I kind of accepted that I will never meet anyone from my original family, and now here I am, meeting my twin brother in a completely different realm, where being part werewolf is normal!"

"Don't forget that you might also be a witch."

Right, when Amora was explaining what she saw in her vision, she also claimed that she felt Maeve's unexplainable power. It is derived from someone with great abilities, and needs to be detained. The power is unexplainable. Something she can't exactly pinpoint unless the answer was flashing bright green in her face. Which to Maeve is even more absurd because not only is she just barely coming to terms with the idea that all her life she has been the same creature she watches little kids dress up as for Halloween, but she was also someone who could potentially grow warts on her nose and cast spells. Okay, maybe not the warts because it was already made clear that witches don't actually look like that, but it's still terrifying to imagine.

"Yeah...do you think I'll get used to it? Not being human?"

"I think so. Emry and I were speaking before I came out here, and she's completely okay with trying to help you unlock this special unexplainable power" Micah smiled when listening to the way Maeve let out a laugh. He let out his own chuckles even, already enjoying the fact that he has a real sister. It was like watching a part of him. Which is almost quite literal because she's his twin and he can already see the similarities when it comes to their features. He's surprised that no one else did. "And I can help you with your wolf, if you'd like?"

"Ah, what's that like!? Is it more Goosebumps or Twilight?"

"I don't know, actually. I never really thought about it. Especially since us werewolves don't shift that often. But what I can say is that it's almost as if a miniature you is stuck inside your brain, helping you make decisions" He reached out to touch her forehead. "Have you seriously never experienced it? I swear I could already feel the little guy running around in my head the second I could talk."

Maeve shook her head.

"Nope" But then her eyebrows furrowed as she really thought about it. There were a few times where she was stuck in situations and she had no idea how to get out of them; but those were: *which dress should I wear to homecoming? And should I sneak out to a party? Should I stay up binge watching the earlier seasons of Love Island UK?* And yeah, the debates have gone on longer than they should, her head always tugging her in two different directions, but never would she have guessed it may be because there is literally another version of her picking the opposite. She liked to call herself undeniably indecisive.

"Well, that's basically it. There's nothing big and flashy about it. I mean we do sometimes go crazy whenever the moon shines a bit brighter, but I wouldn't say it's something that you should brag about to your friends."

"Way to suck the fun out of being part dog" Maeve slumped. "As for bragging about it, I highly doubt I'll be able to do so. Before being confronted, Emry thinks it's best that I don't return to the human world. Puts an easy target on my back."

"I'm sorry."

"For what?"

"Not only was your first family taken from you, but your second is now too. Who knows when you'll be able to return to them. I'm sure they're worried about you" Micah puts a hand to her knee, thumb caressing the fabric of her pajama pants. Thais' pajama pants. The remembrance of her loving adoptive family engulfs her mind then. She is instantly flashed with memories of all the fun times they've had together. Who knows when they'll be able to create another one, if at all. Her face falls flat and she's now back to staring at nothing. Only this time she lets the tears sting her eyes, a few even clumping her eyelashes together.

"But at least they're safe ya' know? With me gone, there's no evil men trying to do anything possible in order to secure their desires. The last thing I want is for them to get hurt" She gives a tight grin to Micah. "You're wrong about one thing though," He looks at her confused. "Not all of my first family was taken. I still have you. And I'm hoping you'll still have me?"

"Yeah, I still have you."

Chapter Seven

"And I'm not being poisoned, right?" It was said with cheeks full of those delicious fluffy pancakes, them having been warmed up in the microwave just briefly before being re-dished to a once hesitant Maeve (because again, she is surrounded by people that she doesn't know, and this could all just be some elaborate scheme to kill her). But after being reassured that everyone ate the same breakfast that she is fully allowed to indulge herself in, finally eating something after days of nothing occupying her stomach, it wasn't long before the buttery smell had her sold and she was scarfing down everything at once. She looked like a rabid animal, scavenging for food as if it was the last meal they would ever eat. If it wasn't for Amir reminding her that she had to breathe in between bites she probably would have choked at some point. Rowan placed a hand to his chest, right where his heart would be and let his eyes close from the praise of his cooking that was represented by Maeve shoving another fork-full of pancakes into her mouth while also reaching for a piece of bacon that he purposely fried just for her.

"If we wanted to kill you, I think we would have done it by now" Foster replies bluntly. He tried to grab for one of the remaining strips of bacon, to only have his hand smacked away by Micah. He was quick to reel the stinging appendage back in, fingers immediately rubbing at the red area while his face had twisted, a whimper rumbling from his pouting lips.

"Saying things like that only gives her a reason to think we are trying to kill her, you idiot" Zenaida says as she rolls her eyes. Foster made a biting motion, smirk resting on his red lips right after. The only response he had gotten was her huffing out a breath before pulling out an empty chair beside Maeve. A gentle smile appeared, and Maeve would be lying if she said that it didn't make her trust the woman. They've only really talked briefly on her first day (and most of it had to do with what shampoo was available), but she was welcoming. A part of her was shouting that no matter what, Zenaida was a girl of her word and if she needed a shoulder to cry on, the tan platinum blonde was that person to reach out to. But then again, Maeve felt that way about everyone she's met so far. Yeah, of course she still has that inkling of a doubt coursing through her, but the other half, the side telling her that these people won't harm her is beginning to win. Especially when she locks eyes with Micah, her brother. And Amir, a man she has been entranced with ever since they met in the dungeon.

It's a feeling that's made her question herself. Yeah, she knows what it feels like to like someone, even love (if she remembers what Reggie means to her), but this pull she has towards Amir is so much more. It's something akin to finding the missing piece to an extremely hard, forty-thousand, all the same color, obnoxiously small puzzle. She's been searching for so long that once she finally found it, a satisfying wave crashes against her and she feels like she can do anything now. It's definitely something she's never felt before with someone else. Not with any past high school crushes and not with Reggie. She mentally reminds herself to ask Micah about it later—because maybe it's another wolf thing. She only knows what she sees on TV, the movies and shows that play, depicting un-realistic and much scarier (or sexier) versions of what the mythical are really like. So she knows that every wolf has their specific significant other; a mate if she racks her brain hard enough. But that idea scares her more than that disgusting dirt cell within the Raba's home. Because if anything about mates are true, then she's tied to Amir for the rest of her life. He is the one she is supposed to be with. Maeve doesn't think she's ready for that commitment. She has yet to explore as much as she liked to. She needs more time.

Maeve looks at Amir once more after she swallows her last bite. He's looking at her as if he can sense her worry. It only makes her suspicions about being tied to him all more alarming. She tries to smile, signifying that there is nothing wrong and the only thing she still can't wrap her head around is the fact that she is currently in another realm sitting in a room filled with werewolves and two witches. But his expression doesn't budge. His lips twitch into a maybe grin, head slowly nodding, but nothing to disintegrate the growing creases between his eyebrows. She moves on. She looks at Micah who sat across from her at the table. After confirming that they were related, he was honestly the only person she genuinely wanted to be around. Everyone else stood on the other side of the room, keeping their distance—probably because an ounce of them feared that she might explode again from anger, still spiraling at her newest rendition of family history. Also because Emry and Amora said to give her space. It was a bit hard for Thais, as all she wanted to do was ask so many personal questions about her life before the kidnapping.

She can't read Micah's expression. He appears to be carrying a brave face but hidden underneath the lipped smile was something far more concerning. He looked like he was worrying. A part of Maeve knew he was worrying. And in all honesty he had all right to be. Where do they go from here? The Raba is probably out looking for them, ready to strike at any moment. Micah is just in his head, thinking about strategic ways to keep the both of them out of sight until they can probably escape the wrath that is three old men dressed in ugly purple robes. But that means they'll have to lay low for another few days...once the red moon has passed.

"Thais has a date–" Zenaida starts.

"Wait what!?" Amir interrupts. He steps from behind Lucas to get a better view of his sister; someone cowering behind the tall and lanky figure of Gabe. "And when were you going to tell me this?"

"Never...?" Thais squeaks.

"—with a girl in her class—" Zenaida tries again.

"And you're lesbian!? Why am I just hearing about this now! I thought we told each other everything!?" The genuine shock and small ounce of hurt residing in the pout Amir gave was quite amusing. Definitely lifted Maeve's spirits about her situation. And it only got funnier when Thais finally stepped from behind Lucas to point an accusing finger at her older brother.

"Bisexual, and I did tell you! But you were too caught up in your stupid video game to listen!"

"That is not fair! You know how hard killing zombies can be. They need my full undivided attention" Amir shoots back with his own finger pointing.

"Please don't tell me you guys also have zombies here?" Maeve mumbles low to Zenaida. The other woman shakes her head.

"That's another realm."

"That's not my fault! Everyone here knows but you!" Thais crosses her arms over her chest, Amir mocking the gesture as he looks at his friends. They refused to make eye contact with him, causing his bulky arms to fall right back to his sides and jaw unhinge.

"I'm seriously the last to know?"

"Maybe stop spending all of your time attached to that dumb game?" Foster snickers.

"You literally hogged the system all night last night!" Amir has now directed all of his surprise on the other man. One who went from smug to offended. And it didn't help when Micah murmured something about it being true under his breath, Foster hearing it and dropping all emotion into a frown. He stared at the back of Micah's head. The other hadn't turned around, brown eyes sparkling under the dining room light, stuck on the way he picked at his nails. Maeve looked between the two (mostly concentrated on her brother, because Foster has gone back to arguing with Amir about who really takes up all the time on their gaming console; which ultimately ended up bringing both Lucas and Gabe in as well), noticing that there was definitely some hidden tension between them. And it appears to be a normal thing, everyone else not bothering to blink an eye when it comes to the side comment. Reminds Maeve of her first day here, seeing Foster in a towel, Micah obviously staring at Foster in said towel. Was there something between them? Her heart squeezed from empathy.

"As I was saying!" Zenaida eventually shouts. She shocks Maeve out of her thoughts. She jumps slightly in her chair, attention then going to the woman. Everyone's attention goes on her actually. The group pauses—Foster somehow had Rowan in a headlock, who wasn't even a part of the argument, while Amir was holding Lucas by his collar. It's amazing to see that neither Amora nor Emry stopped the beginning of a brawl, rather content with standing in the far back, observing, waiting for any unusual interactions. So far everything appears normal. "Thais has a date, and she wants to go shopping for a cute new dress. I was wondering if you, Maeve, would like to join us? Get you some clothes of your own, so you won't have to keep borrowing ours?"

Maeve doesn't know whether that's a jab because Zenaida's not one to share, or if she's just being nice and would like to get Maeve something more fitting to her. Either or, the suggestion has a few people in the group in an uproar. Thais on the other hand is excited by the question, taking this opportunity as a chance to bond with another female addition to the group. Amir and Micah are disconcerted, alongside Amora and Emry who are also apprehensive.

"What part of Maeve's life being in danger did you not understand?" Micah asks indignantly. "Bringing her to the mall is the perfect opportunity for the Junud to just snatch her up. Or anyone for that matter!"

"Oh calm down," Zenaida huffs. "Obviously she'll be in disguise. I just think she would rather get a tour of Kariq Leada than be cooped up in this house for who knows how long."

That does sound nice.

"Micah has a point though, dear" Amora steps in. Her worry is all over her face. "There is a risk that comes with taking her outside. Who knows if the people you pass will be regular pedestrians, or people trying to make some quick cash by helping the Raba? I think it's best that she just stay here for the time being. Once we know it's safe, then we can discuss ways to reveal her to the public."

Way to shut that idea down.

Maeve and Zenaida had shown their disheartening by dimming their grins. Thais had shown it by verbally expressing her discountenance with groaning loudly.

"What if we bring a few of the guys with us? They can be her bodyguards."

"There's still a big risk" Emry steps up. She's firm, more serious than the tender stare Amora gave. "Like Amora said, we don't know who is willing to attack and kidnap Maeve for the sake of a reward. That's possible harm to not only her, but you all as well" A silence fell over everyone as it was obvious that a decision was made. Maeve even began to think of things she could do while being held hostage. Maybe she could explore all of the nooks and crannies that the place had? Count the amount of flowers that decorated almost everything about the house. "*But,* I do think it'll be good that she goes out for a bit" The celebratory shout from Thais was held back by puffed cheeks and a giant smile. "It would definitely help with the information overload we just gave her. Maybe even ease her into the idea that people like us do exist."

It's amazing to see them all talk about her like she isn't sitting right there. Other than that, she is a bit glad that Emry was the lenient one today. She always has had a soft spot for Maeve. And as the two locked eyes, it was like staring at her best friend again.

"But with that being said, I need all of you to keep an eye out. Make sure you're watching her and for any possible enemies. Understand?"

"Aw, do we really have to go? Thais takes forever to shop. Last time we went, we spent at least an hour staring at make up" Rowan whines. His ear was then being pulled by said girl. He tries to pull her off yet she continues to yank and tug while mumbling curses.

"Yes, I need all of you to protect her. The Raba can strike at any moment" Emry says. Amora is quick to jump in, eyes locked in on Micah.

"I need you to be careful as well. We can't have anyone finding out who you really are either. So as far as everyone knows, you're still Micah Loom. Abandoned child who was taken in by a nurse. Understand?"

Micah and Amora stare at each other. But then he nods.

Maeve was astounded by Kariq Leada. She couldn't keep her eyes off the beautiful scenery, entranced by how it wasn't any different from the human realm. She believed it to resemble New York City. She visited there once, a trip taken by the family for some family reunion on her father's side. They were strangely accepting of the Ross couple only housing adoptive children, but then that's when Maeve also found out that Athena was an infertile woman and always wished to bear her own children one day. Unfortunately it was a dream that won't ever come true and she was more than perfectly happy to give that love to kids that never experienced it. The reunion was years ago, hidden deep in the crevices of a memory that could only be dug up if Maeve traveled back to her awkward emo phase from middle school. Heavy dark make-up and the unnecessary need to blast punk-rock music, fourteen-year-old Maeve Ross sends a shiver up her now twenty-one-year-old spine. But it does help her relive the hundreds of big skyscrapers from New York City. Helps her think of all of the neon signs that were attached to any building they could be installed on, the people who roamed the streets, and most importantly the heavy amounts of traffic that was never solved with the pressing of palms to the steering wheel of cars. It was all the same in Kariq Leada. Even the many homeless people that swished around a cup and terribly made signs asking for any spare change.

Rowan was almost a fool to a woman with a stomach that poked from underneath what might have just been an extremely dirty designer shirt. He thought she was pregnant, holding out her hand as she asked him if he had anything to give her.

"Here, let me see" He was reaching to pull out his wallet, fingers wrapped around the black pleather and already giving the woman some hope. But before he was able to really check, his arm was being halted by Foster.

"Sorry, but we don't carry any rons."

And then he was dragging the shaggy blonde closer to the

group that was continuing their way down the sidewalk. Maeve giggled from her spot in the middle of everyone. She didn't know what part was funnier though. The sulking face that Rowan gave as he was being scolded by the other, or the offended stare the woman gave as she watched the duo walk off. But then she was just as fast to move on to her next target that was two lively teenage girls chatting.

It wasn't much more walking after the encounter, Zenaida claiming that they had finally reached the store that would be great for finding a new date outfit. Maeve craned her neck expecting to see something of a small boutique, maybe a stereotypical retail store that played loud pop music and was overpriced. Instead she was face to face with a mall.

KL SHOPPING CENTER

It read across the top of the building in giant red letters. It had to be at least five stories, the entrance being glass push and pull doors, persons of all kinds coming and going from them—most if not all carrying some kind of paper bag with big smiles on their faces but deep frowns on their credit cards. All of the guys groaned at the sight of their city mall, already knowing that Thais and Zenaida were going to spend hours upon hours in the place. And if they planned to keep their word about buying a few pieces for Maeve as well, then it's a guarantee that they'll be roaming the floors all day. Amir is just glad that he wasn't the only man tagging along. Last time he went shopping with his avid spender of a sister, he couldn't feel his arms or his feet. She wanted to buy everything she laid her eyes on, not only leaving the both of them in debt, but they tapped a bit into Amora's wallet. If he wasn't already sore from carrying pounds of clothes in hundreds of bags, he would say he could barely walk from how many chores he had to do in order to make up for spending more than they were supposed to.

He didn't even get anything out of all of the stuff bought. *Wait, no that's a lie.* He got one thing. It was a tacky bracelet Thais spent fifty cents on. It came from one of those plastic pods within a coin machine. He still has it. It lays on his dresser, right beside his bedside lamp. It's nothing like the many pretty bracelets the group of them starred at right now, fingers grazing against the silver and gold with admiration for the metal.

Maeve was intrigued about what she could and could not buy. There was a certain pair of earrings she took an interest in when first walking into the store. They weren't much, just small earrings that dangled a tear-drop shaped kunzite gem in the middle of them. It was a color that reminded her of that halo from the stained glass window. She'll have to ask about them once Thais and Zenaida finish with their dress shopping mission. They were a duo that giggled tremendously once finding anything they remotely liked.

"Come on Maeve, pick out something you like too!" Thais speaks while shoving a dress into her arms. It was an action that had her stumbling a bit in place. The hat she was forced to wear had fallen off from the unexpected jump, tumbling to the floor and landing on the feet of Lucas. Within that moment she is a bit frazzled, because not only is she trying to look at the dress Thais handed to her, but she's looking around for where that dumb hat had fallen. Lucas saved her one problem though by picking the red accessory from the ground and plopping it back on hair that had been slicked back into a bun. But then he placed his arm on top of said hat, using her head as some kind of clutch to rest his body weight on.

"Be gentle with the girl, would ya'?" He chuckled. "Wouldn't want anyone finding out her identity, now do we?"

Amir shoved him off, a low growl resonating from within his throat. It had Lucas raising his hands in the air, mocking surrender, while Maeve was a bit flattered. She couldn't help wondering if it's just because she's beginning to sike herself into believing the whole werewolf mate thing, or if she's just thankful that heavy Lucas no longer leant against her head leaving pressure.

"Oh calm down, there's barely anyone in here. I highly doubt anyone saw her" Thais replies with a roll of her eyes. That's when Amir stepped forward more, flicking his sister in the middle of her forehead. She groaned at the attack, rubbing the spot before shooting her sibling a glare. "Ow fucker! I thought Ms. Loom said you're not allowed to do that anymore!"

"She also said that every time you swear you gotta put a dollar in the swear jar" Amir crossed his arms over his large chest. "But besides that, you really do have to be careful. While there might not be many people here, we don't know anyone's true intention. For all that we know the cashier is spying on a great opportunity to take Maeve. So just be a little more cautious?"

Thais blew out a puff of air.

"Alright fine" She took a step around her brother, looking at Maeve with a grin. And then not even seconds later she's apologizing. Not like she needed to. Of course Maeve is just as scared (because then this would be the second time that she gets kidnapped), but she doesn't think something as small as her hat falling off for what could have been a minute, was that big of a deal. So shaking her head, she began to explain that it was all good on her end and that Thais can return to her happy search for her date dress.

"We should find you something nice too. Who knows what good looking guys you might find out here?" Thais eventually speaks after a beat of awful silence. She wiggled her eyebrows suggestively and then reached for her wrist where she tugged Maeve towards Zenaida (a woman who debated on what pair of blue jeans she wanted, even if they looked the exact same).

The idea of potentially finding a romantic partner spiked a bit of fear in Maeve. Especially when she looked back at Amir, their eyes locking just briefly before it was broken by a tall rack blocking the view of each other. She didn't want to admit to her ears beginning to burn when seeing his eyes shine their gorgeous yellow. It's not like she would mind having someone like Amir being her werewolf soulmate. He's shown nothing but kindness towards her (and it definitely helps that he's really good-looking). He's a perfectly good candidate.

What if she chooses not to be with him though? What if she really does find someone else? Like Reggie. He comes back into the picture and admits to being a terrible person...but he's done some thinking and he wants to be different. Maeve hates to admit it, but she'd fall for it, fall for him; all over again. Yeah, he's chipped at bits of her love with the betrayal, but he could easily re-build it. She loves him, she probably always will. But then there's the other monsters. Eveytime she passes another civilian, she can't help but wonder what they could be. Another werewolf, a vampire, a witch. Was she even allowed to date out-side her own species?

This is more confusing than human boys.

"This may be a weird question," In order to appear noncha-lant, and totally not at all freaking out about the fact that she's having supernatural boy problems already, she keeps her shaky focus on the clothes perfectly displayed around the store. It's not like Thais or Zenaida would notice anyway. They were far too captivated by the sequins that were attached to a blouse. They couldn't keep their eyes off a pretty floral print long enough in order to see the way sweat began to curate around her temple, or the way her fingers curled around a cotton cardigan in order to hide the way her hands were as nervous as she was. But then Maeve lets her brown eyes wander over to the boys playing with giant bras, and hair accessories. If Micah didn't stop Gabe from trying to kiss Foster on the cheek as he pretended to be a girl, then it's possible that they would have been thrown out. The prissy cashier was already staring them down, narrow green eyes looking at the rowdy boys menacingly. "But is it true that every werewolf has a mate?"

A head-turning question it was. Thais and Zenaida stopped their ogling at a cute set of heels in order to look at her with wide eyes and almost an unhinged jaw.

"Why do you want to know? Someone you already have your eye on?" Zenaida places a purse back down on its shelf, before moving onto another bag. She shares a look with Thais—one that says that they know something. "If it's Lucas, sorry but he's off the market. He's kind of already married to me" And while the shock could barely settle from the statement alone, she was raising her left hand where a shiny diamond ring was seen wrapped around her finger. It wasn't anything too extravagant, but nothing too bland either. She would have never guessed that the two of them were in a relationship—the duo not having many interactions since Maeve arrived. Yeah, she's seen them bicker occasionally, but anything relating to being in love until death do they part hasn't come around just yet. Maeve moves her attention from the ring and over to the boys once more. She spots Lucas pointing and laughing at Rowan, someone used as a test subject for the usable makeup products. Red lipstick stained his thin lips and bright blue eyeshadow went way past just being on his eyelids. The ugliest makeover ever doesn't stop Maeve from catching sight of the shiny golden ring also on Lucas' finger. She's in awe.

But also a bit confused.

"But you sleep in the same room as Thais?"

"Technically yes, Thais and I share a room, and then Lucas with Gabe. But that's because there was a time when we were just friends..."

"And then they found out they were tied for all eternity and just couldn't keep from professing their love to one another" Thais fake gags as she walks around another rack, this one full of many dresses. It immediately caught her attention and she was going through the many different designs and select-few sizes.

"So the whole mate thing is real? Like there seriously is someone in this world that I'm destined to be with? How does that work? Is it a destiny thing, or do you get to pick and choose who you want to be with?"

The questions poured out of Maeve because she didn't know

how to stop. There were thousands of running thoughts that just needed to be said and yet her mouth could only muster so many before she was running out of breath. Plus she doesn't think there is enough time in the world for her to list the multiple questions she needs answers to.

"Woah, slow down there hun" Zenaida giggles. "But yes, having a so-called mate is indeed real. Most if not all mythical creatures have one. Werewolves, vampires, fairies, mermaids...It's written in the Haya. Which I'm guessing you don't know," Maeve shakes her head, bafflement through the roof at this point. Zenaida giggles. "It's an ancient text kept in possession by the Oracle. We really only learn the basics in school, like a history class. For example, it may have not been that long ago, but it's definitely something that takes the cake for one of the most historical moments here in Kariq Leada, the Witch Massacre."

Witch Massacre? Maeve will definitely have to ask about that again later. That and along with this said *Oracle*. Aren't they people who're supposed to see all; know your present, past, and future?

"But that doesn't matter. You asked about mates. It's honestly just a shortened way of saying soulmate. Someone that is connected to you both mentally and emotionally. They are the one person in the world that will be able to connect with you on such a personal level, you might end up believing that you're one person" Zenaida finishes with a fond stare. It isn't hard to tell that she's looking past Maeve and staring at her husband.

"And how do you know you've met that person?"

"Oh that's easy," Thais joins in. It appears she has finally picked out the perfect dress. "It may be different for every species, but us werewolves feel as though we are in excruciating pain. My sex-ed teacher says it's because our souls are binding together physically. It could happen unexpectedly, but typically the binding happens when that couple undergoes meeting for the first time. It's like a meet-cute but with a terrible sensation" She chirps.

And oh my goodness, Maeve better not have experienced this in that stupid dungeon when finally being able to see Amir under the flames.

"Yeah, you werewolves. Personally us elves–"

"You're an elf!?"

Why hadn't she known this before!? She swears that she was only surrounded by extremely large dogs that can also be human. But nope, she's also in the presence of someone who's supposed to have pointy ears and be a lot shorter. Her confusion makes Zenaida chuckle. But then she's pushing back her blonde hair in order to show the way that her ears are most definitely pointy. She even wiggled them a bit, the small hoop earrings she was wearing swaying.

"Have been since the day I was born. My husband *is* a were-wolf though. The crossing of our species is what made us realize later that we were mates. I as an elf though didn't feel pain and was instead experiencing this surge of new energy. It was like an adrenaline rush."

"So you are able to date outside your species?" Maeve asks. She wasn't even looking at clothes anymore, neither pretending to.

"Of course. There's hybrids all over this place" Thais responds as she smiles at a perfect set of earrings that would go perfect with the dress. "You can date whoever you want, marry, have children...but the minute you meet your mate that life you made will be turned on its head. So it's not often that you see people with *blended* families. Makes the breaking bond worse."

"You can break a bond too?"

Maybe Maeve should find a place to sit down. This was a lot of information.

"Yeah, but it's taboo. The agony is far too much to bear and it's been told that people tend to commit suicide from how heartbreaking it is."

"And how do you break a bond?"

"I couldn't tell you. I think it involves some sort of spell. Like I said, it's taboo, no one is practicing this" Zenaida then returns to looking at clothes. Or that is until Thais joyfully says that she's going to try on the dress in the fitting rooms. That leads the other two to follow, taking a seat on a nearby cushioned bench waiting for her to come out and show the final product.

It's when a man passes the duo, an uneasy feeling sits within Maeve's stomach. Maybe it just has to do with how the man looks down at her, eyes boring into hers with an evil gleam behind his already so dark brown irises. It's just even as he walks to the opposite side of the store, she can't help but let her anxiety begin to fuel her. She puts her hands between her closed thighs, eyes darting back and forth, nothing in particular catching her attention. Mentally she's rushing Thais, also hoping that the guys will finally join them (because if they forgot, they're supposed to be protecting her! Not playing with clothes). Thankfully Thais must have heard her internal dilemma and had stepped from behind the wooden door to her dressing room. She looked pretty. She chose a baby blue dress, the skirt of it resting only inches above her knees. It had thin straps resting on her shoulders, along with the design of the bust to the torso being tight in a corset fashion, while the skirt was breathable. It flapped about as Thais twirled, a giggle leaving her lips as she adored how she looked in the dress. It was hard not to be jealous. Thais was one of those girls who didn't need pounds of make-up or watch her calorie intake.

She was a natural beauty. One that sparks envy within you as you think back to your own prime youth. Yeah, Maeve wasn't that much older, but finally hitting twenty-one, it's hard not to think about how life is more serious now. A career, health, relationships. It's enough stress to already give a person eye-bags. And Maeve would rather die than have dark rings encase her pretty face.

Maeve watched as Zenaida stood from her spot on the bench, eagerly going up to the other with just as much admiration as one would a mother celebrating their daughter. Maeve would have joined, gushed and squealed and continuously said that this was a dress that needed to be purchased, but as she looked at the duo, this was a more intimate moment. It was something that they obviously have spent endless nights gossiping over, therefore they deserve to take the time to gossip a little more. Maeve actually believed that she would take this as an opportunity to stand and maybe find something she liked; like return to those precious purple earrings.

She could hear the men being loud still, so she glanced in their direction. The cashier had finally interrupted their antics, the lady trying to stop Amir from beating Micah with a mannequin arm. She wasn't getting anywhere. She was shouting that he must give her the arm, but he was far too caught up in chasing Micah.

Maeve felt bad. The cashier was obviously tired of their boyish shenanigans. So putting her shopping on hold for just a moment longer, to finally get all of the guys to relax, she began the short journey over to them. Unfortunately not many steps in she was being grabbed. Panic shot through her and it only increased when she looked back to see that it was that man from before.

Chapter Eight

Maeve tried to rip her arm from out of the man's hold. It wasn't hard to tell that he was definitely stronger than her. He was tall and bulky (his bicep being as big as her head), and the hold he had on her was tight enough to bruise. He was able to keep hold of her, dragging her away without any doubt she would be able to slip away. The man was confident in his catch—a nasty smile stretching his scarred up face, and revealing that he doesn't know what a toothbrush is because his teeth were yellow and rotten.

"Yeah, boss is going to be so happy I found you" His voice sent shivers up her spine. It was deep and gravely. It was rough enough to have her assume that he chainsmokes, and his breath smells heavily of cheddar cheese chips. If the man's obvious attempt of kidnapping wasn't the biggest hint that she should get away from him, his hygiene would have been it. It's why Maeve struggled. She yanked and pulled, dug her heels into the store carpeted floors, and used her other hand to try and smack him away. She was getting absolutely nowhere when it came to freedom, just a lot closer to being dragged out the store and into the hands of whoever this man's boss is.

"I'm not going anywhere with you!" She twisted her arm once again, as she also dropped all of her body weight to the floor. The sudden fall took the stranger by surprise so his grip loosened just enough for Maeve to slither out of his touch. But now she was on the floor, barely able to register that she escaped before she was being grabbed by her leg now. It's obvious that this man doesn't care how he gets Maeve out of the store, for as long as he does. And if that means grabbing her ankle and pulling her against the carpet, then so be it. Maeve tried to grab onto whatever she could in order to keep from leaving, but all of the furniture grabbed just moved along with her. "Let me go! Guys! Help!"

Her last resort was shouting.

She must have been causing too much ruckus now because the man had gotten angry. He looked down at her and then used his height to hopefully spot the many people that she walked in with. It wasn't hard or long before he was locking sight on a bunch of men who took alarm to the sudden screams. Their laughter and minimal arguing with the cashier had come to a halt, faces going stoic as they opened their ears wider for any more potential yells. It was when Maeve had shouted for Micah this time, her plea to be released was heard and the entire group of werewolf men had locked on their target. They all looked at the man, wrath burning their bones. And that fire only continued to spread when watching the stranger bend down to lift Maeve over his shoulder. She pounded at his back, feet kicking. She feels like the biggest damsel in distress. How many times has she had to be saved since being here?

"Micah! Help! Please!"

While the man had sight on exiting the store, the group

of werewolves took it as their cue to pounce. Amir threw the plastic mannequin arm over his shoulder, not even bothered by the crashing sound that happened seconds later. He was already dashing towards the big burly man with full speed—his eyes glowing their gemstone yellow, and a low growl rumbling from within his throat. He had purposely raised his hands, showing off the way his shortened nails had extended into something of claws, along with baring his teeth in order to display the way his canines became as sharp as knives. He looked deadly already, igniting fear in the glimpse that Maeve had gotten of him; but if that's how he looked still in human form, she wonders how frightful he could be once completely shifted into a wolf.

It had to be only a minute or so before Maeve was squealing out from the fear that came with almost being dropped. She was practically dangling in the one arm of the man, head bobbing and hands desperately wishing to find something stable to grab onto. Amir had been the first to attack the stranger. He jumped feet in the air before landing a scratch on the enemy's face; the result being a shout of pain, his one fighting hand used to go to the wound and cover it. He tapped his scarred eye, feeling the way Amir's nails had definitely dug deep enough to draw blood. The crimson color was already cascading down his face in waves, causing his sight to also be just as red. The scratch had only made the man angrier though, his confidence once coming from being assured that he would be able to kidnap the target without a hassle. He was proven wrong when now he is being kicked in the stomach by a raging Micah. The stranger goes flying into the nearest wall, cracking the freshly white paint and scaring the few customer ladies who were getting changed. They all scream as they run out of the store. The kick was a bad move on Micah's part though because Maeve had been let go somewhere in between, crashing into the side of a metal table, the agony of what have been a corner bruising something internal, before she's crashing to the ground where she may have accidentally kicked a rack and that tumbled down on her. She was covered in clothes, only able to hear the chaos that was going on. And the ache that struck her whenever she breathed in made her dizzy. She had half a mind to think about who may be helping her through the stacked shirts. So she just let the person help her, pull any fabric from her body and use her arm to help stand her to her feet. It was when she turned to thank the person that her vision made out the sight of another stranger.

It was a woman. Fiery hair, with an expression being one of determination and annoyance; definitely older. She was also vaguely familiar. It might take Maeve a moment to think about where she has seen this woman from. She must have hit her head during the fall as well. A pulse kept pounding at her left temple, causing great pain when she went to touch it. Her fingers were wet then, sticky and warm. With spotting eyes she looked at the two digits she put to her temple and saw that her own blood was dripping. She was in shock by the sight; blinking repeatedly and holding in the gasp. She didn't want to think that it was as bad it felt, but in reality Maeve wanted to sit down. She could barely keep her eyes open, legs tripping over themselves as she was being guided somewhere by the strange woman.

"I should have just done it myself" The woman heaves as she continues to the exit of the store. She bypassed the fighting men like they were pure background noise—all of the werewolf men having underestimated who they were brawling against. After kicking the one gross kidnapper into the wall, not even seconds later, six more of the same guy approaches with vengeful grimaces and the thirst for blood in their eyes. But Amir, Micah, even Rowan have that same stare. They began to attack each other, warning off all the bypassers and alarming all of the shopping mall security.

Foster had seen that one of the kidnappers was aiming for Micah's head with a steel pole that once housed hanging jeans. Rage boiled within him. He didn't believe that he needed to use all of his strength in order to fend off a few punks, so there was no intricate fighting going on his behalf. Just mindless kicks and jabs that evidently wound whomever is throwing a punch at him. But once seeing that Micah was about to be harmed while his back is turned caused his chest to tighten and his teeth to grind against one another. Foster clenched his fists, hands balled so tight that his knuckles began to turn white. And with a pace he built in order to make it to the enemy in time, he threw his arm back before releasing it in a punch that had the man crashing to the floor. His pole soared, flying past the sight that was that woman still pulling a stumbling Maeve to the exit, and instead into the leg of one of the mall security guards. Maybe Foster would have cared about the wellbeing of someone that was just doing their job and now has a large metal pole jammed right in the middle of his thigh, but he was far too busy with finishing off the man who lay on the ground. He took the man by the neck, casually lifting his large body as if he didn't look like a magazine-issued bodybuilder. And then he began to squeeze. He squeezed until there was a struggle to breathe, and then with force slammed the man onto the ground where he didn't stop until after he dragged him through different tables, lifting him once more so he could be thrown into the body of one of his fellow kidnappers.

"That was a bit excessive don't you think?" Micah pants after being leisurely lethal when simply using his two hands to twist one of the enemy's heads until it was backwards. He kicked the guy's dead body to the ground, pocketing his hands.

"Anything for you," Foster answers with a grin. Whether the response had its effect or not was never revealed because the duo were back into the action when they heard Thais begin to shout.

"I don't think we can let you leave with her. We will be in big trouble. So if you could ever so kindly just return her to us..." It was said with the sweetest smile, eyelashes batting up and down while she motioned to her and Zenaida. Someone who was far less than pleased that Maeve had managed to be taken from their clutches. Day one and they already managed to get her partially kidnapped. There's no way that Amora and Emry would allow them to bring Maeve outside again.

"Sorry, but once the Junud has a task, it's best that we complete it without any complications. So unless you wish to meet your fate, I suggest you please get out of my way" The woman was blunt as she spoke, grip on Maeve getting tighter as she pulled her closer to her side. It had awoken some self-awareness in Maeve, because she was beginning to pull away from the stranger.

"Let go of me" She mumbles, even going as far as kicking the woman in the shin. There was a hiss, but no real damage done to make her posture deter.

"You heard the lady..." Thais' pretty smile dropped into some-thing far more dangerous. Her eyes matched her brother's, a gorgeous shiny yellow that almost puts citrine to shame. She snarls as the other woman pulls out a blade, spinning it around her finger before it's clasped in her hand. "Let. Go. Of. Her!"

That's when Thais launched herself, fingernails expanded into thick claws reaching out to rip through the woman's smooth neck aligned with a thin silver necklace. She was able to dig her nails into the woman's arm, pulling at the skin until open cuts of crescents were given, dark blood gushing and plopping onto the floor in droplets. The woman cried at the pain, before she was letting Maeve go in order to use both hands to grab hold of Thais and throw her into the nearest thing. That being three mannequins once showing off sporty-wear. Now they were knocked over and intertwined with a groaning teenager. Her distraction though gave Zenaida enough time to grab hold of Maeve and usher her to safety. They didn't get far, just into the hold of Lucas before Zenaida was being grabbed by her platinum blonde hair and pulled to the ground. Lucas shouts for her when his wife doesn't immediately give up. She instead recovered from the fall and reached for the stranger's leg to also cause her to topple over. Zenaida took the opportunity to get on top of the woman where she then began to whisper unrecognizable words. Sounded like a different language. Her brown eyes rolled back and the hands she wrapped around the woman's throat began to glow green.

"Alsharu min aldaakhil qim wa'akl ma tabaqaa min al'abria' muhataman jasadah."

The woman was screaming as the words became louder, more

aggressive. Zenaida's hold on her became tighter; and if she didn't plan on causing harm with magic, then she might just choke the woman to death. Only when it looks as though Zenaida was going to succeed, she is being thrown back by a force. She soars across the room, body crashing into the desk that the cashier fearfully hid behind. She screams at the possibility of a dead body, running for the back exit. Maeve understands Lucas' devastation—the way he can only watch his wife become a ragdoll, flying across the room. But he could have been a lot gentler when it came to dropping her on the floor in order to run after her. Maeve is left groaning where she is, weak and completely vulnerable to whoever this strange woman is. Maeve holds back the moans of pain that come, left hand debating whether it wants to clutch her bruised side or her leaking temple, while her right hand helps her wobbly legs crawl what is probably only a few inches. Panic rushes through her more when the blurry version of the woman is seen stalking her way closer.

"Stay away from me!" Maeve throws the nearest item she could at the stranger. It was no help; merely an item that was dodged with a tilt of the neck. If anything, throwing whatever it is she grabbed only made the woman more annoyed.

"It would save me all of this goddamn trouble" She grits back. "But unfortunately I cannot. You shall be coming with me."

Her path was blocked when Micah stepped in. Foster was beside him, arms crossed over his huge chest and coming off more like a bodyguard than a friend. And Maeve would say that he technically is at the moment (hers), if he wasn't standing so close to Micah's back, physique basically hovering over what was already such a tall man. He was like a big and strong wall that would take the blow for Micah if he did as little as blink. Maeve really has to ask about the two of them later...under different circumstances.

"No she won't."

The woman released a heavy breath.

"Why must you foolish animals continue to stand in my way? I find it best that you all just step to the side if you wish to keep your lives."

"And both you and the Raba can shove it up your asses."

Maeve would have laughed if it didn't hurt already just to breathe. She thinks she may have hurt her ribs, or bruised a lung. All she wants to do is go to sleep. That sounds like such a better idea than fighting to stay awake, doing absolutely nothing to determine her fate. But she couldn't fall asleep now, not when catching a glimpse around the huge guy: Foster, to see Micah going in for the strike. All she could really watch is Micah drop to the floor and swipe at her legs before he's reaching out and grabbing a fistfull of her thigh. She screamed at the way his claws dug into her flesh and began to tear into the muscle there. Then he was lifting her by the bleeding thigh and slamming her back down on the ground. A breathy chuckle was given from Foster, and then Maeve was being touched on her shoulder. She stiffened from the touch, afraid that maybe another one of the unknown woman's goons had risen from the dead and was using this instance to succeed in kidnapping her. But craning her neck she had seen Amir. Thais was leaning on his side, a bit battered and bruised from her take on the battle.

"Come on" He lifted her from the ground with ease. The body weight of his sister was non-existent as he helped Maeve to her feet, big arms wrapping around her midsection as he threw one of her arms over his shoulder. She groaned at the motion, face contorting as her body did the same. Amir was quick to hold her still, eyes racking her up and down in hopes of spotting where she was hurting. The mystery of her injuries wasn't hard to decipher though, she had a trail of blood dripping down the side of her face and she was already reaching for her bruised side. Her visible pain had Amir bringing her in closer, having them chest to chest. His concerned brown eyes stared into her hazy ones, a moment of tranquility taking over the both of them.

It was a rush. The aching that came with the possibility of broken bones had vanished, and was replaced with her heart beating at a pace that she deemed unhealthy. Staring at a man she's only met a day ago shouldn't make her knees go weak and her breath hitch as she tried her hardest not to glance down at his pink lips. She wants to blame it on the circumstances. She's going to blame it on the circumstances. No one would be able to think straight if they were thrown into this terrible predicament; so abrupt and unusual feelings are bound to appear. Maeve will excuse her ball of jitters for Amir by saying that she isn't in the best state, and some big attractive man is saving her from it.

She does not need to read any further into it.

"We have to get you out of here while we still have an opening."

Maeve breaks their stare to glance back at her brother and their threat. The woman was lying on the ground, desperately fighting off the ferocious attacks that were sharp claws gunning for any piece of her flesh. She was already severely damaged, and it's mighty impressive to see how well she was still defending herself. She had obviously been trained for something like this. But then she's returning her stare to her surroundings. The entire store looked to be in shambles; clothes and racks, jewelry and shoes are now dangling from random spots. All customers and staff have abandoned the store, but there lay dead and unconscious evil henchmen all about. Walls and shelves were damaged beyond repair and it'll be shocking if this place is scrubbed clean of the many splatters of blood that decorated the walls and floor. While the mall security had appeared, they left not too long after one of their men had been impaled. They realized that this battle was beyond their control. It's still in question about whether or not the police were called, but bets reside on no.

Micah referenced the Raba. If these people worked for them, what even is the point of police officers? They would just be told to stand down under much higher authority. A fight that was supposed to be easy turned more into a bloodbath.

Maeve tried her best to smile at Amir, nodding to show that she agreed. That's when they began to stumble towards the exit. Amir helped guide both his sister and Maeve out of the fight. It was rare that he was seen struggling when carrying two grown girls, but whenever he did, Maeve did her best to lift her weight. She thought it would be best if Thais was taken to safety first, aided to first. So whenever it looked like either one of them was about to fall out of the firm grip Amir had on the both of them, Maeve disregarded that her side returned back to its burn and tried to walk rather than limp along.

Chapter Nine

She doesn't know about everyone else. Doesn't know if they made it out of the fight safe and sound, or whether or not their group faced the same fatality as those men. Amir had claimed that they would be fine, that they've all suffered fights worse than that while living in Kariq Leada. It's inevitable when monsters with this hidden killer entity live in all of them. She was told not to worry, that it's promised that everyone will make it back to the house with little to no harm and they'll be joking about the experience soon enough. It didn't sit right with Maeve though. As the three of them still stumbled down the street, battered and bruised, her chest tightened and a part of her sank. This was all because of her. People she barely knows are being attacked with the intention of death all because she was some stupid chosen one. Makes her think back to the dungeon. She thought about if it would have been better if she was just left there for the Raba's little experiment. She doesn't know the damage that they would have caused if their plan succeeded, but as of this moment, with no intel on a family she would hopefully like to call her friends, she is beginning to think staying was a better choice. Especially now knowing that Micah is her long lost twin brother; someone that she doesn't want to ever see harmed. And yet she left him back in the mall, not only fighting for her life but his as well. A strong part of her wanted to defy the way Amir continued to guide them back to the quiet part of the city where their house is. She wanted to run back to the store and see if everyone was still breathing.

Unfortunately she knows she can't do that before Amir says it. The three of them are already getting weary looks from by-standers; all of them wondering what may have happened; or already knowing because the fight wasn't something small. They had to get back to safety as fast as they could, and allow answers of the aftermath be given later. So Maeve continued to trudge. One foot in front of the other. And when she wasn't thinking about her brother possibly being slashed by that woman, she was groaning from the absence of a car. It would make this trip a lot less agonizing. While she's still clutching her side, gripping at her skin believing that it will ease the pain for just a moment, along with trying her hardest not to pass out from the massive throbbing that was going on to her temple, Thais looked to be doing fine. She recovered fairly quick. It took a few moments but eventually she was removing herself from Amir's hold and walking along fine. She had even built up enough strength to complain about being sore.

"Now I'm going to have to tell Lisa I can't make it tonight."

It was a whine, said as she tried her best to fix her hair. A chocolate color that curled around like bouncy springs. It fell to her shoulders and was being tugged up into a ponytail.

"I'm glad that that's your biggest concern right now" Amir rolls his eyes.

"Well of course! I was really looking forward to our little..." Her cheeks burned red and she grew bashful. Her eyes twinkled and a grin couldn't keep from her lips. "Date."

"Let's get you checked out by Ms. Loom first. Just to see if you need any serious medical attention" Amir nudged her gently with his elbow. "And then maybe I can convince her to let you leave for your date."

It was a sweet moment between the two siblings. The way they shared smiles that proved there was genuine love between them. Made Maeve feel warm. All she's ever wanted was that kind of connection. And while she does have huge love for her fellow adoptive younger siblings, all her life she wanted nothing more than a real family. Now she has one. Micah. She wants that with Micah.

"Thanks. But I highly doubt Ms. Loom or Emry is going to let any of us step foot outside again once they hear what went down" Thais referenced to a barely hanging on Maeve. She looked the worst. If it wasn't for Amir's support she probably would have collapsed by now. "I mean look at Maeve. She looks like she got run over by a truck."

"I'm fine."

No, she's not. She feels nauseous.

"I don't get why she isn't healing faster" Amir voiced his thoughts, large arms tightening around Maeve's waist, ultimately pulling her in so close that they're basically hugging. Amir might as well be carrying her. "She should at least be able to walk on her own. Especially since I'm right here and our-" He realizes what he's about to say so he bites his tongue. Maeve wants to know what it was. He looked a bit nervous. "I just mean, her werewolf gene isn't taking its full effect like it should."

"Wait, so you guys do have that weird ability to heal fast? 'Kind of thought that was made up by movie directors" Maeve blinks slowly. Her words were also a bit slurred. Amir helps her from tripping, so their faces get closer and they're caught staring at each other yet again. It always felt so intimate...intense. He moves a strand of hair from her face, tucking it behind her ear. Maeve tries hard not to shiver from the delicate touch. It's only making her dizzier. So she puts space between them, eyes darting to Thais and how she stared at them with a raised eyebrow and knowing smile.

Okay, but seriously what does she know?

"Yeah, we do. But it appears that you cannot" Thais nods. The trio momentarily stops at the edge of a crosswalk, and the teenage girl raises her manicured fingers to touch Maeve's bleeding temple. It began to clot, so she didn't have to be scared of dying from blood loss. It still hurt tremendously though, Maeve flinching at the touch. "I wonder if it has to do with you being raised in the human world?"

"But shouldn't her supernatural powers be awakened once she stepped foot in Kariq Leada? It's not like she's denying the idea of being a werewolf..." Amir waved a dismissive hand in the air. "Or at least anymore."

He has a point. It's kind of hard not to believe that this is her new reality for any longer. There's no promise that she will be returning home any time soon, and no matter how many times she has pinched herself from seeing something magical, she still feels the pain and is forced to open her eyes wider in acknowledgment. If she was going to wake up from the most insane dream ever, she believes the fear from the fight would have done the trick. Her blow to the table definitely would have awoken her, body dripping in a cold sweat while her hands gripped her bed sheets in an attempt to ground herself. Instead, she's very much awake in a different realm, debating if she wants to continue to walk back to the house or finally let her eyes close and hope that Amir carries her the rest of the way. In the end she went with the second option when the throbbing in all parts of her body was too much and she just couldn't handle the ache for any longer. She completely shuts down, her eyes fluttering close while her knees go weak and she's toppling over. If it wasn't for Amir's quick reflexes, she probably would have fallen into the busy road.

"Maeve!"

She hears whispering at first. It's faint, rushed and filled with aggravation. Appears that whoever is talking is actually angry, frustrations coming out in a hush voice and spiteful words. The voice was accompanied by another, two, three, eventually Maeve believes that she's surrounded by people who were arguing. That's when she's flinching from a bright light hitting her face. It turns the darkness into red, before it's a blurry white. She blinks as she groans from the disturbance. Her body hurts and it was a lot better when she was sleeping. She didn't have to endure the agony that came with every movement. And it's when she subtly announces that she is indeed alive and finally coming to, that all of the quiet voices had dialed down and were mixing with the room's silence. It made Maeve feel uneasy. She continued to blink as she used her shaky arms to sit up. She looked around at her lap, seeing that she was covered by Thais' blanket. She rested in Thais' bed yet again. When her vision was cleared she looked at her surroundings. Everyone from the group was in the room, staring at her. All of their expressions were different, but hidden underneath everyone's eyes there was a bit of concern. She was intrigued to see that Lucas looked to be mad. He stared at her coldly, buff arms crossed over her chest as he tried to hold back his scowl. It wasn't working, Maeve could feel that she had done something wrong.

"Please tell me that I didn't sleep for three days again?" It was said as she raised a hand to her head. The pain wasn't as strong, but it did sting as she tried to caress the wound. Maeve pushed the blanket off of her after, shifting to make her way off the bed. Only as she moved, she groaned from the surge of pain that coursed through her side. Micah was the first to approach, cutting Amir off from being the one to stop her from leaving the comfort of a soft mattress.

"It's best that you just lie down for a bit longer. Back at the mall, you cracked a few ribs."
His warm touch to her arm had her obeying, the pain becoming more bearable.

"She also almost had my wife killed, but that's neither here nor there" Lucas huffs out. At least now Maeve knows why he looks as though he wanted to crack a few more of her ribs. She feels bad about it. She invades these strangers's lives and is now putting them all at risk. She never meant to. Her eyes search for Zenaida. She's not in the room and neither is Thais. All of the guys are, and Amora and Emry. There's some disappointment there. Whether it was for themselves or the group was a question that swarmed Maeve's head, but in a way she knew the answer had to be both.

Lucas was told to leave the room if he wanted to continue with his snarky comments. He took up on the offer, mumbling something under his breath before he left with a slam of the door. The closing shook the room with the wood about to fall off its hinges and leaving Maeve to startle at the loud sound.

"Don't worry about him. He's just upset that Zenaida took a bit of a fall earlier. But she's fine, and so is everyone else" Rowan chimes as he takes a seat at the edge of the bed near her feet. A gentle touch goes to her covered ankle—and while she did get the comfort that he wanted to provide, it wasn't the same. It isn't as sweet as Micah's, or as electrifying as Amir's. She really didn't want anyone to touch her if it wasn't one of them. Which is a thought that's astounding to her, because she just met these men. She shouldn't be comfortable with them so quickly. Especially Amir. Someone she kept glancing back to just to see his reaction.

"What about those people? What happened after?"

She needs to know. None of them have a scratch to show the fight. Or at least anything visible, who knows if they bandaged themselves entirely under the clothes they wear. Almost wants to make Maeve ask if they were hurting; if she could do anything for them to ease the pain. It'll give her the opportunity to finally show her appreciation for a group of people willing to take her in.

"They were a part of the Junud" Foster steps in bluntly.

"Which means the Raba are searching for you" Amora pushes all of the men out of the way, both her and Emry being the main attention with their worry and determination. "And now that they know who is protecting you, it won't be long before they show up here. I wouldn't be surprised if they tried to take Micah as well."

"You guys keep saying *the Junud*. Who even are they?" Maeve asks as she rearranges her posture on the bed. Worryful irises tracked her every movement, looking for signs that she still may be hurting. Nothing obvious, just the little twitch of her lips because she accidentally put too much pressure on her side. Micah helped fluff the pillow supporting her back.

"They're like our law enforcement" Gabe pushed himself from off the wall, hands going into his sweatpant pockets as he had gotten just as close as everyone else. His piercing eyes were just as firm as everyone else's too. Maeve felt as though she was being psychoanalyzed by everyone in the room—when all she needs is answers to the new world that she was dropped into. "They are loyal to the Raba and the Raba only. Species from all over are ripped from their homes, and trained to be these killing machines. They are the ones we see on a day-to-day basis."

"So if an announcement to all of Kariq Leada needs to be made, the Junud are the ones making it" She shifted her attention to Rowan who smiled gently at her. He had to be the only one who wasn't watching her so intently. "A criminal is loose, the Junud are tasked to handle it. The Raba needs someone kidnapped or assassinated, the Junud are there" The mention of kidnapping is kind of a sore subject. Makes her think back to Reggie. She wonders how he's doing, if he took the money given to him and now spends it with no regrets? So is he a part of the Junud? She wants to ask, but there's no guarantee that any of them will even know who Reginald Marks is. Emry might. Or not, if she couldn't see that he was a spy in the human realm. Just another thing that she would have to ask about later.

"And it doesn't help that we're being watched extra hard by them lately. They probably know we're the ones trying to steal the Haya. I'm actually surprised that they're not kicking down our door right now, demanding to search the place" Gabe adds.

"Which is why we need to leave," Emry states. Maeve has never seen her so pressing. No, that's a lie. She gave the same expression when they were back in the alleyway, staring at men dressed in ugly polos.

"Wait! The Haya! Why didn't we think of that before!?" Amir exclaims. His hands are itching to grab onto someone and just shake them about as he lets out the excitement of his new idea. But he kept his hands to himself, instead clapping them together as he drew everyone's attention to him. "There's definitely gotta be some kind of answer in there!"

"I remember Zenaida saying something about it at the mall. Said it belongs to the Oracle," Maeve interjects. Her confusion is crystal clear in a room filled with people who were slowly coming to the same conclusion as Amir. "How is it going to help us?"

"While the Oracle can see all, the Haya is like a written version. It holds the answers to all questions...it can give you insight on your destined future. It's mystical" Rowan ends it by making this weird ghostly sound as he wiggles his fingers and eyebrows. Maeve snickers, but it becomes a giggle when Foster steps up and kicks the blonde with his foot. Probably for making a serious situation into something funny. Maeve appreciates Rowan's efforts.

"All of Kariq Leada is mystical, dumbass. You're literally a werewolf."

He crosses his big arms over his chest, blatantly ignoring the way Rowan jumps up from his spot on the bed and kicks Foster back. Or at least he tried to. Foster is already moving out of the way with a swiftness and nonchalant expression. It only irks Rowan even more and eventually the two become entangled in this strange game of tag—Rowan is always 'it' with a competitor who manages to move out of the way just in time. The game began to escalate with Rowan jumping over the bed in order to grab Foster. He launched through the air, a manic smile stretching at his lips as he set his emerald eyes on the other, who for a split second showed fear. A squeak slipped from Foster's lips when Rowan latched himself onto him, poking and pulling like a nuisance. Their loud tussling had been firmly stopped when they crashed into a nearby dresser, knocking over a bedside lamp that crashes and evidently breaks. Thais is going to be so mad when she finds out. For now, the two men are terrified of Amora who was staring at them with stern eyes and lips pressed into a tight line.

"I swear if you boys don't break it up right now, you're going in the make-up sock."

Make-up sock?

Her words had Foster and Rowan looking off into the distance (still clinging to each other) comically, reminiscing about the few other times that they were forced to shove their desired foot into a sock knitted by Amora Loom herself. It keeps the

pair connected at the ankle, bound together until their punish-
ment is over. Usually Amora has them stay in the sock for a day,
but if they can prove that there is no bad blood between the
two, she lets them go early. So rushing to disconnect from one
another, the two mumble apologies as they create a noticeable
distance between them. They looked like little boys within the
moment. Not these scary large men who can easily tear you limb
from limb. It reminds Maeve of Jax and Aziel. So childish and
so spiteful because they are family to one another. They find it
in their nature to poke at each other, but it's obvious there's no
malice in their actions or words. More so, done in order to seek
some kind of attention.

Maeve smiled at how sheepish they appeared now. It was
funny to see them cower at the glare Amora gave them.

"I don't think we have time to fool around. We need to focus"
Micah's voice was so much lower, austere. His face was cold and
there was no room for a laugh. He didn't like that the group
wasn't taking this problem as serious as they needed to be, and
it was beginning to get under his skin. It's understandable that
they aren't the ones who have a massive target on their back, but
it would be nice if they showed some compassion. He's known all
of these people for almost his entire life, and he was hoping that
they would be worried for his well being. Because now not only
is Maeve in grave danger, but he is too. And if any of them cared
even the tiniest, they would stop their stupid jokes and start
coming up with conclusions to their problem. "Who knows how
close the Junud are to pounding on our door, and here you two
are," His dark brown irises were sharp as he looked Foster and
Rowan into theirs. The disappointment lingered a while longer

on Foster; but that's probably because Micah stared at him just a little while longer. Maybe because he expected more from him—because there was this unspeakable tension that existed between them. Maeve seriously needs to know what is going on. "-playing around like this room is a fucking jungle-gym. As your pack leader, this behavior is unacceptable. You both shall be confronted at a later time. Do you understand me?"

Micah was scary in this state. He had the same energy as when they were still in the dungeon. The two men nodded their heads as they also gave a verbal response. And then it was left at that.

"So the Haya..."

"There's no way we can use that," Gabe interjects.

"And why not? If there's a solution, the Haya has to have the answer" Amir replies.

"Did you forget the week you spent in the Raba's prison? You were there to steal it. How do you expect us to ask the Haya if it's not even in our possession, or the Oracle's."

Amir tried his hardest not to look stupid by the revelation. Maeve tried her hardest not to look intrigued by the new information. So now she knows why Amir was locked away, she just needs the missing details. Why was he trying to steal the Haya anyway? What was he trying to find?

"Why not just ask the Oracle?"

Her question had everyone looking at her. She was baffled by the quizzical stares, because from her standpoint, it was a reasonable answer. The Haya was the Oracle's book, and if Maeve makes a bold enough assumption, everything that is written in it is everything the human rendition can say through their mouth.

"Because they live on the other side of Kariq Leada, stuffed away in the forest. It's hard to find them. It's expected that the only people to ever see the Oracle is the Raba" Amir says. "We don't even know where to start looking."

"Yes we do," Maeve began to leave the bed yet again. Micah protested, trying to push her to lay back down, but Maeve shoved him out of her way. She hissed as her sore body was desperately trying to stay upright. Her bare feet against the cold floor sent shivers up her spine, and the concerned looks made her want to hide away. And yet Maeve stood tall, a new found rush of assertiveness taking over her body. "You said they take sanction in the forest. Let's start searching there. Besides, if the Junud are urgent to capture Micah and I, then it's best that we get out of this house as fast as we can."

It was a bit anticlimactic to think that everyone would immediately agree and start trudging their way through the woods. The group stood around her with dull looks. Crickets could be heard like one would a joke that didn't land.

"And what are we supposed to look for once we get to the forest?" Gabe asks with a snarky smirk.

Emry let out a sound that brought the spotlight to her.

"I think I have something."

Lucas knocks against the wooden door. He flinches just slightly when the hard surface collides with the few cuts and scratches that align his knuckles—yet he stays expressionless, biting his tongue. He doesn't wait long, probably a second or two before Thais' voice is ringing out. There was some last minute shuffling; undefinable sounds that just made that awful gut feeling swirling about within Lucas. His wife was resting in his room, on his bed, which is perfectly fine if she didn't allow

Thais in there as well. The girl liked to touch stuff, liked to keep things neat and pretty. So it wouldn't be a shock if the teenager stepped into a rather messy boyish-room and began to pick socks off the floor. There were times where she stood in the doorframe and criticized the way he and Gabe lived; like how she can smell the week old bowl of noodles sitting on the nightstand.

Thais' feet pad closer to the door and then eventually she's opening it with a slow twist of the nob. She peaks her head through a crack that she created, doe-eyes scanning the lengthy body of who waits. One look at his face and she was swinging the door open, stepping to the side so he was allowed into his own bedroom. Lucas stands in the doorway, eyes kept focused on his resting wife therefore he doesn't have to notice the way Thais rearranged his closet.

"I'll give you two your privacy" Thais almost whispers with a tight smile. Then she's out the same way Lucas came in, quietly shutting the door behind her.

"How are you, snowflake?" As he says it he gets closer. He reaches the side of the bed Zenadia rested on, falling to his knees so they were eye-level. Then with fingers touching her cheek so delicately, he brushed strands of her platinum blonde hair from out of her face, tucking it behind her precious pointy ears.

Humming with a smile, Zenaida melts into the touch. She raises her own hand from out of the covers and holds onto the one connected to her cheek. Removing it, she brings her lips to his bruised knuckles.

"I'm fine, thank you" She notices the way that creases lined his forehead and a storm of rage is hidden behind his eyes. Lucas' shoulders were squared and he refuses to let his guard down even though it's just them two. Turning so she was flat on her back, she then scoots over in order to make as much room as she can. Lucas takes the hint and fills the space. They're both just lying there now, staring at the ceiling, fingers interlocking once they've found each other. Lucas is the one to lay a peck to her knuckles this time, keeping the skin to his lips for just a little while longer before he's resting their connection on his chest. She could feel his beating heart slow from a rapid pace, his breathing evening. "What has you stressed, darling? You know I hate to see you this way" She turns her head to look at him.

"That was serious back there. You could have really hurt yourself."

Zenadia huffs.

"I can handle myself. You really need to stop treating me like I'm going to break at any minute."

Lucas turns his head to look at her. She's staring at him with a frown and stern irises. He doesn't like the expression; he never likes when she's mad at him.

"I'm sorry. I just don't know what I'll do with myself if-"

"Nothing is going to happen to me...to either of us. You're being paranoid again" Fully shifting onto her side, she cuddles up close to her husband. He does the same, dropping her hand so he can engulf her within his arms. He wants to stay like this forever—trapped in each other's orbit, where the only issue is how neatly disorganized his room is now. Zenaida reaches out, cupping his face within her palm. Her fingers begin to trace his face and he lets her. She smooths down his eyebrows, skates her index down the bridge of his nose, and then drops it right onto his lips. Her thumb taps on the pink skin, picking at it.

He chuckles when the feeling becomes a bit too ticklish. Having been locked on his lips, she then darts her sight back into his shining brown eyes, smiling along with him. "I love you...for forever" She whispers.

Lucas's heart swells and he knows hers does too.

"I love you too, forever."

Then finally giving into the temptation, the couple seals their love with a kiss. Zenadia sighs into the way Lucas presses her closer; the way he takes the lead with a gentle force. He rolls her onto her back, laying her body into the mattress while his heavy figure lightly rests on top of her. Calloused hands slip underneath the covers, and pull them back so he is able to see the majority of his wife. She looks as beautiful as the day they met. And she looked absolutely ravishing by how she broke their kiss in order to stare up at him with siren eyes. Lucas holds back a groan, resulting in grabbing the meaty flesh that are her thighs. He dives back in for a kiss to which she giggles at.

"Maybe we should stop while we're ahead?" She laughs at how he peppers her neck with kisses, licks, and a few bites that might purple over. For a response to her though, he hums, nowhere close to stopping his love for her. "We have targets over our heads right now. Who knows if the Junud plans to attack" Lucas lets go of her neck with a pop. He looks down at her smirking. "Plus everyone is awake in the other room."

He places pecks to her left cheek, the right, on her nose, and on her forehead before hovering his lips over hers.

"Let them listen," He whispers. Before he could seal it with one last kiss, Zenaida is pushing his face away with a giggle.

"Go take a cold shower."

Chapter Ten

"Another book?" Rowan asks with hesitancy. Him and the rest of the group surrounded Emry, a witch that unpacked an old box that was stashed away in Amora's attic. It contained many unusual items that were begging to be touched. But with already witnessing Emry smack a pen-shaped antique from out of Rowan's hold, Maeve kept her hands to her sides and willed away the need to rub her palms all over the glass ball that sat within a black holder. It was molded to look like dragon claws, and for a moment Emry and Amora were filling the witch stereotype. All they needed was large pointy hats and a black cat strutting past their feet.

Emry moved fast as she slammed the old book on the dining room table. The cover was made out of leather (most of it peeling from years of multiple use), while the pages were a dusty and dirty brown color. The edges were shriveled and ripping, while the ink of the words were no longer a vibrant black; instead a faded gray that may take squinted eyes in order to see what had been hand-written. It was clearly an ancient text, and while Emry was eager to start flipping through the pages, she also handled every piece of it with delicacy. It was another item that

Maeve wanted to get her hands on. As she watched the pages fly by, Emry intent on finding a certain page, Maeve was furrowing her eyebrows from confusion. While her brown eyes skimmed the words, she either thinks that she hit her head a lot harder than she thought, or it was written in a different language.

"It's not just any book. But one of the most powerful spell-books in all of Kariq Leada. If something is going to be able to find the Oracle, it's this thing" Amora chirps. She was obviously excited. It's been a while since she was able to rummage through old belongings; and so seeing, feeling something that she used to read through everyday brings back a time where she was young enough to test out a hundred different spells.

"And how did you out of all of the witches manage to get a hold of it? Shouldn't Ma'am Letita have that?" Amir asks for everyone.

"Oh she does," Amora lets a mischievous grin stretch at her thin lips. "...have the original of course" She let out a giggle when watching the group stare at her with bafflement but also some impressiveness. They never really took sweet little Amora Loom as a rebel. And Maeve doesn't think she could mistake Emry Young, someone so strict and firm, to have a bit of a rascal hidden within her. "We were young and troublesome. Plus we were in this facility forcing us to behave, or else we should fear what the people of Kariq Leada would do to us. It's only right that we occasionally pulled a prank and rebelled."

"Why did you have to fear everyone?"

Maeve Ross-Whitmore, the one asking all of the hard-hitting questions.

The room fell silent and she watched as not only Amora

became solemn, but Emry (who was still rifling through pages) too. It was as if they were reliving something that was far too traumatizing. But it seems that everyone knows about what made the mood shift, and she is the only one still pondering what was held in the past. But what did she expect? She entered this new realm only a few days ago, and she was still figuring out the place—herself. The rest of them have lived here their entire lives and know all about the history. Like Zenaida said, they learn about this stuff in school.

"Three decades ago there was a Witch Massacre," Emry starts. She had stopped flipping through the spellbook, blue irises glimmering as she looked down at her wrinkly hands. They used to be so small and smooth. For a moment she's transported back to the time that this all took place. She was nothing but a small girl; scared because for some reason her powers were going berserk and she couldn't control them. "It was the night of the red moon. Us witches have always had a weakness to the natural occurrence, but nothing as bad as that night. It was almost as if all of us witches had gone feral."

"None of us could stop what was happening," Amora then continues. She remembers being a little girl at the time too. She recalls a memory; her small and frail body hiding underneath a shelf as she murmured to herself all of the breathing techniques her mother has shown her. And she did it with her eyes squeezed shut, hands covering her ears therefore she was able to drown out the sound and sight of her parents destroying their home with their crazy magic. "And then it was only a matter of time before the witches took their power, their anger, this blood-thirsty rage to the streets where they attacked anyone and anything they set their sights on. At times they even attacked each other."

"That's when the royal family declared war. They set out their best troops within the Junud to fend off all witches."

"It resulted in over four-hundred deaths by the time the moon had passed. Us witches have been trying to rebuild what was once a strong and trusted community ever since...but people have casted us out, still tying us to the killer narrative."

Their slumped shoulders, their frowns, the glaze that covered their eyes as they stared off, cringing at the horrible events. Maeve felt terrible for asking. If there was even a hint that the question would lead to such a depressing state, she would have never asked. For now she will just raise a hand to Emry's arm, caressing it with as much comfort as she can. They looked at one another then, a sympathetic smile meeting one of despair. It was all that was needed in order for Emry to give into her tiny need of reassurance and swoop in to wrap her arms around Maeve for a hug. It was nice. The pair doesn't think they've had such a tender moment in so long. The embrace felt long overdue, and if either of the two felt tears begin to prick their eyes, they didn't voice it. Instead as they broke apart, they wiped at their faces.

"I'm so sorry," Maeve whispers.

"Ah, what can you do?" Emry sniffles with a chuckle. "It's been years, plus we're finally reaching a place where we can all live in harmony again."

"But your families...everything that you guys once were-" Micah interjects. It was painful for him to witness Amora express how hurt and broken she truly is. He's always been so caught up in his pack, that he never truly sits down with the one woman who raised him, and asks her if she's doing okay. He would have ran up and crushed her with a hug so tight, but was stuck behind Foster and Lucas. For now all he can really do is stare from afar and hope that his gaze was enough to cherish. Looks like she got his message by how she smiled back.

"I like to think that the witches were fighting against something, *for* something that night. All lives lost weren't in vain. So cheer up my children," Amora claps with a grin that may have fooled a stranger, but was wobbly to the people who have known her for years. "Besides, we have much bigger problems to work through. And first things first, we must find where the-"

Cutting Amora's words short was the aggressive pounding done to the front door. Squeals of unexpected fright squirmed their way out of everyone's mouth, their bodies having also startled in place. Heads whipped in the direction of the front door, before eyes were darting back and forth between each other. It was the Junud. They've found them. And now they don't know whether they should take the oblivious approach, or try fighting their way through again. It was when more pounding and the strong voice of a woman was heard for a second time that a decision had to be made, and quickly.

"To the basement! Now!" Amora shouts, urging everyone to start heading in the other direction of the house. The pounding got louder and so did Maeve's heartbeat. She could hear it in her ears; could feel it in her toes. Everyone scrambled around her, and she was desperately trying to figure out what to do and where to go in the sea of frightened bodies. Thankfully Amir grabbed hold of her wrist, tugging her along. She looked at him as he kept forward. He was focused, steps calculated as he trailed behind Thais. Now her heart was in her throat. A swelling of adoration couldn't be stopped as her thoughts swarmed with gratitude. Of course any human will instinctively think about themself, to save themself, but Amir made sure to guide her. While for a split moment she believed it to be because she was the one person that they were trying to protect, those thoughts were overtaken by the idea that Amir kept her close because he wanted to. It felt like she was his priority—as if keeping her and his sister safe were the only two life purposes he had.

Maeve willed the fluttering in her stomach away when the danger they were running from came crashing through the front door. Maeve froze in her spot at the attack, eyes going wide when she was met with the face of that woman again. She looked worse with the scarring of their previous brawl. Micah must have really done a number on her. There was a huge gash from her left earlobe to the corner of her lip; bruising could be seen peeking from the collar of her black shirt; and as she stood in the doorway, she could be seen leaning most of her body weight onto her right foot. She was angry.

It's not often that the general of the Junud lets someone slip through her fingers, so now she was growing frustrated. She brought more men with her. Only two could be seen standing behind her, but there's no doubt that more filled the front yard. They probably even surrounded the house, ready to attack from all angles. Maeve has experienced fear many times in her life. She knew how her palms grew sweaty, how her body lightly trembled, and her breathing increased while her chest felt as though it was constricting. Right now wasn't any different as she stared at the woman in the eye, watching a thunderstorm brew within the green as she silently made a promise that this was the last time they would fight. General Harris will do what she has to in order to return Maeve to the Raba. And if that means chopping off the hand Amir still had attached to Maeve's wrist, then so be it. She was making due to the mental plan when appearing in her hand was a blade shiny enough to see your reflection through.

Maeve's breath hitched. It gave her that push to keep following the others. She held her aching side as she was now pushed in front of Amir by the man himself. He mumbled something that Maeve couldn't particularly hear over huge men shouting their war cry as they burst through the front door. All she knew was that it couldn't have been good, Amir's blank expression being the give away.

He better not try to fend all of them off by himself.

Thais had been the one to guide her now. She led her down wooden steps that creaked with their weight. It was dark in the basement, so Maeve looked around blindly. She reached out to touch anything to prove that she was grounded, but she kept feeling nothing but space. At one point she must have wacked Gabe, who groaned, but as she was apologizing her vision had came back. Or she should be saying that Emry conjured a ball of fire, granting everyone their sense of sight some relief. The flame danced in the palm of her hand, astounding Maeve temporarily—because woah, magic is genuinely real, and here she is witnessing it with her own two eyes. It was another thing she wanted to touch. Another thing she wanted to ask so many questions about.

Would it burn her if she touched it? Or no, because she's also a witch?

Does it feel hot holding it like that?

How did she do it?

Her intrusion of a hundred more questions was interrupted when a loud thump came from up above. Almost as if something heavy was slammed against the floor. Maeve and everyone else looked back at the basement stairs, to the basement door, hoping that it wasn't Amir who took such a hard fall.

"We need to move quickly," Amora says as she turns her attention to a brick wall.

"We can't just leave my brother!" Thais then exclaims as she begins to back up towards the stairs. Maeve reaches out to stop her from moving any further. She barely knows the teenager, but she would feel her heart crack if anything were to happen to her. She doesn't think the group would forgive her if anything were to happen. She doesn't think she would forgive herself. And it looks as though Zenadia feels the same because she's also stepping forward. Or well she limped. She must haven't fully healed.

"You're far from ready to fight Thais. You see how easily that woman beat you in the mall. It just being you two up there, there's no guarantee that you'll be making it out alive."

Another thump, a howl.

"But we can't just leave him. He's all I have left!" Her pleads were complemented by eyes filling up with tears. He really was the only person she had left of their family. Their parents died in a car accident when she was only nine, and not once during the years were they able to find distant family. Ending up in the care of Amora Loom was the best thing to ever happen for the siblings. And while she grew to think of everyone she lives with as her new family, Amir was her blood. Never will she leave him behind. "We have to help him. I have to help him."

Maeve felt her heart hurt for the younger girl. She was almost the one to volunteer to help in the fight. But one: with no chance against the supernatural, she will be captured almost immediately. And two: Foster was already raising his hand.

"I'll go-" His bicep was gripped by Micah. They stared at one another, concern mixing with bravery. Sadness mixed with love.

Love.

Oh my gosh.

"Don't worry about me. Just get to safety" Foster removed Micah's hand from his arm to put it to his cheek, nuzzling his face against it. Such an odd sight to see coming from the one man who made it his mission to appear tough and cold.

"You'll come find us after?" Micah whispers.

His question sounded hesitant as another aggressive crash had sounded. Amir could be heard crying out from pain, and within that moment Maeve almost knew exactly how her brother felt. A part of her felt uncomfortable that Amir was upstairs becoming a punching bag for who knows how many men.

"Of course" He laid a delicate kiss to the palm of Micah's hand, the warmth of the peck being so strong that Maeve swears she felt it on her own skin.

"If it makes you feel better, I promise to bring him back in all of his muscled glory" Rowan chirps as he finds his way over to the couple and lays a pat on Foster's shoulder.

"Wait, you're going too?" Lucas asks.

"Well I can't just let my best buds fight off the bad guys all on their own. What kind of friend would I be then?" Blondie holds a goofy grin as he speaks. Doesn't seem like he's taking any of this seriously. A coping mechanism that Maeve grew out of by the time she was seventeen. But she can see right through his bouncing leg and the way his eyes never stay on one person. He was secretly waiting for someone to beg him to stay. When no answer came, with one last claim that they will all return safe and sound, Foster and Rowan disappeared up the stairs.

Just as the group heard more growls and fighting upstairs that's when Amora was cheering from her accomplishment.

"Everyone! Through here!"

Maeve was yet again amazed by the magical abilities of this place. In front of the two witches was a giant rectangular hole that definitely wasn't there before. It was a secret tunnel, dark and cold, and leading to a destination that only Amora and Emry would be able to say. Thankfully this time, this secret tunnel was also a secret to the rest of the group and some reluctant expressions began to splash against people's faces. If it wasn't for Amora igniting her own ball of fire and then taking the first steps through the sudden hole, then no one would have moved. But then Lucas was quick to urge his wife to seek safety, so he helped her hobble her way behind their guide. Gabe saw no one else moving, so he shrugged and took the opportunity to go through next.

"I can't leave him" Thais mumbles once more. She looked down at her hands, picking at her nails. Maeve moved her hand from the girl's forearm and raised it higher to her shoulder. Her thumb caressed the other gently.

"But what if you do stay? You fight and you take a fall that's far worse than what you received in the mall? Do you really think Amir would be able to live with himself knowing that you might not survive?"

Thais looks her in the eye. They just stared at one another, a silent answer being said as she let one and then two salty tears fall. Thais brought her lower lip between her teeth, finally breaking their locked gazes in order to take one last look at the basement stairs. It didn't need strained hearing in order to hear the fight that was taking place. She could hear the way that her brother grunted, the way he howled, how not only he but his enemy were taking blows. She inhales sharply before making her way through the tunnel. Maeve didn't know if it would work. She had no influence on any of them, none of them had to listen to her. And yet she managed to break through the conflicting interior that was Thais. It felt like an accomplishment. Not only was she warming up to the group, but they were warming up to her as well. And it was confirmed when placing a hand to her back was Micah. He smiled at her, a nod in appreciation given before he was giving her the push to move as well.

"I think it's best that the claimed prize gets a move on. This would all be a waste of time if one of them comes down here and takes you" Micah snickered and Maeve giggled along. He had a valid point. So after taking a look at Emry who awaited for the last of the people by the tunnel door, Maeve slightly ducked her head before entering. It was just like she thought...dark and cold. She looked back to see Micah entering only a few steps behind her. Or that was until his collar was being yanked and he went tumbling to the ground. Maeve felt her nerves spike once more, fear that the enemy had finally made their way down the stairs. She trailed her sight from her brother hissing from the pain coursing through his spine, up to the reason of said pain. It was the woman again. Her fiery hair that had once been pulled back into a tight ponytail was beginning to fall from its band, and her clothes were torn in different places, all of it being evidence that she yet again joined the fight.

"This is taking a bit longer than I like, so please be a good girl and just come with me."

The woman: General Harris, looked crazy as she slowly made her way into the tunnel. Her blade from before was still in hand, but now it was covered in crimson blood that could have come from anyone. She prayed that it didn't belong to Amir.

Maeve didn't know what to do. She needed help from someone. *How weak.* She needed someone to fight for her again. *So powerless compared to everyone.* There was no way that she would be able to fight off a woman who might be an assassin. *It would be better for everyone if she just turned herself in.* Micah and Emry made no attempt to join them in the tunnel and help her. The damage General Harris must have done to them was stunning. Maeve looked behind her, maybe the others were still close enough. She could barely see, who knows how close or far the group had already gotten. She felt alone.

"Get away from me" Maeve's voice trembles as she takes a few steps back. She kept her arms outstretched because just the tiniest bit of her believed that her supposed witch powers would finally kick in and save her life. "For the last time, I am going nowhere with you."

"That's not an option I'm afraid. The Raba demands your presence."

The general got closer. Maeve was scared. Her fingers tingle but her entire body tingles. Her breathing began to increase at a pace that she doesn't think she's ever experienced before. *No,* yes she has. When she was in the dungeon, making eye contact with Amir. A hand went to clutch at her chest where she swore that her heart was about to pound out of her chest. Another headache was arising; the stress of everything was putting an ache to her temple again. She thought that if she closed her eyes for a moment, if she just tried to calm down, all of the pain, this frenzy of a feeling would disappear. But General Harris was still making her way over. She still looked crazed as she mumbled about the Raba. Maeve could hear the woman getting extremely close. She could feel her. So snapping her eyes open, an unusual growl ripped through her throat as she now stared at the woman with eyes glowing purple.

General Harris halted in shock.

"I said to get away from me" Maeve clenched and unclenched her fists as she continued to back away. She had no idea what was happening, but the feeling of it all was beginning to feel overwhelming. The pounding in her head was the only sound she was able to hear. The way her body practically vibrated was the only thing she could feel. There was this ball of *something* deep inside of her just waiting to burst out. It's as if being restrained for so long, begging to be released, but there's no way to be freed. "Get away from me!" She shouts. Her voice didn't sound the same. It was contorted into something deeper. Something more animalistic.

"Maeve!" She could distinctly hear Emry. Her voice was hoarse as if trying to get through pain. It only made that ball of something grow stronger. Maeve collapsed to the ground, curling in on herself. A shriek of terror rips through her throat because every single one of her senses are heightened. This was something that she never wants to endure ever again.

"I'm getting you to the Raba one way or another."

The simple brushing of her fingers against skin had Maeve stilling. Her face went blank, body going rigid. And when General Harris attempted to grip her shoulder, the hand was suddenly flopping to the floor with a soft thud. A gasp of shock mixed with the spraying sound of blood coming out of the chopped arm. General Harris' eyes widened as she was now the one to step back with fear. Her blade clanks to the floor as she immediately reaches for her gushing wound. And she even began to curl in on herself when Maeve slowly stood to her feet, this new sense of wrath and hunger corrupting her. She was the hunter now, and her first meal was going to be a pale ginger. All it took was for General Harris to accidentally trip over a rock for Maeve to make her leap and begin to attack. With fingernails that have never been longer than a centimeter unless she got those acrylic nails from a nearby nail salon, they naturally stretched into these pointy claws that ripped open the shirt of the enemy. And then they began to dig into the skin of the woman, leaving open wounds that just added to the pouring blood. She was thirsty for more. She wanted to see General Harris pleading mercy as her flesh was torn from her bones. If she hadn't already been told that she was part werewolf, she would have assumed she was a vampire from how much of that rosy red liquid she wanted to see.

"Maeve stop!" There went Emry's voice again. It's not like she listened though. Instead she grabbed for the general's leg and broke it into a weird curve. The ginger woman screamed out.

"You're out of control! You need to stop!" General Harris tried to kick Maeve but her ankle was immediately being caught and then she was tossed back into the basement. Her body crashed into the wall, cracking under the intense hit. She watched the lady go unconscious, body limp on the hard ground and already laying in her own pool of blood. "Maeve!" Glowing purple eyes trailed over to Emry who was peaking her way into the tunnel. The way Emry stared at her with this ounce of terror could have been the reason why she finally came to; or it could have been the adrenaline rush washing out of her system. Either or, Maeve began to think clearly. She looked at what she had done, looked down at the way her hands were covered in red. She couldn't believe it. Any of it.

The frantic voices of the group came rushing back. They must have heard the danger and came to fight. If only they knew that it was handled—then they wouldn't have come to a full stop upon seeing a trembling Maeve with blood staining almost all parts of her. Warm tears pricked behind her eyes as she felt everyone else's fall on her. She doesn't know what she hates more. Their fear or their disappointment. And as Micah locked his eyes with hers, she knew that she never wanted him to see her like this ever again.

She felt like a killer.

General Harris could still be alive, but the hurt that comes with the idea that she isn't erupts this regret within Maeve.

"Maeve, there's no need to be scared. You're spiraling" Amora tried to get close to her, but the other flinched back.

"No, don't touch me. I'll hurt you too."

"You won't. I know you won't. You just need to take a deep

breath and let me help you" Once again she reached out but Maeve moved away. She was actually growing a bit frustrated that Amora wasn't listening. If this was her finally awakening her abilities, then she has no idea how to control it. Anything could make her go insane again.

"I said don't touch me!" A wave of power whooshed out of her and made everyone stumble on their feet. That scared Maeve even more. Unintentionally she was already hurting people, so who knows what else she's capable of? She had to get away from them. And she had to get away fast. But she was trapped. And it only got worse when stumbling down the stairs was the three men originally fighting off all of the bad guys. Her gaze fell onto Amir. He seemed surprised by the scene, creeping closer. Maeve's heart squeezes. Yeah, she never wants Amir to see her like this ever again as well. But she also wanted to run into his arms and demand he give her some sort of comfort. She feels out of her own body. She feels gross.

"Woah, what happened?"

Leave it to Rowan to not take the hint. Foster whacked him upside his head.

"It's Maeve, she finally tapped into her inner wolf-"

"And her magic."

"So why aren't we trying to console her? She's probably freaking out right now!" Amir had been the one to speak up, his forehead creasing as an intense amount of concern began to wash over him. His sight was hyper-focused on Maeve and the way she stared back at him with watery eyes that don't know whether they want to stay their whimsical brown, or the most entrancing purple. His feet didn't wait, and he was already maneuvering around everyone in his way. His mind was set on reaching Maeve, wrapping his arms around her and saying anything needed in order to ease the formidable sensations that were seeping through her skin and making it known that she didn't feel comfortable. But before he was able to step foot into the tunnel, a hand was pressed to his chest and he was being stopped. His gaze fell to the shorter woman, Emry. Her wordless stare was enough to say that he shouldn't enter, but still said her warning anyway.

"She can't control her powers. It's not safe for you to just walk in there."

He bit his tongue to hold back a devastated whimper.

"Out of everyone here, I might be the only one who can help her. You have to let me go" His gaze went back to Maeve. She looked to have been in agony. He knew she was. She let out grumbled sobs as they held gazes. He wishes he could go back to the time in the dungeon—make the executive decision not to interact with her, resist the pull that was immediately felt when she was thrown behind bars. Because then they would have never met, and he wouldn't have to feel so powerless with the attack of her suffering. Ah, but then she would have been sacrificed. She would have been gone from his life forever, and leave behind a hole in his heart that no other person would be able to fill. He doesn't know what's worse. He also doesn't like that he's come to a part in his life where he has to think like this. He doesn't want to.

He removes Emry's hand.

"You have to let me try."

If there was any doubt that Amir would fail, Emry would

have halted him once more. But it was almost as if she could see the gravitational aura that surrounded the two. She can see how strong it is. It was something that she doesn't think she's even seen between her own parents. So without another breath wasted, she allowed him to enter. Glances of good luck were given on both sides, from everyone. This was a power that none of them have ever seen before and it was making their bones chill. It was an honest thought that if Amir were to fail, then they would have to orchestrate a plan in order to sedate the witchy werewolf.

Amir was slow with his steps. He kept his eyes on Maeve and Maeve only. His hands were raised to show that he posed no threat, and he made sure that his voice was at a steady and casual octave so as to not scare Maeve more than she had already done to herself. It was only when he was reaching a distance that began to violate his safety that her anxiety rose. Her fingers began to tingle once more and out of fear accidentally shot out a blast of magic to the walls around them. It shook the tunnel, rocks falling. It scared everyone due to the fact that the tunnels they hid in were quite old. It wouldn't take much before the whole thing collapses.

"Hey, you don't need to be afraid. I already told you that I would never hurt you" It was said after everyone and everything was stable once again.

"That's not what I'm afraid of. It's me. I'm trying not to *hurt you*" Her hands trembled and she looked down at them. They were the same ole' hands she's always had. No differences. Just that they were glowing purple and induced a new threat. "I don't know what I'm doing. I'm trying to stop, but I can't."

She noticed that he had gotten significantly closer. Close enough where all he really needed to do was reach out and he could potentially grab her. She tries not to make it a big deal, because thinking about it too hard would cause her to become unmanageable again. And the last thing this tunnel needs is anymore damage before they're all crushed under hundreds of pounds of rock.

"You could never hurt me."

"Don't say that," Clenching her fists against her chest the ground began to shake once more. This time it didn't seem like it was going to be stopping. "Please don't say that! I can't control whatever is happening and look at what I did!" She stopped staring at Amir to look past him...at General Harris. She didn't look like she was moving. The slow rise and fall of her chest from before was no longer noticeable. If she didn't already look like a dead body, she most definitely looked like one now. It made Maeve want to vomit. She could feel the nausea coil in her gut already, and if she wasn't trying so hard already to stop spewing random bursts of magic, she probably would have heaved up whatever bile bubbled. "I killed someone! I attacked her! And a sick part of me enjoyed it. So no, don't come any closer!"

Amir reached out just as a giant part of the tunnel fell to the ground behind him. Everyone became startled by the damage, so the need to get to safety was being shouted on both ends.

"We need to get out of here now. Any longer and we might end up trapped!" Lucas was the first to take initiative, ushering Zenaida to the end that they had came from.

"Everyone get out of there!" Micah directs. "Amir, if you plan on doing something, I suggest doing it now!"

"Go, go...Emry get the rest out from your end! Meet us in the forest, near the pond!" Amora pushes a resistant Thais the same way Lucas and Zenaida went. She protests about leaving her brother again, but eventually she stumbles along only able to whine about wanting to stay. Micah was the same way. He refused to leave the uncertainty that is his sister—throwing a tantrum when Foster basically threw him over his shoulder and forced him back up the basement stairs. Soon enough it was just Amir and Maeve...stuck in the crumbling tunnel. And while Maeve was foreseeing the worst, Amir remained collected.

He puts a hand out again, smiling at her. She watches as his eyes glow yellow. Her anxiety was still there, but not as robust as before. There was now a hidden sense of relief, warmth, relaxation.

"Nothing bad is going to happen to me. You wouldn't allow it."

"How do you know that!?" The outburst had the tunnel on the brink of collapsing, it had Amir flinching. It's when she catches it that it makes her situation worse. "See, no matter how hard you try not to be, you're scared of me."

"I'm not scared of you Maeve, but I am concerned. Any longer in here and you'll be crushed. Let me help you" He reached out and touched her forearm. It was a touch that Maeve jumped back on, and caused enough ruin to the tunnel that the exit back to the house was completely blocked off. There's no more light, just a mix of yellow and purple that keep connected.

"I'm so scared Amir" Her sobs echo and the heartbreak is akin to misery.

"I know you are. So let me be your strength" He delicately touched her again, his smile stretching when she didn't move away. He got closer, moving so they were toe to toe. His voice dropped into a whisper as he cautiously dragged his hands over her shaking arms. "Be scared. Be scared every second of every day...just know that I will be here to fend off your fears for as long as it takes."

Then he's wrapping her in a hug where her body falls limp. He's there to keep her from crashing to the ground—keeping her pressed to his firm body where he allows her to cry. And while she feels that lump of power diminish for every second that Amir holds her, the damage that she's done to the tunnel is far too bad and it continues to crumble around them. So while her body racks with grief, he lifts her into his arms and begins to run.

Chapter Eleven

The pond was gorgeous. It was at the edge of the forest; the crossing between the wilderness and the city. It was shielded from citizens by tall green bushes, uncut healthy grass, and willow trees almost being curtains to keep some mystery. It sparkled underneath the descending sun, and small critters were beginning to leave their water source in order to head home. Rimming the sides were large rocks and weeds. Lucas rested Zenadia on top of one, checking her still healing wounds. Thais in a numb distress fell to her knees in the grass, hands gripping the greenery in hopes of some relief. She needs to reel in that all of what she's experienced so far is really happening. It puts her life on its head, because she may have seen her fair share of wolf fights, but nothing as extreme as people dying. Her brother has always tried to blind her to the real world, and it was working so great. Until Maeve appeared. She wants to so badly hate the woman for ruining their lives, but she can't. It's aggravating—fuels her enough to rip up handfuls of grass and stare at the way mud began to seep underneath her fingernails. Amora watched with sorrowful eyes. She knew a day like this would come, it was practically inevitable. While her and Emry have succeeded in their task of keeping the twins safe for a good portion of their life, there was always that poking voice within her, whispering that they'd still have to fight. And with that end result resting on her shoulders, she should have never agreed to become an undisclosed foster mother. She just believed it to be a good way for Micah to form his pack—having been born an alpha, it's known that he will grow to find people he deems loyal enough to be considered his werewolf pack. So she took in strays...all of them instantly being the perfect fit.

It was only her and Micah for a while. Then came Amir and Thais.

Zenaida was next.

Then Gabe with Rowan following.

Lucas was after.

And Foster was last.

She regrets allowing them in her home. Regrets letting them become this unhinged family. Because now she has to watch them fall apart. They didn't sign up to be a part of dangerous scenarios. She wants to apologize. This was ultimately her fault and if anyone is to be blamed, she wishes that they scream and shout at her before doing so to Maeve. Especially Lucas, who was already so angry at the woman for unintentionally harming his wife. He's going to yell curses at Maeve next time he sees her for sure, and Amora is already prepared to take the blow of whatever harmful words he has to say.

"They should have never freed her-"

"Getting upset is not going to help anything, Lucas. And you can't blame Maeve for this. She had no idea that any of this was going to happen" Zenadia tries to speak some sense into her tense husband, and yet he continues to pace the field with a twisted face.

"The longer we keep her around, the more opportunities you have of getting hurt. Have you forgotten about your sprained ankle already?"

The couple looked down at her bandaged foot. It only really hurt when she applied too much pressure. She doesn't see it as that big of a deal. Especially when she's done worse to herself when experimenting with magic.

"Yeah, I did. Because look at me—*I'm fine*. The herbs Amora gave me are working splendidly, and it barely hurts" Zenaida removed herself from the rock. She reached up to hold her lover's face in her hands. They stare at one another with gentle looks. "What happened to me is because I wanted to fight, not because Maeve told me to. If you have anyone to be mad at, you should be mad at me. I willingly put myself in harm's way."

"I don't want to be mad at you."

"Then don't be mad at all," She dragged her thumb over his bottom lip, grinning at how soft they felt. "Just be grateful you and I are still alive and in each other's arms, okay?"

He nodded and sealed it with a kiss.

Or that was until a dramatic gagging sound was heard, along with footsteps rifling through the grass. Turning their heads, the group was relieved to see that it was the rest of their allies and not more of the Junud.

"Gosh, even in the midst of avid danger, you two still find a way to be disgustingly in love. Impressive and gross" Gabe exclaims with more fake retching. Rowan agreed, laughing along as he too held his stomach as though he caught food poisoning.

The wedded couple rolled their eyes, yet couldn't contain their amusement. Thais on the other hand was far from happy right now and was immediately jumping from her spot on the ground to throw herself at Gabe.

"Is my brother with you guys? He's somewhere behind you, catching up?" She went as far as pushing past the others in order to try and get a glimpse into the distance. Nothing was seen or heard as she desperately tried to sniff out her brother's scent. She was coming up blank, and that made her panic far worse than before. If Amir wasn't anywhere close then maybe he was crushed in the tunnel? Maybe Maeve killed him with her powers? What if they did escape and the more of the Junud had caught them? Her breathing increased as she frantically looked around. Micah understood her sorrow, but he couldn't give her the answers that she wanted. He could only wrap his arms over her shoulders and hope that the comfort he is emitting eases some of her worries.

"I'm sorry" He whispers to her. She clings onto him, gripping his shirt as tight as she could. She so desperately wanted his hug to help, but it was only doing so much. The only way she would relax is if her brother strutted through the bushes with his arms wide and the loud announcement that he was far from dead.

"Me too" She whispers back. They share an astute look before breaking apart. *Even if* Micah wanted to say that he knows, that he can feel that his sister is alive and well. He can't explain why he can tell, but he can and that's more than enough for his confidence.

Emry draws everyone's attention by raising her voice.

"Is everyone alright!?" Murmurs of confirmation were given

along with head nods. "Firstly, I want to apologize for putting all of you in this, if I had just done my job a bit better, Maeve wouldn't have even ended up here. Everyone's lives would have been normal and good,"

"But then I would have never met her," Micah pipes up.

"You also wouldn't be in grave danger."

"And she would have spent her entire life wishing that she knew at least someone from her biological family" Micah continues. His eyebrows furrow. "Don't you think that's a bit fucked up?"

"Woah, Micah" Foster intervenes. Micah just pushes the bigger man out of the way, unbothered by how heated he was suddenly becoming.

"If we could have kept you two together, we would have done so. Don't think for a moment that you know what your best interest could have been...because you don't" Amora takes a stand as she moves up beside Emry. She was giving Micah a stare that he liked to call one of those stern motherly ones. He used to instantly fall to those eyes, but it only made the fury in him grow a bit brighter now.

"Oh cut the *for your safety* bullshit-"

"Micah! Chill" Foster's tone hardens. The other whips around and snarls. Foster was quick to bow his head in obedience. While Micah respects all members of his pack, he also is their leader. He shall not be told how to respond.

"Dude, why are you getting so worked up? I'm sure your sister and Amir are fine. They'll be here and we can continue-" Rowan tried and failed as well. Micah growled, eyes glowing purple. Amora and Emry glanced at each other, confused by the suddenly irrational behavior. He was exhibiting the same characteristics as Maeve.

"Micah darling, I think you need to take this time to rest" Amora tries a gentler approach. "Everything's been happening so fast, and you're trying to be a good leader...but you're only wearing yourself out."

"I'm fine" He mumbles. "I'm sorry for shouting. What's the plan?"

"I agree with Ms. Loom, I think you should take a moment. We all could" Lucas adds, which only makes Micah become a bit more irritated. He shall not be told how to act.

"I said I'm fine. What's the plan? Come on, pull out the spellbook."

"Maybe you should-" Thais squeaks.

"I'M FINE!" Micah roars. His eyes flash a dark violet. It must have been the final straw, because Gabe is then tackling the other to the ground. They tussle around for a bit, biting and punching, kicking and scratching as they fight.

"You need to relax! You've just gone from completely normal to berserk within two seconds!" Gabe yells while he has Micah in some twisted hold. It leaves the other man vulnerable and unable to fight back. Or at least he no longer chooses to. He feels utterly drained. The last few days have been a bit too much for him to take and now he's taking those feelings and forcing them into a ball of anger. He's ready to lash out on anyone. Thankfully this final fight with one of his friends was his realization. He should get some rest; he should take a moment to think, go for a walk, blow off steam against someone who deserves it, not the people he loves.

Tapping at the ground, Gabe slowly releases Micah. The leader stays silent as he gets back up to his feet. His head is bowed and with how his features droop, dark circles could be seen underlying his usually bright brown eyes. From all of the current stress he might as well have aged three years.

"I'm sorry. You guys are right, maybe I do need to take a break. So I'll uh...I'll go find us some twigs, for a fire" He lets out a deep breath, bringing a hand to his nape to rub at it awkwardly. "We can set up camp here for the night and figure out what to do tomorrow morning" It's as he's leaving that he apologizes once more. They all watch him go. Everyone but Foster because he doesn't miss a beat when it comes to following after the other.

Amir exits the tunnel with a now fast asleep Maeve in his arms. He doesn't know when she had drifted, but he's glad that she's at peace. His shoes crunch against concrete and rocks. Blinking up at the sky and his surroundings it wasn't hard to tell that he wound up on the more unfortunate side of Kariq Leada. All of the buildings were worn and falling apart. Spray cans littered the ground because the people who lived here couldn't resist the urge to tag whatever they could. Trash exploded out of a nearby dumpster, and it was grotesque to witness a rat as large as his foot jumping out of it with a half-eaten burger encased in its mouth. Amir looked back, the tunnel exit had disappeared. Before him was a plain brick wall (one that he refuses to lean back against, because there was some unknown substance dripping down it, and he knows that he'll shed a few tears if it touches him in the slightest). So heaving a breath, he looks at Maeve and remembers that he must continue on with their journey; because while he was oddly amused by the sight of a homeless man who picked at his bare feet on the dirty ground, Maeve needed safety. He looked back and forth in what he assumes is an alleyway, debating which side he wants to go down. Neither one tells him which way is the fastest to sanctuary.

Didn't Amora say to head to a pond? How did the tunnel lead her there, but not him?

It was at times like these that he wishes he hadn't forgotten his phone. He can picture the small device now. It rested on the floor in the living room, plugged up because it needed to be charged. Risking the low battery would have been better than being stranded—the homeless man staring at him now, to which he had to give a crooked smile to show that he meant no harm.

"Did you kill her?"

"What?"

"The girl," The homeless man points a shaky finger at Maeve. A smirk twitched at his dirty chapped lips. "Did you kill her? Because I know someone who can get rid of the body for ya'."

Amir let his eyes widen as he looked from the man to a sleeping Maeve. He could see why the man thought she was dead. She was nothing but a limp body in his arms, figure almost completely covered in the nauseating blood of General Harris. Amir was quick to shake his head and tighten his grip. *Yeah, they needed to get out of here.*

"No! No, she's alive. She just fell asleep...you don't know anything about a pond, do you?"

The homeless man had gotten ready to respond when the loud opening of a door was done. It was a metal door, attached to the tall building in front of Amir. He should have known that he stood on the side of a nightclub—the music that was once faded background noise became much more apparent. It was a techno-DJ mix, the beat having just dropped as the door collided with the bricks of the building. It was a loud enough slam to stir Maeve from her sleep. And Amir would have welcomed her back to consciousness, if he wasn't becoming vigilant towards the person who made such an entrance. It was a man. He sipped on the remaining alcohol left in a green beer bottle before throwing it so it shattered next to the many others that littered the ground. The way his shoulders slumped and an almost permanent frown kept to his handsome face, he posed no liable threat. Fortunately Amir knew better when it comes to people like this stranger's kind. They could easily manipulate you into thinking that they won't cause any harm, and then before you know it, they're sinking their teeth into you.

The stranger locked eyes with Amir and smirked. He inhaled sharply, sighing from such a delicious smell.

"Ah, werewolf blood. So rich and inviting...you're lucky I got my fill for the day" The stranger mocks with a throaty chuckle. Amir snarls as a warning. The stranger puts his hands up in defense. "Woah, take a joke there buddy. Tasted your species once before, not the best flavor. Too...*dirty*."

"Who knew vampires had a preference? Kind of thought you guys just bit anyone. Kind of like mosquitos" Amir didn't have to comment back. He could have just picked a side of the alleyway and began walking (leave the thousands of years old feud of vampires versus werewolves to the textbooks), but it's always been quite hard for him to hold back against such grimey creatures. They live up to their uptight, snarky and prestigious image. It's exhausting to live in the same realm as them.

"And who knew that dogs like you, are now using people as new chew toys. A pretty one you got there from what I can tell" The stranger inhaled once again, stopping abruptly when the scent had been oddly familiar. His attention went to the girl. She still lay in Amir's arms, face buried in his chest as she tried to return to dream land. All of the noise and voices around her are a bit disturbing. Eventually she became too uncomfortable to stay asleep for any longer and squirmed in Amir's hold. Her eyes fluttered open and once she noticed that she was no longer in the tunnel, she was craning her neck in order to look around. She felt her stomach drop when locking eyes with the stranger. "Maeve?"

"Reggie?"

Micah broke off a thick yet still thin enough branch from a nearby tree. He found satisfaction in the snapping sound. He plucked a few leaves from off the stick before tossing it into the growing pile beside his feet. He looked at the pile as he heaved out a sigh. He scratched at the back of his neck, trying to itch away the guilt he feels for lashing out on his friends. While he's at it, he can maybe scratch away all of the stress that he's been enduring lately. After hearing the truth, and seeing with his own two eyes that he has a long lost sister, his mind has been scrambled. He doesn't think he can believe anything anymore, afraid that it'll be another master lie. He doesn't think he could hate Amora for keeping his true family history hidden. She's had far too much of an impact on his life in order to do so.

Will he hold a grudge, make her work a bit more for his full trust again? *Yeah*, kicking at the pile of sticks, *he thinks he will*.

What she kept from him is life altering news. Not only him,

but Maeve as well. They're a part of something far bigger than he could even imagine. He had no time to mentally or physically prepare for the battles that he would have to go through. And now his whole pack is involved. Innocents that he's vowed to protect and lead with his entire being could be terminated at any moment, and he has no idea how he's going to be able to fight back.

How he'll cope.

It's why he refuses to let his guard down for even a second. He's typically strict. Grown and raised to be the perfect alpha for everyone. But with their new danger arising, he's become just downright beastly. He wants to make sure that he has all of his bases covered—that no one can touch him or anyone that he cares so deeply for.

Micah lets one more sigh slip past his lips as he reaches for another branch. He's already gotten more than enough. Now he's just using this time as an opportunity to really think. It's been a while since he was able to do so (alone at that). He's going to take his time and let the connection to nature really ease away all of the emotion that's been building in his chest. And not only will he be allowed to think about good ways to guide this brewing war in a direction that doesn't end up lethal, but he can also take a moment to think about a few personal things. Tall, muscular, dark handsome features, with a personality that switches between hot and cold *personal things*. He'd love to know if they're ever going to establish what they are to one another. While he knows that right now probably isn't a good time to talk about relationships, it's been years of them knowing the truth. And if he's been present in each of their conversations, then he knows that not much *real* talking has been happening. Just a lot of affectionate actions and the attempt to keep them hidden. It's confusing because everyone already knows about them. They're out and in the open, and yet still keep the public displays to a minimum. It can be a bit worrying. Or a lot. He's heard rumors about being rejected by your mate. It's just as soul-crushing as breaking a bond. And Micah knows that he might as well have his heart ripped out than experience the heartbreak that comes with being rejected by Foster.

"You're a hard one to keep up with. I should know that already though" The one and only Foster Carrington chuckles as he approaches from behind a bush. He pushes the big leaves out of his way, the rustling and his unexpected voice making Micah immediately grab a stick and aim the pointiest side at him. Foster raises his arms, a charming smile reaching his face, while Micah deflates at the sight of his most recent thoughts. "Woah, lower your weapon alpha, I come in peace."

His snickering at the situation only made Micah frown a bit more. Foster was actually like Rowan, privately. He took everything lightly, cracked jokes and could be more on the unserious side. His hypermasculinity would never let him show face in front of the others though, too busy trying to be the dark and mysterious one—when in all reality, Lucas tends to be the aloof one of the group. He's quick to already have his judgements no matter the circumstances. Foster wants to be what Lucas is, but probably won't ever be. And that's fine with Micah because he prefers the light-hearted side of Foster than any other.

Micah drops the stick back in the pile as the other man gets closer.

"You didn't have to come after me, I'm fine...seriously."

He bent down to grab for what was just a big pile of torn branches. He kept dropping a few of them, therefore Foster also leant down to pick up what the other couldn't. Reaching for the same stick their hands brushed and they looked up at one another.

"But I wanted to," Hands still connected to the same stick, they stood up as one, before Foster let Micah take a hold of it alone. "It'd be wrong of me not to check on my mate, no?"

Hearing it made Micah cringe.

"So we're mates now?" He didn't mean to sound spiteful, it's just been years and this has got to be the first time that he's heard Foster actually say it. It was refreshing and revolting all at the same time. Because yet again, the context of what he said it in wasn't as solidifying as wanting, *needing* it to be.

Foster must have picked up on his tone, because his grin was dropping and his eyebrows furrowing.

"Yeah, I thought we'd already established that?"

"Established? Foster, we've never had a conversation about what the hell we are. Yeah, we occasionally do coupley stuff, but not once have you ever tried to talk to me about being in a relationship" Right now isn't the best time to be pouring his heart out, but who knows if they'll get tomorrow, so it's best that he tries. Especially when Foster is going pale in the face. Not the first time he's looked so ghostly whenever Micah takes an opportunity to ease this topic in their conversations. "Don't you want that? Because I do! I do so badly, and you're not helping my heart by making me believe that we can be more than just two people who just so happen to be tied for all of eternity" Silence filled the space between them. "Please say something."

"I'm sorry."

"You better not be apologizing for what I think" Micah pretends he doesn't hear his heart crack. He drops his pile of sticks to the ground as he gets close enough to place his hands on Foster's chest, slithering them up to his face where he was able to hold him. "Foster Carrington, I swear you better not be doing this to me."

"I just don't think I can be what you need right now."

Tears welled up in Micah's eyes.

"No, don't say that!"

"Micah," Taking the hands from off his face, Foster held them for a second and then let them fall to their sides. It was all that was needed for the dam of salty tears to start sliding down Micah's face. "I've already explained to you that I'm not ready to be open with my sexuality."

"But everyone already knows! No one is judging you for it" He tries to grab onto Foster's hands again, but they're pulled away. He latches onto the jacket Foster wore instead. "Please don't do this to me."

"Only the pack knows. I don't think I'm ready for all of Kariq Leada to. I'm sorry, but for now, I don't think we can be together in the way you want."

Foster removes Micah's hold on him once more before turning to leave back to the group. He's not able to make it far when Micah is shouting out from a heart that has been thrown to the ground. It's been shattered by the one person he so willingly handed it to. He's scrambling to pick up the pieces, but just like the sticks, pieces keep falling and he only has so much room in his arms to hold every last part. He's wishing that Foster will change his mind, he'll turn around and he'll clean up what he broke—he'll fix it. Instead Micah is kept to clean the mess himself, met with nothing but a broad back and the distant sound of another's heart crashing to the ground.

"I love you!"

This is the part where Foster is supposed to turn around and hurriedly kiss the living day-lights out of Micah, because he feels the exact same way. This whole argument is supposed to be some test. A terrible one, but a test nonetheless. There's supposed to be rain, and loud dramatic romantic music. They're supposed to soak another in and declare their love, resulting in a beautiful healthy relationship from this day forward.

Where's the kiss?

The rain?

Where's the I love you too?

"I'm sorry, but I cannot be with you."

The both of them fall to the ground with agonizing shouts. The feeling was excruciating. It felt as though their hearts were literally being split into two. They gasped for air. It's known soulmate knowledge that the rejected person was the only one who experienced the heartbreak. Why was Foster also suffering? He should be walking away with a smile and the weight of Micah Whitemore being lifted from his shoulders. Instead he also clawed at his chest, eager to get rid of the tightness. Their vision also began to blur due to being under too much pain. Until they weren't. The frenzy of ache was put to a halt and now the two men lay on the ground numb. It was an interesting feeling. *Nothing*. It was as if all intense emotions had been wiped clean, and now you're a shell of what you used to be.

You might as well be a dead man.

"You used me" Micah says after a beat of just them breathing heavily.

"You're accusing me of a heinous crime that I don't think even the devil himself would be able to commit" Foster got up from the ground, lending a hand for the other to grab. Micah stares before taking it. He missed the way rabid butterflies flapped their wings in his stomach from such a simple touch. Now there was nothing. He felt hollow. He stared at their combined hands willing the butterflies to come back. They *needed* to come back. Micah thinks he's about to cry again, but he doesn't know if it's because he's heartbroken or if it's because he can't feel anything for the man standing in front of him.

"You took everything that I could give you. Asked for everything and more because you knew I wouldn't hesitate...how selfish" Micah removed his hand in order to return to his previous task. The sticks and bringing them back to the group.

"I am doing what I need to do in order to be a better man for you. Never call me something so ridiculous again."

"You're not doing this for me, you're doing this for you."

"And is that such a bad thing!?" Foster was the one frustrated now. He's told Micah countless times what's happened to him in his past. His parents were nothing but terrible to him. From the moment he was born it was evident that his very own mother and father couldn't stand the sight of him. They could never really tell him why they detested him so much. They always claimed that he ruined their life—took away their freedom.

Freedom that they could have maintained if they learned the basic guidelines to safe sex, and didn't just go at it like rabbits. And then in a pivotal moment of his life, where Foster was already in the confusing stage about whether or not he found men sexually attractive, those disgusting parents of his were homophobic. He was scared to confess to them. He remembers being so young and stumbling over his words as he tried to get them out. When finally doing so, the slurs flew out of their mouths so fast Foster swears he heard them incorrectly. They continuously told him that he was revolting, and that not a single soul in Kariq Leada would accept him. What a confusing thing to say to a young boy. Especially as he grew to learn more about his sexuality, that there are indeed people like him out there. Foster believes that he'll always have some internal homophobia—that fear of being outcasted, alone.

He doesn't want that for Micah. He wants the world and more for him.

"I never said it was. I was just hoping that we could have done it together. I wanted to be the one to help you. I want to show you that nothing anyone has said to you before is true" Micah retaliates and Foster scoffs.

"Now who's selfish?" He tugs at the dark roots of his wavy locs for hair, the same time that Micah throws him a glare. Never would he say that his wish to help someone he loves was an act of selfishness. He's a bit hurt that Foster is taking his words and contorting them into something so cruel. Foster sighs, shoulders sagging as the weight of this argument was becoming too heavy. It was bound to happen—they've been walking on the tightrope of this conversation for a long time. But it's best they end it now, before they say things that end in resentment. "Look, I'm not saying I don't care for you. I do. You've got to be one of the best people I've ever met...Micah Whitemore you are the person I want to spend the rest of my life with,"

"So do so! The only person stopping us from being together is you!"

"Exactly" Foster rushed up to the other man and cupped his face with fingertips as light as a feather. "I don't want anything, not even myself, to risk our happiness. I can't give you all of me, and I really really want to" He leant forward in order to connect their foreheads, their eyelids fluttering close. They were able to feel each other, smell each other with heightened senses. Sad to see that it no longer affected each other. "All I ask is that we don't grow to hate each other after this. I still want you in my life."

"Would it be too cliche to say that I'll wait for you?"

They laughed. They opened their eyes, staring at each other. It's mental to think that the soul searching once made Micah grow weak in the knees. Now it felt as though he was staring at a stranger. How do they go back to the way they used to be? Micah desperately wants to go back. And for a moment his wishful thinking might have come true when Foster leans in and places a kiss so delicate on his forehead, that Micah believes he imagined it. He knows he's still stuck in an emotionless state when those same pillowy soft lips aren't the thing that changed, but the way it made him feel did.

"Only if I get to say it back."

Chapter Twelve

Maeve might as well have fallen out of Amir's arms. She flailed about in the man's hold; him trying to help her back to her feet safely while she rushed to be upright in order to see properly. It resulted in a stumble when she was back on her own two feet. Her tripping brought her face to chest with Reggie. The same man who was supposed to still be standing by the club door, and yet now she was breathing in his cologne. It was still the same mandarin orange, papaya, nutmeg and amber that came from some expensive bottle. She inhaled, the scent engulfing her in this warm blanket. For a moment she's flashing back to when they took turns sitting on each other's porch—how the breeze of each season gave her the opportunity to shift closer and then claim that she was just a bit cold. And he would allow her to. He would give his throaty chuckle, eyes crinkling just slightly from amusement and then offering to wrap his arm around her. His scent was lighter then, maybe one or two spritz before he deemed it enough. The exact amount to have her swooning, internally wishing that she could just smell him all day. Taking a whiff of the cologne now, it was as if he bathed in it. It was a bit overwhelming and beginning to clash with the repulsive trash can nearby.

Maeve swallowed down a lump in her throat as she slowly raised her head in order to look Reggie in the eye. They weren't that same stomach-churning red. She recognized them to be that comforting brown that always made her heart leap right out of her chest and into his hands. Everything about him was that nice guy from before. She could have fooled herself into believing that he wasn't the one who kidnapped her. It must have been his evil twin, a clone, because the Reggie Marks who stared down at her, lips pulling into a grin, would never break her heart.

"Maeve, stay away from him" Amir didn't like their close proximity. Detested it actually. Animosity boiled deep within his gut when witnessing Maeve succumb to the irresistible charms of the vampire race. She smiled back at Reggie, the feeling of her heart beginning to thump sporadically being what made Amir grab Maeve and pull her away from him. The abrupt distance had her a bit flabbergasted, but deep down she was thankful. She was sinking into the orbit that was Reggie all over again. And it's best that she doesn't do that to herself—one heartbreak was far too much, and if twice by the same guy, she might as well give up on relationships altogether. "His kind likes to prey on the innocent."

Oh how she knows.

"And your kind likes to pee in bushes, what's your point?"

Amir shouldn't have let his anger out so easily, but barring his sharp canines was his best way to get his already obvious disliking across. Reggie seemed undisturbed. Maeve was quick to step in the middle of the two, a hand being pressed to Amir's chest in order to push him back a few steps. She released a breath when a decent space was placed between them. And while Amir continued to watch Reggie, Reggie watched Maeve. She was alive—unscarred by the Raba. He believed that after being thrown out of the castle that that would be the last time he ever saw her beautiful face. But here she was, dropped into his unruly part of town and attached to a werewolf. He couldn't hold back a chuckle when seeing that yet again, her typical ravishing appearance had been ruined. She looked messy with her curls not knowing where they should be sticking up, her clothes stretched and wrinkled, almost all parts of her smeared in blood, and when seeming to finally find a pair of shoes, they were slippers.

She must have heard his snicker because she was soon looking at him with narrowed eyes and pierced lips.

Must still have hard feelings.

"What are you laughing at?"

"You" He chuckled again. Only this time as he did so, he stepped closer, hands going to his jean pockets as he let his shoulders slump. He was far too nonchalant about this whole ordeal. Made Maeve think that he might have some kind of personality disorder. The many faces that she's seen on Reggie is only forcing her to think that she never knew the real him. She couldn't read any of his intentions before, and she still can't. Amir puffed his chest as he too got closer. He wasn't taking any chances when it came to the vampire. Even if it appears that the two seem to already know one another, maliciousness is never not a thought for evil creatures. "Cute slippers."

Maeve looks down at her feet, wiggling her toes within the comfortable footwear. A heat brushed her cheeks at how embarrassing she must look. She didn't have time to change before the Junud attacked, so she was still stuck in loose sweatpants and some rock band t-shirt the witches helped her into when healing her unconscious body. But wardrobe was the least of her problems. So smoothing out her shirt the best she could, Maeve then tried to stand tall while wiping a few stray pieces of hair out of her face.

"Been kind of busy trying to fight off people trying to kidnap me—oh wait! Didn't you do it first?" Maeve gave an amused expression to Reggie's slightly guilty one.

"I did what I was being paid to do."

Maeve furrowed her eyebrows. He has no right to stand there and hang his head in shame. He's admitting to a crime. And for what? A couple of bucks that he's now caught blowing on booze at some sleazy nightclub? This newfound rage had her clenching her fists. The love that she once had for this man was being replaced with hatred.

"Does it look like I give a shit about the money?" Her anger was rising tremendously. That same nearby trash can blew up and the homeless man screamed in fright before getting up and taking off down the alleyway. Amir looks at the damage Maeve has done already. He starts to grow concerned that more will go wrong if she lets her emotions go haywire. He puts a hand to her shoulder.

"Maeve, let's just go."

She shrugs it off, fiery eyes focused on Reggie. His own liable ones stay on hers.

"You made me fall in love with you," Amir was quick to stare at her with wide eyes. A part of him crumbled.

"You were in love with him?"

A vampire. *Seriously?*

Amir doesn't know what he hates more, the fact that Maeve was in love with someone else, or that it just so happens that that someone is his species' mortal enemy. She didn't answer him. Instead she stalked up to Reggie and shoved him by his chest. He goes flying into the wall. She would say that she's both astounded and frightened by her sudden inhumane strength, but as her eyes glow purple, she's all too captured by the rage that was sprouting. Amir looked left and right. No one was around to witness his miniature freak-out about this woman ready to beat the living hell out of a previous spouse.

Did they date? Or was it just one of those unrequited kinds of love?

Amir looks from Reggie's groaning form that is slowly emerging from the wall, and onto Maeve's powerful figure that is stomping her way over to her target.

Yeah, he can't see them dating.

"You took everything that I've ever expressed to you, and used it against me!" Maeve grabbed Reggie by his shirt collar, pulling him close and then slamming him onto the ground. "And for what?" She watched him struggle to get up. She was a lot stronger than he remembers. But what did he expect? He knew that she had special abilities, the Raba told him so when given the assignment. They never specified what though, just that he should be careful. When he coughed out, using his elbows to lift himself, she used a slipper covered foot in order to push him back down. She stood on his chest. "And for what Reginald!?"

Ah, why must she say the full name? He cringes. "Some lousy bounty?"

Reggie let out a harsh breath when she pressed further on his body. She has reasons for being upset, he gets it. But he's also not going to let her step all over him...literally. So gripping her ankle, he then pulls, tripping her. She gasps from the unexpected move, twisting her body so she was able to catch herself before colliding with the concrete ground. A scoff sounds through her when catching a glimpse of a rising Reggie.

"Maeve!" Amir rushes to her aid. He's helping her to her feet but is instantly pushed away when stable. He's conflicted. He so desperately wants to help; ease her away from a situation that was making her, her wrath. But then again, he wants to see her handle herself. Handle her powers, confront someone who's made her feel so vulnerable. Amir's not given much of a choice on his weighing options because Maeve already made it up.

"You have to understand that it's more than that" Reggie heaves out. He blocked her attempt to throw a punch to his face, grabbing her hand and twisting it so it was behind her back in an awkward position. Maeve shouts from the pain and the ground shakes under their feet. Reggie notices and lessens his grip. Whether it was because of the sudden earthquake, or that Maeve looked genuinely hurt was only an answer that he'll keep in his head. But with his loose hold it gives her the opportunity to shake him off and whip around to try and hit him again. Like before her wrist is grabbed. She uses her other hand, he grabs that too. They're so close. She's breathing in his cologne again. *Why must he smell so good?* "They took something from me...and in order to get it back I had to find you and turn you in."

"You couldn't have done that without involving my feelings!?" She struggles to be released from his grasp. He sighs, letting her go with a force that knocks her into Amir.

"When a heartless monster, you come up with the most excruciating ways to get what you want."

"What?" She didn't sound mad anymore. Just confused.

Reggie raikes a hand through his hair, sighing once more before he's looking Maeve in her midnight purple eyes. They were slowly descending back to their entrancing brown.

"The Raba...they quite literally took my heart."

Maeve laughs. It spits from between her lips, sounding sarcastic and in disbelief. Because what was Maeve supposed to say to that? What was she supposed to think? To do? No normal being would be able to live without their heart. They'd drop dead in an instant, hole in their chest and the faint screech of their soul leaving. Her eyes sparkle as she stares at Reggie. His lips kept in a straight line, not even attempting to match her grin.

"They stole your heart? Seriously?" Maeve looks back at Amir. He would be able to say whether or not Reggie was telling the truth.

The answer was written across his face. With eyebrows furrowed and jaw clenched tight, it was evident that ripping someone's heart from their body was a normal occurrence in Kariq Leada. The smile Maeve wore faded as she was whipping her attention back onto Reggie. Now she was just baffled on how he was still standing on his own two feet—how he was staring at her with this gleam in his eye, lips moving to talk. The curious part of her wanted to touch his chest, let her palm lay flat against his skin and see if she could feel the missing lub dub, lub dub, lub dub.

"Oh my gosh, you're not joking. They really–Oh my–" Maeve couldn't contain her shock. It was like reliving the undeniable truth about different realms and mythical monsters all over again. It was another piece of information that she didn't think she could wrap her head around so easily. A blast of power shoots from her fingertips and a piece of the concrete ground blows up. The trio startles at the unexpectancy and it leads Maeve to blast the glowing neon sign attached to the club.

"I can see that this has been an interesting reunion, but we really need to go. The others are waiting for us" Amir lightly grabs hold of Maeve's arm, urging her in the opposite direction of Reggie. She looks at him, still a bit frazzled yet nods her head. That's when she glances back at the vampire. He looks understanding—hands going into the leather jacket he decided to wear that evening, head hung in shame as he debated whether he wanted to say what always lingered in his head. Was it wrong for her to want him to stop them? Her feet kept aligned with Amir's, she kept pace with Amir, and yet she was practically breaking her neck in order to keep Reggie in her sights. Their eyes stayed locked on one another's, unspoken words being transferred from the stare alone. Her chest clenched at his shameful look, fingers itching to raise the frown that tugged at his lips. Something must be wrong with her. Why must she still yearn for someone who was cruel?

He has his reasons.

That doesn't make it right.

Three years he had her wrapped not only around his finger, but his entire body.

How dare he treat her like such?

He's missing his heart.

Maeve inhales as she turns back around. Whether or not Reggie's morals, Reggie's feelings, the difference between whether or not Reggie genuinely feels an emotion or if it's just a nulled version of them, she shouldn't stay tied to him. It's best that she continue to walk away; stick beside Amir and pray that he too isn't secretly the villain. But the vampire just had to go and open his mouth. Maeve halts in place, air flow constricting and eyes squeezing shut. The hidden excitement she felt as she heard him jog over was bad. The leap of joy she internally did as she saw the man now standing in front of her and Amir was bad. Hearing what Reggie has to say isn't good for any of the trio. Just having him in the way was forcing a low growl to grumble within Amir's throat.

"Let me help you guys."

A few more minutes with her won't hurt.

"What makes you assume that we need help? Thanks but no thanks. Get out of our way" Amir says quite aggressively. But then again he's been tense ever since he laid eyes on the other. Their feud must run deep. Maeve is justled about as the were-wolf man tugs her around the body of Reggie, almost desperate to get her away from him.

"Oh come on, I'm assuming the Raba are out looking for our precious Mae-" *Gosh, she hates how he says her name.* "It's obvious you have no idea where you are, and didn't you say that you needed to get back to your friends? I promise I can lead you right out of this icky part of town."

"I think we can deal on our own. Get lost mosquito."

There was a beat of silence. Maeve and Amir continued on down the alleyway, reaching the end where they were finally able to see the street. Reggie stood behind them with a cocky grin stretching upon his handsome face. The sweat dripping down Amir's temple was enough evidence to prove that the big bad wolf was growing a bit frustrated because he didn't know what to do. Where to go. They could either go left, bypass a group of shady men who smoked cigarettes and drunk booze, or turn right where tussling could be heard from a random group of people forming a circle. Either or direction could lead to a confrontation—one that neither him or Maeve would be able to handle without leaving unscathed. It's also undetermined whether any of them were a bunch of thugs undercover for the Junud.

"I won't even make you apologize for being so rude. All you gotta do is ask" Reggie teased. He walked in front of the duo, proudly stepping out into the hazardous streets that were rumored to be called *Lima*. It was a part of Kariq Leada that the scumbags lived; the homeless, the ones who want to do illegal things without being faced with serious consequences. Amir's been here once. Years ago when Thais accidentally fell into the wrong crowd at school and wanted a taste of the rebellious life. He had to go and save her from being peer-pressured into doing underaged activities. How he managed to find his way out of this place back then, he couldn't say, because right now he was more frazzled than ever before.

Maeve nudges Amir with her arm. He looks at her already knowing what she's about to say.

"We can't trust him, Maeve."

"Is it because of my species? How discriminative of you."

"But it's better that we risk it with him than finding ourselves lost even more."

"I say we listen to the pretty lady."

"I'd rather have my heart ripped out before having to deal with someone like him."

"Ouch, low blow."

Maeve reaches out to lay a hand to Amir's bicep, stepping closer into his space and staring him in the eye. His muscles relax from her warm touch, his lungs release a puff of air because of her sparkling eyes. He's crumbling because of her. That's why he sighs with a roll of his eyes.

"Just until we find the others" She whispers, and he falls at her voice. Sucking at his teeth, Amir then straightens his posture. His muscles harden all over again as he turns to put a firm glare on Reggie—Maeve mentally gawks at the flex she feels beneath her fingertips.

"Fine. Can you please help lead us out of here? We need to get to the forest...quickly."

Reggie's smirk widens and his eyes flash red.

"Anything for my favorite mutt!" He throws an arm over Amir's shoulders, his strength forcing the other to bend under the weight. The werewolf was anything but pleased by the physical contact and pushed the other off of him. Reggie laughed as he stumbled a bit in front of the walking duo. Maeve let out a giggle. This was a Reggie she wasn't used to seeing—and it makes her wonder if this is his actual personality? Nothing like that cool, calm, collected guy who would die if he was caught being energetic for even a second. The two of them catch gazes as she follows him; a lanky figure that walks in front, yet backwards. His smile falters as he becomes trapped in his own head. He quickly turns around, ushering them to follow him down a new street that was barely lit from the many busted lamp posts. "Lucky enough for you guys, I know a shortcut. I should be able to get you there and be out of your hair in no time."

His neck cranes and for one of the last times, looking back at Maeve before putting it on the road ahead of them.

`Chapter Thirteen

Ringing Amir's phone for the third time, Rowan gives up. He listens to the dial tone, a curse slipping from his lips as he throws his hands in the air. He wobbles where he's sitting within a tall tree, fear glazing his emerald eyes before he's instantly reaching down to grip tightly at the branch used as his seat. The risky need for better cell-service wasn't necessary if it meant that he'd almost fall and possibly break his neck. So he shoves his cell-phone within his one hoodie pocket before looking for a safe way to get down. Climbing the bark was a lot easier than getting down, and he probably should have made a plan before clawing his way up a giant tree. A pitched squeal escaped past his lips when the branch that he put his foot on had broken under the slightest weight, and he almost went tumbling to the ground with it. Luckily he had fast enough reflexes to catch himself and attach himself to the tree; hugging it with all of his strength as he wearily stared down at the ground. Thais and Gabe had to hold back their laughter. Before Rowan impulsively decided to scurry up there, they protested. Said it was far too high and extremely unsafe...

That's a lie.

They encouraged it. They patted his back and spewed invigorating words once the ridiculous idea was brought up. It was actually Amora who told him not to climb the tree. She contradicted the way Thais and Gabe cheered for Rowan. Obviously her concern fell on deaf ears and it wasn't long before the blonde man was digging his claws into tough wood. Amora waved it off as the last of her worries and then returned her focus to Emry. The witch was flipping through the spellbook, attention focused solely on the hundreds of words written on the pages. She was so into it that she hadn't even known that Rowan was stuck in a tree until he began to shout for her friend.

"Ms. Loom! Ms. Loom, please help me!" Tears pricked at his eyes while a pout tugged at his lips.

"I told you not to go up there, didn't I!?" She shouts back with hands on her hips. She spares the young man a glance, but is yet again turning her back to him when he stutters over a response. Because she's right. He let the two menacing bastards boost his confidence, and now look at him. Clinging to a tree as though it was his bedroom pillow. He throws a glare at Thais and Gabe, mentally reminding himself to throw a few jabs their way once he is safe back on the ground. For now he can only flip them off and try not to let their laughter ruin his mood even further.

"Ms. Loom! I'm scared!"

The elderly lady heaves a breath.

"Lucas, will you please go over there and help Rowan down" Lucas rolls his eyes while his wife snickers. It's like living with a bunch of children sometimes. While it's typical to see such behavior within Thais, it'd be nice if Gabe and Rowan acted their age. But as he stalks his way over to the trio, he realizes that the three of them aren't actually that far in years. None of them were. Or well except him and Zenaida, they'll be reaching their thirties soon. Whereas everyone but Thais (a senior in high-school) and the two witches (senior citizens) were still in their early twenties. Still, they've reached an age where climbing trees for better cell-service is a bit ridiculous. It's why when Lucas finally reaches the terrifying tree that Rowan can't help but press his entire body to for security, letting out a disappointed breath was called for. Thais and Gabe suck their boisterous laugher back in, figures straightening while they try not to show how much fun they are getting out of this whole thing.

"Alright, come on" Lucas pries with a wave of his hands. He held them out as though he was ready to catch the blonde. Rowan looks down at his possible savior, and at first he's filled with glee. But then he sees the height difference again and only hugs the tree tighter. He shakes his head comically fast, and Gabe spits out another chuckle. If it weren't for Thais elbowing him in the side, he probably would have continued. He resorted to a snicker and pressed lips, thinking that his much taller frame would be able to successfully hide behind the teenage girl. "Rowan, just jump. I got you."

"No!"

"You're not even that high up. You'll be fine. Jump and I'll catch you."

"No!"

Thais is the one to giggle now. While it's cruel to be laughing at a dear friend, she just can't take it seriously. She has to turn around and hide her face in order to keep from falling to the ground laughing.

"Don't be a big baby! Just ju-"

"What's going on here?" Micah's voice appears from behind a bush. Foster moves all of the giant leaves and pines out of the way, Micah then ducking under his arm in order to approach ever so elegantly. A pile of twigs rested in his arms, only dropping them to the ground when Amora states that a certain spot near her is fine. She creates another ball of fire with the flick of her wrist, then shoots it towards the broken branches. Immediately a makeshift campfire is made, lighting up the area. It had gotten dark tremendously fast, the cold night air beginning to prick at their skin. In such a frenzy not many of them were able to dress appropriately—Zenaida was sitting down on the grass rubbing at her bare arms, internally grateful when the bright flames brought her the warmth she was craving for.

Micah turns around to see the tree dilemma, one that Foster was already so amused by. He stood beside the laughing duo, biting back his own growing grin.

"Rowan, why are you in a tree?"

"I wanted to see if Amir had his phone. You know, if he picks up then he's alive," The blonde screamed when his body rocked and he was re-affirming his grip. "But this place has no cell-reception and I climbed up here to get better bars—Micah, please help me down!"

"If you didn't want my help you could have just said so" Lucas sucks his teeth while crossing his arms over his broad chest.

"Alright, don't worry" Micah smiles up at the other, easing poor Rowan's nerves, but then he's looking at Foster. "Give me a hand will ya?" It was all that needed to be said before Foster was nodding with a smirk. Both men approached the tree, Micah holding his arms out and Foster going over to the side. With a simple head nod for the approving signal, dark and mysterious was landing a powerful punch to the tree. A hiss seeped through from the rough texture scratching the skin of his knuckles, but it's worth it when seeing the piece of nature shake. The vibration of the attack loosened Rowan's hold and not long after the blonde was tumbling from his spot. He fell from the tree with a scream, stopping abruptly when instead of landing on the hard ground he fell into the manly arms of Micah. "Ah, look at that. You're down."

"My savior!"

"Again, if you didn't want me to do it, you could have just said so!" With a huff Lucas walks back over to Zenaida and rests beside her. She coos at how hurt her lover looks, reaching out to bring him in for a comforting side hug and a kiss on the head.

Rowan is placed back on his own two feet, and once settled with feeling the ground underneath the sole of his shoes, he's then whipping his head in the direction of two of his barbaric friends. His eyes darkened and a wicked smile stretched across his pink lips. Immediately both Thais and Gabe stopped giggling and became more fearful. They watched as the blonde creeped closer and so they slowly backed away. And then the three of them were running in circles, almost as if playing a more ruthless game of tag. Micah and Foster watched it happen for a few seconds longer—the sight for a moment making them believe that they were back at home, being the rowdy family that they're used to, and *weren't* being chased by the very people who held authority over their heads—and then they joined the others, taking a seat in front of the warm fire.

"I think I may have found it!" Emry exclaims. She brings the book closer to Amora, pointing to the part that she just read. Words mixed with scribbled pictures were fading from extreme use and that's when Amora wished that she wore her glasses. Old age comes with bad eyesight.

"What? How to find the Oracle?" Lucas asks.

"No, to bake cookies," Foster teases.

"I will beat your ass."

"Pfft, you wish Mr. Accent. Everyone knows I'm the strongest here" Foster throws his arms behind his head, fluttering his eyes closed and relishing in his own compliment. But then he was opening them to take a peek at the annoyed older. "Did you see how I just punched that tree? Sick, wasn't it?"

"Oh, shut up" A smack was given and right there the two of them would have joined the running trio when it came to tussling with one another, if it wasn't for the sudden loud rustling happening within the nearby bushes. Heads whipped around and conversations halted. Rowan guided Thais and Gabe back towards the group, while Micah was easing his way to his feet, muscles tensing and jaw clenching. He focused his hearing in on who the possible intruder may be, but the steps were just a bit too light; the heavy breaths of a person panting was indescribable. For a moment he believed that they had been discovered. The Junud had found them—the Junud was ready to attack, kidnap and kill whoever they needed in order to fulfill the wishes of the Raba. So Micah let his sharp canines show, nails growing into long claws as he crept closer to the shaking bushes that had progressively gotten louder and more aggressive. Years ago he vowed, not only to his pack but to himself that no matter the danger he will always be the first to fight. He will do what he needs to in order to protect every single person he loves. So not bothering to look back and see if the others were also ready to pounce, Micah puffed his chest and flexed his muscles while awaiting the final few moments before the intruder was revealed. The branches cracked and slashed against each other, leaves shaking and crunching. The anticipation of who was on the other side was only making Micah more anxious, glowing purple eyes darting back and forth, desperately trying to seek out where exactly they might be popping out from.

He needed to know if there were more of them.

He couldn't get a read on anything.

But then the greenery in front of his very eyes began to spread, splitting down the middle and letting a leg poke through. That was all that was needed for Micah to strike, hand moving so fast to the normal eye that pulling the person the rest of the way was like a blur. A scream vibrated through the trees that disturbed the birds who rested in their nests. Micah let his claws sink into the flesh of the intruder, the pitched shout getting louder. Dribbles of blood left the wound and cascaded down the tan leg, too painting the hand gripping it and the fresh green grass beneath. He didn't have to look to know that a few of the others immediately ran over to also inspect—so it wasn't long before a few more bodies hovered, their piercing irises staring down at one person who decided to cover their face from fear.

"Please don't hurt me!"

The stranger's voice was frail, squeaky and evidently filled with sobs that matched with the clear droplets that could be seen dripping from off their cheeks. Micah was quick to let them go, nails going back to normal so now his palms rested over the injury that he had done to an innocent. His chest tightens from guilt and he's quick to take a step back. That's when everyone is able to see that the stranger wasn't a part of the Junud. They weren't an enemy at all. It was a child; a little girl. She was so tiny compared to the big men that towered over her. Their faces that had to be terrifying. They genuinely looked like what they are: monsters. If it wasn't for Zenaida hobbling over, pushing in between Lucas and Gabe then the group would have just continued to stare at the poor girl. Her entire body shook, legs curling in towards her chest so she resembled one of a ball. Her crying had gotten louder, mixing with the still sound of nature. It only made Micah feel worse. He wanted to apologize but it was getting caught in his throat.

"It's a girl," Rowan announces.

"Well don't just stand there and stare at her! Move! Make some space. You're probably scaring her even more" Zenaida is waving them away, pushing at some of their chests. They stumble over their own feet as they rush to create that space. While it's only a few steps, it definitely created a difference and now the beaming crescent moon was striking the child. It made her look pure, made her tan skin shine and the blood that painted her wound glimmer. When Zenaida bent down to delicately touch the innocent, it was a trigger. Instantaneously the little girl flinched away. She scrambled to her knees and tried to trudge as far away as she could. She didn't make it too far though, the cuts on her leg kept her from crawling so she ended up collapsing. She fell on her behind, teary blue eyes darting from face to face of person to person. She raised one hand, thinking that the small appendage might be able to do something against a pack of werewolves.

"Please don't hurt me! I'm sorry! I'm sorry!"

Zenaida gave a gentle smile, inching a bit closer.

"Oh darling, we're not going to hurt you" The little girl shifted her eyes over to Micah. Zenaida didn't have to turn in order to know. "Or at least not again."

That doesn't help the way Micah feels. His ears heat and his lips flap open and close, unable to form the proper apology. He doesn't want to say something simple and then the sympathy he feels comes across untrue. So for a moment he's just watching Zenaida try to speak to the little girl, while his brain is still scrambling to piece together what sounds the most appropriate. He wasn't used to saying sorry, and even when he did, it wasn't because he physically harmed someone to the point that they felt the need to steer clear. It was typically for something miniscule, like stealing the last slice of cake out of the fridge even after Rowan took claim of it. But what he's done will never be as small as stealing cake, and now he's more choked up than ever before.

The child hissed as she moved her leg. Blood gushed and the pain the wound caused was enough to ripple throughout her entire body. Her shaky hands reached for it, trying to stop the agony. But again, her small limbs could only do so much, and she can only keep her hands on the cuts for so long.

"Let us help you," Zenaida took a step closer. "There's not much we can do, but at least we can wrap it. To stop the bleeding" She held her hand out once more, fingers wiggling while she let her face quirk into a pretty smile. Zenaida made sure to be patient with the little girl; letting their eyes connect and an unspoken conversation be said through them. "Just take my hand, and we can help you."

There was a second, then two. The child looked at everyone who stared at her. Her eyes lingered on Micah who shied away from the cautious look. She looked back at Zenaida who outstretched her arm a little longer. Ten seconds and then eleven. She bit at her lower lip before reaching out to connect her hand with the woman's. A silent cheer vibrated throughout everyone's heads. The child was helped to her feet, her small body stumbling into Zenaida's, to which she was held tight with a slight rub to her back.

"Come on," It was a bit hard to guide a limping child when one is limping already. So with the help of Lucas and Thais, both were guided to the campfire where Amora and Emry awaited.

They looked to have already prepared a tea from nearby herbs found and the help of their powers. Witches had always been connected to the four elements—fire, water, earth and air —along with their emotions. The more confident and powerful they feel, the better their powers work. Wielding a ball of water above the blazing fire, they tossed in the freshly grown herbs. Their fingers wiggled mystically, Emry throwing her left arm out and flipping her palm upward where she then balled her hand into a fist. It was a sight to see a rock emerge from the ground, shaking the Earth momentarily and then float absentmindedly in the air. Her fingers crossed and poked, making weird motions, all of it being directions for the rock and the new shape it was forced to create. Minerals chipped and fell off, hitting the grassy ground with soft thumps. But soon all of the magic stilled and the finishing product was a lumpy version of a mug. The little girl was far too entranced by the magic, not being able to hold back her awe. Her eyes brightened alongside a smile when the curated tea plopped itself inside of the makeshift cup, then danced its way over to her eager hands. She stared down at the hot drink, silently wishing to see the show all over again.

"Go on, drink. It'll help your wound heal" Amora grinned. The child looked between the witches and Zenadia, only raising the rock mug to her lips when the woman nodded.

Slowly she raised it to her mouth, sipping lightly, the caution of it being something poisonous lingering in the back of her head. Even as a child, she knows the dangers of her world. This group of people could have had some psychic conversation where they decide to finish the job. Already have hurt her enough and wishing that she doesn't run off and tell someone in Kariq Leada, the idea of having her congest deadly tea would be the best way to keep her silent. And then all they have to do is hide the body in a forest that no one enters anyway. It was deemed inaccessible after the Junud (under command from the Raba) made an announcement that no civilian is allowed to enter the forest under any circumstances. There wasn't a reason why, but it's not like anyone bothered to ask. Everytime a new rule is added, it's best that everyone just nod in acceptance. Having always been just a little more curious within an already inquisitive species, Micah and his pack sniffed around for answers; eager to find the reason for such a sudden new law. The only reasonable answer is that it's where the Oracle lives...and no one is allowed to talk to the Oracle.

No one is allowed to read the Haya.

No one is allowed to be more powerful than the Raba.

"What are you doing out here? What's your name?" Thais speaks with a voice so soft it might as well have been a whisper. She moved beside the little girl, dropping to her knees. They held gazes, only a faint flinch coming from the child when Thais raised a hand in order to push a piece of snow white hair behind the little girl's ear. It was a good way to distract her from the way that Micah approached, a veiny right hand ripping at the bottom of his shirt, until a long strip dangled from his clutches.

"My name's Olivia. My family and I were camping, and then I had to use the bathroom. My mom-"

"Camping? But no one is allowed over here" Zenadia wonders as she begins to hover her hands over the child's bleeding leg. Micah walked over and slowly went down on one bended knee. Olivia saw the male werewolf and moved her leg away quickly —to which he also flinched and looked at the little girl with sorrow. He'll probably never earn the trust of this specific child ever again. She stared at him with so much terror he was ready to pass the ripped shirt to literally anyone else and go wallow in self pity on the other side of the fire. But Zenaida grabbed his forearm, stopping him from moving. "Hey, hey. He's not going to hurt you. He's just going to wrap your cut."

Olivia stared at Micah. Micah stared at Olivia.

And then he was clearing his throat.

"I'm sorry," That was harder and easier than he expected. He swallowed before continuing. "I didn't mean to jump on you like I did. I was just trying to protect my friends. I thought you were a bad guy. I really am sorry for hurting you. So please let me help heal you. I have this," He held up the cloth swaying from the slight breeze. Olivia looked at it briefly before her blue eyes were locking back in on the man holding it. " I'm going to wrap it around your leg, to stop the bleeding for a little while. Is that okay?"

She waited again, debating within that tiny head of hers. It was an agonizing wait that will either make Micah feel worse or boost his self-esteem right back up.

Olivia nodded.

Micah nodded. A smile couldn't keep from stretching at his full lips. And then with nibble fingers he was reaching out to securely wrap the ripped piece of shirt around the child's leg. She hissed, and that's when Zenaida started to whisper inaudible words. Her hands glowed a vibrant green, and seconds later Olivia's scrunched face was contorting into something far more soothing.

"This won't magically heal you, but it'll stop the pain for now" Her hands stop glowing and Zenadia is letting out a few heavy pants. Using magic did always drain her of energy. Lucas was quick to be right by her side, hand going to her back and silently making sure that she was doing alright. With a head nod and light pat to his chest, she confirmed that she wasn't going to pass out...or die.

"Where is your family now?" Micah asks as he wipes any dirt from his pant legs. "Where did you guys take camp?"

"I think it's best that you find your way back to them and then get back to town before it takes word that you're out here" Thais says next.

"Why are you guys out here?"

All of them sputter. They glance between each other, ignorance passing between their eyes and unsubtle mouth movements. A few shrugged and others tried to appear nonchalant. The last thing they want is for some random child to know what they plan to do to. Doesn't help suspicion when everyone begins to blurt random things.

"Treasure hunting."

"We got lost."

"Meditating."

"Picking fresh fruit."

Yet again they were all staring at one another, this time with expressions that are calling each other idiots. Olivia was blinking up at them with blank eyes. They either had her confused, fooled, or not buying whatever they were trying to sell. Olivia let out a giggle and all of the adults let out a heavy breath. Thankfully Micah had been the one to take the ignitive and reply to the child with a lie that actually makes sense. Or at least he tried to. With everyone giving different answers, he was scrambling to put together a sentence that has to do with at least one of those things. He smiled at the little girl.

"We were looking for something...kind of like treasure hunting, and our map led us to the forest. But while we were looking we might have gotten lost, so we decided to build a campfire for the night and go home in the morning."

"Yeah, and then we started to pick some fruit and try meditating-"

"Not needed Rowan" Micah grits out while elbowing the blonde with his elbow. The other groans at the rather aggressive attack, bending over as he slowly walks away. He finds a seat beside Amora who instantly brings him in for a side hug and begins to coddle him like he was an overgrown baby. Doesn't help that he feeds into the touch by letting his green eyes go big and round and have his bottom lip jut out dramatically. Rowan attempts to childishly stick his tongue out at his leader, but it goes unnoticed when Micah has his back to the other and his attention is solely on convincing Olivia that they weren't bad people. "But enough about us. We need to get you back to your parents. Who knows what lurks within these trees. Do you know where you guys set up camp?"

Olivia is sitting where she is, humming as she begins to think. She looks around the dark woods, blue eyes trying their hardest to decipher which way that she had been dragged from (courtesy of Micah and his sharp claws), and yet everything looked the same at night. All bushes and trees, tall blades of grass, and dirt paths blended into one. She feared that she wouldn't be able to give an answer. The panic showed on her face—eyebrows furrowing as her lips dropped into a frown.

"That way?" She pointed left; and yet her voice was against her. It squeaked while her shoulders slumped and her finger unwillingly deterred.

"Are you sure?" Olivia bit her lip, eyes darting back and forth all over again. She wasn't sure, and the question only made her all the more scared and confused. She shook her head, face going pale and eyes dimming from their once youthful glow. "How about we search in the morning? You can stay here with us, and then we'll search for them when the sun comes up. I promise we'll keep you safe."

Olivia appeared hesitant. She didn't know these people. And they haven't really given her a reason to trust them, besides the fact that they are willing to patch up the damage that they've done. And the group understood. It's not like they can trust this little girl either. She could secretly be a spy—manipulating the group by her vulnerability of being so young and the cuteness that came from her plump cheeks and tiny body. She could be a shapeshifter Junud for any of them know, ready to strike when the final guy closes their eyes for the night. The stare Micah and Olivia share is long, deep. But breaking the intense eye-contact was her as she smiled bright. Her eyes turned into crescents and she was shaking her head in agreement.

Micah won't say it out loud but something felt unbalanced within that moment. His stomach twisted and yet he was pulling his lips into a tight grin.

"I'll take first watch."

"No, I will," Foster interjects right after. He steps forward from the background, hands going to his hips. "Did you already forget your major meltdown? You need to sleep for a few hours—throughout the whole night. Maybe then you'll be able to think better. Be more prepared for tomorrow when we find the Ora–oomph" This time Foster was the one elbowed in the gut. He glared at the culprit, coming face to face with a cheeky Gabe. He motioned to the still sitting child only a couple of inches away. Olivia looked drowsy, eyes threatening to flutter shut and body swaying slightly. She let her head fall onto Zenaida's shoulder. "Like she's going to remember. She's practically asleep" Gabe doesn't lessen up, making Foster roll his eyes with a sigh. "-when we find our *treasure*...or whatever."

"It's my job to make sure that all of you stay safe though. I promise I'll wake one of you when I feel tired."

"No you won't," Amora snickers. She knows Micah like the

back of her hand. All of them do. Which is why they know that the leader will force himself to stay awake by any means possible. It was a few months ago when he almost broke his toe because he wished to stop his eyes from closing. Every time his arm would go limp, the heavy wooden staff he would tie to his hand would fall right onto his foot, occasionally striking his toes and causing him enough pain to jolt awake. If it wasn't for Lucas waking because a bug crawled up his nose, Micah could have done some serious damage to himself. "Come take a seat beside me and rest a little. No harm will come our way. Just because you're the pack leader, doesn't mean you also don't have to be taken care of."

"Just the first watch. An hour at most. I pinky promise" He holds his smallest finger out for all to see. No one moved to interlock though, all just staring at him with deadpan faces. Micah slumped. He wasn't typically one to throw in the towel so easily, but as Amora stood (letting a leaning Rowan fall over) and place her warm comforting arms around Micah's much larger frame, he felt fatigue wash over him. His mind and body was exhausted, and the green grass looked a lot more comfy than a hard dirt ground should.

"Sleep," The elderly lady looked at everyone. "All of you. You've been through a lot today. I may be old, but I'm pretty sure I can fend off a rabbit."

Not much was said after that, just the occasional murmurs as they tried to find a comfortable spot beside the warm fire. It wasn't long before Rowan threw his head back and began to snore, and Lucas held back his pout because he wasn't able to cuddle up beside his wife due to Zenaida wishing to keep Olivia in her current position.

Chapter Fourteen

"So..." Reggie turned on the heels of his black boots facing the couple who followed his heavy footsteps, arms going in the air before resting his hands on the back of his head, a smirk teasing at his pretty lips, and brown eyes twinkling with interest. Those same irises bounced back and forth between Maeve and Amir, the suggestiveness circling within them making Maeve's lower stomach swirl in unsettlement. She clasps her hands behind her back then, shuffling a bit to the right in order to create space between her and the werewolf she once walked beside. She tried to make it unnoticeable, appearing unphased by the cheeky gaze Reggie kept upon her. She failed to do so when he let out a snicker. She could feel the tips of her ears burn and she became thankful when Reggie finally tracked his vision over to Amir— one who was less than pleased that the annoying vampire was speaking anything other than directions. They've been walking for what feels like eternity but might only be an hour.

It was around the fifteenth time that Maeve had complained about her feet beginning to ache within the cute slippers, that Amir grew frustrated and traded their footwear. So now he dragged his much larger feet within shoes that he assumed to be his sister's, while Maeve comfortably clomped around in sneakers that clearly have seen better days. Not only, but it's been a while since he last ate anything and he could feel his stomach rumble; along with his eyes becoming heavy from the lack of energy.

Running from danger can be a bit draining.

If he was allowed to sleep beside the rat that chewed on a moldy piece of garbage, he thinks he'd take the opportunity. Because then at least he'd get a break from walking through Lima; a place that he feels as though he's been walking in circles. He swears he's walked past the same graffitied building three times now, each time a new colorful picture or word being added. If it wasn't for Reggie saying that they're almost there then Amir would have lost his mind. He would stomp his slipper covered foot down on the wet gross concrete and shout that he and Maeve will find their own way. And to top it all off, all of this irritation, agitation, and tiredness, made the vampire appear more than insufferable.

He believes the groan he let out was excused.

"Aw, don't be so grumpy...I just wanted to know how you guys met. Last I checked, Mae was being held captive."

"And who's fault is that?" Maeve clicks her tongue, arms now crossing over her chest while Reggie mouths an apology. "But we met in the dungeon. He helped me escape."

"Just like that? How so?"

"Why do you care?" Amir eventually speaks with narrowed eyes and with lips that were pressed into a thin line. "Shouldn't you be more focused on how you should be begging for Maeve's forgiveness."

Reggie rolled his eyes.

"Yeah, I'm the bad guy wah, wah, wah, moving on."

"I think we should focus on making it to the forest," Maeve's stomach grumbles. "Or finding a place to eat."

Amir nodded along, placing a hand to his own stomach where he could feel it growl at the mere mention of something tasty to ingest. The trio halts as they look around, trying to see if they were anywhere near an open late restaurant. Luckily enough with a sparking neon sign, and a flickering arrow, literally pointing them in the direction, a diner was seen. It was a small building; two large glass windows showing the classic aesthetic. A singular waitress could also be seen, wiping down a counter. Reggie nodded his head in the direction, the other two catching the hint and seconds later the three of them running across the street. They pushed through the single door, hearing a bell chime as they entered; it mingled with the faint sound of some 80's jazz music playing through a hanging speaker within the corner. To the left sitting in a booth was a group of four, two girls, two boys (presumably on a double-date) and they chatted animatedly, not bothering to spare the newcomers a glance. Or that was until Maeve listened to one of the girls laughing loudly, and her curiosity got the best of her so she looked over. She locked eyes with a blonde with brown eyes, a smirk pulling to her lips that were painted over with red lipstick. Maeve grew embarrassed from getting caught therefore she decided to give a crooked grin back and then scurried to stand beside Reggie who was already ordering. Amir took the time to use the bathroom.

"Get whatever you want, I'm buying" Reggie says as he pulls out a little brown pouch. He shakes it within his palm before pulling out a singular gold coin. "Catch," He flicked it into the

air from off his thumb, Maeve instantly reaching out to catch
Kariq Leada's version of 'cash'. Wonderfilled eyes observed it, and
nimble fingers touched every crevice and imprint. She would
have said that it resembled a token from the human world, one
that a child would use for an arcade game. But this was a bit
bigger, a bit heavier. It was shining under the barely lit fluorescent lights hanging above them, and it had an angel imprinted
on both sides of it. Maeve brought it closer to her eyes, narrowing in on the slightly distorted face of the man with wings. The
lightness and confusion she felt as she stared, was the same as
when she saw Micah for the first time. *When she saw that stained
glass window.* The angel could be just some form of symbolism
for this realm and yet here she is feeling as though this person
was real.

"It's the previous King...before the Raba took over and made
this place a real shit show" Reggie speaks. He breaks her out of
the trance the coin had on her, a new interest in the backstory
for the unknown angel. *Guess she was right.* "It was after he helped
stop this major massacre way back when-"
"The witches."

Reggies was shocked by her knowledge. *The werewolf must
have told her a few history facts after rescuing her.*

"Yeah" He took a seat on one of the cushioned stools placed in
front of the counter. She followed his lead. "Uh-" He cleared his
throat. "When I was still a fleshling, my mother used to tell me
stories about the royal family. Said that they were this picture
perfect family that lived in this beautiful castle up in the clouds.
The King, the Queen, and their four children."

"Please don't tell me it was that ominous castle you brought me to?"

"Unfortunately. But I was told it was better than what it looks now. It was something straight out of a fairytale," *Isn't all of this?* "The royal family would even host these giant parties that anyone and everyone was invited to. My mother had shown me pictures of her attending a few of them. She looked beautiful each time" There was a sadness behind his eyes; as if a distant memory was resurfacing and it was not only nice to revisit but rather painful. "It was a time where all of our species lived in harmony."

"And then?"

"The massacre. It was like our realm was crumbling right before everyone's eyes. And once the queen had been pronounced dead, it was as if all hope had been lost. She too was a witch."

A frown couldn't keep from Maeve's face. It appears that the people of Kariq Leada have been suffering for quite some time. And they're going to continue to, in silence, because they fear the people in power. It has her heart pumping faster, her shoulders squaring. If she's supposed to be this *chosen one,* (someone that's going to give the Raba what they want) then maybe she can turn that prophecy of theirs against them. If not, she'll surely try. She doesn't know much about this place, but it's beginning to grow on her, the people, the sights. They could definitely use a bit of hope again.

"If the people were upset, I can only imagine how the family felt."

"That's the real kicker," Reggie let out a laugh. "The King chose one of his children as the new ruler—his youngest, his daughter. I remember this part the most because my father used to say that she had to be the most beautiful girl he's ever laid eyes on. My mom would threaten to hit him with a sandal if he didn't change his mind and say it was her." The duo shared a giggle. "But it wasn't long after the daughter was crowned that she disappeared. It's rumored that she was whisked away into the same forest that you guys want me to lead you to, not being seen ever again. The King was willing to search every inch of Kariq Leada with the help of the Junud in order to find his daughter, and yet nothing."

"Even to this day?"

"Yup, there had been no sign of her body anywhere. It's what made more rumors start, my sister once telling me that she realm jumped because the pressure of being queen was something she didn't want. Being so young and hearing this, all I ever wanted to do was meet her. To see if she was this beauty that was supposed to be a gift, a new beginning for us all. But of course this was all before me and who knows if my family was even telling me the truth."

Maeve placed a hand on his bouncing thigh. It stilled under her touch and they were now looking each other in the eye. She gave a grin.

"Doesn't seem like you believe that."

Reggie shook his head, heaving out a breath.

"Of course not. Because not long after the daughter had been claimed to be missing, the King passed and the only people left to the throne were the final three children. All sons, and you won't believe who they are."

"The Raba."

Reggie nodded.

"Such a compelling story, huh?" It was then that Amir finally stepped from out of the bathroom, a much happier expression taking over his face. Looks like all he needed was a severe bathroom break—his form walking that much straighter and almost lighter. It didn't take a genius to know what he released behind closed doors. He plopped himself down in the seat beside Maeve, grabbing for the menu and scanning his eyes over it.

"You guys already ordered? Gosh, I'm starved."

"I always have been told that dogs like you have a never-ending hole for a stomach," Reggie replies with a smirk. Because just like that, the intimate conversation he and Maeve were having disappeared and they were back to business. It kind of left her disappointed. Never in the years of her knowing Reggie, has he talked to her with so much tenderness. It was nice. It was allowing her to see this new side of him that she didn't think he had. Amir glares at his comment. "Get whatever you want, I already said I'll pay."

"Really?" Amir's narrowed eyes and clenched jaw shifted into something more relaxed. Something more surprised and glad.

"Yeah, kind of hit the jackpot with my last job" His eyes moved to Maeve's and she let out a quiet gasp from his insinuation. She punched him in the arm, mumbling something along the lines of *douche*.

"What happened to you being the bad guy, let's move on?" She then chuckles with raised eyebrows.

Reggie shrugs.

"Eh, I'm beginning to think for every second that I'm here with you, I need that constant reminder" They were staring at each other again. The slightly different browns that were their eyes were being compared, they were being searched, conversed with words that only they could hear. Stupid Maeve was falling for his charms again. She was leaning in, feeling herself being drawn into that same man who stole her heart all that time ago. Her hand slithers a bit further up his leg. What was he doing to her?

What was she doing to him?

Making it so easy to be engulfed by anything and everything that is Maeve Whitmore. Stealing his breath away and intoxicating him with how amazing she smelled.

Amir clears his throat.

He was still sitting beside them. He was still listening to them, still watching and listening. And yet it was as if he wasn't. Maeve and Reggie practically jumped apart at his loud clearing —cheeks tinting red and hands going to their laps where they had to act as though they didn't want to keep touching each other. The sight angered Amir. His jaw clenched and he had to deter his sight back to the menu that he was crushing within his hands. How dare Reggie? He can't just ruin Maeve's life and then try to come back in and save it. He wasn't allowed to. The waitress came over, on her right palm holding a black tray there was a white bowl and a filled glass. She smiled as she placed it on the counter in front of the vampire, giving everyone the sight that he hadn't ordered much but a bunch of fruit and some water.

"Can I get you guys anything else?"

"Could you give us a minute more?" Amir asks with a tone much lower than anyone expects.

The waitress wipes her hands on her white apron before

shoving the tray under her arm where she nods and walks away. It's when she enters through the swinging doors to the back kitchen that Amir can't contain the burning he feels in his chest. Because he felt it all. Felt the way that Maeve and Reggie had that romantic pull towards one another. They were slowly rekindling a fire that never needed to be ignited. He could feel the undeniable attraction that they have for one another. It was demeaning.

So gripping the side of Maeve's stool, he wiped it around, spinning her so she no longer faced the insufferable vampire, but him instead. Maeve squealed at the turn, hands going out to grip Amir's biceps in order to steady herself. She also let her breath hitch upon noticing how close they've gotten. Never in her life would she have imagined that she would quite literally be stuck between two good-looking men; and the both of them were fighting for her. Or at least she thinks so. It's still a bit blurry with her and Amir, while with Reggie it'd be dangerous to ever explore her feelings for him again. Maybe it's best that she just rejects both of them? She should explain that a relationship is something that she's not looking for right now. Saving herself and hopefully everyone else from whatever the Raba is planning is currently holding the top spot; and then returning back to her adoptive family is number two. There are definitely a few things she rather accomplish before she dives deep into the complication that is romance and dating people related to mythical creatures.

But then again it's quite hard to ignore the way that her heart jumped for joy when she found herself staring into Amir's eyes this time. She watched as they shifted their pretty yellow again, making the butterflies fluttering throughout her stomach wish to fly out of her throat and physically show everyone the way she was feeling. The warmth Amir's arms continued to protrude and surround her with, she could melt in her seat. She didn't want to admit to the difference between the two men, but it's there. Maeve is ready to say one person, but is secretly wishing for the other.

"I don't like that you're forgetting that I'm right here."

That was sexy.

His gravelly voice vibrated throughout her body, making her hot and thighs squeeze tight.

"We were having a conversation" Maeve chokes out.

"You guys were practically eye-fucking each other" He leaned in closer, his breath fanning her lips. She's on the brink of kissing two men tonight. What a show for the people in the booth. And then Amir lowered his voice a bit more, practically whispering as he stared ardently into her eyes. "And I rather rip my eyes out than have to see that again" He leaned towards her ear, having her shiver as his lips touched her cartilage. He was caging Maeve in, her body morphing around his and trying extremely hard not to touch all over the hard muscle that was pressing against hers. Amir was looking at Reggie now—the other man staring back with eyes shifting red as he popped a grape into his mouth. "Or I'll just rip his eyes out instead."

"I'd love to see you try, mutt" The vampire stands from his chair, and at the same time someone bumps his shoulder. It was one of the boys from the booth. He looked to have been heading to the bathroom when the run-in happened. "Excuse you."

"Sorry man" The guy says, barely looking back. He keeps

heading in the direction of the bathroom, Reggie observing his figure as he walks. It was when a hand went up to push at the door, did a sleeve roll down and a wrist tattoo was shown. A sword with an X put over it. Reggie's eyes go wide before he's stepping closer to Maeve and Amir, face and tone going serious.

"We need to get out of here."

"What? We just got here, and Maeve hasn't gotten anything to eat" Amir stands as well; and *wow* the testosterone was wafting throughout the room, filling Maeve's nose and making her head a bit fuzzy and body warm. The vampire took a step, so did the werewolf. Maeve was about to be squeezed between two men's chests.

"The Junud, they've found us. We need to get out of here now" He motioned his head over towards the table where now three of the four spoke quietly. It even looked as though they were getting ready to leave. "Try not to look suspicious, but be efficient. Once out of the diner, take a left and then keep going down two more streets. It shouldn't be long before you start to see the entry trees to the forest."

"Why are you saying it like you're not coming?" Maeve asks as they slowly head towards the exit. Her eyebrows furrow and a sinking hits her gut.

"Well someone has to hold them off" Reggie winks.

Maeve lets a sad smile take over her concern. She's grateful for the help he's given them, and hopes that this isn't the moment where it's their last. She mentally scolds herself for thinking that way. There's no way this is the last time. Reggie could easily take on four Junud members—or at least she wants to think he can. She doesn't necessarily know what he's capable of, as the only person she's seen him take on was herself and the most fighting spirit she has is self-defense.

"Thank you...for everything."

"Eh, wouldn't want a beauty like you to be captured again, now would we?"

"Maeve, come on" Amir holds a hand out which she takes. He's guiding her out the door right as three Junud members are seen creeping in closer. The last she sees before she's being pulled down the street is Reggie turning around to throw a punch, landing the attack on the cheekbone of one of the girls.

Chapter Fifteen

It was when Amir came to a stop at the end of the street that Maeve assumed that they had made it a safe enough distance to finally stop running. The duo looked left and right, taking multiple glances behind them to see if anyone was chasing; to see if Reggie had gotten away and was now catching up. Only the streets were steady. There was rattling from midnight creatures bumping into litter, and the occasional drop of water striking a puddle due to a leaking drainpipe. They could hear an occasional car drive by from a street over, and if they strained their ears hard enough they could hear a couple fighting from the apartment complex they stood below. Maeve squeezed Amir's hand out of fright and nervousness

This was a lot.

She had gone from living a pretty boring and scheduled life, to something where if she takes a break she will either be kidnapped or killed. It fueled her veins with a thrill that she has never experienced before—or well besides the one time that the Ross family took a trip to a nearby amusement park and she was dared to go on one of the tallest and fastest rides the place had to offer. Her knees were weak and she knew she was going to vomit if she didn't find a place to sit. There might not be a need to throw up right now, but she can say that her knees were beginning to wobble. Her entire body was shaking; she was cold and tired. She was scared and worried.

That fear heightened when the clomping of shoes sounded from out of an alleyway. Their necks snapped in the direction of the sound, and as it got louder Amir grew cautious. He pushed Maeve behind him. Thankfully he did, because not long after, jumping to kill was a man dressed in all black with these stunning giant brown and gray wings flowing from out of his back. A roar ripped through his throat as he outstretched his hands where long and sharp claws protruded. His eyes were an evil yellow, locking their sight on the smooth flesh belonging to Amir. The two men went tumbling to the ground, scaring Maeve with a shriek and a lamppost lightbulb bursting.

"Maeve, keep running! Keep going straight like Reggie said!"

The two men tussled on the dirty ground. It looked as though the enemy had laid a nasty scratch to Amir's cheek, blood already trickling out of it and giving the other man confidence. Luckily he wasn't able to land another attack because Amir struck him in the neck, temporarily choking the other and having him stumble away as he tried to regain his breathing.

"What about you!? I can't just leave you here!"

"I'll be fine."

Within the same time, he's hit in the back, forcing him to crumble to his knees. He grabs the Junud member by his ankle and throws him to the ground with an impactful slam.

"His fighting skills prove he's a low rank soldier. Shouldn't take long to finish him off" It was when the Junud was getting up with a growl that Amir then lets his own claws come out and he's baring his canines for all to see. "Now go!"

She's reluctant as she watches Amir go for a punch. She's slowly jogging away, eyes still kept locked on the scene. And then her irises go huge as she witnesses something that she doesn't even have the time to shout before it's happening. Coming up from behind Amir was another Junud soldier. One of the girls from the diner. She must have escaped in order to help. She didn't look physically dangerous, besides the matching wings of the boy and the fact that she was swirling a giant green orb within her hands. She threw it into the back of the were-wolf. Amir falls to the ground with a wounded cry, only having enough strength to turn and see who'd struck him. His face hardens as he sees the girl, such a menacing stare being wiped from his face when he's being lifted by the guy and being thrown into the apartment building.

"AMIR!"

Maeve has never raised her voice like that. Never has she felt so sad but also furious at the same time. She's staring at the crack his body made, then looking down to see his limp form barely moving on the hard concrete. Tears welled up in her eyes, then they broke through and cascaded down her cheeks in streams. She wished to run over to him, check his pulse and make sure that he was still alive. Only she wasn't allowed to when his lying body was being blocked by the sight of the boy and girl. The same boy who was supposed to be going to the bathroom, the same girl who gave her that unsettling smile. And for a second she thought she was doomed. There was no way that she was strong enough in order to take down these two Junud members.

Especially not with powers that she's had no training with. She took steps back as they took steps forward. All they had to do was reach out and take her. But then they had to go and open their snarky little mouths.

"It's unfortunate that we had to kill not one but both of your boyfriends" The girl giggled. Her fingers twitched and it was disturbing to see her raise already bloody hands to her face where she licked some of it off. No, Reggie can't be dead. And neither can Amir. "With one touch, I'm easily able to poison my victims."

Good for you *Poison Ivy*...

"A specialty us nature pixies have."

"I thought pixies were supposed to be nice" Maeve managed to tremble out. She almost tripped over a crack in the sidewalk, managing to catch herself in time and stumble into a wall. Worse than actually tripping. Now she's cornered. *Fan-fucking-tastic.*

"Ah, you mistake us for those primp little fairies. They're the goody-goodies" The woman flicked her hair back at the same time as the man who let out a shrill laugh. They looked absolutely wicked. Their eyes twinkled with vice intentions, their lips lifting into huge curves. "But don't worry, I won't hold the little mistake over ya'. It fills me with glee telling everyone that they should fear me" She's about to reach out and wrap her glowing hands around Maeve's neck, but before she could, she's being shoved back by a blast of power.

"No, get away from me!"

Having fallen to the ground, the Junud then stare up at Maeve with shocked faces and speechless throats. They've been warned about this girl—have been warned about her entire group of friends and what they might have to look out for. But the energy they just experienced, the force that caused them to smack the back of their heads off the cracked concrete, was nothing like they expected. It was much stronger. It was vigorous and full of passion, filled to the brim with emotion that might have been revenge for what they did to Amir. The same man who she now knew was still alive because he let out a breathy moan as he struggled to get up. Whatever magic the lady had thrown at him had really done a number on him. She let a smile twitch at her chapped lips, a new surge of glee spreading throughout her chest as she could feel the motivation Amir was prepping himself with. He was going to protect Maeve until his last breath. Judging he still released heavy breaths that came from his mouth and nose he didn't count himself dead just yet.

It was just a bit difficult to stand, his arms and legs wobbling enough to let gravity pull him back down.

"You people really need to leave me alone" Maeve starts as she pushes herself off the wall. The Junud soldiers are standing on their feet. They're a bit scared of the way the woman goes rigid, her eyes flickering between purple and the once shy brown. Her fingers wiggled unknowingly, tingling with power that was already lifting trash cans from off the street corners, and cracking car windows that were parked. "I've already made it pretty known that I don't want to be a part of whatever plan your precious Raba are trying to do. So just go away!" Her shout made a gust of wind hit the boy and girl, their bodies flying across the street and into a rusted mailbox.

These low ranking soldiers hadn't planned to battle someone like this. They were still in training. But of course the Raba

needed all hands on deck. If you spot the girl and her lousy pack
of foolish dogs, they are to proceed to do whatever it takes in
order to bring her back alive. Witnessing her knock their breath
from right out of their chests, they're beginning to think they're
far too young and far too inexperienced to be fighting someone with this caliber. Panic is seen lacing their appearance and
they almost come to an agreement to wave the white flag. They
were scared of the way that she now descended upon them, an
uncontrollable power taking over her body.

"I'm afraid we can't do that" The girl pixie grunts. She uses
the mailbox to help bring her to her feet. Staring at Maeve,
she shook her head and remembered her oath. She worked for
the Junud, worked for the Raba. She willingly signed her name,
promising to complete any and all missions handed to them
whether their lives may be taken or not. She's serving her leader,
a trio in robes who has and will continue to give them anything
they ask for. It's been ingrained that she shall treat them like
Gods—she shall fight for them like they're Gods. And if that
means standing up to a woman who can't quite figure out how
to relinquish the power that was building within her, then so be
it. "It is our job to return you to the Raba, and returning you is
what I shall do."

The girl threw her arm out, an open palm to the concrete. A
green glow brightened with every second that she continued to
stand where she was and chant in a language that Maeve couldn't
understand. The ground shook and parts of the sidewalk, the
street began to crack. All eyes fell to the platform under their
feet, it shifted and crumbled, giving enough room for dirty roots
to sprout from underneath. They slithered their way over to

Maeve's feet like a snake until they were able to wrap around her ankles and secure her in the spot where she stood. The Junud soldier was ecstatic by her capture. An almost defeated line was pulling into a smile so large she could have been mistaken for a cartoon character. She began to laugh maniacally, putting her other hand out to only strengthen the already tough roots. They crawled up Maeve's legs with a speed she could barely keep up with, and they tightened for every second that she struggled to be set free.

"Bringing you in would be life changing for me" The girl says. It sounds as though she was speaking to herself, eyes darting between her hands and a panicked Maeve. But then with wide eyes beaming with glee darted up to meet with the same woman she had encased in multiple plant roots that smelled like dirt and sewer. "Everyone would see how far I've come! I can finally prove to that snotty general that I too can be just as good as her" She whipped around to look at her colleague. He stood behind her, jaw dropped slightly in awe, eyes glistening as he nodded along to everything she said. "*We* will never be pushed around again. Us low ranks will finally get the respect we deserve."

Why can't she just find a better way to do that?

Maeve found these soldiers' dedication just a tad bit creepy. She writhed under her restraints.

"Let me go! Let me go! Let me go!" She shouts before her mouth is being clamped shut by another root. She threw her head back, thinking the disgusting piece of nature would be removed from her lips, but instead it only brought her head back upright, seeping dirt past her lips. Maeve swears that if a slimy worm crawls into her mouth thinking it's their new home then she will probably find a way not only to kill every single worm in the world but before she does so, shove a handful up the ass to the person who put her here. Her animosity grew with each cackle the girl and boy gave. It grew when seeing Amir try to get up once more, but fall into the nearby building wall. Dark lines could be seen sprouting on his arms and neck, tracing the outlines of his veins and making it a struggle for him to breathe. Maeve wanted to scream out for him, go over and make sure that he wasn't about to die right then. The only thing stopping her was these stupid roots that didn't hesitate to squeeze.

Maybe if she just tapped into her power again then she'll be able to set herself free? *Sounds easier than it is.*

Shoot. Nothing.

Shoot power, shoot. Still nothing.

Come on! She groaned at the inability to do anything involving her werewolf or witch powers. Everyone makes doing magic look so simple. With a wave of their hand, with a flick of their wrist, with a dumb chanting of a spell, it's been shown that it doesn't take much to make a ball of energy release from her hands. She feels thick for not knowing what to do. Right now she doesn't have time to sit and think either. Lives are in danger and she's feeling as though her lungs are about to collapse the longer that she's in these roots.

"Ah, I can already feel the official Junud badge already! No one will ever look at me like a low rank again."

Maeve was really getting tired of this girl's monologuing. Yeah, it was a bit interesting to listen to her motives, but the ranting is just going on and on. She's beginning to repeat the same things. Either kidnap, kill, or release already. It was an irritation that

Maeve only felt for fictional villains—movie or television ones that speak through all of their time, giving the hero an opportunity to find an escape plan. Maeve looked around, searching for her escape plan. There was a broken window from the apartment building. It must have shattered when Amir's body was thrown into it. The jagged pieces littered the ground, all shapes and sizes ranging from it. One particular piece glimmered from a streetlight and looked to be her perfect weapon. She moved to grab it, being stopped when one last thick root swirled around her torso and clamped her arms shut to her sides.

You've got to be kidding me!

It was shouted through a closed mouth and more wiggling. Her brows turned down and her jaw clenched. Her muscles stiffened and her hands balled into tight fists. Her eyes shaded purple as she moved to lock them onto her target. Her knuckles began to turn white and crescent indents were created from her nails into her palms. The violet glow that surrounded her hands was enough to get the mean pixies to look at her; and the way she managed to rip the tangled roots from off her was what had them alarmed. Shaking an arm loose, she then uses an iron grip when it comes to taking hold of the large one that is surrounding her upper-body. Her fingers roll around it, and her skin begins to collect more of the dirt. Her lip curls and her face contorts into a scowl. Without removing her sight from the enemy, she rumbles out a growl from her throat and tears the thick piece off of her. The girl lets her knees buckle, hissing when the pull had been so strong that it ripped it apart. Magic users tend to have a connection with the forces that they project, therefore physical damage to a creation of theirs, can ultimately cause damage to the person.

It's unknown whether or not Maeve picks up on it, but it doesn't matter. She looks down at the rest of the roots struggling to regrow and once again wrap around her, a new resentment for nature tugging at her big heart for the pretty plants. And as she opened her mouth to let out a shout from annoyance, there was the amazing sight of her canines having grown exponentially longer. Not only that, but her nails, ones that are usually manicured to perfection were growing into these ugly claws. They stretched inches and became thicker. They shaded from their typical matching skin tone to a mixture of yellow and brown—as if saying that she hasn't taken care of them in weeks. The tips of them were pointed and sharp enough to slice through the roots like scissors to paper. She uses those claws in order to break free, shredding them until they are limp on the ground. Screams vibrated out of the girl pixie's throat, matching the way that her creations didn't hold the same life as before. Maeve is a terrible person. She's relishing in the sounds of weeping nature and the girl who dares encase her in it.

She gave one last swipe to her ankles where the remaining trap rested. Freedom washed over Maeve as she stepped out of the pile of chopped up roots, inhaling as she rolled her shoulders back. A vicious grin stretched at her pretty pink lips. Power filled her veins, touching the tips of her toes, tingling her ears. Never has Maeve felt like this. While it was familiar (matching how she felt in the tunnel) this time she wasn't petrified of it. Now she felt anew. She was relishing it. Maeve locked in on the two pixies. She raised her arms, glowing palms facing the two Junud soldiers who stared back in both wonder and terror.

"Maeve!" Amir had shouted it. He was standing, but most of his body weight was pressed to the cracked wall. "You don't know how to control yourself just yet! Don't do anything!"

"But they poisoned you!" Her anger seeped through and now the ground was shaking for a different reason. "They need to pay for what they did. Especially if you-" She looked back at him, eyes dimming back to their normal brown as she observed his battered and bruised form. The black lines that tainted his skin were spreading. It was all over his face. "Especially if you die..." Her whispering had fallen on deaf ears as she attempted to blast a wave of energy towards the pixies.

"Maeve no!"

His protest had been too late. The attack had been done and the two enemies were being hit with a purple wave. Screams from the torture bounced from wall to wall of building to building. It's surprising that none of the residents took wonder at the loud afflictions, peaking their heads through their windows and checking whether or not someone was actually dying—if they themselves were in danger. Besides the pixies pleading that Maeve stop, them wishing for mercy, the streets were still quiet. Curtains and doors were still closed, no ears pressed against their walls wishing to get a listen.

And then there was silence.

Maeve dropped her hands, along with her body. She was on her hands and knees, chest heaving up and down as she tried to regain her energy and strength. She watched as her claws transformed back into her normal nails, along with feeling her canines retract just a bit in length. Allowed her to press her mouth into a firm line, matching the way her mind too was blank after the events. She can't believe she just did that. But it felt great. Slowly lifting her head, Maeve glanced in the direction where the pixies once stood. It was empty, a void of space. Shifting her irises downward she was allowed to see that there lay a pile of ashes where their feet used to be planted. It reminded her of when Emry took care of those frat guys, witnessing how instead of their corpses lay on the ground, drifting dust, and piles of ashes lay about. It must be the way that all low rank Junud members die.

Just another thing she would have to ask about.

At this point it'll take years before she is completely satisfied with all of the answers to Kariq Leada, and to all of the people that lived here.

"Maeve," She doesn't know when Amir stumbled his way over, but he had and he plopped himself on the ground beside her. More so he fell on the ground beside her, groaning from his suffering. He clutched at his chest and it's assumed that whatever that girl did to him, whatever poison she injected into him was taking serious affect and now attacked his heart. She stopped relishing in her success at defeating an opponent all on her own in order to rush to Amir's aid. She doesn't know how she'll be able to help him, but she could at least try. She doesn't know the limits to her witchy abilities, therefore she doesn't know if she can cast some sort of spell and magically heal him.

"Amir! Oh my God!" With shaky hands she is placing them against his chest that was rising and falling tremendously. He was in desperate need of oxygen that his lungs feel as though they are being deprived of. Amir coughed, he moaned, his face twisted into pain and Maeve was scared that this was the end for him. "What can I do? How do I stop it?" Without wanting to feel like a pervert or thinking she was taking this opportunity to see how toned he really is (even though she is quite impressed by the imagery) she lifted his shirt in order to see the initial wound. It sprouted from his back, a morphed blob of black taking center and then sprouting all around.

"You go find the others" He breathes. He sounded oddly calm for someone who was dying. He probably came to terms with his fate...just like Reggie. She doesn't think she can lose two people tonight. She doesn't think her heart would be able to take it.

"What? No, I can't just leave you here. What if I help carry you? The forest shouldn't be too far now. Ms. Loom and Emry should know what to do" Maeve tried to lift Amir from the spot he laid. Only he didn't budge. She wanted to assume that it was because she was too weak from her powers, that Amir was just a really big guy and she couldn't lift him so easily. With how he removed his arm from out of her hold, it was because he didn't want to get up.

"No, I won't make it in time. But you need to go, before any more soldiers show up."

"What am I supposed to tell everyone? They're all going to be heartbroken. Your sister..." Maeve looked him in the eye, vision blurring with tears. She tried to give a hopeful smile but it became crooked before falling into a frown. "*I'm* going to be heartbroken" She sucked back a ball of snot that dared to dribble out of her nose. "There's still so much I want to talk to you about. So many werewolf things."

Amir chuckled, raising a weak hand to where hers laid on his chest.

"You have everyone else. I'm sure they can tell you anything you want to know. Micah could tell you anything."

"It's not going to be the same" Her eyes shifted to the side momentarily and Amir had to crane his neck in order to find them again. He let the corner of his lips twitch into a grin.

"How? Even Zenadia can give you insight...seeing as she's married to a werewolf" He coughed and any ounce of light-hearted amusement had been washed away and replaced by concern. They don't know how much time Amir might have left, but Maeve internally promised to stay until his life slips away. She doesn't want to see him die alone.

"They're mated," Amir furrowed his eyebrows. "I don't think she or even Micah would be able to tell me about mine."

"What are you-?"

"I know this isn't the right time," She let out a breathy laugh. "And I know this isn't the right place to be asking this, because we barely know each other...I actually think it's only been a few days, and I'm still extremely confused on how this all works. But I can't lie and say that I haven't felt this connection with you ever since we met in that stupid dirty dungeon, and I-"

"Blue dress," He interrupted her. "Your rambling is cute and all, but I'm still dying here and I'm going to pass before you get to the point."

He chuckled and she blushed. He called her cute...or well her rambling which is embarrassing, but it's still a compliment she's willing to take. She smiled along, wiping at her face. She inhaled sharply and mentally prepped herself for what she was about to say because for some reason her heart was beating a bit fast and she could feel her body get hot. She was nervous, fearful. She had no idea what Amir might say for a response; and with that could be his last breath, leading her to take whatever he says to the grave. She doesn't quite know what answer she's looking for.

"Are we mates?"

Amir's eyes widened comically wide. It would have been funny if they were in any other situation

"What-Why?" His face twisted and he was curling in on himself, hand leaving Maeve's in order to clutch at his chest where he felt the burn. She felt it too. There was this tightness that squeezed her, made her chest sting, and the discomfort was becoming unbearable.

"I have to do something!" She panicked as she watched him writhe on the ground. Her hands hovered over his body, not knowing where to touch, how much pressure to place. And it didn't help that he kept swatting at her in weak attempts, still urging that she continue to search for the others. Her mind bustled and a nervous frustration was poking through, leaving her clueless. Tears ran down her cheeks in waves, hands trembling as she finally allowed them to rest on Amir's chest. He instantly grabbed for her wrists and they halted to stare at one another. "Please just let me try."

"You need to go" Amir's voice was hoarse, barely noticeable from the whisper-like volume he tried to protrude after clearing his throat. "Like you said, it's only been a few days...no need to worry about me" A crash sounded and Maeve instantly snapped her head up in order to inspect. If it was even possible, her heart pounded even harder, it ran even faster. There had been no physical sign that someone was near, but her gut was a warning in itself. Someone was creeping closer and it won't take long before they spot them. "Go. Go now."

"Not until I help you!"

"You'll never be able to. You need to leave Maeve."

"How do you know? Just let me try! I promise there can still be a chance."

Another crashing sound, along with a grunt. It was louder so whoever, or whatever it is, they weren't too far away.

"Because witches can't heal people!" His shout was enough to make her stop breathing. No. That can't be. There has to be a spell. Some kind of magic potion that he can drink. If she could just get him to Amora or Emry—she dropped her head to his chest. She hated that she couldn't hear his heartbeat. It was so faint it might as well have stopped altogether. She doesn't want to hear that though. Doesn't want to hear the deafening silence that was her taking the life of a beloved friend and brother. Sobs fell from her lips while Amir wrapped his fingers around hers in a hold. "I'll be fine Maeve. But you won't if you're captured. All of this would be for nothing."

I would have died for nothing. He didn't have to say it in order for her to know.

"I'm so sorry," Maeve croaks. Lifting her head she was met with Amir's precious smile. Droplets fell onto their entwined hands before she tightened it. She thought that maybe if she squeezed hard enough, part of her would revive him. She thought that maybe if she cried heartbroken enough, the tears would soak his skin and wash away all ounces of poison that flooded his veins. "I'm so, so sorry. I didn't mean to bring you into this. I didn't mean to bring anyone."

"None of this was your fault."

"But maybe if I had just fought back a bit more then-"

"Then we probably would have received the same fate" Amir reached out to caress her face. His eyelids drooped and he was staring at her in all of her blurry beautiful glory. "You can't change what's already written. It's okay. At least the last thing I get to see is you" Clanging and the sound of a strangled voice. It must have been around the corner. "Now go. Please."

She didn't want to leave him. Didn't want his last breath to be taken on a dirty concrete ground surrounded by no one that he loves and cares for. But Amir removed himself from her, urged her in the direction of the forest. The sound of footsteps got closer. She stood. She looked down at him with sorrow and guilt. He couldn't do much but smile up at her and encourage her to start running. She was hesitant. She could stay, fight off whoever was coming and stay with Amir for a bit longer. But shaking her head and complying to his final wish she turned and took off in a sprint. He watched her go. Watched as her curly brown hair bounced with every step; and her tears getting swept up in the wind before falling to the ground in her wake. He felt himself go lighter as she craned her neck to look at him one last time, luscious lips parting to mouth her final apology.

"Yes. I am" He said it slowly, pronunciation better than anything he's said in the last few minutes. But that's because Maeve was already too far away in order to hear. His eyelids fell shut and the last thing he was able to bask in was the hard sound of feet stopping beside his head.

Chapter Sixteen

Micah let out a whimper. He let out a groan. It was quiet at first, it came out in mumbles along with his face contorting. His eyebrows creased inward, causing waves to shape on his forehead; and his eyelids squeezed tight; while his plump lips flopped into a frown that was so deep it looked as though he was suffering from a heinous nightmare. He twisted and turned on the hard ground, his weight flattening the fresh grass and crushing small daisies he didn't even know were sprouting. He moaned again, this time louder and with the curling of his body where he clutched onto his stomach in search of some comfort. This feeling that sprouted throughout him...it was different. It's definitely something that he's never experienced before; his confidence, his energy, his power. It was all reaching a limit he didn't even know existed. And if he doesn't let even an ounce of this new potential free, he just might go ballistic. There was a tightness in his chest that made him breathe heavier; his eyes stung with fresh tears; he felt undeniably weak yet capable of doing anything all at the same time. This new sensation was indescribable—promptly waking him from the slumber that he and everyone was supposed to be deep within by now.

Amora stopped the entwining of flower stems and then craned her neck to silently check in on him. At first she believed nothing to be wrong (probably a small case of parasomnia that came from a bad dream), but then she noticed that he was actually awake. Micah batted his eyelids open, right as he struggled to lift himself by his arms. They felt wobbly, fingers bending and nails digging into the ground for more stability. One last whine slipped past his lips, and his skin was paling. He tried to regain his vision, but with fear vibrating throughout his body, it continued to blur; it was strangely shaky and if it didn't stop soon he knew he'd get a headache. That is if the sudden ringing that strikes his left ear didn't already begin to do that. It was loud and it was pitched. It was enough to make Micah let out a shout, one hand going to his ear ready to rip it off in order to stop the agony. The other dug deeper in the grass, nails lengthening and then puncturing the dirt so it gathered underneath the growing claws. Amora doesn't remember getting up, doesn't remember letting her perfect flower crown drop to the ground, and she most certainly doesn't remember making her way over to Micah so fast, cradling him close to her chest.

"Micah! Hey! What's wrong!?"

Between his suffering and Amora's loud worry, it didn't take long before the rest of the group was being awoken. Rowan let out a sound of annoyance, not taking the disturbance to his surprisingly peaceful and comfortable sleep nicely.

"What's going on?" Emry asks, while at first being sluggish eventually making her way over to the tense duo. After seeing the tears that cascaded down Micah's cheeks, all drowsiness was wiped clean and she was moving over to her friend and said friend's indirect son with a quickness she only ever uses during a fight. "What's happening?"

There was no given answer, because even Micah himself wasn't able to form any words. He just continued to be cradled in Amora's arms, letting this formidable feeling ruin him from the inside. He gasped for air and suddenly his eyes were rolling back.

"You guys have to keep it down, Olivia is still sleep...ing. Is he okay?" Zenaida speaks.

"I don't think he'd be doing that for the fun of it" Foster says with disquietude. His eyes were blank, dark and less than happy by Zenaida's lack of perception to everyone who isn't Lucas and Thais.

He also had to dig his heels within the dirt or else he feared he would run up to Amora and shove her out of the way. Because if he's being completely honest, he wanted to be the one to hold and comfort Micah. It was almost a need actually. For what he can remember, Foster alway had the urge to keep the other man wrapped in his arms, to be the one to protect him when it's fairly obvious that he refuses to be taken care of. Even with the rejection back in the woods his fingers twitched, itched to touch the warm skin of Micah. He wanted to keep his body so close that they basically became one. He wants to hear his thumping heartbeat and find a way to calm it to something much more relaxed. Sitting back and watching Emry try to cast a spell over Micah's thrashing form could only hold him back for so long. His patience was thinning—his arms crossed and he tapped his fingers against his biceps. He gnawed at the corner of his bottom lip. If one stared at his face hard enough, they would be able to notice the way every now and again his scowl would shift into gloomy eyes and a soft frown, a pure moment of concern.

"Obviously you dipshit. I mean, what's wrong with him!?" Zenaida glared.

"Well you asked if he was okay? And with the gift of sight that comes from your ocular organs," Foster glared back, posture straightening and jaw tightening. "-you would be able to fucking see that he isn't."

"I was sleeping not even a minute ago! You really expect me to comprehend what my fucking *ocular organs*, are looking at!?" She really wanted to stand from her spot on the grass; maybe even stand toe-to-toe with him, chin tilted upwards while she shoved a finger in his face. She wanted to prove that she wasn't intimidated by his larger frame. But precious Olivia laid in her lap, asleep beginning to toss from the sudden chaos and all of the loud voices that came with it.

With a huff and Lucas becoming a human wall, blocking any sight Foster could have of Zenadia. Foster rolled his eyes before refocusing his attention onto Micah. He feels as though he'd just missed something, a bit confused why Micah was now resting calmly. He was limp within Amora's arms, the only small movement in his chest being the indicator that he was alive. Foster couldn't resist anymore and rushed to be by his side. Emry put a hand to his chest after he fell into a squat. He reached a hand out ready to relay some form of comfort. Eager eyes darted over at the witch, a spark of vexation hidden within.

"We have no idea what's going on. You can't just touch him."

"It's not like he's going to give me some dangerous disease" Foster scoffs before pushing her hand away from him, and then once again reaching out to place a hand to Micah's shoulder. It was instant to see Micah waking up gasping for air, letting out a cough a few times. It would have been thought that the man had just recovered from almost drowning. He was in a hasty fit as he was pushed to sit up, a hand going to his chest while he heaved. The others widened their eyes, too rushing to get a closer look. Olivia had finally awoken, rubbing her irises with balled fists and a pout.

"Micah?" Foster tries.

"Maeve..." Micah snapped his head around to look at him, eyebrows furrowing and a slur trailing as he slowly whispered his twin sister's name. But then his irises were becoming saucers and he was fumbling slightly as he stood. "Oh my God Maeve!" That's when he began to run in the direction of the creepy and big bushes that ultimately surrounded them like a cage. It might be a little hard to find his way out of the confusing territory, but eventually he'll find his way. He'll find his sister. Only before he could make it too far, Gabe was stopping him from going any further by clutching onto his arm and pulling him back.

"Where're you going?"

Micah turns around, ripping his arm out of the hold. Gabe raises an eyebrow, brown eyes searching the face of his leader. He was beyond frazzled.

"I saw Maeve."

"What do you mean?" It was asked by Thais, her approach being more out of curiosity for her brother than the newbie werewolf. She intended to stand beside Gabe and just listen in for her answer, but got a little too excited and found herself pushing herself in front of the man so she was looking Micah in the eye. "Did you see Amir?"

"Well it wasn't that I was *seeing* her, I *was* her" Confusion struck the eyes that stared at him. They've never heard of this before. It's an ability that only the Oracle has—that the King had. "It was as if I was looking through her eyes."
"So where is she?" Emry wonders. Her heart leaped for joy. Yeah, she may have lost her for the second time when she's supposed to be the responsible guardian, *but* at least she isn't dead. She will still be able to give the Ross' some sort of good news.

"She was running down a street" Micah closes his eyes. As he tries to remember, his temple begins to throb and he's quick to raise a hand to his head where he believes applying pressure to the part that hurts, some of the pain will be eased. Glimpses of himself, of Maeve, running down the street appeared. He heard her panting and how her heart thumped sporadically. He could feel her fear and the tears that fell down her face due to heartbreak. But hidden underneath all of the prototypical emotions were those same immense electrical feelings; and they were surging this unexplainable power throughout his body, making him believe for just a second that he was invincible.

"Is my brother with her?"

Micah thinks back. He can see dark and cold abandoned buildings; dirty streets littered with anything and everything; a skinny black cat just ran by (well that's bad luck); there was barely any lighting, Micah has to strain in order to focus on street signs. *Barryside Road.* Why does that sound familiar?

"She's on Barryside Road, do any of you know where that is?"

Rowan stepped forward, expression neutral from the panic

he was growing for Maeve. He knew what that part of town was like. He used to live there, many years ago, witnessing first-hand how terrible the place was. The horrific people, the run-down places, the way that there was nothing to live for over there and yet people rather suffer than find a way to thrive.

"That street isn't too far from here," His brooding tone was suspicious, because Rowan Hathaway was never one to brood. It's not like anyone stopped to wonder where this grim attitude came from, moreso focused on how Micah took a step back, ready to take off in the direction of the bushes again. "I can easily find her."

"Well then let's go. Lead the way."

"That street...it's in Lima" Everyone looked at each other with irises widening into globes, mouths popping open in silent gasps. It's blatantly obvious that all of them know of such a place— because who wouldn't? It's a part of the city that parents tell their kids is filled with dangerous things, dangerous people. *"It's off limits"* Amora used to tell Micah. *"I don't ever want to hear that you've been over there."* It's notorious for the heinous conspiring between thugs and the poor; filled to the brim with grime and pests contagious of rabid diseases. "It's best if I go."

"Alone? You can't do that? You'll be mauled the second you step foot on the street" The bafflement was said by Foster, who can't picture his best friend even looking in the direction of Lima. There was a whispered "No offense", that Rowan didn't bother listening to.

There was nothing to be offended by. He never told anyone about his history; where he came from, what his family is like, how he was raised. Or at least he didn't tell them the truth. Way back when he was first taken in by Amora, literal bull*shit* might as well have spewed from his mouth—because right then, when he looked Ms. Loom in the eye and gave her a bright smile, he told her lie after lie. He said he lived on the northern side of Kariq Leada, the more wealthy side that everyone typically called Thari. He said he grew up with both kind and loving parents (no he didn't, his mother disappeared when he was three, and his dad was a drunk). He explained he lived in this nice, fancy house where if he shouts, an echo would shoot throughout the three floors. (Oh how he wishes. He lived in a crumby spider infested apartment, where occasionally they had to shower with cold water because they couldn't afford to pay for heating.)

Before Rowan was known for beaming with delight and not being the smartest, he considered himself detached. Stepping out of Lima, he completely transformed himself. He bleached his hair, changed his style, and flipped the switch on his personality. Taking a deep breath in, he claims that meeting Ms. Loom was a fresh start. But then he giggles to himself because he can't believe his life had come full circle; being in Lima and fighting for his life.

"I um—I grew up there" He didn't mean to flinch. It was something he did in fear of everyone hating him. He's lied to all of them for years. "I lied to all of you about who I am" It was hard not to cower away from the muddled stares that he was receiving. Made a new bashfulness engulf him, his nervousness growing bigger and stronger for every second that no one said anything. "I'm not actually from Thari. I never was. I didn't have this picture perfect life I always told you guys I had. I was born and raised in Lima."

Silence. One. Two. Three–

"I think I speak for everyone when I say that I'm speechless," Micah says. He looks around, hoping that someone else will chime in. Except the space was quiet; no one could conjure the proper words in order to settle the anxiety that brewed within Rowan. Because what does it change? Unless the next thing he says is that he's been a serial killer all this time and the pack is his next target, where he originally grew up is something they can just shrug off. Of course they're a little upset that they've been lied to for years now, but none of them are running to rip his throat out from an ultimate betrayal. "I mean, it doesn't matter what part of the city you grew up in" Micah approaches the blonde and puts his hands on the other's shoulders. "And this might sound cheesy, but from the moment I met you, I knew you were sincere" There were smiles rising into soft laughter between the two. "You're our friend Rowan. A part of the pack. You've given us no reason not to trust you,"

"The reason is that I lied...for years. Taking away the story I made up about my childhood, none of you know anything about me."

"Do you still like to read comics?" Foster asks with a raised brow.

Rowan furrowed his own at the question. What does that have to do with his entire existence being false?

"Yeah why?"

"Is your favorite color still green?" Thais asks next with a grin.

"I guess so," He shrugs. Liking a certain color isn't something that's a big deal, so he didn't necessarily change that about himself.

"And do you still think you cook better than me?" Amora asks which got a few snickers. Even Rowan couldn't help but giggle, remembering the many times that the two debated about whether or not they were the best chef in the house. There were even a few times that they made the rest of the group take a vote. Who won was never finalized out of the fear that choosing one over the other would result in possible strangulation. It's always been quite nice for Rowan to reminisce about all of the good times he gets from this newly built family of his. It's something he's alway wanted when he was little; and now here he is, being embarrassed by people who are way more than a runaway mom and loser of a father.

"Will I still have a room if I say yes?"

Micah shook his shoulders as if jostling the blonde werewolf awake. They smiled at one another while the rest laughed at what was becoming another heartwarming moment.

"Don't you see? We don't care that you're from Lima. Even though you've had to do some minor rebranding, you still kept true to yourself. The Rowan Hathaway that you are today, is the same Rowan Hathaway you've always been. We're going to love you all the same."

"But now with a shit ton of questions," Lucas chuckles.

"Yeah, like how even with a life swap, you're still girl-less. Real tragic man" Gabe snickered beside Lucas from his lame boy-ish joke, the two eventually sharing one of those manly handshakes where they end up snapping at the end. Rowan raised his fist at the two, but there was no malice behind it. He rolled his eyes before returning his stare to Micah in front of him.

"I just don't want this to be something that gets me shunned, ya' know? I never had anybody living in Lima, and then meeting and having you all...it'd really hurt to be casted out" Emerald eyes welled with tears. He wanted his new personality to be someone that was nothing but positive and goofy energy, feeding into a trope that made no one ever question his loyalty. And with that came emotions that he typically had to put on a show for; be dramatic. But as he looked at all of the faces that he's grown to love and appreciate, these raw feelings that surfaced and tracked down his cheeks wasn't his character. It was the real him through and through. He was only proving Micah's point. It's almost as if he wasn't lying about who he was, but more so using it as a crutch to be himself confidently.

Lima is a place where if you're not tough, you're bound to be eaten alive. So Rowan became that, and he fended for himself. Leaving was removing that mental burden, and *oh* if he could express how relieving it was.

"It's going to take a lot more than lying about where you used to live in order to be casted out of the pack" Zenaida claims.

"Try putting all of us in danger because of who your parents were and why our so-called 'kings' are tied to it" Gabe then says without any consequential thought behind it, earning him a smack to the back of his head by Thais. "Ow, what!? Too soon?"

"*Speaking* of, I think it's best that we go find Maeve now," Micah said.

"I can lead you right to her."

Chapter Seventeen

She was almost there. Maeve was almost there. She could see the tall trees belonging to the forest, gorgeous willows dancing in the night and appearing to be the fragile shield in order to keep people from entering. Her legs burned as she inched closer and closer to the end of the street; her having stopped running a long time ago and eventually paced into a sluggish walk, internally praying that she didn't have to deal with any more enemies for the time being. She doesn't think she's mentally or physically capable of fighting; and if someone were to randomly attack, it wouldn't take much for her to give in.

Goodness that makes her sound weak.

She shook her head to get rid of the thoughts. It only makes her think about Amir—how she could have done a little more to help, to save him. Her stomach swirled with misery and so she wrapped her shaking arms around the area. A small piece of her believed that if she clutched hard enough the terrible despair would evaporate and the only depressing thing she would have to deal with is explaining what happened to the pack...to Thais. But the sorrow wasn't leaving and the brutal imagery of Amir dying on the hard ground was on repeat. Her fingers grip onto her shirt, pulling tight at the fabric. This is painful. For a moment she believed that she could feel the poison too. Her body grew hot and her breathing was rapid; her knees wobbled and she was tightening her hold.

She wiped her eyes, drying all of the tears from before. She didn't think she would be able to shed anymore, every last drop being dried from her body the moment she let them freefall over Amir's body. Her final tear was the one she let drip onto the palm of his hand, dampening his skin and being the last gift she could ever give him. But with her brown irises against her, she could feel her vision blur and her lower lip begin to tremble. It was when she caught the loose string to Amir's sneakers (which she should have at least gave back, the poor guy laying dead with a pair of cute slippers on) and tripped onto the hard ground is when she let out a particularly loud groan.

No point holding back the tears now.

She sat on her knees, body leaning forward in order to curl in on herself, hands slamming down on the concrete sidewalk completely disregarding how painful it felt and the way that it began to scratch and cut up her hands. She also let the sound of glass shattering and bulbs popping, late night critters squealing from fright and cracks from buildings ruin her.

Makes her realize that she can't even cry without something going wrong.

"Why did it have to be me?" She sobbed.

"Ah, pretty lady what's wrong?"

Maeve immediately lifts her head, neck craning in order to look up at the random voice being directed towards her. It was some man. He looked way older than her, not too tall, and carrying more fatty weight than muscle. With the sly grin that stretched at his lips surrounded by peach-fuzz, a dark gleam twinkling his soulless eyes, Maeve felt a shiver go down her spine. It was obvious that this man shouldn't be trusted. He looked hungry for her—in which way is entirely up to him and whatever heinous thoughts that brewed in his creepy mind. Maeve scrambled to her feet, creating distance between them. Her showing even the smallest amount of fear was enough to have the stranger lick his lips.

"Oh, there's no need to be scared. I just heard you crying and I wanted to see if there's anything I can do to help" He put a hand to his chest, fake sympathy lining his features.

"Thank you, but I'm okay" She turns on her heels, once again setting her sights on reaching the forest; the pond; the rest of the pack. Before she could get too far though the man was grabbing hold of her wrist. His meaty fingers wrapped around her skin, tugging her back and almost into his chest. She cringes at his touch, body tensing.

"Wait wait wait" Maeve stays planted, watching as the man approaches her, almost coming toe to toe, and giving her an all access pass to how his breath reeked of booze and cigarettes. "I saw that you were on the ground, did you hurt yourself? I'm a doctor, I can help patch you up" He glanced down at her knees where indeed there had been a wound. A small trail of blood dripped down her leg—it must have happened when she tripped (in too much distress to notice). He also turned her hand around where scratches were done to her palms. "Come, I have every-thing upstairs in my apartment."

He tried to pull her in the direction of where it's assumed that he appeared from. But obviously refusing to go with anyone like him, Maeve twisted and slithered her hand out of the man's grip. He didn't like that. His smile dropped into a frown, eyebrows drooping and his stare becoming more powerful.

"No need, really. I'll clean it myself when I meet up with my friends."

Slight alarm must have rung throughout the stranger's head, because he looked back and forth for these said friends. The streets were empty, and it didn't look as though anyone would be approaching anytime soon. Had the man raise an eyebrow, calling her bluff.

"It can get extremely infected in a short time. It's best if I help you do it *now*," He reached for her again, this time digging his nails into her forearm while gripping. "So come on."

There was no twisting herself out of this one. She tried digging her heels into the ground but that did no justice. She tried using her other hand to help pull her arm away, but that only made him hold on tighter—any more and he'll pierce her skin, which is another wound that he'd *help patch up*. Maeve let out a frustrated huff, angry with herself for always finding herself in these situations. At this point she might just tape a sign to her back that tells everyone to go ahead and kidnap her. The stranger continues to pull her in the direction of a darkened alleyway, no sign of a door that could lead to a possible apartment. But then again, why would a part of her even believe that this man was telling the truth. His original plan was to find a damsel and have his way with them. Unfortunately Maeve was his target for the night. Stomping her foot down, she wasn't about to plead mercy to this sleazy man.

"I'm not going anywhere with you. Let me go!" And with a defensive reaction, she threw a punch to the man's left cheekbone. His hold on her dropped and instead went to his bruised cheek. He was turned away from her, a perfect blind opportunity for her to run away as fast as she could. But as she whipped around to take her head start in a possible chase, she ran right into the broad chest of what appears to be another man.

Is the population eighty percent men and twenty women?

She's surrounded by the opposing gender, seeming to always be stuck within their clutches. Maeve yelped from the impact, stepping back as she rubbed her now sore nose.

"That's an impressive left hook."

Wait...

"Rowan?"

Maeve blinks once, then twice. Her heart leaped for joy when he didn't disappear—him just standing there with his typical goofy grin. She thought she reached the point where he would vanish and she's left to hallucinate about whether or not she's ever going to actually meet back up with the group. That's why she jumps into his arms, more than excited when she doesn't fall right for him. He wraps his arms around her, squeezing tight and it only reassures her even further. Eventually he places her back on the ground, letting her silently gawk at his presence.

"And me too."

Looking around the blonde was none other than her twin brother Micah. He tried not to make it noticeable that he was relieved to see Maeve alive and well, but it was evident when

286 ~ NEVAEH BRAGG

she's giggling and then rushing to give him a hug as well. It felt
amazing. To be held so securely by family. There was a warmth
there that made her relax for what feels like the first time in forever. They molded into each other, relishing the moment where
their only family was safe and sound.

It only made Maeve think about Thais.

She parted herself from Micah, ready to confess what has
to be her biggest sin; only before she could, the stranger from
before was heard throwing curses, and following it was the cackling of Rowan. The siblings turned to look at the commotion,
being met with Rowan pointing and laughing at the creepy man
who was now tied up in an awkward position; his restraints
having been his clothes. The stranger wiggled about on the concrete almost completely naked. How Rowan managed to do that
in such a short time is astounding.

"You're going to pay for this!" The man grunted as he tried to
land any hit to the legs of the blonde, but of course the attempt
was dodged and he only looked more foolish. His face was beat
red and the glare he wore was about to become permanent. Between his giggles Rowan shoves his hands within his pant pockets and then leans down to become eye-level with the stranger.
His crooked smile never deters as the two hold gazes; it actually
only widens and he begins to look wicked as it doesn't match
the inimical glaze that covers his shining green eyes. Within that
moment, Maeve was actually scared of him. Only makes what
she has to say all the worse.

"You think I'm scared of scum like you?" Rowan's smile falls
and he becomes all the more menacing. "But if you wish to have
your debt paid, bill me. The name's Rowan Hathaway."

The two men stare at one another for a moment or two, the stranger letting his eyes scan over the handsome face of Rowan; observing his figure and letting the rusty gears in his head turn as he tries to remember where he must have heard that name. It was blatantly obvious when the man realized—his tied up body trying to desperately scramble away from the other, face going pale while terror covered any previous animosity. Rowan stood back up to his intimidating height, looking down at the shaking man with eyes that he let shade to a pretty ocean blue.

"Hathaway!? F-Founder of *Fangs!?*" Founder of what? "Look, I didn't know she was with you. If I had...please don't hurt me" Maeve found it astonishing to see what a simple name could do to someone. The creepy stranger was trembling, eager to protect himself more than ever. His eyes darted over to her and Micah, silently pleading that they tell the blonde to stand down. Only before the message could be sent, Rowan is letting out a growl and the stranger is yet again looking the other in the eye. "I wasn't even going to do anything! I swear!"

Maeve was tempted to roll her eyes.

"So you wouldn't mind if I asked?" Withdrawing his hands from his pockets, he threw his thumb over his shoulder, pointing it in the direction of Maeve. "I want to know why she punched you in the face if you didn't plan to do any harm. It'd suck if you were lying."

The man aggressively shakes his head.

"I wouldn't. Not to you. Please," The man looks at Maeve and Micah again, becoming frantic. Whatever threat Rowan had imposed on the people in Lima all those years ago is mind-boggling. Watching the blonde grip at the man's chin in order to get his attention back, and said man cowering back at the touch, Rowan was a different person. Gone, was the man who made jokes that were so stupid. Gone, was the person who matched the energy of the sun and had the soul of an angel. Now he's a threat that kicked the stranger in the stomach, rolling his eyes intensively when the other groaned in pain; pleading to be left alone. "I was only trying to help. Come on, pretty lady, tell him."

Rowan punched the stranger in the face, spitting on him as he lay on the concrete with little droplets of blood spilling from his mouth...maybe even little droplets of tears falling from his eyes as well.

"You shall not call her that," He grabbed the lying man's head by his hair. Or what was left of his hair. His teeth grits as he continues, and Maeve is a bit scared to go up and tell him that he's taking it a bit far. They could have easily left the moment that he was tied up. "Dirtbags like you use it wrongfully."

He slammed the man's head down onto the ground. A smirk twitched at his lips when watching the split and more than enough blood began to spill.

"Alright Rowan, I think that's enough. I think he got the hint" Micah states with a step forward.

"Yeah, let's just go back to the group" Maeve chimes, finding her voice. "There's something that I really need to tell everyone. So let's just go."

Or maybe Rowan could spend the rest of eternity causing physical harm to this stranger, leaving all of them stuck in their spots and never having to tell the unfortunate news of Amir's passing. It'd save her eyes from witnessing the stream of tears that would fall from the others; the gooey snot that would tremble from their noses as they tried their hardest to keep composure. She'd be able to save her ears from hearing all of their sobs—the way that they mixed their sadness for the fallen with their newfound hatred for her and just letting Amir die so easily. Her chest twists and nervousness bubbles within her stomach. She couldn't stop her anxiety from showing, and hopefully for now Micah will believe it only has to do with being in Lima for so long.

Rowan stomped on the man one last time, before he turned on his heels and started the journey back to the others. Only as he's passing Micah, the leader grips his bicep that causes the blonde to halt in his spot. One looks ahead while another watches his side profile. Internal conflict was brewing past beautiful emerald eyes and it only made the other pairs of brown show worry. Only made telling the truth about their dead loved one all the more hard.

"Are you alright?" Micah's voice was low, stern, and yet all the more intrusive. His grip fell so their hands swung beside one another, knuckles brushing. It took a second, but eventually Rowan cranes his neck to look back, their eyes locked in what appears to be a conversation that only the two could hear. Blinking once and then nodding his head, an answer was given.

"Yeah, I guess being here is just having some weird affect on me" Rowan chuckles letting a hand swipe through his hair, to then huff out a breath and let his arm dangle beside him. He attempts to smile, to ease any doubt Micah may still have, but it only makes his eyes pierce into his just a little harder. He's observing every breath and twitch Rowan may have done. If there was even the tiniest hint that he felt any different, the leader would do what he could to help. Looking around, he doesn't know exactly how he'd help, but he's sure he'll come up with something. Rowan was a dear friend, he was family, there's no way he would just let him suffer. Especially when he's done so much for so long already—hiding away all these true pieces of himself out of fear. "I think it's best that we leave" He was back to looking out into the distance. A snicker escaped as he took his first step back to the forest. "You know what they say...old habits die hard."

Micah nodded, agreeing that it's best that all of them finally return to one another. But as he's following, he stops abruptly and quizzically stares at Maeve. His eyebrows furrow and he takes the moment again to look around him.

"Where's Amir?"

Maeve froze. What was she supposed to say? More so, how was she supposed to say it? And wouldn't it be better that she was with everyone so she didn't have to relay the news for a second time?

"That's actually the thing I needed to tell you guys."

"Well then, where is he?"

"I think it's best if we get back to the group before I say."

Rowan snickered yet again.

"What? Is he dead?"

His question was meant to be lighthearted; a way to calm her squared shoulders and give her the cue to release the breath she inhaled long ago. But her silence was killer. Both men looked at her with prodding irises. They stood in front of her with an intimidating stance. She had one wish coursing on her mind, that being she hoped the ground would open and swallow her whole.

It had done nothing of the sort, having kept firm under her feet and forcing her to face the curiosity of two of Amir's friends. More of those tears struck her eyes and she willed them to stay where they are. At what point is she going to think that she needs to be stronger than what she is? People are in danger, someone died! It should be about time that she found even an ounce of courage and did something.

"Wait, Maeve...is that it? Has Amir been killed?" Micah swallowed a lump that had gotten stuck on the last word. She could feel his terror. She could feel his rage. Whether it was for her or the enemy, it didn't matter because she was willing to take the blow. Amir had already done so much for her, and she couldn't have helped him in the slightest. She deserved to take all of the harsh emotions that will erupt because of this. And if this was how Micah was reacting, she's beginning to imagine how Thais will. "Had he been killed!?" He lets out in a shout this time. Maeve flinches but does end up letting out a squeaky reply.

"Yes."

"N-No. You're lying" Rowan's voice cracks. "Where is he actually? Did the Junud capture him as ransom? Come on," He grabbed Maeve by her arms and shook her. Her breath hitched from the force, scared that he was about to bash her face in just like he did to the creepy man. "Don't tell jokes like that!"

"I'm not," A tear fell down her cheek. "He was trying to protect me and was poisoned by a pixie that was a part of the Junud."

"FUCK!" Micah screams. It startles Maeve and the entire street had gone almost pitch black due to every streetlight lightbulb having been blown out. The only thing that could be seen was the way that his round eyes glowed a bright purple, revenge lacing every crevice of the entrancing swirl of violet. "I want the Raba's head on a silver platter."

Chapter Eighteen

Pushing back a few more large leaves belonging to various plants, eventually Maeve was granted the sight of a glorious pond. It glistened under the moon that was slowly but surely going down, switching with the sun. It's then that she realized that she'd been making her way through Lima all night, fatigue of everything finally hitting her ten times over. It also didn't help that she heard the crunch of a fresh apple. She was extremely hungry and ready to dive head first into whatever food that was offered. But of course stuffing her face had to wait, because first things first: announce her return.

Rustling of the bushes had the rest of the group snapping their necks, ready to do whatever was needed depending on the people emerging from them. But once seeing that it was nothing more than the trio, the pack let humongous smiles take their faces alongside leaping from their seats and giving enthusiastic greetings. Maeve had been the one to receive the most hugs, (almost) everyone expressing their worry and how they were all so glad that she was now safe. Emry couldn't even hide the relief she had when finally having Maeve in her arms; their embrace being tight enough to have the younger of the two gasping for air. Didn't stop Maeve from smiling warmly after they separated, just as joyful to see the witch.

She was pretty glad to see all of them too actually. They give her this comfort that made her feel secure and oddly enough loved. Thais was caught looking behind them, confusion written on her features. Maeve could feel her heart sink. She didn't want it to be so soon, but it was expected for the sister to realize that one particular person is missing. Any smile Maeve had was wiped clean and now she frowned from shame. She approached the teenage girl, a gentle hand going to hers.

"Where's Amir?" Foster wonders.

Ah, so Thais wasn't the only one who noticed. But then again, it'd be strange if no one took notice. While Maeve has only known him a few measly days, she can already tell that he has a presence. He has this nurturing entity that lures not only her, but everyone else around him in. It's refreshing.

Micah and Rowan look at one another before turning their attention to Maeve. So did everyone else. And while she knows this is about to be devastating for all of them, she couldn't keep her glossy eyes off the already saddened face of Thais.

"I'm sorry-"

"No..." Thais rips her hand out of Maeve's. Her bottom lip wobbles and her brown irises sparkle with fresh tears. "No, you're lying. How could you just–please, tell me he's okay. He has to be!"

"Thais, Amir had been killed. I'm so sorry. If there was any-"
"He's all I had left! And you...!" Thais shoved a finger in Maeve's chest. This was the anger that Maeve was prepared for. It's best to just let her let it out. Maeve was even willing to take a few

punches if it meant that Thais expressed her depression for this situation. She knows she'd react the same way if she found out her family suffered the same fate. "You're the reason he's gone!"

"I know. The Junud had found us and he was willing to fight for me. Sadly, I was of no help. He had been poisoned before I had the chance to warn him."

"Y'all should have left her in the dungeon when you had the chance."

Lucas didn't have time to think about the words before they were dripping from his tongue with venom. It matched the way he glared in her direction, standing tall with flexed arms crossing over his chest. Micah was quick to turn and look at the other, sight just as firm and menacing. Maeve didn't need the help though. She was beginning to see that the damsel in distress act was only making things worse. That's why it's understandable for them to be very upset. Amir was more than just a lousy friend that occasionally gave good advice. He added value and sought to encourage the weak. It's rather shocking that he hadn't been born to become a pack leader; already holding so many of those morals, and even being the one to take over whenever Micah wasn't able to.

There is no way that Micah was going to let a spiteful Lucas (or anyone for that matter) wish ill on his sister though.

He wants to loop it in with the fact that he was protective over anyone he held close to his heart—especially since this particular person possesses the same DNA as him—but then again a part of him knows it's because he had thought the same once. He doesn't want to point fingers at a dead guy, but Amir is the only one to blame for his death. If he hadn't pushed to save Maeve when being rescued himself, then she probably would have been sacrificed already.

Micah wants to make up for his few moments of ruthlessness. "Watch your mouth!"

"It's the truth! None of us would even be in this mess if she was left behind. Better yet, if she never came here!" Lucas fires back with a step forward and a puffed chest. It was a test of strength, of power, to see how far he is willing to go against his own pack leader. It was an occurrence that never happened unless Micah was being far too unreasonable. Right now Lucas was crossing a boundary; letting his canines stretch and a scary growl to rumble from his throat. Micah stepped up just as furious, and that was the beginning of their pheromones flying through the air like someone spraying air freshener. Maeve wanted to scrunch her nose in disgust. It smelled like rotten fruit and molded trees.

"Lucas, you are being quite harsh. It's not like we would have expected for any of this to happen" Zenaida speaks from her spot in the back of the group where she was shielding Olivia from a possible fight.

The little girl is a new sight, a new addition. And she seemed to also already be staring...quite intensely actually. Maeve has never been so uncomfortable under the gaze of a child before— and that's saying a lot, when she lives with three children for siblings, each and every single one of them occasionally bursting through her bedroom door and just standing there to bother her. Eventually Olivia does look away and Maeve is turning her focus back to Thais. She had fallen to her knees, tears mixing with snot and hands clutched tight to her chest where she was forming into a ball. She was completely and utterly devastated by the passing of her brother, and Maeve is the last person that should be comforting her about it. She did so anyway. Slowly descending to her knees, the witchy werewolf woman reached out to touch Thais's shoulder. She should have expected the jump that came along with it. The poor girl probably wanted to be alone right now. She didn't want to hear all of the mushy crap that is her brother now being in a better place. She wanted to see him come running from out of the bushes and then hug her as tight as he could.

"No, don't touch me" She grumbled. Sounded like she wasn't as angry anymore. Or if she was, she was hiding it behind all of the despair that covered her once bright aura. "I agree with Lucas. They should have just left you in that stupid dungeon."

Maeve sighs.

"I won't sit here and say that I'm not hurt by that," Because she was. It hasn't been long since they've known each other (and that's why it was so easy for some of them to just flip a switch and show their hatred) but Maeve was foolish to believe that she and Thais were getting along fairly well. "I do understand though."

Thais lets out a laugh. One so boisterous that it halted the quarrel of the others. She threw her head back, eyes squeezed shut as more droplets fell from her eyes. But then the fit stopped and she was silent. The air around them had gone still, except for the slight breeze whipping past them, matching the soft howls of the creatures who lived in the forest alongside them. She wiped at her face, rubbing salty tears and green snot all over her arm. It was promised that someone would have commented about how unsanitary that had been, but given the serious atmosphere, all attention went to how a glare reached Thais' face and her lips were pressed into a thin line.

"You can look to the left and see your brother...I can't. So until Micah takes his last breath, you will never understand."

Maeve turns her head in order to look at her twin. If he wasn't already frowning because of the death of his friend, his features couldn't help but sink from what was said. Micah's shoulders fell and he did his best to ignore the eyes of everyone. They kept tracked to his feet, the front of his sneaker bumping a rock and skidding it a few inches from where it was before. He knows that he shouldn't be taking anything Thais said seriously (all of it being her grief talking), but then again there's a part of him that feels a bit hurt. Before meeting Maeve, he always filled that sister-sibling role with Thais and Zenaida. One was younger and one was older. And while he's no Amir, he always believed that he was their brother. Selfish of him to be thinking about his own feelings when one of his closest friends had just been killed. Maybe it's his way of mourning—move on without expressing the feelings that were slowly but surely collecting into this big pool of darkness. Hiding his hands behind his back, he uses his nails to begin picking at the skin around his fingers.

"Listen, I know this is a terrible time in our lives right now. We lost someone so dear to us, and I promise—I promise, that this hurts me too. But tearing each other down is only making everything worse " Thais snaps her neck, throwing her glare at Ms. Loom instead. It didn't sound like she was sorry for Amir at all. She was standing there, hands flailing as she defended a woman who popped into their lives four or five days ago. The teenager doesn't know whether or not she's angry that her brother isn't getting the recognition he deserves, or astounded that Amora Loom's loyalty had moved on so fast. Amora spent years personally getting to know her and her brother. She doesn't know anything about Maeve. It's insulting. "We must keep our heads, or else it'll make it that much easier for the Raba to succeed."

If Thais could scream, her voice would be hoarse and everyone would be covering their ears.

"How can you say that!?" Her disbelief covered her pretty features. Tears of animosity were showing again, and she was quick to wipe them away. "How can you stand there and just..." For a moment she had to rack her brain, millions of thoughts jumbling together into a spiral of things she wants to say but can't. "It's as though Amir meant nothing to you. Like we didn't just invest so much of our lives into you!"

"That is not what I meant, and you should know that. I loved Amir like he was my own. I love all of you as such."

"I don't believe you" Thais shakes her head. Her hands tremble but then again so does her entire body. She wipes at her brown eyes once more but what was the use? The tears kept coming and there was no telling when they would stop. Ms. Loom felt her heart squeeze. This wasn't the Thais that she recognizes. She looked so fragile standing there—any moment she was about to collapse, shatter like a vase falling from a sturdy table. Gosh, why must she kick the legs of it? Why must she just stand there and watch as the delicate piece of glass slowly falls. Amora attempted to reach out and catch her, save Thais from crashing into a million different pieces. But the teenage girl stepped away, refusing to be held by someone who she wanted to trust so desperately. "I can't be here. I don't want to be here."

"You can't just leave" Gabe interjects. He approaches, hand reaching out to grip onto the other's wrist. It stops her from running into the forest that was whispering her name. "It's guaranteed that the Raba knows who you are. The Junud probably have our faces plastered all over, and who knows who might try to hurt you. You're not safe on your own."

"I'm not asking for your permission" She snatched her arm back before turning on the heels of her shoes. And with a speed that was unmatched, she was dashing past the greenery. Gabe turned to see if anyone was going to say something; ask that she stop, maybe even go after her. But they all kept still. Either they glanced away to avoid contact, or they watched the spot where the girl once stood.

"None of you are going to go after her?" Irritation could be seen morphing onto his face. His hands balled into tight fists, knuckles beginning to turn white. He hid them behind his back, more truth on how he feels coming forward in his actions then the words that were getting caught by this tongue. "Micah? Ms. Loom?"

"She should be fine" Micah mumbles. He refuses to make eye contact, sight solely focused on the way that a particular tree to the left swayed as if dancing with the wind. He tried not to cringe at the way Gabe roared. He stomps his way over to the leader, and it's then that brown meets brown.

"What the fuck do you mean!?"

"If I'm being honest, it's highly unlikely that she'll be harmed. The Raba wants Maeve only. The only ones who really need to watch their back are the ones who are at the core of this all, which is Maeve, me, Ms. Loom and Emry. Thais will be fine" Micah rolled his shoulders back as he gave a once over to Gabe's flexed build. "Now you need to stand down. And that's an order."

Gabe let out a snicker.

"Are you serious right now!? Anyone could recognize her and use her as bait! Are you that much of a selfish douchebag to not be concerned for her!?"

"What did I just say about insults?" Amora exclaims.

He refuses to be disrespectful to the elderly, therefore he snaps his lips shut and rolls his eyes instead. He finally takes that step back from Micah.

"I'm not saying I'm not concerned. Thais is like a sister to me-"

"Then how dare you just stand there!?"

"Because I already said that there's an unlikely chance that the Raba, or the Junud are going to go after her. Thais isn't stupid. She knows to keep a low profile."

"Doesn't mean she's safe!" Gabe shouts again. Looking closely, you would be able to see that the tips of his ears were shading the same red as his cheeks. His hostility was becoming apparent. Micah stared. He was completely unbothered that one of his companions looked ready to throw a fist and land it anywhere for as long it caused harm. "And if none of you plan on going after her, then I will."

"Gabe..." Rowan tries.

"You can stop me, but not her?" A scoff. His grin was sarcastic. "Unbelievable."

And without another word, without another glance, Gabe was taking off in the same direction Thais went.

Chapter Nineteen

The silence between them was awkward now. No one dared say a word as they circled one another; the vigor in the conversation being too much for all of them, and now they couldn't keep still. Lucas paced the same spot. His steps had been so repetitive, so strong and heavy, that looking down at the grass anyone would be able to see the indent he had created. The ground was warped and his shoes were starting to get muddy with uneven grass clippings. Not even the soothing words of Zenaida could stop him from getting so caught up in his head. Foster kept opening and closing his mouth like a gaping fish, body and brain fighting against each other about whether or not he should go over and comfort Micah. It's not promised that he'd respond well, possibly still sour from their exchange in the forest—the rejection of their souls entwining. Foster just hopes that Micah understands.

He decided that he'll leave the talking to Ms. Loom while he takes everyone's silence as a moment to mourn his best friend

He drops beside the glistening pond, fingers reaching in to touch the cool water. He sighs when seeing some of the small fish swim away.

"Please don't beat yourself up about this" Ms. Loom almost whispers when approaching Micah. She delicately places a wrinkled hand to his arm, thumb creating circles against his skin. He's grown so much. He once was such a tiny baby being cradled in her arms. When he'd cry, Amora would scoop him up and place soft kisses to his temple before whispering anything and everything relating to him being safe with her. It could have been the hums of a lullaby, or the fact that he was a naive child, but within seconds he would clamp his lips shut and stare up at her with tearful round eyes. It'd be impossible for Micah to curl up in her lap now. So the best she could do is bring him in for a hug, keeping their embrace tight so all of her love could be felt even after they separated. "There's no way you could have known that things would turn out this way. You're thinking with your head like you should be. Once all of this is over, I promise we'll all have the chance to let our hearts experience everything it feels and more."

"Amir's dead because of me."

"No, Amir's dead because of himself" She cups Micah's face, his droopy eyes finally locking onto hers. Her chest tightens. She always hated seeing him so upset. "He made the decision to go after Maeve. He made the decision to fight those pixies. His fate was sealed the same time he made up his mind. The only thing you did was be a leader."

"Doesn't make the losing of a pack member any better. I could have done a little more. Maybe if I had-"

"You couldn't have done anything" The duo looked to the left to see that it was Maeve. She was stuck in place; feet planted to the grassy ground as she looked at nothing. Her vision kept forward, eyeing anything and everything that was in front of her. She saw the swaying trees, saw the way that the sun was slowly rising from the horizon, could even see the two people that she was addressing with her words. But her dull brown eyes never deterred from the line that they had created. She had become captured by her own mind.

This; all of this, was her fault.

It kept repeating, eventually becoming a chant that she found herself mumbling slowly to herself. And it's something that she'll keep saying for as long as needed, even willing to say it to Micah so he doesn't—not for a second—think that any of this was his doing.

This; all of this, was her fault.

"Amir didn't want to be saved. Believe me, I tried all that I could."

Maeve moved. Or well her eyes did. They looked at Micah and Amora. But she wasn't the same. They appeared to have aged everyday that she had been in Kariq Leada—the once mix of marvelous browns, draining into a pit of darkness where one isn't able to know if they are naturally that dull. And she may have been looking at her twin brother alongside his guardian, but they couldn't feel the stare. It was going right through them; or going past them; or her sight just wasn't there at all. She had become a shell, and now her body needs to catch up with her new mentality.

All of this was real. All of this was happening to her right now, and there's no way that she can deflect any longer. She witnessed a man die right before her eyes. She watched a woman bleed, because she was the one to have her doing so. All of this power, this strength—creatures and monsters—the fight between good and bad—all of it was real and Maeve needs to accept that this is her life. Her choices matter, they create the path she will be walking on. And depending on whether or not she wants to live through this prophecy or not, she needs to start making smart ones.

"I could have tried to find you guys sooner. You wouldn't have had to fight alone."

"So both of you could end up poisoned and dead?" *I would have lost three people.* It was hard to read what exactly Maeve was feeling, but a part of Micah knew it had to do with remorse. And sadness. And anger. "I know I'm the last person who should be saying this, because I'm still learning the logistics of your guys' realm—that all of this could even exist outside of a movie," She chuckled dryly. And for a second she looks at the rest of the pack. They all look so disconnected. Just like how she feels. "But everything that happens is calculated. All of you are so calculated. And a part of me knows that Amir dying wasn't because one of us made a mistake. There shouldn't be any blame placed. Just the celebration of who Amir was."

"You speak as though you knew him" Lucas spits. He's held back when Zenadia holds his arm. So he keeps scowling. "You met him a few days ago. You don't know that he deserved way more than what he got."

"I'm not saying that."

"Instead you're trying to make us all forgive you for luring him to his death. Had he not vouched for you, he wouldn't be lying breathless somewhere. You're right, Micah shouldn't blame himself, we should all be blaming you."

The way his eyes blazed with a fiery madness would have

pinched Maeve's heart yesterday. She probably would have cowarded away from how he was barking at her, shrink away into a
ball of the imagery of him ripping her throat out with animosity.
But with their distance, with what she's experienced in the many
hours that she's spent in this new world, it's hard for her to
feel any fear from the man. It only made her want to stand her
ground even further. Prove that she isn't the enemy.

"You're missing the point-"

Lucas pushed his wife off of him and stomped his way over to
Maeve. She won't lie and say that her heart didn't jump a bit, that
her stomach didn't bubble with an ounce of fear from a frightening monster, but she stayed standing. Her stare hardened to
match his, and she puffed her chest trying to assert just as much
dominance as the man who towered over her like a building to a
pedestrian. She wasn't going to let this man intimidate her any
longer. He didn't know her, and she didn't know him. And if he
just for a second let his pride fall, then they could reach common
ground and maybe even be friends.

"You killed one of my friends!"

"No, a pixie did. So the only person you should be angry with
is the now pile of dust on one of the streets. Or be angry at the
people who sent them."

"If you didn't-"

"That's enough, Lucas!" Micah shouts. Words got caught in
the older man's throat then, hands balling into fists so tight that
he began to shake. He huffed out a breath before turning around
and stalking back over to his wife. She is almost instantly reaching out to comfort him. Maeve wants to roll her eyes yet keeps
them forward. Lucas is a man-child who needs to release his

emotions in other ways than hostility. "This topic shall now be dropped and we will revisit the unfortunate news that is a fellow friend's death once the prophecy has been avoided. I promise Amir Miller's life will never be forgotten."

"Prophecy?"

Heads whipped around to see little girl Olivia peeking from behind Zenaida.

"Forgot about her" Rowan says.

Maeve personally couldn't forget about someone she was never introduced to.

"We should just leave her here and hope for the best," Foster grumbles. He got an evil stare from Zenadia, arms immediately wrapping around the frail frame of the little girl. Foster smirks as he shrugs.

"My mommy talks about prophecies all the time. She says that they can be really helpful but also really dangerous."

"Mom?" Emry whispers. She crosses her arms over her chest, thoughts immediately swirling and plans already forming.

"What else does your mom talk about?" Zenaida says sweetly. She bends to Olivia's height, gently taking hold of one her hands. "Does she say anything about the Raba?"

It's a bit weird to interrogate a child, but then again this is a major hint to where the Oracle may be. If assumptions are correct, this child is the descendent of the all knowing.

Olivia nods her head.

"Mommy talks about them a lot with dad. They always get so angry. Say they're bad people" She tilts her head, sparkling eyes looking up at the sky as she uses one of her tiny fingers to tap at her chin. "She also whispers to herself a lot. Especially while sitting in front of a mirror. She asks me not to interrupt her when she's working. Says what she's doing is really important, but I think it's because I'm clumsy and mommy likes to keep a lot of candles lit."

The joy the pack had gotten from the rambling of a child was far more than enough to refill them with a new hope. Through all of this darkness, finally...*finally* they were getting some light.

"Is it okay if we talk with your mom? When we bring you back? It's really important and she might be able to help us" Emry's asking while approaching the little girl. Her fast behavior scared Olivia, and she was a bit hesitant to respond.

"O-Okay" She batted her long eyelashes, bottom lip protruding into a pout.

"Okay great! Then let's get a move on! Which way would you say you saw your family last?" Amora wonders at the same time that she jogs over.

Again, the hastiness of it all was enough to have Olivia hiding away. She whimpered, clinging to the back of Zenaida's legs. It was obvious that she didn't like the way Ms. Loom approached with an aggressive take on happiness, and so the elderly lady giggled while making distance between them. "Sorry, it's just that we really want to find this treasure of ours. And we're hoping that she can help us. It sounds like she's really smart."

"It's okay," The child whispers. Then she's pointing to the right. "I think we were camping that way."

Chapter Twenty

"Thais! Thais! Stop running and listen to me!" Gabe shouts. While he liked to consider himself a rather fit guy, he was beginning to feel the burn within his legs. Having had to chase after a person who was already so far ahead, he pushed just a little bit more past his limit in order to catch up. Sweat dribbled down his temple and his lungs gasped for air. Thais' figure was a blur in the wild forest, slim body blending in with millions of trees and large leaves. If It wasn't for the bright red shirt she wore, light-washed blue jeans being paired with it, then Gabe guarantees that he would've lost her.

No, he wouldn't. He couldn't. One whiff to the air and he would be able to pick her scent from a crowded room. Finding her in a place where everything smelled like dirt and the occasional flower, pfft, light work. Citron, jasmine, and teakwood. Inhaling she invaded his nostrils. She was to the left of him, a good distance in front. It wouldn't take long before she reached the city again. Hopefully none of the Junud are nearby. If it's true that they do have pictures of each of the pack members, if they were told to memorize their faces, the poor girl will be taken before she even realizes. The horrific thought of them torturing her for answers turned a flame on within Gabe's stomach. He'd personally rip the Raba limb from limb if they laid a finger to her head.

So he must stop her before she gets too far.

He looked left then right. He glanced up at a tall tree, checking the angles of which he could climb and then jump from. Maybe if he climbs and then dashes from tree to tree, he'd be able to land a few feet in front of Thais. Right before she renenters the city. So with a heavy breath leaving his nose, he pushed himself just a little bit harder, building momentum. Then with a jump, he grabbed onto a thick tree branch, swinging himself forward. It was a force that had him flying through the air, and with just his luck he was able to catch a glimpse of Thais. She must have known that one of her pack members was following, because suddenly she's picking up speed. She wished to be alone. Just for a moment she wanted to rest and let her head wraparound what is going on in her life. Unfortunately her urgency only makes Gabe more dedicated, almost desperate to reach her and be the one to help level her head. She wasn't thinking clearly—this all from grief, the sadness that her brother will never return to her, and the guilt that there was nothing she could have done.

The wind attacked Gabe's face as he raced to keep pace with the girl. His coarse hands gripped onto rough bark while his feet wobbled when he sought balance. There was one particular tree that he underestimated. It was rotten, dying second by second, and yet blurred by the need to reach Thais, he took his chances by jumping onto the nearest branch that he could reach. One minute he was almost touching the clouds and the next he was feeling his heart pounding as his stomach sunk. His arms flailed, reaching for anything to keep him afloat. But with the speed that he was falling, everything snapped and began its journey down alongside him. He tried to hide the way that he was scared. Instead of letting his brown eyes tremble, he had shut them completely. And he willed away his screams, clamping down on his tongue—but couldn't contain the shout when his back was being slammed into a thick branch, his heavyweight breaking through it. So he released his howls, letting it be the last time he was heard for he ultimately met his demise against the hard cold ground. He should have never laughed at Rowan.

Karma. Sucks ass.

He crashed. He laid still as the wind was knocked out of him.

As Gabe was sprawled out, the image of Thais was the last thing his mind lets him remember. Only as he lay where he is, he couldn't help but think what splattering from a height that large would feel like. Surely not like this. He thought it to be non-painful. It'd be a quick death, where the last thing he was allowed to do was shout for help. It wasn't supposed to be lumpy, squishable, even warm. His fingers twitched. He felt what he laid upon, expecting the unsettling feeling of grass. Instead this was much softer. Much smoother.

His body rumbled and his ears were met with a few animalistic sounds. Before he knew it, he was being moved, large form hitting the real ground with a grunt.

"You're heavy as shit."

"God, is that you?"

Blinking his eyes open, the sun struck him directly in the face, blinding him. He attempted to block the light, but his body felt immobile and he could only groan at the blows he took. For a moment he believed this to be the part where he begins to cross over. He laid on his back, limbs just barely stretching as he matched one of a cartoon character where their soul ascends from their body.

"Oh wow, you must have hit your head on the way down."

The sun no longer burned Gabe's face. It was being blocked by a figure that looked strangely like Thais. She stared down at him with the sun shining just perfectly over her head, that it resembled one of a halo. He must be seeing angels. Hopefully he gets to meet Kariq Leada's king. What a pleasure that would be. For now he'll just be glad that he gets to at least have someone familiar help him climb towards the sky. So with a shaky hand he reaches to touch Thais' pretty face, hand cupping her cheek. She smiled down at him as though he's gone insane.

"I'm glad it's you."

"What are you talking about? You're not dead" She smacks his hand away, the action pulling him from whatever daze he placed himself in. Then almost instantly Gabe is shooting upright, head snapping back and forth as he checks his surroundings. After touching his body and seeing that he was kept planted and not suddenly floating, he snaps his neck in the direction of Thais. He watches as she fixes her shirt, watches as she too looks around before a grin is reaching her lips and she's jogging over to pick up a sneaker that was sticking out of a bush. She hopped on one foot as she struggled to put the shoe back on.

"What happened?"

"What do you mean? I saved you" It was said as she walked back over to him. The curly brown hair that she attempted to wrap into something cascaded back down to shoulder length when she reached out to help pull Gabe to his feet. "I shifted and broke your fall. May have bruised my spine, but you're welcome."

He chuckled as she made an animated pained face.

"Yeah, thank you" They shared a smile. "Why'd you do it though? You were so close to-"

"I couldn't let another person I care about just—I smelled that you were in danger and came running. Luckily I caught you in time" She took a few steps back, and Gabe reached out slightly before letting his arm fall back to his side. Whether Thais caught the movement or not she bothered not to speak about it. Instead her smile became crooked and she urged for an escape. "I'm still leaving. Don't follow me, and don't try to persuade me to come back."

"Why not?" He took a step and she moved her sight off his saddened eyes. "Being alone at a time like this isn't safe. Who knows what might happen to you."

"I refuse to be around people who make it seem like Amir was just another person walking down the street. He was my brother Gabe, one of your best friends. You can't stand there and make it seem as though I'm being irrational right now!"

"I'm not."

"So what if something happens to me? At least I'll have properly mourned my family before I join him."

"Don't you dare speak like that!" Thais was a bit startled from Gabe's shout. Was a bit startled by the way that he randomly appeared in front of her, toe to toe, hands gripping her arms and bringing her close enough that their chests were pressed together. They stared one another in the eye, brown clashing with brown in this search where they tried to read each other's thoughts. But of course only so much can get across from simply looking at another, and if they wished to properly communicate they needed to open their mouths. Gabe sighs, lifts his grip and removes himself from in front of the girl. "I'm sorry. It's just-" And for a brief moment he's reminded of all those years ago.

Looking through the crack of the bedroom within his old family home. There's tears streaming down his face as there's so much red. On the floor, in the bathtub, lining the once so tan and beautiful skin of his lifeless mother. He didn't know what to do then. He was scared and alone. Should he have checked on her earlier? Should he have seen the signs? Maybe. Wouldn't have made him feel so useless—naive him searching for someone to hold him and tell him that he's going to be okay. It wasn't until he fell into the hands of Ms. Loom that he knew what he saw was traumatic. Yet it can also be used for the future. He can stop others from doing the same, no matter how they choose to. And he was doing so by attending conventions and events, discussing such heavy topics with others who may have been on either side of the spectrum. So excuse him for getting riled up. He didn't mean to get aggressive. He already lost his mother and an amazing friend. He refuses to hand over Thais as well.

"I just don't think you should speak like that when you still have so much to live for. And I know saying that isn't going to magically change your perspective, but it's the truth. You're not wrong to be upset about Amir, I agree that the pack should have handled his death way differently than how they did...but you also can't go running out into danger because of that anger. The last thing any of us want is for you to leave us too."

Gabe's shoulders slumped and he heaved a sigh.

"If I can't stop you from leaving, then I'm coming with you. I can't just sit back and let you run face first into dan-" He was cut off by Thais wrapping her arms around him in a tight hug. "-ger."

"Thank you" She whispers and Gabe could feel his body warm. He smiles at the sight of her clinging to him and he too wraps his arms around her.

It was tranquil then. There wasn't a worrisome thought.

Then bushes rustled, there was an ache in the temple...darkness.

Oomph! Rowan was whacked in the face by a giant green leaf. It had to have been just a bit bigger than his head, also covered in the morning condensation so droplets of water splashed onto his lips and cheeks. He aggressively takes the piece of nature and rips it from its stem, feeling the nectar leak onto his palm as if bleeding. Blondie tosses it to the ground with a final glare, but his narrowed eyes and lips pressed into a line eventually trail up the long figure that is Lucas. The older had been the culprit; walking in front of him and initially being the one to push anything blocking the view. But Lucas Davis is also an asshole. So while he did use his abnormally large hands to clear a path for his wife, his care for anyone else had become just like the broken leaf that was slowly becoming buried by dirt. And maybe if this *was* the first time that it happened, Rowan would have just let it go—he would have mumbled curses and then secretly formed an attack of revenge. But *no*, this had been the fifth time Lucas let Rowan get smacked by some stupid piece of nature. The only good that came out of the leaf is that it wasn't as harmful as the few branches that struck his nose. He wouldn't be surprised if a bright red and purple bruise had blossomed on the bridge, contrasting against his lighter skin. And while he was already upset that he continuously got hit due to Lucas' inattentional blindness, he was embarrassed. It's embarrassing to have a pretty girl walk beside him and then without warning be struck in the face by a giant leaf! It's only right that he exaggerates how much this has affected him.

"Dude! Can you maybe warn a guy before you let the shit go!?" He rubbed at his nose, too, wiping away some of the water that still clung to his skin. Lucas glances back, met with the menacing stare of Rowan. He snickers, yet still feigns innocence as if he didn't even know that his friend was being whacked. And at first maybe he didn't. He kept his attention on the trail in front of him, following behind his pack leader and Olivia (a little girl who occasionally mixes up her left and her right). So blaming him for the first or second time was tolerable. The third, fourth and fifth...it's unlikely that he didn't hear the way Rowan dragged out his pain.

"Oh relax, it's not like I knew you were being hit."

"I bet you didn't. You're always so far up Zenaida's ass. Tell me, do you bring a flashlight? I would assume it's pretty dark in there" It wasn't necessarily the funniest joke, but it did get a few chuckles out of Maeve. Hopefully it'll erase the memory of him and his new hatred for any greenery. Lucas on the other hand didn't take too kindly to the response and was whipping around. He had a fist balled up, knuckles clenching as he raised it into the air. He was ready to throw a punch; using violence and anger to communicate like always. It's a worrisome trait that he refuses to talk about. It's believed to be connected to his years before the pack.

To a family that refuses to speak about.

But before he could lay the hit, Olivia was heard shouting with glee.

"There it is! Our tent!" She excitedly pointed to a red triangular tent that contrasted against all of the green and brown. Rowan blew out a relieved breath. He had just been saved. Lucas was forced to back down and return his attention to the more pressing issue that is to bring a little girl back to her family...*and* hopefully speak to her mother. "Mom! Dad! I'm back!" She let go of Micah's hand, running off without heeding the warning that she needed to be careful. The closer they got to the campsite, the more deserted it looked. The firepit had been put to rest; the once perfectly stacked branches now a burnt mess. The plastic cooler of food had been tipped; snacks and beverages were spilled, and ice that hadn't already melted was sprawled about. Even a foldable table had been broken in half, contents of a board game thrown all over and ripped.

"Olivia, I don't think-"

The tent rustled about, the zipper moving down and giving everyone seconds before another person was about to be revealed. Quickly Micah and Zenaida were the first to begin guarding the child, pulling her behind them where she squeals and a new spark of fear racing through her chest. Defense mode was activated within the adults and if Micah hadn't already learned his lesson with Olivia, he would have jumped the bones of the person who left the tent. Instead he stayed put. Everyone did, waiting to see the face of what is presumed to be a man.

"Daddy!" Olivia yells in delight. She squirms out of Zenaida's protective grip and then dashes into her father's unexpecting arms. He looked surprised and utterly thankful when he felt the warmth of his only daughter back in his arms. He thought he lost her forever. He thought the Raba skeemed a plan, and the most valuable thing they could have taken from him was his pride and joy. But she was back, and she was well. She appeared to be just as excited to see him as he is her. They engulfed each other in the tightest hug, a few tears having even been seen leaving the corners of his eyes.

"Oh my darling, I thought they took you. I thought they'd robbed me of one of my most precious jewels."

"I'm fine dad. These people helped me" Olivia motioned to the pack of werewolves that collectively emerged from the forest and stood tall. While their nature came off intimidating and confident, they had provided nothing but warm greetings and precious smiles. The man nodded, silently thanking them for the protection of his daughter. He'd have to thank them verbally when they've settled. "Where's mother?"

Olivia's father grew stiff. He looked to the left, eyes now shaking and distant. Slowly his arms unwrapped from his daughter and it was obvious that his mind was suddenly captured by something that he doesn't know if he should say. The poor child looks left then right. She stands on the tips of her toes, round eyes searching over her father's shoulder because just maybe her mother is hiding behind him. Olivia didn't let her disappointment show when there was nothing but more forest. Instead she bounced slightly before making a mad dash for the still standing tent. And it was almost as if she had gone deaf because she refused to listen to the way that her only guardian was telling her to wait.

"Olivia my darling, I have something to tell you. Something devastating."

It was extremely easy to hear the way the father's heart was ripping into two.

"Mom's not in the tent, did she return home?"

She was curious as she approached her dad once more, melting into the arms that lifted her into them and cradled with a love that he hopes she can feel even days after. Micah and his pack had gotten closer, ears peered for whatever was about to be said. Because while they did the noble thing and returned a child to their family, they are now able to fulfill a personal mission.

The tall man let out a breath as he slowly pulled a purple crystal from his pants pocket. It dangled from a silver chain—a makeshift one that the man must have scrambled together in order to keep the gem safe. Maeve was almost immediately entranced by the beautiful piece of jewelry. The color, the sparkle, the glamor of it reminded her of the precious earrings she saw in the mall. She felt drawn to it. Her legs began to move and her fingers itched to touch the precious crystal. But before she was able to walk over to the small family, her wrist was being grabbed by Emry that almost had her tripping. It also broke the hypnosis the gem had on her; Maeve blinking as she looked at Emry with slight confusion.

"Olivia..." The man sighed. "I unfortunately have to relay the news that your mother...she's been cursed. She's now trapped in this very crystal" He raised the gem to his daughter's eyes. The purple glimmered in front of her irises; and no one is able to tell whether or not she's in awe or about to cry from devastation. Her tiny fingers slowly reached out, just barely touching the cold crystal before she retracted much faster. Her bottom lip protruded and her round eyes started to blur over with fresh tears. "I'm sorry darling, I tried to save her, but the bad guys— you remember them right?" Olivia shook her head, wiping the falling tears from her eyes. "The bad guys were just too hard to fight off."

The small child wrapped her arms around her father again, burying her face in his neck as she let her sobs free. Her frail form shook and that's when her father began to calm her with soothing words and gentle pats to her back. The man looked up from his daughter, gaze falling on the group of bystanders. He was a bit confused about why they still stood before him, he wondered what they could have needed when they already returned Olivia to him. He looked all of them over. None looked like a poseable threat—none looked like they were ready to steal whatever was left at the campsite. Then his eyes landed on Maeve. His breath hitched. He knows now.

Olivia cried for what felt like hours but was only a few minutes. Her distress managed to whisk her to sleep, where eventually she lay comfortably in her father's arm, trails of tear stains lining her cheeks. So he brought her to the tent. The small family disappeared behind the flaps, and that's when the group moved in closer. They looked at the destroyed camp. It was unsettling to witness what the Raba or Junud had possibly done to what was supposed to be a fun family event. Now it was just a heap of dirt and trash, almost everything a broken mess. Emry trailed a finger over what was supposed to be a badminton net (and

now was nothing more than a tangled mess and snapped poles).
Rowan sniffed about the tipped over coolers, stomach growling
slightly from the smell of frozen foods. It was a new morning
and he hadn't eaten anything yet. And needing to fulfill that
hunger, he secretly ripped open a bag of sandwich meat before
scarfing it down. Maeve and Zenaida saw from the corner of
their eye and gave matching disgusted looks. Blondie took notice
of his audience and grew red ears. But that didn't stop him from
swallowing what was left in his mouth, knees bending so he was
able to lift a dented soda can from under a tree branch.

"What?" He cracks the tab open before tilting his head back
where he's able to chug the beverage. It was when there had to
be a gulp left that he outstretched the can and offered the rest
to one of the women. They immediately shook their heads with
grimaces growing deeper. Rowan shrugged before downing the
rest. Once he was done he crushed the metal cylinder within his
palm before tossing it over his shoulder. Appears that he isn't
one for the environment.

The father of Olivia reappears from the tent. He was reticent,
but there must have been millions of thoughts, millions of questions that bustled about within his head. Micah approached the
deadpan of a man first, the rest following. It was when the group
was close enough that a book was then pulled from under his
arm. It was wrapped in leather, worn and torn from years of use.
The gold detailing—swirls and stars, loops and what could have
been cursive writing—was what kept the old piece of literature
looking decent enough to capture the eye of any passersby. It
was definitely interesting enough to make Emry want to touch
it, her older fingers tracing the spine of the thick pages. A tiny

smile could be seen reaching her face, ounces of pleasure tingling her toes as she felt the bumps of what was obviously something handcrafted. She couldn't wait to dive deep into all of the mysteries and words that were written on all of the pages. Pages that had become ripped and an ugly tan color, splotted with ink and other indescribable marks.

"It belonged to my wife" The father waved his hand within a circular motion, and then not even seconds later the broken picnic table had been repaired. He dropped the book upon it with a heavy thud, then swiping any dirt or dust from the cover. There was no title, just the creepy molding of a blue eyeball. Maeve shrieked when she saw it move, startling the rest. Olivia's father chuckled. "Maybe I should introduce us...the name's Arnold Tume, and this here is Haya. But he doesn't like to go by such an official title. Call him Yaya, he responds well to it."

"Who would have thought books have preferences?" Foster snickers.

"Well of course. It's truly believed that almost everything here in Kariq Leada is alive. Whether you know or not is up to them."

Lucas scoffed while crossing his arms.

"I highly doubt *everything*—not this rock-" Lucas is the next one to let out a scream. Having tried to prove his point he picks up the nearest rock that was beside his feet. Then he smugly looks from the older man to the mineral within his hands. Never in his life would he have expected to be connecting gazes with a rock. It was staring at him, blinking with a stare so blank it might as well have been staring right through him. It was oddly unsettling and he was quick to throw it across the camp. There was laughter and teasing, with Foster and Rowan using their fingers to poke him as if other pieces of nature were slowly creeping up on him. "Thirty-four years of living and *never* have I looked a rock in the eye before!"

"Our entire city would be converted into buildings and technology if the people knew that natural entities like trees and rocks lived. Fear would spark and with that fear would come chaos. Now don't get me wrong, there are a few of us who know the truth, but if the entire city knew, the Raba would get involved. And with the powers that my wife possess, she needs all the magic she can get."

"I have so many questions," Micah says through a breath. "How do you have the Haya, I thought the Raba did?"

"No matter how hard you try to secure this kind of magic, it always returns to its owner."

"And your wife...she's the Oracle?"

Arnold looks him in the eye. They stare at each other for a moment, the elder debating whether or not speaking the truth would cause great harm to his daughter. He gives when catching sight of Maeve from his peripheral vision.

"Yes. But you must not share this information with anyone. No one but the Raba knows who we are. If anyone were to catch sight of us, we are to say that we are just a family of witches."

"Why? It's to believe that your wife is one of the most powerful beings in all the realms" Emry asks. "Us witches worshiped the Oracle from a young age. She is everything we wished to be."

"The same reason you came to find her" Arnold states lowly. His eyes glaze over with this anger and then he's shaking his head. He opens the Haya and begins to hastily flip through the hundreds of pages. It's quite impressive to see that each old sheet of paper was written from top to bottom with print small enough you might need a magnifying glass. Whatever was written in the book must be written with grave detail. "Once the king had passed and the Raba began to rule, we were forced into hiding. No one was to dare look for us, because any random person may be the key to their demise."

Arnold stopped at a particular page. In big cursive letters: Micah Whitmore could be seen writing itself on the page. They were in shining gold letters as they appeared, sealing in a normal black ink when finished. And then within a second, the rest of the page and the one after it was being stamped with more detailed calligraphy.

"What is it saying?" Micah asks with wide eyes. He wanted to drag his fingers over his name. He was wondering how a book is able to do such a thing...know who he is.

"Your existence," Amora says. "The Haya-" Pages flipped sporadically, eventually landing on a part of the book where it looked as though a page had been torn from it.

"Yaya."

"Right, Yaya. It can tell you anything and everything. So with one breath, it would be able to tell you every time you took one since the day you were born" Amora continues. "But I'm quite shocked to see this...I thought it was impossible to destroy this piece of literature."

Arnold touches the ripped page, dragging his finger along the jagged edges of where it used to be. And then with a motion that looked as though he was pulling a string, emerging from the book was the missing piece of paper. Everyone watched in astonishment. Which is a bit surprising in itself. Maeve should be the only one who has her jaw to the floor. She didn't get to witness the mythical and magical things that can happen with a flick of the wrist. The others did. And yet here they were profoundly watching a page of a book float through the sky and land in the hands of the same person who didn't believe any of this was real two days ago.

"Only the Oracle can create a mark of any kind. And this tear had been the last note she made before her unfortunate entrapment" Maeve looked down at the paper resting between her fingers. It felt thin enough that if she touched it too much then it would dissolve. She and everyone else was staring at the back. There was nothing on it. Just a blank sheet that had obviously seen better days. But as she was getting ready to flip it over, see if the other side matched this one, it began to glow. "My wife, she always talked about some prophecy. Said in due time that there will be a confrontation of some kind between two powerful people" The glow calmed into a light shimmer where golden words were being written on the sheet in real time. There was no pen putting them there, and there was no hand raised in order to magically scribble. It only took a few seconds, a minute at most before the paper stopped glowing and it had yet again been a simple piece of paper.

One that cannot be contained shall be filled with darkness
Destroyed by the truth, terror shall be the demise of all
Rising throughout the rubble there is a chance of survival
Light is the balance
Only one, fatality is life

"Well that doesn't sound good at all" Rowan says as he leans just a bit closer to Maeve, looking over her shoulder in order to see the words for himself.

He gets a light punch to his shoulder by Foster, to which blondie throws one back. Why must he get assaulted for saying the truth? He couldn't have been the only one who felt an overwhelming sense of insecurity. He couldn't have been the only one who suddenly felt his chest go tight from uncertainty. If that was Maeve's prophecy, they should all be worried least a little bit. They don't know what any of what was read means. They could guess every possible answer, and they'll only be able to figure it out when the time comes. Another issue that they have: they have no idea when this prophecy is supposed to take place!

"I wish I could tell you more about it, but my lovely crystal for a wife holds all the answers," Arnold attempts at a joke but it only lands with Rowan. He lets out a snicker behind his hand. Maeve stands beside him though, stoic like the others. She narrows her brown eyes on the paper within her fingers, pink lips moving slowly as she mouths the words to herself. She was hoping that the repetition would give her a clue, give her something within her distant memory that would make all of this make sense. But the longer she stood there flickering back and forth through the sentences, nothing more than a headache was being brought on. So she huffed, shaking her head and then belligerently flipping the paper around.

Maeve came face to face with her own face. It was a drawing —with black ink and thin lines, the details of her facial features were staring back at her; almost as though she was staring in the mirror. It was astounding, and it made that little part of her that was still in disbelief about all of this excited. Her stomach flipped and she briefly glanced up at the rest of the group, wondering if they were all looking at the same thing. Luckily she wasn't the only one a bit stunned. Micah looked the most intrigued with the picture. His sight was glued to the paper. His lips were pressed firmly in a line. There was confusion behind the expression; as if he wasn't looking at a portrait of his twin sister. It almost appears as though he was expecting something else. Maeve tried not to think about it too hard though; refocusing on the paper and how this is the one thing that proves that this is what her life is.

"Wow, Yaya even managed to capture that little twinkle you always have in the corner of your eyes" Rowan blurts with a soft smile. Red flush covered Maeve's cheeks, darkening and growing hotter when she caught Rowan's gaze. She quickly turns away, rushing to hand Arnold back the piece of paper.

"Did your wife tell you anything else? Anything that can help us?"

"I'm afraid not. But this prophecy," He exhaled. "Understand that it's a lot bigger than what's being presented to you. It's not as simple as a hero defeating a villain. Mental casualties are inevitable."

Emry steps forward, gently pushing Maeve behind her.

"You have no knowledge about any of this? A clue of any would be extremely helpful."

Arnold carefully places the paper back inside the book.

"The only thing I can remember is her constantly rambling about the Prism."

"The Prism?" Amora couldn't hold back her gasp. She scurried to stand beside Emry, whacking her wrinkly hand against

Arnold's bicep. "As in, can suck in any magical entity, *that* prism?" There was barely a nod before Amora was squealing in happiness. "Oh how I've always wanted to see it in person! It's such a powerful weapon disguised as something so casual. It's magnificent!"

"Uh, please explain for all of the confused people in the back," Zenaida says. Her hand was raised but then it's dropping back to her side when Amora is whipping around to face her with sheer joy. It was a bit surprising and Zenaida was not expecting the way Ms. Loom bounced over and shook her with force. She felt like a fizzy bottle of soda by the end of it.

"The Prism is exactly as it sounds. It's this giant crystal, bigger than my palm" She holds out her hand and uses the other to reference a point. "And with a spell, a chant, whatever you wish to be locked away for all of eternity, said thing or person will be pulled into the prism and unable to be set free. Ah! It's a witch's dream to be able to hold it...even if it's for a second."

"Sounds like a fancier version of a prison" Foster states.

"It's not," Emry replies. "While inside, you are punished. Depending on your moralities depicts your fate. And if we manage to trap the Raba with it, I can guarantee you they will face consequences as gruesome as having your body melted layer upon layer" There were looks of fear and disgust. "It's all an illusion of course. So while you do feel the pain and agony that is your skin peeling from your bones, that's all it is."

"How does one stay on your good side?" Rowan wonders. He got a few chuckles, but seriousness was seen hidden behind his emerald irises.

"Okay so what about this Prism? Do you know why the Oracle

would have mentioned it?" Micah continues the conversation. He crosses his buff arms over his chest, an eagerness creasing his forehead and making his eyebrows downturn. Arnold's looking at him quietly again. Up and down, before directly into the dark brown eyes that never deterred from his own. He was thinking, and he was thinking hard. Something wasn't right and yet he couldn't quite pinpoint what. He darted his sight to Maeve. Back to Micah. He tilted his head using a finger to tap at his chin.

"Twins...it confuses me why the prophecy wouldn't nudge towards that narrative."

"Excuse me?" Micah raises an eyebrow.

"A great deal of power must consume you," Arnold maneuvers around Emry in order to get a much greater look at the human version of a lousy picture. Then without warning the man is taking a large whiff of Maeve's scent. His eyes closed before they were widening once again, face contorting into something less than pleased. Maeve watched and believed it was because she didn't smell the greatest—which she'll take full credit for; she's still covered in dried blood, and from everything she's experienced after that, she probably relates to filth. She tilted her head to sniff at her armpit and shrugged.

Not bad, not the absolute worst either.

She would be grateful if they ever come across a shower though. Some fresh clothes would be nice as well. Ah, she could also go for a pair of shoes that weren't five sizes bigger. "Have you ever felt uneven?"

"I'm sorry?" Maeve glances at Emry to see if she can distinguish what this man is trying to say. She appeared just as clueless.

"Have you ever felt as though a part of you was missing?" Amora asks then. "Like no matter what, you always feel off."

Maeve looks at her, a bit confused by why she appeared to be ashamed. But then she's shaking her head, looking back at Arnold who is more than suspicious now.

"Not that I know of. I mean I have spent a good chunk of my life believing that my family didn't want me. Maybe that's what you're...*smelling?*"

"No. This is deeper than that. I can't quite say what, but something is wrong here. None of this is aligning with the prophecy" Arnold steps back and begins to pace. "But it has to. You were the one on the page. Ah, why must they trap my wife now?"

"Because they knew we were coming. And we'd really wish to be at least one step ahead, so if you could please elaborate a bit more on the Prism-"

"Yes," Arnold stalks over to Micah and grabs for his wrist. He tries to pull away but Arnold is a lot stronger than he looks. Flipping his hand so his palm is facing upward, incoherent words are being mumbled while the older man is waving his own appendage over Micah's. "The Prism, it's hidden in plain sight. This charm, it'll help you find it" He drags a finger across the other's wrist before moving it outward and pointing in the direction of the deep forest. "Can you see that?"

With a twinkle in his eye and the corner of his lip quirking upwards, suddenly a long green line is floating throughout the air and past the trees and bushes.

"Yeah."

Arnold whips his head around when not only hearing an answer from Micah, but from Maeve as well.

"What? Am I not supposed to?"

"Marvelous!" Arnold beams with a giggle. "I've never seen anything like this before! There's an insane connection here."

"Is that like some twin joke? Because I hate to burst your bubble but twin telepathy isn't really a thing" Maeve slightly cringes as if she's relaying the most devastating news. Only Arnold hasn't deterred from glee in the slightest.

"Oh no, this is much more than that! Ah, maybe this is what the prophecy is hinting towards!? It doesn't reference two people because you're supposed to be a team. Work as one."

Be one.

Micah and Maeve look at one another inquisitively. He too was a part of this prophecy?

Of course he is.

Why wouldn't he be? He's literally her twin brother, they share the same DNA.

The only reason the Raba aren't after him so adamantly is because they still believe him to be dead.

Then why wasn't he also in the picture?

This was the start of a very strong and long lasting migraine. One where Maeve will be needing to take more than just three pain reducing pills.

"None of this makes any sense" Micah shakes his head. Apparently he can't wrap his mind around it either. Or he doesn't want to? Maeve does know that he feels scared, worried, or more so completely thrown off track.

"Never said it would. Just know that you two are the key to saving us all."

"Yeah, no pressure or anything" Lucas scoffs.

"No, I mean, how can you assume that I too am a part of this prophecy off of a simple charm? Maeve was the only one who-" Micah was cut off by Arnold placing a finger to his lips.

"An assumption. My wife is the only one who would be able to tell you if I am correct or not" The man pulled out the crystal waving it around. "You and your sister are connected a lot more than you are to think, and that charm was proof. But if you still doubt my abilities, you can always try asking the Oracle. There's no guarantee you'll get an answer though."

"Is that all?" Zenaida wonders. "I feel as though you are speaking in code at this point, and if we want to find that Prism before the Raba do, then we must get a move on."

Arnold was again tapping at his chin, looking up into the sky. Squinting he was able to see the moon that was slowly but surely still switching places with the sun.

"I have covered all that I can. I wish you all the best of luck. We shall be needing it when the time comes."

"How do we know when it has?" Foster asks.

"The sky would go red and we shall be overcome by horror."

"Why must everything sound so depressing?" Rowan groans. "Couldn't you guys be a part of something more bright and filled with rainbows? Like a prophecy stating that if you don't compliment ten people in one day then you'll be turned into a cupcake."

"If only it were that easy" Amora chuckles before being the one to take the initiative that was walking back from where they came from. The rest started to follow.

"Oh!" The group stopped from Arnold's shout. "And thank

you...for returning my little girl to me. I really don't know what I'd do with myself if something happened to her."

Everyone gave their farewells with more questions and less answers.

Chapter Twenty-One

Thais blinks. Once then twice, her eyelashes clumped together with the remaining amount of mascara that she doesn't even remember putting on. She knows that she's looking around, she can feel her brown eyes move in every direction trying to remove the blurry haze that was making her eyes hurt. But everything is dark. That's not an excuse, her eyes were made for this. And yet the only thing she can really see is the circular shape that was a large dancing flame attached to what might be a silver rod. Three times, and then four, blinking she was seeing the orange and yellow hue finally become something of fire that appeared to be floating. Thais had been lying down, her spine already aching from whatever hard and lumpy surface she had been placed upon, therefore seconds later she's sitting up. Her temple immediately begins to throb. Ache bounced about her skull with a soreness that she hasn't felt since Amir encouraged (forced) her to do his intense workout routine. She brings a hand to her head believing that applying pressure would ease the pain, and yet the touch only makes her hiss and retract right after. The limb falls beside her landing in a pile of something wet and grainy. A squeal slips from her lips, and a startle vibrates throughout her body when her own voice echoed many times over. Wherever she was, the place was deep and hollow. It was also fairly cold and she can already feel the tips of her fingers begin to freeze over.

All of this only made her the more curious, all the more concerned. She reached for the supposed ground once more, fingers consciously digging into what felt like dirt. She felt around. All of it felt like dirt. Thais squints trying her best in order to fight through the pulsing that began to spread throughout her entire head. She trips and stumbles in order to stand, a strike of fear holding a place in her chest when she falls onto her knees, the palms of her hands being the only thing stopping her from going face first into what it was she stood on. Once again she was reaching for her temple where the agony was becoming all too much. She wouldn't be surprised if her head was quite literally splitting open, because it sure felt like it. It was frustrating. Her fingers dug into the dirt, the grime collecting underneath her nails. How would she be able to find Gabe and get out of wherever she was in if she couldn't do more than stare at the ground!? Thais snaps her head up (instantly regretting it when a vibrating pound became stronger behind her eyes the more she stressed), she looks left than right. Not like it would do much though. The fire above only held so much light, and the last thing Thais needed was to see what the corner of a stone wall looked like. Her arms shake as she struggles to lift her body. Eventually she makes it, knees ready to buckle, and there was a thought that she suffered from more than just a hit across the head in the forest. Her entire body feels weak and at any moment she just might vomit.

"Gabe?" No answer. "Gabe?" There was the sound of shuffling a bit of groaning, only it sounded like a bit of a distance. "Gabriel!?"

"Mmm, what? Where-?" Ah, there was his voice. At least now Thais knows that he's near and that he's alive.

Bong!

"Ah, fucking—damn that hurt!" And now she also knows that he managed to find a way to hurt himself. She won't judge him too hard, he's probably just as blind as her right now. "Thais? Where are you? Wow my head!"

"I'm fine. I'm somewhere near. I can hear you so that's good" She could hear him begin to move some more and so she followed his lead. Stumbling over nothing, Thais is limping in no particular direction until her hands are coming in contact with something cold, hard, and even a little grimey. She recoils almost immediately, wiping her hands on her pants. "Ah, gross."

"Where are we? And why can't I see anything?"

"You're asking the wrong person" Thais says as she reaches out once more. Her knuckles brush against the cold and grimey object, yet controls her reaction with the simplicity of a contorted facial expression. It's solid, sturdy and almost circular, leaving her blind touching to imagine all of the possibilities. It's when she fully engulfs the object with her palms is she coming to the conclusion that she is gripping onto a bar. Her face lights and she begins to pull. Metal screeching is a faint hiss to her ears and now Thais is quick to move her hands all over the rust that had been collected. "I think we're in a prison. There's bars..."

"See if you can find the door!" Gabe sounds more optimistic and less confused with the basic premise of his surroundings.

Movement could be heard on his end, tapping and light curses following. Thais doesn't have to be told twice though, as searching was something she planned to do whether Gabe instructed or not. Her feet shuffle, no more than inch steps between, the fear of tripping over anything always in the back of her mind. And it's when she moves over more to the right does her hand push against a big block. No, it wasn't a block. It matched the material as the bars and was more round. Her index finger grazes the piece and just the tip of her skin is grazing an oddly shaped hole.

"A lock! Shit, that means we really are locked up."

"Language."

"I think me cursing is the least of our problems " Gabe wouldn't be able to see it, but Thais definitely rolled her eyes.

"Your brother would find a way to hurt me beyond the grave if he knew that I just let you speak like such, so carelessly."

Thais scoffs and bangs her hand against the rotting metal. That's when the lights come on. For a moment it was so coincidental that Thais believed that that's all it took for them to get their vision back. She was tempted to bang against the bars one more time in order to see if these unveiled lights would shut back off. She didn't need to when she was more so glad that she was finally able to see Gabe's face again. She got as close as she was able to, knuckles turning white as she gripped the thing keeping her captive. Gabe was a mirror to her actions. His dark irises scanned every inch of her body; from the wild pieces of hair sticking up from her head, to the way her encased toes wiggled about her shoes. For the most part she looked unharmed, but he was still a bit curious about her health when seeing how sickly she looked.

"Are you okay!?" He asks. He reaches an arm through the minimal space between the bars. It was obvious that he wouldn't be able to touch her, and his disappointment was noted. Thais shakes her head.

"Yeah, you? You're looking a little pale."

"I have a raging headache and all of my muscles hurt, but besides that, I think I'm fine. You don't look so hot yourself though. Do you think something was done to us?"

Thais parted her chapped lips to speak. Only as the tiniest squeak of words were being said, another voice had been the one to answer.

"You both have been injected with a venom, stripping your body of most if not all energy. A great tactic used when one doesn't want their opponent to be at full capacity for a fight" The newcomer sucked their teeth, deep dark eyes observing the way that the two captives were even able to stand. "But I should have known that being a werewolf you two will be burning through it rather quickly. A quick nap and glass of water, you should be fine."

"What do you want with us!?" Gabe shouts. He slams a fist to his prison, and the very person...very people are quick to snap their heads in his direction.

It gave him the perfect opportunity to look at three older men —ones who very rarely show their face, and yet cause the most destruction. They didn't dare try to return Gabe's glare, didn't even want to appear menacing in the slightest. They kept their backs straight, hands intertwined behind them, and housing expressions that show they know that they've won. Snarky really. The corner of their lips were lifted just barely and their eyes gleamed. The duo should have known that they were kidnapped by the Raba. There was no one else in all of Kariq Leada that made them feel like targets. Or well besides Stacy Lyte in Thais' art class. A blonde-haired, blue-eyed perfect student who was after the same academic arts scholarship. She made it her every-day goal to ruin Thais' chances in getting it. A true menace she is. And she's probably celebrating when noticing that Thais has been missing from school.

Thais doesn't know what she hates more right now. Stacy, or these old men dressed in the ugliest robes.

"Ah, that's where you're wrong" The middle man gets closer. He's testing Gabe, seeing how hard the man will grip onto the metal before he downright seizes the opportunity to choke one of the kings. Qayid chuckles when watching the other take a step back. "It's not what I want from you, it's what I need. Our destiny has been stolen from us, and it's only right that we get what we were promised."

"The chosen one. Your friend, Maeve Whitmore...give up the location of her whereabouts and I promise to spare your lives."

"So what? Before you were going to kill us no matter whether we told you or not?"

The youngest Raba smiled before shrugging.

"We like to leave a clean trail."

"When the prophecy has been fulfilled, we guarantee the both of you the security in a new life. Protection, and the means to anything your heart desires" Fakhar voices with a slow head nod.

Made it seem as though he just made a promise that he cannot take back. Consequences will be had if he does.

"Well I guess you're just going to have to kill-" Gabe starts but before he could finish, Thais is telling him to wait.

"You would have to promise not just for us, but the rest of my pack as well."

She looks a bit shameful. And it doesn't help that Gabe is staring at her in disbelief. But could she be blamed? Maeve is the sole reason she had lost her brother. It's only right that she be sacrificed.

"Thais! No, what are you doing?"

"Of course," The Raba tower over her imprisoned form. They stare at her wickedly; already sinking their metaphorical claws within her selfish wants. "No harm shall come to you or your precious friends. You'll be living a life that you can only dream of. Once this is all over, you'll see how much you've won."

"No!" Gabe rages. He's banging against the bars, desperate to get Thais' attention. Unfortunately, it looks as though the poor girl had already fallen for their hollow words. "You can't do this! Thais, don't say anything! We can find a way-"

"SILENCE!" The Raba says at once. Qayid swings a hand around and the power he lets out is sending Gabe flying back into the wall. He hits with a grunt, falling to the dirt ground with a moan. He hadn't been hurt all too bad, but he'll definitely be feeling that in his back later. Thais watches in horror. Her eyes are wide and for a moment she's awoken. She can see how much evil is truly radiating off of these men and it terrifies her. Her arms wrap around herself, a false sense of security being given. Because maybe if she believed hard enough, then she can imagine that Amir is the one holding her. Just like he did all those years ago when they found out their parents have passed. She was a mess then, so she felt like a wreck even more now.

"Thais...please..." Even while suffering, Gabe found it in him to croak a protest. He was trying to crawl back over; knees and palms digging into the dirt with every unstable move. His back burned and the headache he was just getting over was back and worse than ever. The throbbing exceeded past his temple and engulfed the entirety of his head—feeling as though if there was anymore pressure then he just might pop. "You can't."

"Anything more out of you and there will be consequences!" Qua snaps. He lifts a hand, fingers curling around into a claw shape. Right then Gabe is lifted to sit on his knees. His eyes go round and fear is quickly painting his face red. His hands go to his neck where thick veins are beginning to protrude through his skin. He scratches at nothing, desperate to get rid of whatever was blocking his air flow. He probably looked like an idiot—he looked useless. Grunting he tries to fight through the restriction of oxygen, only able to fall to the ground inches from the metal bars. Gabe gasps, he's silently begging to breathe again, but it's obvious that Qua wasn't going to release him until Thais gives an answer.

Even then it's not assured.

"I-I-...I don't know."

Why withdrawal now? She wants revenge and this was the perfect opportunity. So why withdrawal now? Thais glances at Gabe. He's turning blue, eyes ready to fall out of his head, and it's impressive that he isn't already dead. She looks back at the Raba. The look of disappointment that overcame their eagerness was terrifying. Any glee that they may have felt diminished within that second—becoming dark and angry.

"You don't know?" Qayid asks bluntly. Qua tightens his hold on Gabe. His choking was torture and Thais started to scratch at her arms from the sound.

"Let him go! Please, you'll kill him."

"You don't know!?" Qayid asks again. This time his voice is raised and he's as close as he could be to the bars. "What do you mean you don't know!?"

Thais starts to sob. She doesn't know what she fears more: the sight that is Gabe's eyes rolling to the back of his head, or the way Qayid was spitting with his words. She probably would have said that they were equally as horrific but Gabe was literally tearing her heart in half. She could feel it ripping right down the middle, one side being tugged out of her chest and into the loose hand of the dying man.

"Please, please," She fell to her knees, hand pressed to her chest where the pain was becoming unbearable. "Release him! He's done nothing."

"He's deterred your mind. A defiance to what your kings ask of you" Fahkar grumbles. He does lower Qua's hand though, breaking the magical grasp that it had on Gabe. The loud and large inhales that came after it though were relieving. The werewolf had become a fish out of water. He was inhaling, exhaling, desperate to get every ounce of oxygen back into his lungs. He coughed and almost choked from how fast he tried to breathe—deciding to rest on his back where his eyes opened and closed in a dizzy haze. He tried to speak but it was nothing more than hoarse words. Croaks of a crushed windpipe made all communication between him and Thais no longer. It'd be a miracle if she knew what he was trying to say through a weak reach.

"Thank you" Thais sighs.

"Where will be able to find Maeve Whitmore?" Qayid questions.

Thais slowly raises her head, brown eyes meeting black soul-less ones.

"In the forest..."

"Thais" Gabe rasps. She looks at him through the glassieness that were her tears collecting on her eyelashes. She shakes her head in despair.

"I have to save you."

"Where in the forest? Let me guess, to meet up with that grimey maggot Oracle?" Qayid snarls. "Of course," Then he's snickering with a sickening grin. "It's unfortunate that they won't get much out of a rock. Where would they go after?"

"I don't know. Seriously. I left the group by then."

She and Gabe look at one another, before she's darting her sight back onto the three kings. What a wrong move. They saw right through the stare, Qayid using a finger to forcefully bring her up to the bars. The side of her face is being pressed into the metal with a bruising strength. More tears fall down her face and Gabe is left to grovel at the scene.

"You do. Tell us, now!" Qayid then screams in her face. She flinches and right there she's scared enough to pee herself. This is where she dies—it was inevitable.

"Don't" A shaky inhale. Gabe uses the metal bars to help stable himself when trying to at least get back to his knees. "Thais, don-"

Heeup.

"NOOO!" Thais screams.

Gabe shakily looks down at his chest. He doesn't think he could even comprehend what just happened to him. Straight through, a spear had pierced his body. His velvety-red blood dripped from the hole, staining his already dirty clothes. Immediately he's locking gazes with Thais, the life draining from the brown irises she's always loved to look into. She's banging her hand against the prison, careless about whether or not she breaks her wrist. And her shouts only got louder, her shaky body became weaker, her sadness and hatred exceeded its limit when watching Gabe's body fall with a hard thump.

"Tell me where the chosen one is or accept the same fate."

Thais is allowed to fall from the metal, sinking into a heap of her own despair. Her head is down, her eyes are closed, and she's sniffling back any snot and tears.

"Please forgive me" She whispers. Then slowly she's lifting her head and locking eyes with the people who so ruthlessly killed her friend. "Fine."

The charm, the green line that only Micah and Maeve were able to see kept getting brighter; becoming a sparkly lime green for every step that the group took in order to reach the Prism. It also could have been debatable whether or not the line was getting thicker, becoming more of a trail than just a string that they just happened to be attached to. There was only one thing that was different for the twins though, and it was considering Arnold had put the charm on Micah, he was the only one who could feel the intensity of them getting closer to their prize. It was a tingle, something akin to being itchy underneath the skin.

The closer they got, the stronger the itch became. And no matter how hard he scratched at his wrist, it was still there and it was still aggravating. He wanted it gone. Going at the pace that they were, it felt like the agony wasn't going to go away anytime soon. Excuse him for being a little pissy because of it. So when Rowan started to complain that his feet hurt, Micah whipped around to glare at the blonde.

"Stop whining for five minutes-" Micah and the rest of the wolves clutch at their chests. Amora rushes to his side, Emry to Maeve's. Zenaida is questioning her husband, while Foster and Rowan lean on one another. It wasn't painful, just tight. And as fast it came, it was gone.

"What the fuck was that?" Lucas swallows.

"Why? What happened?" Zenaida wonders. "Are you alright?"

"Yeah, I'm fine" He looked at the others to see if it was mutual. Head nods were given in return. "It was as if this pressure was squeezing my chest."

"I also feel really sad all of a sudden," Rowan says.

"Like a part of me had just been stripped out of my body" Foster continues.

"And all of you felt this?" Amora asks with furrowed eyebrows. You could see the gears in her head begin to turn.

The group of wolves look at one another, yet again shaking their heads in agreement.

"Something bad happened. Thais and Gabe, they're in trouble."

"What do you mean?" Micah wonders.

"Back when you were little, I used to read books about your species—learn how to properly take care of you. And in one of

346 - NEVAEH BRAGG

the chapters, there was a brief mention of packs being connected. Once you've been accepted, you guys are emotionally tied."

"But then wouldn't we be able to feel everything that each other feel?" Maeve asks. Her brain might explode if she's given anymore information about herself. But then again it might explain why she can properly guess what Micah is feeling. Or that could just be a twin thing.

"Not particularly" Amora denies. "This connection you all have, it still proceeds boundaries," She inhales sharply because what she's about to say next is depressing. "It only appears whenever you have lost one of your own."

"You mean, when one of us dies!?" Micah unintentionally shouts.

Their stomachs turn when Amora gives no answer.

"So that means..." Zenaida lets out a gasp instead of finishing her sentence. She falls to her knees before anyone is able to catch her. But it doesn't take long before Lucas is at her side, trying to keep her from fully collapsing in on herself. Tears could be seen welling up in her eyes, and a terrible memory flashes past those same irises that she uses to stare off into the distance. She doesn't say it very often but these people are her family—and it's painful to even think that something as cruel as death has overcome them. Her heart is going to suffer if history repeats itself.

"Wait," Rowan itches at his head. "If this is true, why didn't we feel it when Amir died?"

Eyes flickered over to Maeve. Her own widened into saucers. They were quietly asking for a reply, and yet she was unable to give one.

"You said he was poisoned" Lucas growls. She was thankful to see both Micah and Rowan take a step in front to defend her.

"Because he was! One of those stupid pixies shot him with their power and he practically died in my arms!" She also wanted to say that she could feel his life slip away, that her heart yearned to be with him even in the afterlife. But that's such a selfish thing to express. They could care less about her queries involving Micah as her mate. "Why would I make something like that up?"

"I don't know! Maybe you're working for the Raba!?" Everyone froze. Even Emry who couldn't believe what she was hearing. If Maeve was a part of the Raba's plan, then so was she. So was Amora. So were all of them, because in the end, they've been linked from the beginning and this is how their story is supposed to happen. "You've been working with them all this time, and this dumb prophecy involves a sacrifice of some sort! If not a soulmate, then what? A pack member? A brother!?"

"I think you're jumping to conclusions, Lucas. Chill, dude" Rowan replies.

"Show me the proof that she's not! Let's not forget that ever since she came here, our lives have gone to shit. And it's only been what? A few days? A week!?"

"We've given you the rundown about who Maeve Whitmore is, there is no room within my guardianship that granted her the access to be scheming with the Raba" Emry joins. Her stare was cold, piercing blue eyes beaming lasers throughout Lucas' just as scary brown ones.

"Yeah, like we can trust you. You're probably working alongside her, you witch."

Amora walks up to the taller man and slaps him. The sound

was loud enough to disturb the birds that rested in the trees, and the force was strong enough to leave a red print to his cheek. Lucas kept still, head permanently stuck to the side where he stared at the ground.

"You will *not* speak to an elder that way, do you understand me?" Nothing. He didn't move, he didn't speak. Amora got closer. "I said, do you understand me?"

"Yes" It was soft and defeated. She removed herself from his personal space, letting out a deep breath.

"Listen, I know this is all confusing. You're all hurting and tired, and I get it! But this hesitation, this doubt, I will not tolerate it any longer! From this point forward, if you are afraid that we cannot overcome this prophecy, then proceed like Gabe and Thais and begin to fend for yourself...and we all saw where that lended them."

"Ms. Loom, that's a bit cruel" Foster mumbles.

"But it's the truth! So I suggest you all learn how to bite your tongues for just a little longer, or else you'll end up with the same fate."

Maeve nodded along to the soft murmurs of everyone. Amora Loom can be quite frightening when she wants to be. And she would have just continued on like everyone else who followed Micah with sulky expressions, if she wasn't a little too caught up in what Lucas let slip.

Soulmate?

So she was right?

Amir was her mate?

And she just let him die so easily.

Her mind was spinning and her heart was beating sporadically.

Or maybe he wasn't dead? Like Rowan said, none of them felt it.

But then how would he have survived?

"Hey, Maeve, are you alright?" Pulling her from the circling that was her thoughts was none other than blondie himself. He reached for her hand, pulling away when she stared back at him startled. But she enjoyed the touch. It was warm and definitely the comfort that she needed right now. So looking down at the pale limb that swung mindlessly between them, she combined their hands. He looked down at it too before looking back up at her.

"I'm fine, just a bit *frazzled*."

Rowan chuckled at her wording.

"Well, I've been known to be pretty good at unfrazzling people."

It was nice to see her lips pull up into her best attempt at a smile.

"What does that mean?"

"Oh I don't know," He swung their hands high and low, his footsteps just a bit lighter. His eyes sparkled, and he looked undeniably handsome right then. She never wants anyone to take away his joy. It'd be too heartbreaking. "One tactic I got is telling a plethora of dad jokes."

"And suddenly I'm feeling better than ever" Maeve removes her hand from Rowan's and creates space between them. He smirks and then pulls her back by wrapping an arm around her waist. She giggles when his fingers poke at her side.

"Too late, I can already feel the jokes brewing."

Chapter Twenty-Two

"If you step on the back of my shoe one more time, I'm going to take it off and shove it so far up your ass you will feel it in your throat," Foster growls. The steps he was taking had come to a halt, allowing the person behind his anger to accidentally run into his back—also proving that they were way closer than they needed to be. It's an invasion of personal space the big and broody male much rather not have infiltrated unless one is Micah Whitmore. And considering it's a sightful knowledge that Micah is upfront leading the pack while also making small talk with Amora, anyone else shall feel his wrath. Or not necessarily wrath, but a decent amount of anger from someone who almost had their shoe taken off for about the third time within two minutes. Turning around so fast that he had become a blur to the plain eye, the shoe-stepper-oner was now face to face with a glaring Foster.

Fucking Zenaida Davis.

The corner of her lips curled sinisterly when watching the fire behind Foster's eyes burn with annoyance. She had always been similar to an older sister. One that was a nuisance when she had spare time on her hands, but demanded to be alone when she sought silence. Moments like these he (and the rest of the group) remember that she used to have a family before them. She often tells stories, absurd ones that make you believe that she had a big one. Only it was quite the opposite, explaining that a small apartment housed her parents, her, and her little sister Jane—plus a stray cat that occasionally appeared looking for food. They jokingly called it Garfield due to its resemblance to the cartoon, and the fact that it particularly enjoyed pasta days. Unfortunately besides the cat, the small family had been tragically murdered when they were being robbed late one night. Having been working a late shift at a nearby gas station, she was the only survivor. But once returning home, screams of horror escaped her throat as unexpected eyes scanned over the bloody scene. Their bodies were sprawled in different rooms, a struggle evident when trying to flee the scene. With shaky hands and a bottom lip that won't stop quivering, she fell to her knees gazing into the soulless eyes of her younger sister.

"Kinky" Zenaida smirks. She winks, tilting her head slightly and letting a gleam of playfulness and mischief shine through. It wasn't the best time for her to be that irritating sister he never had, but her smile was enough to make that fire within him diminish...a little bit. "Though I do have to say, I think you should leave such foreplay for Micah."

"Stop stepping on my shoe" Foster grits his teeth. He tried to keep his menacing composure but was immediately crumbling. His face grew red and the embarrassment was so visible it was comical. His eyes darted to the left and he pressed his lips to a straight line. "Either walk in front of me, or stop walking so close behind."

Zenaida raises her hands in mock surrender. A sly smile aligns her lips as she slithers around the other's bigger form. It leaves Foster standing there, a bit of fear striking his chest as he thinks about all of the secret sexual moments between him and Micah. They were intimate and definitely not something that another pair of eyes needs to see. So while what she said may have just been a little bit of teasing, it is quite scary to think that she has caught the duo during one of their most private times together. Inhaling and then exhaling deeply, Foster thought it'd be best if he didn't think about it too hard. He rubs his hands over his face, in the process raking his hands through his hair.

His shoulders slump as he turns back around to continue along with the group...only everyone is gone. He animatedly turns his head left then right, eyes blown wide and muscles flexed. He'll probably never admit to it, but he's nervous. The charm Arnold gave led the pack back into the city. After about an hour of roaming throughout the forest, doing loops around the same trees, and the assumption that the dumb spell was broken, eventually they were led under a willow tree and out of the endless sight of greenery. They had to keep low, hide within the shadows and stay as close as they could to roads that were empty. They didn't know where the Junud were hiding—didn't know when they planned to attack.

It could have been said that it was difficult for them to hide —but just blend in with the crowd. Walk and dance beside the hundreds of people that crowded the streets. Pretend to shout and cheer with strangers who swallowed alcoholic shots back to back. And pump your fists in the air as sexy women dress you in funky sunglasses, a colorful hat and throw paint on you. Foster can still taste the dark blue that was supposed to be thrown at his chest, and yet managed to land on his lips (which he mistakenly decided to lick). Thousands of people, persons from all corners and sides, crooks and crannies of Kariq Leada leave their homes and now stalk the large streets. Smiles that stretch and eyes that twinkle in delight, no matter who you were or what your supernatural species is, fun was the only option. Foster easily recognized it as the infamous *Kunant Festival*. The only who hadn't was Maeve; an awe overcoming her as they descended further into the happy madness. She was trying to look at everything all at once, basking in the amazing energy that all citizens were experiencing as they danced to music that was appearing from somewhere.

"This is perfect. Move with the crowd. Just stay alert and keep track of each other. The Junud are smart, but being able to spot us in a crowd this big...that's a clash even another werewolf finds difficult to differentiate between" It had been said by Emry at the time. She tried to keep a blank expression, something professional, and yet there was that glimmer of worry that reached the corner of her blue eyes. While she had been taught to be optimistic about her missions, the further she continued on with this one, her gut just wasn't agreeing. Something terrible was going to come out of all of this. Or maybe she's just worried by what Arnold hinted towards. Red sky, horror...she shivered when thinking of all those years ago. Her eyes stung with tears she refused to let fall. She believed to be immune back then because she was far too young for her powers to ever reach their full capacity. She's much older now. Her and Amora both. They're going to feel that overwhelming surge of power that just can't be contained. They

can become more animaltic than the actual animals. Witches go mad; eager to get rid of that ruthless feeling no matter what they have to do.

"*Well if we're going to play the part of party-goers, then we might as well look the part too*" Amora grins. Then before any of them knew it, she was waving her hand around in a circle. Within seconds the entire group looked like everyone else in the realm. They were all dressed in completely different outfits than before: a shirt, pants, and sneakers. It was trendy enough to be considered a part of a festival, but casual enough that if they were spotted by the Junud they could run away without any faults.

While everyone felt glad that they were finally out of the clothes that were beginning to smell and visibly show how unhygienic they've been, Maeve had to be the one that was most grateful. She was wiped clean of everything she had been through. No blood, no dirt, no sweat. Her top was a white cropped knitted sweater, where the only thing covering the sight of her breasts was a matching tight white lace bralette. Her pants were a bright pink pair of cargos, and her shoes were those white sneakers that she's been meaning to buy since forever. She felt all over her body, scoffing in disbelief. She even reached for her hair where she felt that her curls were back to their usual perfection and not just a heap of frizzy tangles.

"*Wow, you're like a fairy godmother!*" Maeve squeals. She looks at everyone else and they appear to be just as perfect. It's impressive that Zenaida has a glittery makeup look going on around her eyes. Made her wonder if her makeup had been redone as well. Amora waved her off while blowing raspberries.

"*Pfft, fairies can barely do that simple spell. It's why they stick more to handling magic involving the care of our world. Besides this is a measly masking spell"* Amora let out a hum as she curled her lip in thought. *"Kind of like Cinderella, so maybe you're right?"*

"So what? We're all going back to our rags at the stroke of midnight?" Rowan jokes while tugging at the loose pastel yellow shirt he wore. A giggle came out of everyone before they were tasked to get back to their original plan. Follow Micah to the Prism.

Foster keeps repeating the orders of keeping an eye out for the Junud, but also make sure that he always knew where the rest of the group was. So for him to lose them in a sea of people so fast, the ounce of panic he desperately tried not to feel was brewing in his chest. He continued to look left than right, looking over the many heads that still bobbed to music, looking through arms that were raised up high. It wasn't until he was pushing through a group of men that were cheering on their friend who was chugging down the biggest glass of beer ever known, that Foster saw the side profile of Micah. It wasn't hard to find the rest of the pack after.

His fear grew when witnessing a stranger bare his teeth wide for every step that he gets closer to Micah. How are large fangs, long sharp claws, and evil red eyes not suspicious to anyone? There's no way everyone's that drunk that they can't understand that someone dangerous is lurking.

"Micah!" He can't hear him. He's just a little too far and unfortunately enough the music was getting louder. "Micah!" The evil character was getting closer and it won't be long til he sinks his claws into the other's beautiful skin.

And then thunder cracks. That catches everyone's attention. Looking up, they're suspicious of the weather that was supposed to be sunny for the rest of the day. And yet clouds were rolling in and there was a high possibility that it would rain. Having been one of the people to glance up at the blue sky, Foster took notice that it was turning pink. Plop, something wet had just struck his cheek. *Great, now it's sprinkling.* His lips drop into a frown when right after it begins to downpour. And of course none of the party-goers seem to care, this only fuels their drive to continue on. It may even hype them even more, deciding to face the repercussions of pneumonia tomorrow.

None of this feels right though. Foster's oversensitivity to everything was at an all time high, and now with an even more cheerful crowd, he lost sight of Micah and his possible enemy. He begins to frantically push through everyone. In the midst he falls into line with Lucas and Zenaida, the both of them just as anxious.

"I think we've been spotted, I just saw Micah being followed."

"Us too. We tried to get closer but then we saw the sky change color and lost him" Lucas claims.

"Yeah, don't you find it weird that we're the only ones who noticed?" Zenadia adds. She encourages the two men to look around, and as they glance within the crowd, an eerie atmosphere overcomes the once jovial streets.

"Yeah, it's almost as if they're oblivious–" Foster waves a hand in front of a woman's face. She doesn't flinch in the slightest, she doesn't ask what he's doing, she just continues on dancing. "Nothing. They must be under some spell."

"But by who?"

The trio continue on, eyes peered more than ever as they try to find their friends. It's when they're reaching central park that

Lucas catches sight of Micah. He's alone, but from the corners Rowan and Maeve are seen approaching from the right, while Amora and Emry are entering from the left. If any of them had just been a little faster, then they would have been able to save him from the man that was diving down from the sky. Hisses slipped from his tongue, his fangs protruded, and black nails stretched from underneath his nail-beds. He was growling, drooling as he tried to slice at the other. Micah was doing his best to hold him off. He was using all of his strength to keep fingers from digging into his neck, and he was also straining his neck the furthest he could into the green grass to keep from getting bit.

"Micah!" Maeve shouts.

Everyone dashes over, ready to help. Foster had been the one to reach him first, and with insane strength rips the high rank vampire off. He was grabbed by the neck, claws of the werewolf digging into his pale skin. He screeches when being pulled, grunting when his back hits the tall stone statue of the old king. But Foster doesn't let him rest there. He stomps over, a snarl rumbling from deep within his throat and his eyes begin to turn a dark green. His canines began to protrude past his lips, and when flexing his fingers his nails grew two inches longer and to a point. The vampire didn't need much time to regain his strength, standing once more within seconds. He wanted to roll his eyes at the subpar intimidation tactic, but resulted in cracking his neck and rolling his shoulders back before dashing towards the other. They meet in the middle with the vampire taking the first hit. He's gripping onto Foster's shoulder, digging his claws into him and then flipping him onto his back. The large man lands on the ground with a hard thud, hissing from the shock that traveled up his spine along with reaching for his newly required wound. He looked at it, raising his shaking right hand in order to see the damage properly. Blood oozed from the crescent marks in flows. It could have been believed that he was stabbed with how deep the cuts have been, how red and bloody his shoulder was becoming. It'd take a bit longer for it to heal properly. But taking a second to remove his attention from all of the throbbing, all of the pain, he was looking at the enemy. He was smirking wickedly at the rest of the group, fangs flashing and knuckles cracking. It was clear that taking Foster down had boosted his ego, and he was ready to go after the rest. Only as he was taking his first step, his ankle was being grabbed.

The vampire wasn't given any time to realize what was happening before he was also dragged down. He was slammed, chin hitting the ground with an impact where his jaw crunched. Foster slowly made his way back to his feet, grumbling curses under his breath. He still held onto his shoulder, but with how much anger he endured, he was more so focused on killing the person who did it to him. Reaching down for the vampire, he let his own claws dig into the man's thigh. A screech was heard. Foster was holding onto him so strongly that he was on the verge of ripping all of the fat and muscle that resided there out.

"Get off of me, you runt!" The vampire shouts. He attempts to swipe at Foster with his claws for hands, but misses when the werewolf is grabbing his forearm. He doesn't waste a second to snap the appendage in half, the crack mixing in with the scream he let out from agony.

"You don't want to fight me anymore?" Foster sneers. "Fine,

you can fight one of my buddies then. Lucas! Heads up!" And then as if the vampire weighed absolutely nothing, he was being lifted by his broken arm, and then tossed through the air in the direction of the others. Maeve shouldn't have been disgusted (considering she had done something similar to General Harris), but she could feel bile rise in her throat when witnessing the man's arm come right off his body and stay within the grip of the werewolf. His body on the other hand soared until he was captured by Lucas. He was caught by the hair, fingers ripping at the black wavy strands.

"Please hurry, he's getting blood all over my clothes" Zenadia relays her comment with an eye roll. She begins to wipe at the light-blue shorts she wore and then reaches higher to swipe at the long sleeve mesh shirt that was designed with a collision of colors, the structure of the top resembling one of a butterfly spreading its wings. She looked genuinely upset that there were a few droplets that now stained her fabric.

Even if she was already soaked from the rain, blood was the least of her problems right now.

"Anything for you, snowflake."

Then without another second wasted, Lucas wrapped his hands around the vampire's neck. He flexed his muscles, made sure his fingers wouldn't slip, and then *snap*! Within a simple blink, the vampire's head was broken, facing the opposite direction. His lifeless eyes were wide and now staring into Foster's victorious ones. Lucas let the man's body drop to the ground carelessly, kicking his side when watching him twitch slightly.

Once the air settled and everyone was positive that the

vampire was dead, Micah was leaving the side of Amora and rushing to the side of Foster.

"Are you alright? It looks even worse up close" He starts off by holding the other man's face within his palms, but with the haste of making sure that he wasn't silently dying, Micah's hands were touching all over—checking for bruises and purposely avoiding the largest gash that was being clutched in hopes of less blood spread. "Maybe Ms. Loom can quickly poof up a bandage and we can wrap it. Just for the time being...and then once we get the Prism, we can head to the nearest hospital so you can-"

Foster raises his good arm, a few of his fingers reaching for Micah's chin. He tilts the other man's face up, the message in the movement being to look one another in the eye. Oh how Micah wished that it made his stomach flutter like before. How he wished that the touch set a fire off throughout him like before—making him melt and become a puddle of lovesick emotions only Foster is able to clean up. Frowning Micah removed the hand from his face, and Foster could only chuckle before returning it to his shoulder.

"I always find it really cute how much you worry for me."

"If only that comment reached my heart," Micah reached out to push Foster's wet hair from falling too far into his face. And as he's retreating, he lowers his voice into a whisper. It could be a little hard to hear him from the pitter patter of droplets hitting the ground, but right then Micah didn't care whether or not his voice was heard. Being this close to someone he so desperately wanted to call his mate, he needed to express how much this wasn't hurting him. "Please understand that I miss you, so why must you dismiss me like I'm a stranger?"

Foster looks down at him with confusion.

"Alright love birds, wrap it up!" The joking tone came from Rowan, and everyone else completely unaware that two hearts managed to break without even cracking. "We still need to find that Prism! Plus, big man over there is looking a little pale. Shouldn't we patch him up?"

The duo didn't listen and continued to swirl within their own bubble.

"This is just as hard for me as it is for you," Foster responds with furrowed eyebrows and a hold much firmer to his wound. "You make it seem as though you're the only one who ever put effort into this relationship."

"Someone who's putting effort doesn't go and reject the other —ah!" As Micah stomps his foot, and as the rest of the group is looking at the couple with revelation, the charm has taken its unsettling effect again. It'd been a lot stronger this time; only less like an itch and something akin to being shocked. He's quick to grab his wrist, gasping at the continuous tingle that shoots up his arm. Foster asks what's wrong, but Maeve is already beating her brother to the answer.

"I think we found the Prism."

She raises her hand, index finger pointing past the couple and in the direction of the old king statue. The shimmering green trail is shining brighter than ever before and if she listened hard enough she could even hear a faint twinkling sound. It added to Maeve's awe of Kariq Leada's mystical and magical energy.

She's the fist one to run over to the statue, brown eyes drawn to the bottom where beautiful carvings are surrounding the name plaque. It's intriguing to finally see what this King's name was; written boldly, all capital letters, in the middle of the piece of metal, a shimmering gold being the eye-catching color. She parts her chapped lips in order to mumble the name. *King Amal Payne.* It felt heavy on her tongue. A sense that she is unworthy to be speaking something as simple as the name of someone who used to be so powerful, so loved, so trustworthy by his people. She then lowered her sight to the brief description of who he was.

KING AMAL PAYNE

△

Loyal ruler of all Kariq Leada

It didn't take long before the other's joined her. The padding of their feet could be heard jogging the small distance, and Micah's mumbled annoyance for the charm eventually reached her ears. He complained something along the lines of matching the dead vampire—ready to rip his arm off if it didn't stop aching. While his whining was a bit funny to listen to, she did want to help him. She didn't know what it felt like, being privileged enough only to be able to see the spell. And for all she knows this could actually be a painful thing for Micah that she doesn't want him to be going through any longer. So listening to him groaning only fueled the need to find this all-mighty Prism and finally put an end to his misery. It's when she's scanning the statue that she thinks about the charm a little more and wonders when it will wear off. Does it just magically disappear when they have it in their hands? Will it never go away? Does Arnold need to be the one to stop it? She's hopeful for the answer to be the first one; just the grazing of their fingertips to the Prism and the extreme version of a GPS will vanish.

"It's hidden in plain sight..." Emry is the one to speak after a silence settles over everyone. She's making her way to the front, unknowingly using a lot of force in order to push others out of her way. She glares at Rowan when he makes a snarky comment about it, and Maeve finds it a bit odd. While she had always known Emry to be rather tough—don't take shit from no one— her aggression within the moment was unnecessarily to say the least. She blinks at the older woman who's narrowing her eyes on the name plaque. Then as best as she can she's glancing up at the pouring sky. She's alarmed when witnessing the sky begin to shade darker from a cotton candy pink. Maeve isn't allowed to voice concern for it though when watching Emry be forced back, flying through the air before crashing to the ground with a shout.

"Emry!" Amora screams and then runs over. Maeve lets her eyes go wide and lets her jaw unhinge, disbelief in what just happened stun her body for a second and then two. By three she's in control of her legs again and she's running over to Emry as well. She kneels on the other side of the old lady, hands beginning to shake when it looks as though Emry didn't plan on waking up.

"What just happened? Is she okay?" Maeve blurts letting herself finally touch the wrinkly hand that was laid out unmoving. She holds it towards her chest tightly.

"She was struck by what I assume to be a protection spell. The king must have put it on the Prism so it isn't stolen by the wrong people" Amora places a hand to her friend's forehead, closing her eyes and inhaling deeply. It's when she exhales that she reopens her lids and gives an answer for health. "Thankfully she's just unconscious. Given some rest she should wake up in no time."

Well that's a relief to hear. Maeve doesn't think she'd be able to take another death. Or at least a death that means something to her. So releasing a deep breath, she relaxes. But only for a minute. Because not too long after she's tensed from the unknown that is retrieving the Prism from wherever Emry saw it in the first place. She's craning her neck from the old ladies and onto the group that didn't know where to look. At the statue, at Emry...at Foster who could possibly be dying from blood loss. Everywhere is a dilemma and they haven't even gotten to the hardest part yet.

"We're doomed!" Rowan exclaims. He throws his arms up into the air to drop them back down to his sides. Then with an exasperated huff and a deep frown, he's plopping to the ground in this grieving defeat.

"No doubt with that attitude" Zenadia mocks.

"We just need to focus," Micah states firmly. He doesn't know what he dislikes more: the way that this charm was overtaking his entire arm, or because his entire pack was becoming a bunch of mopey-mops. "Foster, we need to find something to secure your arm" They look at their surroundings, which is nothing more than stone, a nearby playground and loads of grass that has a dusty Junud member lying in the distance. Eventually Amora pluck a few pieces of the greenery and stands. She swirls it between her fingers, hands glowing as her magic begins to take effect. Then after making a stretching motion it is presented that she made a large bandage out of grass.

"Use this."

The grass infused bandage floats its way over to Foster and then wraps itself tight around his shoulder.

"Okay, now what about the Prism? We don't even know what Emry was looking at" Lucas comments.

Micah returns to eyeing the statue. He's looking at King Amal in the round pieces that were his stone irises. It was as if the statue was gazing down at him. He remembers when he was little, he was terrified of the sculpture. It just looked too real, every crease and crevice crafted to mimic the man perfectly. If Micah wasn't reassured that it was nothing more than a giant rock pelted by tools, he would have continued to believe that it was really him held captive by Medusa's abilities. He was always told that it was okay, that they carved it that way so no matter what, everyone will know that King Amal will always be watching over them. He'll be there to protect them. But it just never sat right in his gut, and he doesn't think it ever will. He drops his gaze from the face of the old angel and back down to the plaque. He read it over, and over, and over. Nothing seemed out of the ordinary.

Name.

Shape.

Recognition.

Name.

Triangle.

Recognition.

Triangle?

Triangle! Prism!

"It's the damn plaque!"

Chapter Twenty-Three

"What?" Rowan blurts. He keeps whipping his head back and forth between the small piece of metal and his friend. He was trying to decipher the same clues that Micah managed to see through, and yet he believes that his bimbo image was beginning to become true. He just didn't understand. Even after narrowing his precious green eyes on the name plaque, he still couldn't see what the leader had blithely figured out.

"The Prism, it's the plaque" Micah reads his friend's confusion and points at the triangle in the middle of the words. "Or maybe it's in it. Right there. It has to be."

"Okay, but how do we get it out? I don't think you want to end up like a roasted old lady" Zenadia says while throwing a thumb over her shoulder, pointing in the vague direction of Emry. And she's a bit startled when nudging her for the comment was her husband. He looks down at her with a head shake, secretly telling her that that last part wasn't needed. Her ears burn and she's quick to divert her sight to the ground, refusing to feed into the stare for any longer.

"We should have asked Arnold before we left. He had to know that it was here, so he must know how to get it" Foster says.

"You understood what he said? All I heard was "Maeve is the chosen one. Wah, wu-wah, wu-wah, wah, wah."

Refusing to respond to Rowan's supposed-to-be laughable commentary, Foster rolls his eyes. Then he's turning to look at Maeve. He crosses his arms over his chest—where he temporarily forgets he's been clawed open—to cringe from pain and then lower his wounded arm back to his side. Disappointment. Not his best when attempting to look more mean and mysterious. Micah shakes his head, letting a grin just gently tug at the corner of his lips. Foster only grew more as a softer soul; his awkwardness showing just barely as he fluidly asked Maeve a question.

"Do you have any ideas...Ms. Chosen one?"

She looks at him ready to shake her head no, but then her eyes brighten as an idea comes to mind. It's after she rests Emry's hand on her stomach, standing to her feet and letting a crooked grin appear on her face, did she reveal her thoughts.

"That's it! Being the chosen one, it's also like being the secret key to everything. Like in the movies...the super confident, not-like-the-others main character is conveniently able to do anything."

"You're kind of a bland main character then" Lucas grumbles. Zenadia is the one to nudge him this time. Only instead of feeling ashamed, Lucas sucks his teeth with an eye roll. Maeve would say that she's even the least bit phased by what Mr. Accent said, but by now she's learned that the only way to tolerate his pessimism is by being flattered by it. Even negative attention is good attention—so she'll just flip the snarky remarks into the idea that she's just so insufferable that it plagues his mind; drives him so mad that he just has to say it.

Oh Lucas stop it, you're going to make me blush.

Maeve restrains herself from flipping him off, but not from biting her tongue.

"I didn't ask for your opinion side character...I'm simply explaining my idea" She could hear the few snickers that left Rowan, she could see them too. Being hidden by his hand. Lucas narrowed his eyes on her. Really, what is his problem? She can only feel sorry for putting them in this position for so long. And after everything that the witches continue to say, it was bound to happen. It's only unfortunate that people outside of the family managed to get wrapped in it all. "We're reaching that no more options limit, and unless anyone else has a better idea, I really do think we should go the cliche route."

It was quiet, any other comments or opinions being swallowed—because she has a point. If the old king placed a charm around the Prism, there's no way any random creature could come up and use their powers in order to take it. More security would be needed if it were that easy; not just some lousy park ranger who typically slept in his car when he's supposed to be keeping his eyes peeled for any possible danger. So stepping out of the way, a large path was made. Maeve tried to keep her chin high as she walked closer to the name plaque, but she's not going to lie...she's scared. What if she tries to reach for it and it just forces her back like Emry? Not only would it hurt, but she'd be incredibly embarrassed. Lucas would be given full right to laugh in her face. And she refuses to let someone as rude as him be able to point a finger in her face and shout that he told her so.

Sucking in a heavy breath, Maeve raises her hand. She doesn't let an ounce of the oxygen leave her lungs as she slowly descends her hand down. Her eyes begin to squint close, fear pounding at her chest, as her fingers are coming in contact with the cold metal. It's when she witnesses her fingers, her entire hand, begin to disappear in the middle of the plaque that she lets out the breath from a gasp. Her eyes bulge open and her panic is replaced by excitement.

Magic is so cool!

She retrieves her hand a lot faster than she did putting it in, brown irises watching as she wiggles her unharmed fingers. The others gather around when seeing that she's standing perfectly fine. They too are in awe. They've heard about how powerful King Amal used to be—Amora saw it—so to see someone be unscathed from one of his charms is amazing.

"Oh my god, she was right!" Rowan says happily. Lucas huffs. The others smile.

Maeve joins in with the joy before diving her hand back down in the invisible hole. She doesn't think she's experienced anything like this. She was just waving her hand down in a huge void, nothing but empty space. No walls, no bottom. But when she moved her hand a bit to the left, she could feel her knuckles brush against something cold. It scared her, the fear of the unknown shooting a tingle up her spine. She had to mentally reassure herself that it was nothing but the Prism that she had touched. Letting her fingers touch the point, the top of it—feeling the smoothness, the shape, it'd become obvious that she definitely found their prized weapon. Scooping it from the void that it floated within, she pulled it out for all to see. Amora had even temporarily left Emry's side in order to get a glance.

It didn't look to be all that special. It was definitely a Prism.

It was made out of some kind of purple crystal: Tanzanite. It shined without any light and was rather light for a rock that filled the entirety of one of Maeve's palms. The citizens of Kariq Leada marveled at the sight, internally celebrating the win. A win that didn't last for long. Because not long after it was sitting within Maeve's hands, was it being removed from them. It was pulled away from her, flying a few feet across the air and into the possession of someone else. They watched it go, worry becoming fury when coming face to face with the enemy.

"Thanks for returning such a precious family heirloom. Our dear father had always been quite stingy when it came to his personal belongings" Qayid grins.

"How did you find us?' Amora asks.

"We have eyes everywhere. You can't step foot anywhere without me knowing about it" But then his smile quirks into a smirk and his black eyes are beaming with mischief. He then holds his hand out, flipping it so it's palm up. Resting within his wrinkly fingers is none other than Thais' cellphone. There was apparent tension brewing when witnessing everyone flex. Amora looked to be suffering the most though. Veins were ready to pop from out of her neck and her hands were balled so tight into a fist that her knuckles began to turn white. "Your friend also let me borrow her phone. Apparently you can track people on these things now."

"Where the hell did you put her!?"

"I shoved her down in the dungeon where all nuisances deserve to suffer" Qayid hated the glares, the stares, the animosity that was being given from his people.They shall only be looking at him as though he was one of the almighty Archangels. He was one of their kings, and they shall treat him as such. His expression hardens and he loses the playful bite to his words. "For the friend however, I made sure he laid in a puddle of his own blood."

It would have been assumed that Amora attacked. She let all of the stress come out as an angry frenzy. Gabe was family. She loved him just as much as everyone else; as a child of her own, and now he's gone. He lays cold, unable to be held by any of his friends. But instead it had been Micah. He moved in slow motion, everything did. Or at least to Maeve it did. One moment she was listening to an old hag speak so vile, and then the next she's watching her twin brother jump and attack Qayid. And it wasn't because he bravely ran and attacked the Raba, but more so that he did it after fully shifting. His wolf form leaped through the air, his large furry body casting a shadow over her face temporarily. His face was huge; it morphed into one that resembled an actual wolf (a snout, a mouth bigger than her head with teeth that were carved into points, and violet eyes as hooded slits). He was a dog...currently. He was an animal; and he barked as he landed on top of Qayid. Micah was only able to get a scratch in, it going across the entirety of the man's face before he was being shoved off and forced to the ground.

"How dare you lay your filthy paws on the Raba!" Fakhar rages. He shoots a fireball from within his hands, it only inches from landing on Micah before it curves the other direction and strikes a nearby tree. The greenery is set aflame, and yet no one speaks on it. All eyes are back on Amora, the one to deter the shot. The natural blue that are her irises flicked between it and red, while she stalked closer to the brown, black and white mixture of a wolf.

"How dare you try to strike my son!"

Micah is upright again. He shakes his fur before bending low a growl rumbling. Maeve scoots closer to Rowan, seeking comfort from the giant animal that could literally snap her in half with one bite.

Qayid belts out his laughter. One hand covers half of his face, drenching it in his thick crimson. It slipped between his fingers and glided down his arm like water would a glass. It was a terrible sight. Watching the elder laugh with his entire stomach, head thrown back and voice so loud he disturbs the birds resting on a powerline.

"Your son!? You really believe we don't know who he is!?" His assertiveness had all of them flinching. He looked wicked as he stared down at them with his one good bloodshot eye. "How foolish do you really think we are! God damn, you wolves are pathetic and dumb!" His smile stretched when watching the terror burn behind their tough expressions. The slow backing of their steps satisfied the sadistic part of him. He stood straight and tall then, voice lowering. "What challenge would this prophecy be if both of my dear o' sister's children died?"

"What?"

Maeve says it unintentionally. But the one word is enough to put the spotlight on her.

"Ah, there she is. The one that I came for."

"What do you mean your sister? My mother?"

Qua groaned. For being the elderly, you'd really think they'd act more mature. Kind of ruins the whole menacing bad guy image.

"Must we explain everything? We really need to get going."

"You'd think Habun would birth intelligent children" Fahkar grumbles.

"Habun? As in King Amal's only daughter Habun!?" Zenaida wonders. "I thought she disappeared all those years ago?"

"Well it was either run off or be murdered...I think she chose wisely" Qua chuckles lightly. These men are deeply disturbed. They've known everything this whole time. It was only having to be patient—something that they've mastered. But now they've become too eager and are willing to do anything in order to succeed.

"We'd be terrible kings if we didn't have all of this already planned."

"Alright, let's finish this. The red moon should be approaching in a few short hours" Qayid moves a finger and suddenly Maeve is feeling her body moving from its spot. It's when she's about to glide right past Micah does he whip around using his tail in order to knock her back. The force was strong enough to push her into the large body of Foster, knocking them both to the ground with grunts. Then within seconds he transformed back into his human self. His clothes tore when shifting before, therefore he now stood nude. But when it's expected to see more of him—his ass and dick—he's actually being covered by a white light? A cloud? A bright white energy? It wasn't something anyone dwelled on though. They were all too caught up in the sight that was Micah standing tall, eyes and hands shading white as well.

"She's not going anywhere with you."

The Raba have never looked scared until now.

"Y-Your power-" Qua is in shock.

"Contain him. Now!" Qayid states firmly. He quickly gathers hands with his brothers, the trio glowing just as bright as Micah. They begin to chant unrecognizable words in sync, bodies floating. Wind picks up around them, and now the others have to station themselves in order to keep from tumbling away.

"Micah!"

"Get out of there!"

"No! Stop this!"

They were all shouting, hoping that any of their attempts would make this fight come to an end. The wind only became stronger, their words drowned out. Micah could be seen cringing, moaning as he's slowly collapsing. He falls to his knees, gasping for air. Maeve tries to push through the storm, they all do. But no steps could be made.

"It's you. You're the source we needed" Qayid stops chanting to laugh mechanically. Then he sighs with satisfaction. "Just like it should be, the first born with all the power."

Then with one last stare into Maeve's eyes, he, his brothers and Micah are gone.

Chapter Twenty-Four

"No! No! NO! NO!" Foster shouts as he pounds against the ground. "They fucking took him! Just wait until I get my hands on—AAHH!"

"Ms. Loom, what were they talking about when it came to Habun? Their sister?" Zenaida spews so fast that it was hard to even interpret what she was saying. "What does that mean? Maeve and Micah are royalty? They're related to those-those freaks!?"

"Can we discuss the implications of all of this first!? Micah is the one they really needed. So is he the real chosen one?" Rowan wonders.

"I don't know. I don't know!" Amora stresses. Her bulged eyes are staring at the same spot Micah just stood in. "T-The woman I met all those years ago wasn't Habun. She was Miriam Whitmore. Beloved wife and future mother. There was never a moment where I believed-" She gasps. "The vision."

There was a feeling of forever; hours of wasted time being stuck in the same position, eyes closed, and a drowsiness that made her limbs ache from stiffness. But then Amora is opening her gorgeous blue irises, a blurry haze covering them. It was a fuzziness that she needed to blink away, possibly use a few of her fingers in order to wipe away the small clumps of crust that were itchy and made her feel dirty. Only as she attempted to raise her arms, she felt stuck. She was pressed flat to the surface she lay upon. It was hard, cold and squeaked if she wiggled her hips too hard. The inability to do anything besides turn her head, and wiggle her phalanges, removed the remaining blinders. With irises widening and panic settling in the way they darted all over the room she was in, she struggled to set herself free. She was being held down by a force, her ankles and wrists encased by imaginary cuffs. As best as she could she lifts her head, desperate to get a better glance at her surroundings. There wasn't much to look at though—white covering everything it could from top to bottom. There was a giant light hung above her, the fluorescent rays being as bright as the sun; making Amora squint and wish that it be moved from anywhere that wasn't directly down on her face. To the left she could see the faint outline of a door.

A padded door.

Said padded door now opened with a creak that burned her ears enough to make her cringe and shift about some more.

That's when she saw them. They were covered in silky pearl gowns, dragging across the floor yet collecting not a speck of dust. Hovering above their heads were purple crowns; intricate detailing swirling about the thick material. Vines, flowers, and curves that make the trained eye want to trace it to the very end. Five came in at a time—towering figures that would have reached the ceiling for it hadn't been built to accommodate their bodies. But Amora couldn't help but keep staring at giant white wings that were protruding from their backs. They all looked to be different, the layering of the feathers, how big and small said feathers were in certain places, whether there was a silver sparkle that was attached. Mesmerizing really. And Amora continued to stare when one of the women stepped forward and began to speak.

"Maeve Whitmore. Please understand that this is for your own good" The woman approached nonchalantly. Her hands were clasped together underneath the long sleeves of her robe. She looked the furthest from contrite, expression emotionless as she gazed down at Amora. That was another thing that made the elderly confused. She was Amora Loom. Why address her as another? Trying the best she could, Amora tries to look at any part of her—seeing that her typically pale and wrinkly fingers matched one of a youthful colored female. Black nail polish was chipping and a singular silver ring was loose enough to begin falling off her middle finger.

Maeve.

Maeve from when?

"We should have approached you sooner. This kind of power..." The woman sighed. *"It can't be held by only one. But don't worry, we can help. Trust us."*

"How did I not piece it together!?" Amora's shout startled the others. She was shaking, her pupils were beginning to dilate. She looks up at the sky. The sun was descending and the peaks of something far more ferocious were rising. It made the sky less pink and far more red. "I'm running out of time."

"Ms. Loom, please tell us what's wrong?" Zenaida asks softly. She even approached the older woman with a gentle touch to her shoulder. Only she wasn't able to get much out besides the tumbling over words and incoherent sentences.

"The red moon."

It was a croak, being coughed out by Emry. Happy smiles reached the pack member's faces (a genuine concern being that she might have died), and Maeve was the first to rush to her side and help her back to her feet.

"Witches are about to experience what we did all those years ago...and unfortunately Amora and I won't be immune to it."

"Well there has to be something we can do! How about we hide you guys somewhere safe? Just until it passes? No one will be able to harm you and you won't be able to-" Maeve suggests. Only she's put to hold when Emry raises a hand, shaking her head.

"Nothing can be done."

"What about Maeve then? Isn't she also part witch?" Rowan wonders.

All eyes shift to her. Excellent questions that no one has answers to. Because that's what it is; what all of this is. Nothing but a confusing mess of questions and never enough answers. Maeve has been confused and conflicted about Kariq Leada since she's arrived, and never was she given enough time to digest one thing before she was being thrown into another. Whether it be a good something else, or a bad (which is the side of the coin that she swears she keeps flipping to), she could conclude that she has whiplash from this overload. And now she's expected to give some kind of opinion to possibly being overcome by this dangerous 'red moon'; before the topic shifts and she's diving head first into something else. It'd be nice if she could breathe before she has to respond to these people, but there's no way. They're all staring at her, demanding her to say something even though she genuinely has nothing to say.

This is terrible!

But they all know that already. What do they want her to say? She doesn't know what to do just like the rest of them. None of this was making sense. She was raised by a happy human home. She was taught to believe that these fantasy creatures were nothing but a dumb idea one day. She used to spend the weekends with a few girl friends from school, dreaming of what their imaginary vampire boyfriend looked like. But at what time does she stop reeling in the fact that her (almost possible) vampire boyfriend came true?

"I believe her to be an angel" Amora eventually says. Saved Maeve from having to comment. But it doesn't help with the steady growing list of questions. Everyone was a bit confused. "The Raba are telling the truth about their family tree. My vision, I was wrong. Maeve was being *housed* by the Archangels. And no normal Kariq Leada citizen is able to touch the clouds an angel walks upon."

"Unless they've done a spell," Lucas said.

There he goes again. Being Maeve Ross-Whitmore's biggest hater.

Maeve shakes her head.

"It'd give an answer to why I couldn't exactly say what her other species was. Angels possess a power so strong that it's untouchable...it becomes unreadable for defense."

"Okay so now she's a werewolf, a witch *and* an angel?" Rowan wonders. This almost impressive snarky grin pulls at his lips, green eyes going up and down her frame. It feels wrong, taking his stare as something more than just a stare, but she took the opportunity and blushed.

"Crossing our fingers that the other two, werewolf and angel (more specifically the angel) gene cancel out the witch. It goes for any hybrid. The stronger gene dominates the body while little flashes of the weaker gene appear here and there" Emry then said.

"You guys need to go. It's guaranteed that they took Micah back to their castle. Emry and I will stay here" Amora reminds as she raises her head to look up at the sky. Didn't look like the rain was letting up anytime soon. The moon was rising just a little bit higher. She chuckled as she strangely felt some inner peace for all of this.

They're going to make it.

They just have to.

"And then what? We don't even have a way to get up there?" Foster says.

Only the sound of rain hitting everything fills the space between them. Maeve's ears perked inquisitively when the sudden sound of shoes padding against the grass became clear. Entering into the light was someone she swears she'd never see again. Tears began to collect in her eyes, and Maeve ran over. She threw them into a hug, sobs smearing into his shoulder.

"Reggie."

Chapter Twenty-Five

"How are you still alive!? Those pixies told me they killed you!" She couldn't stop hugging him. She left his arms to take a good look at his face, before bringing him back in to feel his body. She didn't want this to be a dream.

"You really thought I'd lose to some lame pixies?"

That's when her happiness deflates and she's looking up at Reggie with sadness.

"Amir had" She whispered it, voice soft enough to make you think you didn't hear. But Reggie had, and he was stiffening because he had.

"That's what I want to talk to you about."

"What?"

"Who is this vampire, and what's he doing here?" Lucas grumbles. A growl rips through his throat, but that's when Maeve notices that all of the wolves are angry that Reggie's here. Their bodies are flexed, and they stare at him with disgust.

"Am I supposed to be scared of a few puppies?"

"This is a...*friend* of mine!" Maeve jumps in. She stands in the middle of three men glaring at another man. "He even helped guide Amir and I through Lima."

"Funny that a pesky little mosquito is calling us that?" Foster then adds, not hearing Maeve in the slightest.

"Amir's friends? That mutt of mine used the same lame joke."

"Wouldn't surprise me if you killed him" Lucas replies.

"Woah, hey! Let's not jump to random conclusions!" Maeve shouts.

"Why'd you do it? He already called dibs on Maeve?" Rowan laughs, and Reggie simply sucks his teeth.

"I am a person, thank you! And we should *not* be arguing right now when we have my brother to save, Thais too!" She shoves at both Rowan and Reggie's chest, forcing them to put distance between them. "So while it's nice to see that you're alive, unless you have a way to get to the Raba's castle, I suggest you leave."

Reggie gives one last flash of his middle finger to the wolves, and then he's smiling nicely at Maeve again.

"Actually I do," He begins to dig his hands within his jacket pockets, reaching in for far longer than needed. There's no way that his pockets are that deep—or maybe they are, and it's just another magical thing; this one you can buy at any clothing store. But eventually Reggie is pulling out two familiar glowing balls, and Maeve lets excitement fill her stomach. "I still have two portals left."

"This is perfect."

Maeve reaches to hold one of the portals and someone behind her scoffs.

"While I hate to say it," Emry begins to speak. Her killer look was locked on the vampire, jaw clenched tight and fingers waiting to wrap around his neck. Honestly if Maeve wasn't still so fond of him, she would have joined the wolves—being one, if not the first to rip the man to shreds. "But this is our only option as of now. And while it may be hard, we need to push our feelings to the side and focus on saving Micah and Thais."

After letting out responses that were grumbled and hidden underneath their breaths, there were mumbled agreements. Reggie snickered. It was all Maeve needed in order to step to the side and throw the portal to the ground. She didn't take any precautions. She let a smile stretch across her face as she did the best she could to remember what the castle on a floating landform looked like. Luckily nothing went wrong. The ball collided with the ground before expanding into a large oval. She marveled when seeing the humongous stone beauty.

"Good luck" Amora smiles.

"Will you be alright?" Zenadia asks while grabbing hold of the elder lady's hand. They give each other that soothing touch, a way to ease the fear that was spreading throughout their chests. Amora nods with a tight smile.

"I think I'll stay back as well" Reggie interjects while taking a step away from the portal. Maeve whips around to look at him with furrowed brows. "Just don't think it'd be a great idea if the Raba saw me again. Can't risk them getting mad and ya' know...crush my heart."

"Not just scared?" Foster asks. But he didn't wait for a response, he was already walking through the portal. The other wolves chuckle before following behind. Zenaida blows Ms. Loom a kiss and then walks through after her husband.

Maeve looks at Emry. A droopy smile becomes, and suddenly this moment is bittersweet. So many things can go horribly wrong. Rushing up to Emry, she wraps the lady in the tightest hug she can manage. She held back the tears in her eyes.

"Keep them safe for me, will ya?" It's asked towards Reggie, sparkly eyes being too innocent for him to say no.

"Anything for you, Mae" The vampire nods. "Oh, here. You'll be needing this in order to get back" He gets as close as possible in order to place the remaining portal ball within her hand. "Come back, alright?" She could feel his breath, smell his cologne. Closing her eyes, she inhales sharply before nodding.

Then without another word she steps through the oval. It closes and disappears.

Maeve stumbles when she exits. She and the rest of the group gaze up at the giant castle. With the sun gone it appeared less elegant and more spooky. The red hue from the rising moon gave everything a wicked imagery. The tall green grass looks rotted and scratchy; the few thick trees dropped leaves but housed annoyingly loud crows. And it didn't help that the heavy rain continued to pour. They were all soaking wet, cold and in a less than cheerful mood. All in all, they wanted to save Micah and Thais and put an end to all of this. It's only been a few days but the adventure is damaging. Their bodies ached and their stomachs grumbled. They hadn't been able to do anything to stay healthy, purely running off anxiety and adrenaline. Maeve doesn't know how those main characters from action movies do it. Constantly moving, constantly worrying about whether or not the rustling in the background is actually the enemy. After this, she's going to be needing a really long vacation. Something involving a whole body massage and an all you can eat buffet.

"Okay so what's the plan?" Rowan questions.

"I don't know, go in and try to find Micah and Thais?" Zenadia answers.

"The place has got to be crawling with Junud members. This is the Raba's big moment, they don't want any disturbances" Lucas joins. "If we just barge in there, of course we're going to get attacked."

"I don't see any other way to get in?" Foster then says.

"What about our escape tunnel from before?"

"Again, there's no way that they left any part of the place unguarded. I'm actually surprised that the front doors aren't being watched."

"So let's see" Maeve voices. She shrugs her shoulders while taking a glance at the ginormous double-doors. "We won't know unless we go in. Foster, Rowan and I will go find Micah, while you two search for Thais."

"That's suicide" Foster blinks.

"I don't see you coming up with any better ideas. No one here has any idea actually. So I think we should just go with our gut, and right now mine is saying to storm the place" Maeve didn't mean to sound rude. She just believes that she's reached the point where she is ready to rip her hair out. This was going to end, and it was going to end now. "Here," She places the portal ball within Zenaida's palm. "Use this after you find Thais. We'll meet back here. If you feel as though we're taking too long, just go."

"Woah, woah, woah. We can't just leave you."

"You can, and you will. At least some of us need to get to safety" She faces Foster and Rowan. "At any time, you run and save yourselves too. I don't need anyone else getting hurt, or dying because of me."

The duo nods.

Chapter Twenty-Six

Foster and Lucas had been the ones to open the front doors to the castle. There had been that same screeching sound; loud enough to pop the ears of anyone. Rowan stood in front, claws and canines on display just in case a Junud member wanted to surprise attack. But once noticing the foyer was as empty and silent as the first time Maeve was here, blondie quit flexing and stood upright. His green eyes looked back and forth, up and down, desperate to find anyone ready for a fight. Eventually he was simply left confused, stepping in the middle of the red carpet and yet no one. The rest followed his lead, eyeing up all of the glorious antique material the further they walked in.

They startled when hearing the doors close on their own. But they startled even worse upon hearing an echoed scream.

"Micah!" Maeve shouts.

The group looks at one another. For a moment reality sinks in. They're all about to go fight for their lives. It's not certain all of them will make it out—which has to be the scariest part out of all of this. Maeve has never been one to fret over life and death. As cliche as it sounds, she typically lived in the moment. Whatever was going on right then, right there, that's what she thought about, that's what she dealt with. But now...now she's praying in her head, begging to whoever will listen, that she be the one to keep her life. She was praying that they all did. She wanted this to be something that she can say she survived from.

Stare holding firm and determined, they all mentally agree to the plan once more before splitting. It's watched as Lucas takes hold of Zenaida's hand before guiding her left. They enter through an archway, disappearing the further they enter the new room. Maeve, Rowan and Foster immediately dash up the large staircase when hearing Micah scream out in agony again. It's an awful sound; like nails on a chalkboard. Maeve's used to hearing her loved ones kick and cry—Jax absolutely loathes going to the dentist (which he wouldn't have to do if he ate anything other than junk), Bailey tends to be spoiled by their parents therefore she throws a tantrum when things don't go her way, and Aziel is just so emotionally sensitive anything can make the kid shed tears—but nothing can compare to the shouts she's listening to right now. It's terrible and Maeve would rather rip her ears off than have to keep listening to it.

"I think he's this way!" Foster directs. He's pointing to the right, up the shorter amount of stairs. Both Rowan and Maeve would have followed if she wasn't yet again enraptured by that one piece of stained glass art. She was much closer to it this time. With a steady hand she raised her fingers to it, letting them just barely graze the cold and smooth surface. It's when the tip of her index had touched the kneeling woman's purple halo that every-thing felt fuzzy and Maeve swore the world was spinning far too fast. She clutched her head, eyes beginning to roll into the back of her head as she then gasped for air.

"*Remember, we're doing this for the sake of the world. Don't you want to keep your family safe?...Or well, what's left of it?*" It was some faceless woman talking to her. She wore all white. Actually everything was. The entire room, the bright light that shined down on her. Maeve had no idea what was going on but she felt conflicted. This was something that she needed to do, and yet the smallest part of her didn't like how she felt strapped down. There was nothing physically restraining her and yet she couldn't move.

"*Yes, I'm willing to do whatever. I just don't want this 'power' in me anymore.*"

"*Do understand that this might hurt. It's as if-*"

"*I don't care, just hurry. I can feel it getting stronger.*"

"*Maeve! Maeve! No, don't do it!*"

The shouting came with loud crashing and a jumble of other voices. It was chaos that made her head hurt. There was this unsettling ring that burned her ears and pounded at her temple. She craned her neck in order to see who could possibly be interrupting. Shock and confusion slipped from her lips as she spoke their name.

"*Amir?*"

"Maeve, are you alright?" Blinking, she was back in the castle. A hand was on her shoulder and blondie was standing beside her. "Foster thinks he found the room...you look like you just saw a ghost."

Call her crazy, but she thinks she really did.

"No yeah," She narrows her eyes on the picture. She doesn't know what weird spell it had just done to her, but she doesn't think she'll be touching it again anytime soon. "I just think this place is really getting to me. Do you know who these people are?"

Rowan raises an eyebrow as he too looks at the glass.

"It's the king and his daughter. It was created the moment she was crowned Queen of Kariq Leada" That's right, her mother was supposed to be the queen. Does that make her a princess? Maeve doesn't know if she'd be able to handle that prissy life-style. It seems fairly difficult to rule over an entire realm. She can barely handle all of the rude customers from her waitressing job demanding to get their food for free because it was just a tad bit cold. Don't yell at her, she's just the one bringing it out. Take the time to stomp into the kitchen and shout at the cooks. "It's a legendary image to be honest. Everyone here has at least seen it once."

"Why?"

"It's never been confirmed but I've been told it's because the king had favorites. He loved his daughter way more than his sons. And so when she went missing all those years ago, he used this picture as a tribute to her. You couldn't go anywhere with-out seeing it on a poster or in the news."

"No wonder they're so cruel."

"I'm sorry?"

"I just mean, when they speak about this prophecy, they always go on about finally taking what's theirs'. Well what is theirs? The throne? Power? Respect? They've probably been so overshadowed by my mom, that they want to use this as an opportunity to be in the spotlight finally."

Maeve sighs as she can tell Rowan just wasn't getting it.

"Are you siding with the bad guys right now? Because let

me tell you, they've always been terrible people. Especially to us wolves."

"No I'm not siding, I'm just saying I can see where they're coming from. They're going to use this prophecy to be the most powerful therefore no one, not even King Amal can say they're unworthy" She began to trail up the stairs Foster spoke about. "And you heard what they said, they've known all along. Of course they're going to pick on the one species we were told we were."

Rowan bites at his lower lip, thinking as he watches Maeve ascend the rest of the stairs. He takes one last look at the stained glass before following her footsteps.

The duo walk down long hallways, turn various corners, and try to be as quiet as could be when almost every little move they make causes an echo within the empty rooms. Foster is standing behind a pillar, brown eyes stuck to the sight of two men standing in front of a huge rectangular door. Dressed in all black and expressions as blank as could be, it's obvious that they were a part of the Junud. Rowan and Maeve quickly scurry over to meet the other, almost scaring him when their steps were just a little too light.

"He's behind that door, but as you can see, we have company."

"So let's just take them out real quick?" Rowan bubbles. He cracks his knuckles ready to step from behind. Only he's stopped by Foster's good arm, keeping him from walking too far.

"That's going to sound the alarm for the rest of them to come out. And who knows if Lucas and Zenaida made it down to the dungeon just yet."

"We probably shouldn't be out like this either. Someone can

easily come around the corner and spot us. We need to find somewhere to hide for the time being" Maeve then suggests. She looks around, smiling when seeing a cracked door back the way she came. So grabbing Rowan's wrist, who grabbed Foster's, she dragged both men into the room. Once in, she closes the door softly.

"I think I'm going to be sick," Blondie gags. Maeve chuckles out of amusement (because where did that come from?). He was just fine two seconds ago. What could have made his stomach bile rise? She would have asked if she wasn't turning around and being met with the most vile sight.

She gasps. The three of them were in a bedroom. A female's bedroom; with an insane amount of pink, the floral patterns, the lacy trim that was attached to anything it could. A large bed was in the middle of it all, fluffy white pillows covered in silk pillowcases. The sheet and blanket were tucked and laid into perfection. What was gruesome about it was the hundreds of bloody hearts that were scattered all over the room. Crimson covered what could have been the gorgeous decor, and it stained what was obviously so pure. Maeve was surprised to not have smelt it the moment she walked in, but the hearts are rotted and are leaving the most horrid smell to ever touch her nostrils. She pinches her nose, turning to the side so she doesn't have to look at the sight any longer.

"I can taste it," Maeve chokes. "We need to get out of here."

She's about to open the door again when she's halted by Foster.

"Wait look, they all have some sort of name tag" With absolutely no care or nausea, Foster lifts one of the hearts from the ground. Moldy blood attaches itself to his skin and both Rowan and Maeve have to hold back from vomiting once more.

"Gross dude, put it down!"

"Camila Shaw" Foster looks at his friend. "Hey, wasn't she that nerdy witch in our science class back in senior year?"

"The one who swore she was better than the teacher. Like we get it, your powers help you calculate formulas properly" Rowan groans with an eye roll. Must have been an annoying girl to be classmates with.

"Yeah, I think this is her heart."

"What? Ew! Put it down! We have to get out of here or I might actually puke."

Maeve is intrigued by this though.

"Wait, do all of these belong to witches?" She wonders. Is this why they've been disappearing?

Foster picks up another heart reading the tag.

"Uh, Henry Mule" Foster is quick to drop it to the ground, ears shading red. He clears his throat. "I uh, I knew him. He's a witch as well."

Rowan smirks.

"How well did you know him?" He's wiggling his eyebrows and Maeve joins in with the teasing too by making "oouu" sounds.

"All you need to know is that it was before Micah. Mind your business."

"Speaking of you and Micah...are you guys mated?" Maeve interjects. That makes Foster flustered even more. He was beginning to look like a cherry. He didn't know how to make his large frame less awkward.

"No," A hand is going to the back of his head in order to scratch his nape. Ew, it was the bloody hand and now he has it in his hair. "I um, I sort of rejected him back in the forest" Maeve was surprised, but Rowan was in complete disarray. "But that's not what we're supposed to be discussing right now! We need to figure out how to get into that room."

"My heart breaks for you guys" Blondie mockingly cries. "I actually ship you two more than the ones who are married."

"I appreciate your blessing," Foster sarcastically said. "Now how are we going to get into that room?"

"I can try to use my powers. Witches are able to put someone to sleep, right?" Maeve says with a wave of her hand. She still doesn't know how to work her magic. In some ways she's just happy that nothing's blown up for quite some time.

"Of course! Ms. Loom used to use it on me all the time!" Rowan exclaims.

Maeve wasn't even going to ask, and Foster wasn't going to help explain. They were just going to have to let the information linger and possibly ask about it later.

"Okay, then let's go. Put the guards to sleep, creep in, and get Micah back" Foster encourages. Rowan was immediately agreeing, actually being the first one out. He dramatically inhaled, indulging in the scent that wasn't decomposing witch organs. Maeve was the last to leave, something having caught her eye as she exited. One of the old paintings was crooked, tilted in a sense that was far too precise in order to just be an accident. And she knows curiosity isn't the best for their situation right now, but there's part of her that is itching to fix it.

Or see what it may lead to.

So resting on her tip-toes she flinches with each step. She doesn't want to squish some poor person's heart. When she reaches the painting, she's just about to touch it when her name is being called.

"Maeve! What are you doing?"

"There's something wrong-"

"Worry about it later! We need to get to Micah now!"

"Let me just," That's when she tilted the frame back into place. As she does so the sound of a click rings throughout the room. Maeve looks back at Foster and Rowan, wondering if they heard it too. Seeing as they had, they were skeptical about it as well.

Maeve pulls back the painting, and is astounded to see that it was an opening to a secret compartment. What she managed to find in it was even more appalling.

"Are you sure you're going the right way? I think the entrance might have been that way" Zenaida comments while her and Lucas turn yet another corner. It was as if she was walking around a maze. These underground halls felt like confusing tunnels that if you don't make it out, you'll die trying. Sue her, but Zenadia felt like she was going to die trying. She's seen that same rat chewing on that same piece of hard bread four times now. Now that means they're either going in circles, or the rat is following them. To taunt them.

"You have to remember that this isn't my first time being down here. I know where I'm going."

"I know, I'm just getting anxious. What if Thais is hurt? What if none of us make it out in time?" She gently hits his forearm while her face is filled with worry. "I don't want this to be the end for us."

Lucas stops in his tracks, turning so he can pull her in for a hug. She melts into the embrace, breathing in his scent—one that has always calmed her. She closes her eyes and tries to will away all of the scary outcomes.

"We're going to be okay. Thais, Micah, everyone is going to be okay. You just have to trust."

She nods along to his words, but she doesn't know if she can allow herself to believe them. Something about all of this isn't sitting right with her.

"I love you, forever" Zenaida whispers. She looks up at her husband, trailing her hands upward so she can card them through his outgrown hair. He gazes down at her, letting his lips pull into a smile.

"I love you too" Slowly they collide into a kiss, lips joining into a dance that just proved that the universe had gotten this right. Had gotten them right.

Unfortunately ruining their romantic moment had been loud clapping. The couple broke apart, snapping their necks to the left of them. Because of course they couldn't just save Thais without any more hassle. The nuisance, General Harris is sneering at them from a distance. She looked like a wreck. Her missing hand was stitched and covered by a metal plate. Her broken leg was wrapped in a cast. And all of the cuts she received turned into scars, ruining her once flawless skin.

"Cute."

Her voice was hoarse.

"You couldn't have given us some privacy?"

"I thought you were dead."

General Harris thought she was dead too. But before she

could, her fellow members helped bring her back to safety. They saved her life.

"Well then I hate to relay the terrible news. Fortunately you don't have to dwell on it for too long. You'll be dead" She pulls out a sword and then is seen charging towards them. The wedded couple jump apart when she gets close enough. Then when she's turning around with a swing, Zenadia ducks, and brings a leg out to trip her. She's falling, until she's being grabbed by Lucas and thrown into the nearest wall. The tunnels shake and her body colliding with stone leaves a cringey sound. He goes to lift her limp form, but is being stabbed in the leg by a small blade. General Harris smirks, pulling it out and then slicing at his cheek. Lucas feels helpless as holds onto his leg, kneeling as he moans from the pain.

"Lucas" Zenaida calls. General Harris throws a punch to Lucas's right cheek, knocking the poor man to the ground. The red-head can't relish in her win for too long because she's being tackled to the floor. Zenaida had thrown herself at the evil woman, rolling them backwards by a few inches. She manages to get a few punches in with Harris, but is then being punched in the side, and then kneed in the stomach. She's glad she hasn't eaten anything.

General Harris goes over to Zenaida and grabs her by the hair. Screams are heard from the pull, but then they're hushed when her head is being slammed into the wall. Once, then twice, and Zenaida has definitely broken her nose. She was dizzy, a ringing piercing her ears. Lucas' voice was muffled, and the only thing she could feel was the warm sensation of her own blood falling from her temple.

"Ugh, get off of me" Zenadia slurs. Her hand glows green and with a flick of her wrist, the general no longer has a hold on her. She flew to the ground actually, grunting when the wind was knocked out of her. Lucas bit his tongue as he stood to his feet again. He growled, brown eyes shading into a dark yellow. As he cracked his neck, his teeth were longer and sharper. As he wiggled his fingers, his nails extended into long claws. And with one look at his wife—his battered and bruised wife, he howled. Tearing right through his clothes, he shifted into his wolf. A giant beast who's back was almost touching the ceiling. His fur was all black.

Lucas was barking before he was leaping through the air and onto the red-head. He didn't hesitate to show her the enormous teeth that will be ripping her flesh from bone. With a heavy paw, he raised it and slashed at her stomach, reopening old wounds. Blood splattered and General Harris screamed. He'd done it a few times, just scratching away at her skin as though she was some sort of chew toy. It was when Lucas went in to snap both of her legs with his own, he was flinching. A whimper squeaked from out of his throat. He would have bothered to shift back and see what she had done to him, but then she grinned. She looked wicked as she stared into his eyes. It made his hatred burn.

"At least I didn't bash your head in."

Lucas growled at the implication. It had also been enough for him to finally kill her. With a widened jaw, he sunk all of his knives for teeth into her neck. He dragged her from under him and then clamped down. He could feel the snap of her bones, taste the iron in her blood on his tongue. Then to make sure that she wouldn't ever be coming back, he twists and rips her head from her body altogether. He spits her out, head bouncing and then rolling inches away. He snarls at a dead General Harris before limping over to his wife. She was still conscious, that's good, but she didn't look in the best condition. He uses his head to nudge her, his snout lifting her head by her chin. A weak smile tugs on her lips as she feels him.

"Please tell me she's finally gone" She got a head nod and some soft humming. "Well okay then, let's finish finding Thais" She struggles to stand and that's when Lucas yet again uses his head to nudge her. He taps at her leg, a signal the entire group uses when they are asking another to get on one's back. Zenadia doesn't refuse. In her agonizing state, she will more than willingly take a ride. It's when she gets on that Lucas falters from her weight. A burn overcomes his entire right side. "You're hurt" She tries to get off and yet he shakes her back on. "Lucas, I can try my best to walk. If you're seriously injured I don't want to strain you any further."

Doesn't seem like Lucas cares. He shakes his head with a huff before starting to walk down the hallway. They have to bypass a mutilated general, but that's okay. Lucas only uses a paw to push her head off to the side.

The couple are only walking for a minute more before Lucas nudges Zenadia that they've reached the dungeon. It was behind a door; locked by a lock just as old and rusty as the rest of the place. Being placed back on her feet, Zenaida raises a hand. She tucks some of her platinum hair behind her ear.

"Walan kasr" She whispers it while turning her wrist. The lock snaps in half, falling to the dirty ground with a clank. Zenadia stumbles into her husband's side, clutching the side of her head.

"She must have really got me. That bitch, now I have the biggest headache known to man."

She recollects herself before grabbing the door handle and entering. It squeaks as she pulls it open. The Raba truly need to invest in some oil. The hinges on their doors are getting pretty stiff. It's an ear-sore and doesn't help the throbbing that Zenaida wished away with some simple rubbing. The duo creep in, keeping not only their eyes but ears open for any other possible Junud members. But it was as if all danger was a second thought when weeping could be heard from three cells over.

"Thais?" Zenaida calls. She got some shuffling. "Thais, is that you?" More shuffling with some heavy breathing and even louder sobs.

"Zenaida!? Over here! Over here!" The teenage girl sticks an arm between the bars, waving it as she was no longer crying out of sorrow, but happiness.

The couple run over. They're met with a disheveled Thais Miller. She has a few bruises on her face, and it was stained with tears alongside dribbling snot. Zenaida does the best she can to wrap her arms around her. The hug was awkward and broken not long after. It made Zenadia rush the process of breaking another rusty lock, swinging the metal bar door open and then securing the frail teenage girl in the warmest and safest hug she could ever give. They fell to the floor, Thais using the opportunity to cry out any of the remaining tears she could still produce. She gripped onto Zenaida's shirt, curling the fabric within her fingers; believing that if she held on tight enough she would finally be grounded.

"They killed Gabe. They did it right in front of me" Bloodshot eyes peered into the older woman's. Zenaida's heart broke as she looked into the soul of a changed girl. She was so broken, so petrified. "He was only trying to change my mind. He didn't want me getting tied up with Raba, and so they killed him. I'm so sorry" She leaves Zenaida's hold in order to crawl over to the opposite cell. Laying in a pool of his own blood, a lifeless Gabe stared back. Thais cried more waterfalls while looking at him. She reached through the bars trying to touch him one last time. She flinched when feeling how cold he was. "I'm sorry. I'm sorry. I'm sorry. Oh please Gabe, please forgive me. I didn't mean for this to happen."

Lucas got closer and was easing his head in between Thais and the cell. He was trying to slither his entire body, but that's when she began to panic and refused to leave Gabe all alone.

"No! He has to know how sorry I am. Please!"

"Thais darling, he's gone. You can only trust that he knows" Zenaida uses her words to encourage the other back. Thais detaches from the cell, but is still rooted in her spot. She's motioned to get on Lucas' back. "You're going to be okay."

"But Gabe-"

"Gabe is also going to be okay. I bet he's lending us his strength" Thais is helped onto Lucas. He's so warm, and his fur is so soft. From a sitting position, Thais slowly finds herself lying down. She nuzzles her face deep into the neck of her friend, eyes closing. She's exhausted. Hopefully no one would mind if she shut her eyes for a second or two. Thais couldn't remember if she asked or not. She just knows that Zenaida was saying something along the lines of her being safe now so she can relax, and that it's best that they get out of here.

Amora and Emry sit on a bench that was nearby. It was cold to the touch, sending goosebumps up their arms. They kept their distance as they sat, the only contact coming from their eyes; and the only sight being how terrified they were for the next few minutes. Reggie awkwardly stood in front of them, brown irises glancing everywhere besides the elderly women. His shoes, the deep red moon, the way an already berserk witch was running after an elf before being tackled by another witch. He cringed at the attack, taking a step back, even though he wasn't close enough to be spotted, and it was highly unlikely that he would get caught up in the tussle. Emry must have seen it too because once the first witch literally made the other witch turn into ashes, she was speaking montonely.

"That's going to be us any moment" A soft breath pushes from her nose. "If I live through it, I wonder if I'm going to remember it all? I hope not."

"Why?" Reggie blurts. He doesn't care, but the hanging silence left an open space for the question. Someone had to say it or the depressing tension will only get worse. He didn't like seeing two old ladies mope. It made his skin crawl, and made him feel slightly uncomfortable. But once both of the women turn to look at him, he wishes he never said anything to begin with. Because now Emry glared.

"I never saw what Maeve saw in you-"

"Well that'd be weird if you did. You look like my grandma."

"Bite your tongue, vampire!" Amora gasps. Reggie shrugs. Emry rolls her eyes.

"How long have you been tracking her?" Emry asks. Her grip on the bench rail was seen tightening. Her pupils were shrinking and her irises were beginning to change into a red. Reggie could see the evil. "How long have you been preparing to crush her heart?"

"There was originally no romantic intention-"

"Then what? It was after you got a good look at her that you decided you were just going to charm your way in. Be handsome and flirty to just hand her right over to the Raba!" Emry stood from her seat, hands clenched tight into fists. They also began to spark with a darkened version of its typical magic. Cautious Reggie stood tall, resisting the demonic need to defend himself. He'd only respond if he was attacked first.

"You have to understand that I did what I had to do in order to complete my mission,"

"And so you did so by playing with a precious girl's feelings?" Amora is growing a bit enraged too—and that's when her ocean blue turned into a ruby. He curses underneath his breath. Reggie then glances up at the night sky and sees that the moon was finally in place and it shined its garnet rays upon Kariq Leada. Maybe he can talk his way out of this?

"Being heartless, cruelty is the only option when it comes to decision making. I was far more focused on retrieving my award than I was Maeve's feelings."

Emry's face goes blank and that's when he knew that his words meant absolute shit to this woman. She's raising a fist as she charges towards him.

"I am going to make you suffer!" Reggies is quick to move out of the way, but somehow underestimates Emry's abilities. Without having to turn around, she's tossing an ice spear behind her, it going through Reggie's shoulder. He stumbles from the hit, groaning from the rather unsettling impact. But still refusing to sharpen his fangs and release his claws, he just pulls the spear out of his shoulder and tosses it to the ground. It shatters beside Amora's feet and then she's letting out a shrill.

"How dare you throw that at me?"

"It wasn't intentional. Besides your friend here is the one who created it in the first place. Blame her" He motions to a snarling Emry, someone who is pulling huge brown roots from within the park grass. They hovered over her like ten tentacles, wiggling slightly as they await their orders. Unfortunately they weren't allowed a directive because they were being sliced down with a simple slash of wind. Emry takes her attention from Reggie and places it on the woman who responded with her own powers.

"Must you always be such a nuisance!?"

She pushes Amora back into the bench with her own gust of wind.

"You insult me as though we're teenagers still. Looking at your face now, I'm beginning to realize how much I actually despise you."

Running from her spot, she jumps high, the bracelet on her wrist transforming into a knife that fits perfectly in her hand. It's silver and has her name engraved on the handle. She's ready to dig her weapon into any part of Emry, but is halted when she's kicked to the ground. She slams into the grass, rolling over when the impact cracked her spine.

If Reggie knew that they would have tried to kill each other, he wouldn't have pointed fingers. Now he has to go do damage control.

Emry begins to chant spells as she throws a blow of power

at Amora. She successfully blocked and dodged most, only being hit and seared by three fireballs. Her pale skin melts, burning and flaring red as she struggles to lift herself back to her feet. Emry runs and grabs hold of Amora when she's close enough. She grabs onto the other's wrist, throwing her over her shoulder, before dragging her slightly with momentum, and then with as much strength, tossing her body against a nearby lamppost. Amora lay on the ground, unmoving and what might be breathless. Reggie's eyes go wide. He looks from one old lady to the other, shocked. Emry was smirking in triumph.

"Always was the weakest" Then snapping her neck in the direction of Reggie her anger flares once more. "Now you."

Reggie doesn't waste time, using his much faster speed in order to get behind Emry and restrain her with his arms. She jerks around to find an outing—grin devilish when she slips an arm out and throws a punch to his stomach. Reggie is caught off guard, allowing the elder to then jump and grab him by the arms and flip their positions. She pants between chuckles, all of them landing on the tip of his ear. Reggie's irises shade rose and his fangs extend. He throws his head back, butting Emry in her forehead, and then is quickly turning around where he grabs her neck with one hand and begins to squeeze. He can feel the crushing of Emry's throat within his palm. It's a wonderful sensation. The pumping of her tasty heart was vibrating throughout her entire body and he was beginning to wonder what she tasted like. Reggie brings her in closer, only squeezing tighter when she starts to hit him. She coughs, she gasps for air. He lets his nose touch her neck, inhaling sharply where he then throws his head back to sigh dreamily.

Then without warning he's using his thumb to bare her neck and sink his teeth into her. Emry shouts from the pain. She also flinched when there was a sting that came with the puncturing of her skin with his teeth. It had an inflamed feeling, and she could feel the way that he injected her with some of his venom. It soared through her veins like endorphins, and then it wasn't long before she was falling limp in Reggie's arms, fast asleep.

"There," He lays the woman on the ground. Then he wipes at the corner of his lips before fixing his wrinkled shirt. "That should keep her out for a few hours."

Chapter Twenty-Seven

"Why must you bring that?" Rowan asks as his face contorts into one of distaste.

"I believe it needs to be returned to its rightful owner. Now shush so I can concentrate" Maeve says as she returns her focus to the two guards who refuse to move in even the slightest. She inhales as he raises a hand. She doesn't know if this is something conducted by a spoken spell, or if she needs some kind of potion, but she guesses she'll find out the answer when she attempts to put them asleep. Images of her watching the two men slowly yawn flood her brain. And then she's imagining that they are leaning against the wall from drowsiness. They can't stop blinking, forcing away the heaviness that pulled their eyelids down. But the tranquility that comes with sleep sounds great, and the men are eventually sliding down the wall. Their heads loll to the side and their breathing steadies. Maeve would have thought that it was nothing but an illusion in her head if Rowan wasn't then congratulating her.

Her hands dim from purple. *When did they start glowing?* And she's blinking in order to see if the guards were actually on the ground. They were. They had gotten comfortable enough to curl up like fetus babies.

"It worked, now come on" Foster is the first to move out of hiding.

The trio are cautious as they approach the sleeping Junud members. They open the large door as best as they could without waking them, and then are slithering inside. Turning around they're met with a ballroom. It was huge. The ceiling was high and decorated in old art—the colors having faded from their once vibrant shades and hues. The architecture was as gorgeous as the rest of the place. All of it was carved and cared for with intricacy. Swirls and curves. Jagged lines and indents, all in the right spots, in the best ways. The floor was polished wood, shining underneath the large chandelier that housed thousands of sparkling crystals. Maeve would have gawked at how beautiful the room looked if she wasn't just as detesting the torture chamber that was placed in the middle of it all.

It was some giant metal machine. Wires and pumps were connected to it, and its motors created indescribable sounds. The worst part was seeing where all those pumps led to.

Micah had been strapped to a table, arms and neck being poked by plenty of needles. He looked to be trembling in pain as he laid strapped where he was—whatever the machine was called sucking something violet from out of him. He shouts in horror and Maeve has to dig her nails into her arm not to do so with him. She couldn't describe it, but she could almost feel the torture as well. Tight; is the closest she can come up with. Almost as if being squeezed, crushed.

"Oh my god, Micah" Her voice cracks.

Maeve, Foster and Rowan run over. They don't immediately touch him, just let their eyes do a bunch of scanning. Micah looks worse up close. He was growing skinny, face pale and irises almost faded. They all wanted to remove him from this horrendous machine, but don't quite know where to start. Maeve tries to take a needle from out of her brother's arm, but stops when he begins to shout louder.

"What's this?" Rowan wonders as he taps at a glass. It was tall and round, and was filled with the liquid being pumped out of the pack leader.

"I'm so glad you asked!" A booming voice crept from out of the shadows. No one was surprised to see that it was Qayid. It was all of them. Fakhar and Qua too; tailing their brother with matching menacing stares. Foster did his best to hide Micah behind him. "This is my way of getting what we need. The striped magical abilities not just from anyone, but the chosen one" He lowers his voice. "I should have known some lousy witch wouldn't be enough."

What?

"You're the reason all of those witches went missing?" Maeve asks firmly. She moves from around the machine and is bravely standing in front of the Raba.

"Even us kings have our faults. For a moment we actually believed our plan to fail. And what other great magic source to grant us our wish, than witches? We just had to find someone who was strong enough" Qayid waves his hands with a grin. "As you can see, there was no one who stuck...but then we caught wind that you're still breathing and suddenly everything is falling into place all over again. Besides, no one is truly going to care that a few spell casters went missing when the entire realm has it out for them."

"But I'm the one you want. The chosen one. Let my brother go."

"See that's where you're wrong" Having suddenly disappeared and then reappeared behind her, Qayid twirled a curl of Maeve's hair before flicking it away. She whips around, shaking away the goosebumps this man gave her. He chuckles low. "The Haya fooled us all. It is inscribed that you are the one to be the source of this invincible power, and yet it is the first born. Like it should be."

He grinds his teeth.

"What's so special about the first born? They're older, so they get everything?"

"WRONG!" Qayid shouts in her face. He's snapping his head to the left. "Where do you think you're going!?" Without having to order, Fakhar is throwing a hand out. Heads turn and they're able to see Foster and Rowan trying to help (a now unpinned) Micah towards the exit doors. They stand where they are frozen."I don't expect you to understand" He returns his attention to Maeve and grips her by her chin. She instantly reaches to grab his wrist. "And I just don't have enough kindness in my heart to explain it to you. Just know that angels are selfish, and I deserve all of the power your pathetic mother received."

He throws Maeve to the ground.

A bell chimes.

"It's time!"

In rushes a few more Junud members, stone cold as they restrain the trio of boys. Foster manages to knock only one of them unconscious before he's being tackled by three more. Qayid reaches for the glass full of violet power. He winks at Maeve before gulping it down. She wonders how it tastes? Like air, or water? Maybe it's grape flavored and her brother's powers taste like a jolly rancher. The elderly man is seen sighing contently as he finishes the glass, letting it slip from his fingers and shatter to the floor. His eyes shade entirely black and wings sprout from his back. He holds both of his hands out and instantly his brothers are at his side. They connect palms before rising into the air. White light shoots from out of their eyes and mouths and then they're phasing into one another. It's disgusting really. They're almost melting into one body.

On three sides of a head, there were a set of eyes, a mouth, and a nose. Two more pairs of wings shoot out of their back, and they begin to flap. The gust of wind is enough to make Maeve turn away. Fine with her, she didn't want to watch the grueling imagery that was this one person growing two more pairs of arms and legs. A true monster is what they looked like in the end.

"Soon no one from any realm will be able to stop me!" The monster's voice was contorted. Three different pitches combined into one. "'Adeu quat ruasa',"

"Holy shit, what do we do!?" Maeve shouts. She was hoping that one of the guys would be able to give her an answer, and yet she was met with silence. She moves her eyes from off of the meshed mess that used to be three separate uncles, and onto her friends. They were still struggling to be set free from the Junud. Except Micah, he must have passed out from all of the suffering.

"Almalayikati! zudani bialquat walquat walshari hataa 'uhaqiq raghbati."

"I guess it's up to me—Hey!" Before she's able to release any of her magic, she's being grabbed by a Junud. He's trying to get her to the ground, but she wiggles about. "Get away, I'm trying to save the world!" Her lip curls and frustration reaches her voice as she uses her strength to get the guy off of her. She elbows him in the face before taking his arm and flipping him onto his back. When seeing him down, she reaches for the gun within his holster and cocks it back within seconds. Her eyes flash all white before she's letting a bullet fly into the man's head. Part of his brain is flying onto the amazing wood floors. Her eyes return to normal, but only for a moment. And within that moment she feels guilty. She just killed someone. Then her eyes are back to white and her tight grip on the gun returns.

She fires one, two, three at the men holding her friends hostage. Four, five, six, they're dropping like flies. Foster and Rowan look between the dead soldiers and Maeve holding the weapon. They won't lie, they're a bit scared of her.

"Tajealuni la yumkin waqfuha."

"Go, now" Maeve demands. Foster scoops Micah into his arms and is already making his way out the door. He stops when Rowan isn't following.

"Come on."

"But what if she needs help?" Rowan protests. He watches as Maeve turns to face the Raba.

"This is something beyond our help! We need to go now!"

Rowan shakes his head.

"No, I'm staying. You take Micah to safety, find the others."

There was no changing his mind. Rowan was already jogging further into the battlefield, picking up a random piece of metal that must have fallen from the machine. Foster clenched his jaw, debating whether he wants to stay or go. He looked down at Micah. He looked so sickly. Nodding, he wishes the duo good luck before leaving the room.

"I'm the chosen one, therefore it's my job to stop you!" Maeve shouts. Hands that were beaming with a violet hue, she began to throw surges of power at the Raba. It knocks them from their concentration, the spell getting caught in their throat. One hit in particular strikes them to the ground. They moan as they raise their shared head. All six irises glare at her. They rise to their feet, and that's when the intimidation sprouts. Maeve steps back, hands in front of her for defense.

"You can't stop me. The ritual has already commenced!" The monster stomps his foot and the ground shakes. Maeve is thrown and is unable to notice the giant ball of fire that was flying towards her. Rowan does though, so he's shoving her out of the way. They go crashing to the floor. Blondie lands on top of her.

"Are you alright?"

"I told you to leave!" She yells back. Maeve pushes him off of her. Weird to see her eyes constantly shade from brown, to purple, to white. A loop that Rowan is strangely getting lost in. "Leave this instant."

"Yes your maje—No," Rowan shakes his head. "I'm here to help."

"With what? Dying?"

"Well I just saved you from getting torched, so you're welcome" He grins.

The conversation is short lived when the Raba is yet again throwing a blow of power in their direction. Maeve pushes

Rowan out of the way before holding her hands up. A shield surrounds her and the blast fizzles into the air. She waits a second more before using her power to shoot yet again. It definitely leaves an effect but nothing strong enough to knock him down. Maeve is growing irritated that this monster wasn't being harmed, leaving her shots to get more sloppy. She focused on getting at least one hit to their face, trying the tactic that is temporarily blinding them. It left her vulnerable to her surroundings. So she wasn't able to notice that a sharp blade was being morphed out of an arm. It elongated and was trying to attack from the side. As it surged to hit Maeve, it ended up piercing Rowan right in the stomach. Yet again he had jumped in, this time leading to a fatality. The blade contracts and Rowan falls to the ground with a thump. Time stills and Maeve is watching her friend fall to the floor. She watches as velvety blood oozes out of him and makes the polished wood slippery. She shouts as she rushes to his side. It's just before she can get to him, she's being flung into the power sucking machine.

Her body crashes into it, and she can whole-heartedly say that it's worse than when she hit that shelf in the mall.

She lays within the bent and broken scraps. She could feel the ache of her muscles, feel the burn of all of her new cuts. She's actually ready to just give up and let this be the end for all. But as she slowly turns her head, she's looking at Rowan. His chest rose and fell slowly. He still had some cheerful wonder behind his green eyes, chapped lips twitching into a smile.

"Now where were we?" The monster's voice says. "Tajealuni la yumkin waqfuha. Aghmurni bikhataya saqitina,"

Maeve presses her lips into a straight line, fingers curling into fists. She struggles to get up at first, but then her eyes shade white and she's standing on her feet. She stalks over to the Raba, hands raised and already blasting more of her power. It causes damage this time. The monster is hit, stumbling into a stone sculpture of a naked woman. The statue crumbles, but the Raba still uses what's left of it to throw big and heavy chunks at Maeve. She successfully dodges them; there being a moment where she almost is hit by the last piece, the head.

"You can't stop me Maeve Whitmore. I am destined to be your ruler!"

"Show me the fine print then" That's when she's applying all of her pressure onto the Raba. They howl in pain, but then suddenly both the monster and Maeve are floating. Maeve's body extends, and her mouth is opening wide. The perimeter of her body is glowing white. Large wings are ripping through her skin and she screams from the pain. Light is coming from out of her mouth and the Raba grows excited. They continue to chant their spell.

"Yes, yes! The prophecy shall be fulfilled. Aghmurni bikhataya saqitina, waismah lah 'an yurshidani 'iilaa ma hu li!"

The Raba's body too is being extended. But when it's believed that he will be soaking in the remains of Maeve's soul, it feels as though theirs is being taken in return. Fear furrows their eyebrows and pain is punching them in the gut. They struggle to be released from the torment, and yet are held in place. The Raba's eyes roll to the back of their head as their soul in the shape of a black wave is leaving their mouth and into Maeve's. Lights of the ballroom flickered and the walls of the castle shook. Soon Maeve clamps her mouth shut and is looking down at the monster with her own all black eyes.

"Angels are selfish" Maeve's voice was different. It was lower, mixed with an unrecognizable entity. "And I deserve all of the power you pathetic men have never received."

With one final blast, the Raba were vaporized right before her eyes. They were dust that descended to the floor slowly, being swept up in whatever direction the breeze was moving. Maeve too fell to the floor. She coughed, gasping for air.

Then for the first time since she entered the castle, she could see clearly. Her brown eyes twinkled with concern as she darted her attention over to Rowan. He was already looking at her, flopping an arm out to show that he still had a few heartbeats left. She ran to his side, cradling his limp body within her arms. Tears slowly fell down her face.

"I'm so sorry! This wasn't supposed to happen" She caresses his face. She uses her thumb to brush away the few tears that fell from his own eyes. "There has to be a way I can heal you! I have all these powers now."

She places a palm onto his chest, but he shakes his head and tries to remove her touch.

"Maeve..."

"Don't try to stop me. I have to try. I'm not letting another person die because of me."

Then with a white hue, a surge of power is pumping throughout Rowan.

Chapter Twenty-Eight

The portal had been opened. It glimmered as it displayed central park. Reggie can be seen panting as he sits upon a metal bench. The group debated whether or not they should step through. It was Zenaida who opened it. The second she saw Foster running over with an unconscious Micah in his arms, she urgently threw it against the ground. It was when she noticed that Maeve and Rowan weren't behind them, that she regrets doing so. Time is ticking and it's already been ten minutes.

"We need to get going," Foster claims. The ground shakes and Zenaida shares a cautious stare with him. "Everyone through."

Lucas would have stepped through with Thais first, but as he walks, he's crashing to the ground with a whimper. Thais tumbles, groaning. Zenaida is quick to kneel beside her giant wolf for a husband.

"Shift back. You're hurt" She pleads. Lucas is unresponsive. He lays in the grass, staring off into the distance. The rain had finally stopped and he was allowed to see the night sky in all its glory. The sky was no longer red, nor the moon. It looks like something out of a movie. The stars twinkled and gleamed, while the moon had its marvelous faint blue shine. He felt at peace. He wouldn't be able to show it, but as he gazed at the moon, a proud smile overcame his heart. Maeve had done it. His eyes are slowly fluttering close. He could only really make out the hazy figure of his beautiful wife. "You're bleeding!" Zenaida gasps. "How long have you-" She looks back into the grass. Squinting she can see a trail of scattered blood leading them right to where they are. "No, no, no. Stay with me Lucas, okay? We're going to step through the portal and get you to the hospital. Just shift back."

An ugly sob falls from her lips when her husband doesn't move an inch. He isn't moving at all. Foster stumbles and Thais grips her chest. For a second their air flow is halted and they have to pant. But then their hearts break and they know the outcome. Zenaida crumbles. She falls into the dead body of her loved one. She could literally feel her heart being ripped into shreds, all of the tiny pieces casually falling to the ground as if they were mindless leaves. She feels incapable of moving. The only purpose she served now was to mourn over the only person she was meant to be with. There was no light in her life anymore, and depression was surrounding her mind.

"Zenadia we have to go," Foster says gently.

"I'm not going anywhere without Lucas!" She shouts.

No one knew what to do. Foster would physically remove her if he wasn't busy carrying Micah. Thais was nowhere near strong enough to push, pull or carry Zenaida across. He was left to stand there and watch streams of Zenaida's tears clump Lucas' fur.

"We're here!"

Flying in with wings the size of another human, Maeve touches down beside the group. In her arms was Rowan. His face was turned away, but once stable on the ground, he uncurled from a ball. He leaves Maeve's arms completely, smiling sweetly to the rest. It was a smile that didn't last too long when his and Maeve's ears were being met with devastating news. Zenaida's body wracks even harder as she hears the truth for a second time.

"Oh, I'm so sorry for your loss" Maeve approaches the woman. She kneels while putting a hand to Zenaida's back. Rubbing in a comforting matter, soothing words are traveling throughout the other's pointy ears. "You're going to be okay. Lucas is always going to have you in his heart, and him yours. You will have your time to grieve. We all will. But for now, it's time to let go."

Zenaida raises her head. She looks at Maeve through teary eyes. Maeve smiles with a flash of her brown irises going white, and suddenly Zenaida is nodding along. She wipes at her eyes, looking down at the face of her husband in wolf form. She sniffles back snot, and then lovingly brushes his fur back. It's the last she sees of him before she's being guided through the portal. The rest follow, and it closes behind them.

Their presence is startling to Reggie—the vampire jumping up from his spot on the bench and greeting the group. He takes notice of them looking down, so he tracks it. Right, he has two unconscious witches beside his feet. Raising his hands in surrender, Reggie pleads innocent.

"I didn't kill them, I swear!"

Chapter Twenty-Nine

The group steps over the damage that was done to their house. A few broken windows, a busted down door. All of the furniture was smashed, and precious possessions were no longer. That fight had really done a number.

"Hopefully the shower still works" Thais grumbles as she finds herself walking up the stairs. She looked like a zombie, eyes staring at nothing but everything at the same time. And her tone was far from its bubbly squealing. Zenaida is two steps behind her, mouth clamped shut unless she wants to cry even more. She thinks she'll skip a shower. She just wants to go lay down. Her chest tightens and tears well when she finds herself entering Lucas' room. It's an instinct to grab one of his many dirty hoodies from off the floor. She brings the collar to her nose so she can inhale her husband's scent, and then flops herself onto his bed where she's able to curl up in his blankets. It's when the entirety of the world stills that she can't hold the tears back anymore and she lets them hit Lucas' pillow like a broken dam.

"I'm starving," Rowan grumbles. He lays Emry down on one of the couches before taking off towards the kitchen. Reggie mocks his movements when it comes to laying Amora on the other couch. After he takes a stand beside Maeve near the tarnished front door.

"I'll just lay him down in his bed" Foster comments next. He's talking about a still sleeping Micah. A head nod from Maeve is all he receives before dark and mysterious is heading upstairs as well.

Maeve turns to Reggie then.

"Thank you," Her smile is sweet. Matches the one she gave him from the first time they met. "Without your help, I can only imagine we would have made it in time."

"Eh, it's no problem. I've always wanted to have bragging rights over a dog."

She giggles, and then she's remembering.

"Oh and here," She removes a bag that she created from a ripped curtain from across her body. Reggie stares quizzically but waits for her to unwrap the gift before saying anything. "It's just something I managed to come by while saving everyone" She lifted the final layer to reveal a beating heart. It had a name tag on it like all the rest did in that room.

Reginald Marks.

"My heart."

"Well don't just stare at it, come on, put it back in" She motions for him to have it, and he has shaky hands when taking hold of it.

He can't believe it. It's been three years since he's become someone without a heart. Someone without emotion and feelings. He's been waiting a long time for this. He bites his tongue as shoves the bloody organ back into his chest. He hiccups at the sensation. Stillness, and it's as if nothing has changed. But then he's feeling it all at once. He looks Maeve in the eye and his heart pounds sporadically. He cups her face within his hands, and then without being able to deny it any longer, he gives her a kiss. Maeve gasps from the action. Her eyes go wide and she doesn't know what to do with her hands. But with the way Reggie's lips feel so full, so soft against hers, she is falling for the charm. Her eyes flutter close and she's complying.

The sad part is when she's just getting into the rhythm, Reggie is pulling away.

"Fuck, it's even better now that I can feel you." Maeve's knees wobble. She grins crookedly. This is what she's wanted. Reggie. She leans in for another kiss, only this time he denies her. "No, because there's something I need to tell you."

"I'm sure it can wait."

"It's about Amir," She steps back, newfound interest taking over. "He's alive."

END OF BOOK ONE

Written Within the Stars

The door was humongous. Doubled and rounding into an arch at the top, it softened what may have come off intimidating. The golden doorknobs have never been touched—or at least never by a bare hand. The two guards who stood in front of it wore gloves, the color of them matching everything else in the place: snowy. Detailing was nothing short of various shades of gold. Curves and swirls sprout from the bottom of the fiberglass and then spread into intricate designs, where if you look hard enough you might be able to see the historical stories that were embedded within the shapes and lines.

Approaching the giant door, it was already being opened before the person wishing to be on the other side was close enough. Not a single creak or squeak could be heard from the hinges, but a presenting whoosh is heard once the doors are forcing all of the air to be pushed in one specific direction. And then there's a loud slam when it's being closed behind the newcomer. Another blast of wind has their robe being lifted from the ground, floating elegantly back down where it's being dragged upon further entry into the room. Not once was the clothing lifted. But it's not like it needed to be. Dust didn't exist where they were, and the shiny marble floors were clean enough to eat food from.

426 - Written Within the Stars

The person stops walking once they're in the middle of the room; their sight is nothing much but five red thrones being occupied by five more people. Not people, *Archangels*. They were extremely tall, with cotton white wings attached to their backs. They didn't express how they were feeling once seeing their guest —they didn't express anything at all. They just continued to sit where they were, fingers gripping onto the arms of their chairs a little bit tighter. Their faces were blank, yet the way their eyes moved up and down their guest's frame was enough.

A woman. Caramel skin and chocolate brown hair.

"I demand that you leave her alone."

The one in the middle. The angel with the strongest glow, the biggest wings, the tallest chair. She held her chin high as she stood from her seat, raising an eyebrow as she clasped her hands together in front of her.

"Who are you to give us orders? Your father was one of us, and he wasn't allowed more than a compliment to our ruling."

"You know what this plan will do to her. Death is the only outcome" The other tries to assert dominance by rolling her shoulders back, letting her brown eyes go ablaze.

"One life will not be saved at the hands of thousands of others. We're moving forward with the chosen one, and you are to no longer challenge us. Do I make myself clear?"

"You're wrong about this. About her!"

"*I said,*"Do I make myself clear, Habun!?'"

She shakes her head.

"You don't know what you're doing!" The angel woman flicked her wrist and immediately those giant doors were being opened again. Storming through them were the guards. With unmatched speed, they reached Habun, grabbed her arms and dragged her away. "You can't do this! You're going to kill her! You won't be able to contain the darkness either! Evil will spread and the city will fall!"

"You know nothing."

Habun is being tugged out the door when she meets the angel woman's glare.

"I know my daughter."

Acknowledgments

How does one go about saying how grateful they are? Do they implement it through their work? Do they take the time to go to everyone who was involved and verbally express their gratitude? It's hard to sit and think of the best way to say thank you. So I'll just be saying it: Thank you. Thank you to everyone who saw my book and decided to give it a try. Whether it was a story that was satisfying, or a story that made you want to return it, I appreciate your time. Without people reading, I wouldn't be able to pursue my passion. I also want to thank everyone who helped push me to continue on with writing. My friends and family. Without their support, without their constant reassurance that I am doing great, I would have stopped writing. It's been long grueling years of pressure and doubt—not knowing whether or not my skills are good enough. But here I am, and I'm not going anywhere. So again, thank you to everyone involved, thank you to everyone who reads, and thank you to me, myself and I.

Milton Keynes UK
Ingram Content Group UK Ltd.
UKHW032043180324
439698UK00001B/53